ALIX JAMES

THE MEASURE OF TRUST

THE MEASURE OF A MAN COLLECTION,
BOOK TWO

A PRIDE AND PREJUDICE VARIATION

Ebook ISBN: 978-1-957082-34-9
Paperback ISBN: 978-1-957082-35-6

Cover Design by GetCovers.com
Cover Image Licensed by Period Images
Background image licensed by Shutterstock

Blog and Website: https://alixjames.com/
Newsletter: https://subscribepage.io/alix-james
Book Bub: https://www.bookbub.com/authors/alix-james
Facebook: https://www.facebook.com/ShortSweetNovellas
Twitter: https://twitter.com/N_Clarkston
Amazon: https://www.amazon.com/stores/Alix-James/author/B07Z1BWFF3
Austen Variations: http://austenvariations.com/

Contents

Dedication

To the one in whom my heart trusts.

Chapter One

"BLAST THIS INFERNAL MUD!" Elizabeth Bennet muttered under her breath. She tried to wipe a slimy splatter off her riding gloves as her horse trudged through the soggy autumn fields, its hooves heavy with the weight of the mire.

Hertfordshire had not even been experiencing any extraordinary measures of rain this autumn. But the fields had become irredeemable marshes—a complaint Elizabeth had largely ignored when she heard anyone speak of it until she became the one to accidentally try wading through the quagmire.

"You should have stayed home, Lizzy," she grumbled. Jane had warned her, but no, she simply *had* to call on Charlotte, even though her ankle was still tender from the day before when she had slipped most ingloriously on the path back from Oakham Mount. So, what was her solution?

A horse. A bloody *horse*.

And as the carriage horses were wanted on the farm that day, the only alternative had been her father's riding horse—a temperamental beast with a penchant for putting his head between his front legs and pitching his tail in the air whenever the fancy suited him.

Which it had earlier... Thus, the muddy gloves.

But for Charlotte, Elizabeth had been willing to put up with a little discomfort, perhaps even a little danger. Charlotte had been suffering from what Elizabeth could only describe as low spirits this autumn. Indeed, that was a generous term for the way poor Charlotte had been feeling, and she found little comfort in her mother's admonishments or her younger siblings' carelessness. And so, Elizabeth had been making the trek nearly every day of late, hoping to lift her friend's spirits even a little.

The horse's hooves squished into another soft bit of earth, and being as displeased by the notion of slogging through another swamp as his rider was, he lodged his feet in the ground and refused to move forward. Elizabeth uttered one or two indelicate phrases about the horse's parentage, but rather than fight with him again, perhaps it was best if she turned back and found firmer ground. Just... Where was that? She leaned slightly forward, inspecting the earth below for a promising path.

That, however, proved to be an ill-judged notion. The moment her weight shifted, the horse tossed his head and snorted, and then his front feet popped a few inches off the ground in a menacing threat to rear if she tried to make him go where he did not wish to go.

"Easy now," she coaxed. She would get nowhere by telling the horse exactly what she thought of him, so perhaps gentle manners might prevail. "Just a little further, and we'll be back on solid ground."

Another rabid-sounding snort and the horse subsided long enough for Elizabeth to pull him away towards firmer footing. There, now, they were getting somewhere. Just a little farther on, and they would be on the road. And she would be hanged before she tried to cross these marshy fields again before next summer. Shortcut or not, her petticoats were already several inches deep in mud, and she was starting to shiver. Just a few seconds more...

But fate, it seemed, had other plans. As they approached a particularly waterlogged section of the field, the horse's feet seemed to just... stop. He splashed up to his knees, and then his head went down, his body wrung to the side in a slithering hop... and Elizabeth felt, just for an instant, what it would feel like to fly like a bird.

A pity she could not land like one. Elizabeth hissed when she splashed into the wet grass, rolled to her side, and then surveyed herself with a groan. Good heavens, she was a slimy wreck! There was another gown ruined.

But that was not the worst of it. Pain shot through her already injured ankle as she struggled to sit up, her hands sinking into the cold, wet mud. The horse, its eyes wide with panic—or malice, she could not decide which—thrashed against the sucking earth and splattered her with more of the infernal stuff. Not that it made any difference now, though.

"No, no, no!" Elizabeth gasped. "Don't you dare try to run off. You got me here. Now, you shall... Ooh!" She grabbed whatever leather was within her reach and pulled herself to her feet, wincing as she put weight on her throbbing ankle and tried to reach for the dangling rein.

Where was she? Elizabeth steadied herself by resting a hand on the pommel of the saddle and sought her bearings. She should never have taken the shortcut.

"Let me see... There is that stand of oaks, and the lane wrapping around, and oh, drat. Had I not got farther than that?" She shaded her eyes and turned about one more time. There was the marker for Netherfield, just around the bend. And that meant that she was still three miles from home.

There was nothing else for it. She would have to climb back on that pompous, twitchy beast somehow. She certainly could not walk home in this condition, but just now, hobbling three miles back to Longbourn on one good ankle seemed a great deal more appealing than getting back on that recalcitrant brute. He had done nothing today to earn her regard.

With a heavy sigh, Elizabeth gathered her skirts and braced one arm over the saddle to keep herself from falling as she tried to walk. And thus began the long, painful trek back to Longbourn.

FITZWILLIAM DARCY FINGERED THE brim of the hat in his lap as his friend, Charles Bingley, strained to look out the carriage window. The autumn air was crisp, carrying with it the promise of change and new beginnings—that was the poetic way Bingley had described the weather. He had hardly ceased chattering since they left London, and now he was busy pointing out every building with which he had already become acquainted in the little village of Meryton.

Darcy obliged by glancing out the other window and nodding agreeably whenever Bingley seemed particularly enamoured of something or other. "That there is the bookseller's," Bingley informed him—as if the sign in the window was insufficient to the task. "You recall that fine first edition I showed you the other day? Well, that is where I found it. Odd thing, too, for I should never have thought to find... oh, and there is the haberdasher. I was a little concerned there would be few options outside of going to London—you know, a small village like this. It is a very respectable shop for all that. And there is the milliner. They had a very fine beaver that I admired immensely, and I think I shall look in on it again after we have concluded our business."

"We are not here to purchase a hat," Darcy sighed as he pinched the bridge of his nose. Drat this wretched headache—would it never leave him in peace? "In fact, we are very nearly late for your appointment with Mr Philips. We shall not have time to make ourselves presentable at the inn before we are expected."

"I suppose we ought to have left when you recommended," Bingley confessed. "But I thought surely it was not so very critical, as I expected the roads would be quite good. A real shame about that downed tree we had to go around. Fancy, a two-mile detour just to go around a tree!"

"Would you rather drive off the road and get the carriage wheels stuck in the mud?"

"No, no. It is only that it seems like it should not have been such a bother. But Mr Philips seems an easy chap. I doubt he shall mind so very much."

"I always mind when people waste *my* time," Darcy grumbled. But the complaint was lost on Bingley.

Some minutes later, the carriage stopped directly outside the legal office of one Mr Walter Philips, solicitor. Darcy gave his jacket a cursory dusting, wishing he did not feel so badly on account of their tardiness that he refused to stop at the inn first, as planned. Well, Mr Philips was a solicitor from a small village. Surely, he had seen gentlemen arrive with creases in their trousers before.

They entered the office and were asked to wait a moment, but before they had even taken seats, Mr Philips himself came to greet them. "Mr Bingley, Mr Darcy," he began, his tone heavy with regret, "I am afraid I have some unfortunate news. The lease for Netherfield has been taken by another party. I sent a letter to inform you only yesterday, but it appears it did not arrive in time. I do apologise, sirs."

Bingley's face fell, his enthusiasm draining away like the colour from his cheeks. "But... How is that possible? We were in negotiations, were we not? I had hoped to establish myself in a house before winter."

"I am very sorry, Mr Bingley, but another presented himself only two days ago and was willing to offer far more generous terms if the owner would agree to consider leasing to him, in preference to you."

"We had a contract, man!" Bingley's ears were turning red, and Darcy drew himself up in surprise. Bingley was not the man to lose his temper, but his looks now bordered on very vexed, indeed.

"In fact, Mr Bingley, we did *not* have a contract. That was the purpose of our meeting today. Thus far, we have only discussed details, and you have performed your due diligence, but there was nothing legally binding on either party. I truly am sorry, sir, but I am merely the one managing the contract. The decision was Mr Northam's, as Netherfield property belongs to him. And once the other contract was signed, he departed for Bath, as he means to make his residence there. I am afraid there is no possibility at this point in asking him to reconsider."

"But... Well, this is dashed indecent. Shoddy business, I should say! Who is this other party? Was he made aware that the property was under consideration?"

"I am afraid it is not within my purview to disclose any private matters, but indeed, he was made aware of your interest. Thus, the reason for his... exceeding generosity toward Mr Northam."

"I should have been at least given the opportunity to match his offer!" Bingley protested. "I daresay, most indecent. I shall make a formal complaint, I shall, and—"

"Mr Philips," Darcy interjected firmly, "we thank you for your time." Darcy held an arm before Bingley, inviting him to extricate himself.

Philips nearly sagged; such was his evident relief, but Bingley was not quite prepared to surrender. "Well, I... I shall write to Mr Northam myself, I suppose. This should not have been carried on in such a way."

He continued posing similar remarks, more to himself than anyone else, as Darcy ushered him out. His expression was that of a broken man, and in the short span of time it required to descend the stairs, he had gone from blaming Philips and Northam to questioning himself.

As they stepped into the carriage, Bingley turned to him, his brow furrowed with confusion. "Darcy, what more could I have done? I was prompt to answer all correspondence. My man in London looked over everything and said nothing looked out of the ordinary. Is it not irregular for a property to be let out from under one's nose in such a manner?"

Darcy nodded. "Indeed, it is. These transactions usually take weeks, if not months, to complete. The last letter you showed me, a mere four days ago, gave no indication of any other interested parties."

Bingley sighed. "That was what I thought, too. It is a shame, Darcy. Netherfield had everything I'd hoped for. I dearly wish I had been able to show it to you."

"A pity," Darcy agreed, though, for his part, he was already more than ready to quit the area and return to the comforts of home. The pounding in his head was growing steadily worse. "You will show me the next one."

"Of course, but..." On impulse, Bingley leaned out the window and called out to the coachman, "Take us along the North Road before we turn back, would you? I would like to catch a glimpse of Netherfield, even if it is no longer to be mine."

Darcy studied Bingley's profile, noting the sharp disappointment etched in his features. Bingley was a chap whose every emotion played loudly across his face, but Darcy had never seen such extreme peevishness over a simple missed opportunity. He was not without sympathy, but surely, the matter did not warrant this level of disappointment. "I do not think it advisable to drive by the property. You only torture yourself needlessly."

Bingley lifted his shoulder. "It is a lovely prospect, Darcy. I did want you to see it if for no other reason than that once you do, you will not doubt my taste."

As the carriage rolled along the country lane, Netherfield came into view, its stately façade rising majestically against the backdrop of the Hertfordshire countryside. Indeed, it was a property worthy of admiration, and he could understand Bingley's attraction. They did not drive directly up to the house; instead, they took a road that ran parallel to the property from which they could see most of the manor.

"It is a fine estate, Bingley," Darcy remarked, his tone measured. "But there will be others."

Bingley sighed, his gaze fixed on the retreating image of Netherfield as the carriage rolled on. "I know, Darcy. It is just... I had such high hopes for this place. The promise of a new beginning, a chance to establish myself."

Darcy nodded, his mind already turning to the practicalities of their situation. So, it was not the loss of this particular house that had Bingley so crushed but the delay in all the things he had looked forward to. To become more like Darcy—that had always been Bingley's unstated desire, and though flattered, Darcy often wondered if he was the proper standard by which Bingley ought to be measuring himself.

Well, there was nothing else for it now. They would need to redouble their efforts to seek new opportunities for Bingley to secure a suitable property. It was doubtful they would have any luck at all until spring, and there was certainly nothing to be done at this moment. And indeed, nothing when Darcy could hardly concentrate over the clamouring bells in his head that made his eyes ache and his skull feel as if it were ready to split apart.

Darcy shifted his hat a little lower on his brow and leaned toward the window, trying to let his thoughts trail into that gentle autumn breeze that rustled the remaining gold in the treetops.

Chapter Two

"Bingley, look there," Darcy said, pointing towards a figure on the side of the road. "Is that a young lady? And... is her horse lame?"

Bingley squinted, following Darcy's gaze. "By Jove, I think you're right, Darcy. She appears to be in some distress."

Darcy rapped on the roof of the carriage, signalling for the driver to stop. He alighted as the carriage rolled to a halt, his long strides carrying him towards the lady in question. The young woman was covered in mud from head to toe, her skirts caked with the stuff. She stood beside a horse that looked equally worse for wear, its chest and legs mired in bog that was beginning to dry.

"Miss, are you in need of assistance?" Darcy inquired.

The lady had continued walking with her head bowed as if meaning to pass him by, but when he spoke, her eyes lifted to his, flashing with a mixture of frustration and embarrassment. "Unless you have a magic wand to turn back time and prevent me from ever getting on this wretched beast, I am afraid there is little to be done, sir."

"Well, I have no wand, and I never met anyone who could work such arts—useful though they might be—but it looks to me as though an injured ankle and a rather awkward state of discomportment are your chief troubles at the moment. Please, is there anything that may be done for your assistance?"

"Oh, I should think not, for that in itself would create further complications. Think what would be said of me if I accepted a ride from a stranger?"

Darcy turned about, scanning the road in each direction. "Do you happen to see anyone about with whom you are acquainted?"

One of her eyes narrowed faintly, and a corner of her mouth turned up. "Someone will be along eventually. Or I will simply hobble home as I am. As you see, I am not entirely lame, and I have already managed half a mile in this... state."

"Miss, I have no intention of arguing with you, but it is clear that you cannot continue much further. Look here. Permit me to introduce myself, and we shall not be strangers."

Her mouth turned up even more. "That silly line only works in children's books."

"Naturally, but as there is no one else to overhear me, I had dearly hoped you would not call me out on my lazy reasoning. I am Fitzwilliam Darcy of Pemberley and my friend—" he gestured over his shoulder and saw Bingley walking toward them after talking with the coachman— "back there at the carriage is Charles Bingley. We would happily offer you a ride back to your home, Miss...?"

"Bennet," she supplied, her voice clipped. "Elizabeth Bennet of Longbourn. And while I appreciate the offer, Mr Darcy, I couldn't possibly impose. I am not fit to be seen, let alone to soil the upholstery of your fine carriage."

Bingley, who had joined them during the exchange, chimed in. "Nonsense, Miss Bennet! We insist. It would be our pleasure to see you safely home."

Miss Bennet hesitated, her gaze flickering between Darcy, Bingley, the carriage, and the muddy road ahead. "I suppose I am not quite so well off here as I would like to appear. But the upholstery in your carriage..."

"No bother at all," Bingley interjected. "For, you see, I had a picnic blanket in the boot, as the weather is fair, and I had intended on an afternoon of celebration on the lawn of... well, that is not to be now, but I already had my coachman cover the seat for you."

She wetted her lips and looked down at herself, surveying her gloves, her gown, and the boots that were so thick in mud it was a wonder she even kept her footing... and swallowed. "I suppose the usual fears of a lady who finds herself suddenly dependent upon the aid of two gentlemen whose characters are unknown to her are abysmally lacking in this case."

Dacy stepped marginally closer. "I do not follow, Miss Bennet."

She held up one hand, spreading the fingers of it to display the crusting mud over her gloves. "You would have to be desperate, indeed, to try to take advantage of me. It would ruin your expensive coat."

Darcy nearly choked on a laugh, even if holding it back made his ears feel like they might rupture. Had she meant to be impertinent? Or was she simply so out of sorts that the words and thoughts jumbled together in her mouth until they came out sounding gloriously amusing? "I assure you, Miss Bennet, you will be as safe with us as in your own father's carriage."

She frowned, a crease appearing under the cracks of mud over her brow as she deliberated. "Well, what about my horse? Frankly, I do not mind leaving the brute here to rot, but my father seems unaccountably to like the rogue. I think he just likes being contrary."

"The matter of the horse is quite simple," Bingley replied. "We can fasten the reins to the back of the carriage and lead him. What say you, Miss Bennet?"

She swallowed, her eyes flicking to Bingley, then back to Darcy. "It does sound better than walking, but you do not know what you are offering. Are either of you gentlemen single?"

"Single?" Bingley chuckled a little. "Whatever does that have to do with…"

Darcy put a hand up. "We both are. I can guess at your concern, Miss Bennet. We shall be discreet, but I cannot, in good conscience, drive away without seeing a lady safe on the road. I could never look my own sister in the eye afterwards."

She shot one more caustic look back at the horse, then nodded wearily. "Oh, what is the use? I am a tragic enough sight as it is. Perhaps no one will recognise me."

Darcy doubted that very much. Miss Bennet was already fixed in his mind as one of the most unique creatures he had ever encountered, and those who knew her well could not help but spot her at fifty paces, even if she was covered in mud. But he kept this thought to himself as Bingley tugged the horse's reins from her hand, and Darcy offered his arm to help her hobble to the carriage.

"Oh, I do not think…" She drew back, eyeing his coat. "Sir, I cannot possibly…"

"Your concern is touching, Miss Bennet, but what you 'cannot possibly' do is walk unaided. Without leaning on your horse for support, how do you mean to make the carriage?"

"With a great deal of stumbling and more mud on my knees, I should imagine." She made a wry face. "Very well, but I will touch only your glove, sir."

Darcy, fighting back a smile at her frank words, offered his hand to assist her to the carriage. "I assure you, Miss Bennet, a little mud is of no consequence."

Miss Bennet's lips twisting into a droll smile, accepted his hand and limped away, leaning on him even more than he had anticipated. After some torturous distance, she climbed into the carriage, taking great care to keep her skirts from brushing against the plush velvet. Bingley and the coachman had secured her horse to the back of the carriage, and a moment later, they were underway.

"You will have to give some direction to the coachman. Which way is your home?"

Miss Bennet sat ramrod straight, her hands clasped tightly in her lap, her gaze fixed resolutely out the window. "Two more miles to the southeast, I am afraid."

"Two miles?" Darcy repeated. "However did you mean to walk that distance?"

"One step at a time, sir," she retorted, but not without a sweet little smirk that took the bite out of her words. "I imagine that is the way most people walk."

"You must have been enjoying quite a long outing. I take it your ride did not go as planned, Miss Bennet?" Darcy ventured.

"What gave it away, Mr Darcy? The mud or the fact that I was trudging along the road like a vagrant?"

A flush crept up the back of his neck as he stammered an apology. "Forgive me, Miss Bennet. I did not mean to pry."

Miss Bennet's expression softened slightly. "No, forgive me, Mr Darcy. It has been a trying day, and I am afraid my temper has got the better of me—not least in the matter of the horse. I might have still been mounted, had I made some little effort at getting along with that ill-mannered cad."

Darcy permitted another small smile, but hid it away immediately, lest Bingley should see it. He wanted to knead his forehead and massage away some of that infernal throbbing, but at least Miss Elizabeth Bennet helped to distract him. She was one of the few things that had, oddly enough. "I was not aware that it is ever incumbent upon any lady to make herself agreeable to a... a cad, did you say? Some creatures are better left alone, lest you injure yourself in trying to redeem them."

The mud on her cheeks somehow faded when compared to the brilliance of a genuine smile from her. Egad, the lady *did* have fine eyes, which sparkled just so in the light from the carriage window. "Well said, Mr Darcy. And now, you and I may be friends. There, I have not done such a wretched thing in accepting a ride from you, after all."

That might be the first time a lady had ever evoked such an easy laugh from him. Darcy forced himself to look away, for it would not do to wonder what she looked like, properly cleaned up and turned out for... oh, say, a ball. No, it would not do to imagine that at all.

"I say," Bingley asked, "how did you come to be so..." He cleared his throat and gestured to her person. "... besmirched?"

"I tried to take a shortcut," she sighed. "And I did not realise that nearly every field around here is doing its best to join the ocean."

"Yes, that is a deal of mud. Has Hertfordshire suffered more rain than London this autumn?"

"No, that is just the shock of it. No one can discover why it is so, but the irrigation channels have all flooded over and broken down any earthen dikes set up to divert the water."

Darcy narrowed his eyes. "Interesting. I wonder where the water has come from if it is not raining overmuch yet this season."

"The lake, I suppose, but it does not bode well for winter." Miss Bennet's brow furrowed again. "Or next spring, when the farmers must harvest winter wheat and plant new crops."

Darcy had begun to let his eyes wander over those very fields out the window, but at her words, they snapped back to her. What a... singular thing for a young lady to mention or even think about. "Indeed," he agreed. "It does not bode well at all."

They rode in relative silence for a little while until Miss Bennet straightened, her eyes on something out the window. She bit her lips together and tried to restrain a sigh. "Mr Bingley, I beg your pardon, but did you say this was your carriage? Pray, ask your coachman to let me out just over the ridge there, behind the stand of trees shielding the road from the house beyond."

"But we have not delivered you to your home," Bingley protested. "I would not force you to walk in your condition."

"I would rather endure the pain of walking than other... indignities." The lady grimaced.

Darcy leaned to look out the window. A cluster of young ladies was walking on the path ahead, with much giggling and tomfoolery between them. One of them pointed at Bingley's carriage and squealed in some delight, and Darcy was certain he caught the phrase "rich men from London."

Miss Bennet groaned and sank back into the corner, looking away.

"Friends of yours?" Darcy asked.

"My sisters," she hissed as a hand covered her cheek from the window's light. "I only hope Jane does not look up and recognise Papa's horse behind the carriage. Lydia never would note that sort of thing, but Jane... oh, please beg the driver to slow down and let them pass before we reach the turning of the road! I would rather not make a scene."

Bingley gave a short command, and they heard the feminine chatter dying away as the girls passed on. Miss Bennet gave a great roll of her eyes and released a shaking breath. "Well! There's a relief. If Lydia had spotted me in your carriage, I am sorry to say that Mama would have shackled me to one of you unfortunate creatures before sundown."

"Oh, surely, you jest, Miss Bennet," Bingley laughed. "Nonsense, for it was only a matter of helping a lady in distress. No one could fault you for accepting, what with an injured ankle and all. I should like to present myself to your father and assure him that your safety and reputation were properly seen to."

Miss Bennet cast a weather eye over him, then her gaze shifted to Darcy, and she raised a brow. "You understand, sir. I can see that much."

Darcy dipped his head. "Unfortunately, I do, Miss Bennet." And the last thing he felt like subjecting himself to just now was a noisy bunch of girls who were hardly out of the school room.

"Then you will understand that I mean what I say when I beg you to let me out before we are quite in sight of the house."

Darcy nodded. "Indeed, Miss Bennet. Bingley, have the carriage stop just there." He pointed to the place she had indicated.

"Oh, very well. It seems rather ungallant, though." Bingley rapped on the roof and said something to the driver.

Miss Bennet shifted on the cloth Bingley's coachman had laid down as she gathered her skirts and prepared to disembark. "I must thank you, gentlemen, once more. With any luck, I shall not have to endure the embarrassment of meeting you again."

"Why would that be an embarrassment?" Darcy asked as he disembarked and reached to hand her down.

"Because I shall never have any credit in your eyes after such a miserable first impression! It would take me months to redeem your opinion of me, and I daresay there would be little reward in it for either of us. No, sir, far too much effort. I shall bid you a good day, and you shall return to London or wherever you are bound, thinking that all Hertfordshire ladies are accident-prone and barely civilised."

His mouth turned up a little more—dash it all, he could not help it. "And what will you think of gentlemen from London?"

She tipped her face up to him with a thoughtful expression, puckering her mouth. Darcy almost chuckled aloud at how the drying mud on her cheek stretched, caked, and cracked as her features moved. "I think they are not all cads, sir. Some of them, but not all."

"Well, that is a relief. I would hate to have such a remarkable lady alive in the world and thinking ill of me."

She looked away long enough to take the reins Bingley passed to her, then shot him one final, impish look. "I believe you are assured of my good opinion, sir. Little as that matters, I can at least grant you that. Good day, and thank you again for your kindness." With that, she turned and made her way toward the house, disappearing around the bend without a backward glance.

Bingley sighed. "It truly is a pity about Netherfield, Darcy. With neighbours such as Miss Bennet, I am certain I would have been quite happy there."

Darcy shook his head, and this time, he did remove his hat to massage his forehead. "With neighbours such as Miss Bennet, Bingley, you would have found yourself wed before Christmas."

Elizabeth winced as she stepped out of sight of the gentlemen's carriage, her ankle throbbing with every movement. Oh, if Mama ever heard of this...

If Mama ever heard of this, Elizabeth would find herself bundled in a fast coach for London with her mother and a clergyman trying to chase those poor gentlemen down.

But they truly had been kind. Certainly, there were worse ruffians a lady could find herself compromised by. She glanced back over her shoulder, ensuring that the gentlemen were well out of sight before letting out a long, painful sigh. The horse, drat him, was all friendliness now, and he nuzzled her hand. She patted his shoulder absently.

"We dodged a bullet, you miscreant. It seems no one saw our little misadventure."

Limping towards the house, Elizabeth braced herself for the inevitable confrontation with her family. Mr Hill saw her limping up the drive and immediately came to take the horse. "Shall I help you inside, Miss Elizabeth?" he offered. "I shall call Mrs Hill to attend you."

"No, no, that will not be necessary." She sucked a breath between her teeth and hopped a little on her good foot to make it up the steps to the house. No sense in exciting Mama more. Let her believe it was no more than the same sore ankle from yesterday.

"Lizzy!" Jane, her eldest sister, exclaimed as she caught sight of Elizabeth's at the door. "What on earth happened to you? Why, you are covered head to toe!"

Elizabeth grimaced, holding up a hand to halt her sister's concern. "I know, Jane. It is a long story. Could you help me get cleaned up before Mama sees me? I'd rather not have to explain myself just yet. Or ever, really."

Jane nodded and quickly ushered Elizabeth upstairs. Together, they worked to remove the mud-caked clothing and tidy Elizabeth's appearance. It would take a full bath to get some of the slime out from under her nails and the roots of her hair, but hopefully, Mama would not have cause to look too closely. That walking dress, though… she would have to sneak it out to the washbasin herself before Hill had a look at it.

Once presentable, Elizabeth descended the stairs; her breath caught in her throat as she noticed the muddy footprints she had tracked into the hall. Oh, dear… perhaps Mama would be too preoccupied with asking her sisters what they had done in town to notice before Elizabeth could clean it up.

But Mama was not in the sitting room to notice. Nor was she upstairs, nor even in the kitchen talking to Hill. Guilty conscience, perhaps, but Elizabeth could not be easy until she knew precisely where her mother was and if there was any chance the details of her little afternoon outing might have been discovered.

She did not have to look long, however. Elizabeth was just returning to the hall when her mother burst through the door, both hands framed in the air.

"Girls!" she cried, her voice echoing through the house. "Netherfield is let at last!"

Well… This was… fortuitous timing. There was no better way to distract her mother from the fact that she had just ridden home alone in a carriage with two wealthy, single gentlemen than for her mother to have something better to gossip about.

Elizabeth knotted her shaking fingers behind her back, willing the nervousness to remain at bay while she smiled serenely for her mother. "Is that so, Mama? How thrilling."

"Aye, and do you not want to know who has taken it, Lizzy?"

Elizabeth sighed. Mama would not rest until she had divulged every last detail of the new tenant. She nodded, resigning herself to the inevitable gossip that would follow. "I am all anticipation."

"The man has come from the north with a large fortune," Mrs Bennet proclaimed, her voice filled with barely contained glee. "And his name, girls, is Wickham."

Chapter Three

"How was Charlotte today?" Jane asked.

Elizabeth fluffed the bedcovers and thrust her chilled legs under them, shivering as she tugged the blankets up to her chin. "The same. Jane, I truly am concerned for her. She hardly eats, she has no interest in anything—even painting screens. You recall how she used to love that?"

Jane nodded as she tucked herself into the other side of the bed they shared. "She took so much pleasure in it. Why, I recall her sitting in the garden for hours, trying to duplicate the look of the spring bulbs or the bumblebees. Has she truly lost interest in even that?"

Elizabeth shrugged. "She says it makes her sad to try because she can never get her paintings to turn out just as she wishes, and she is weary of the attempt."

"Oh, dear. Surely, there must be something to pique her interest. What about the piano?"

Elizabeth blew out the lantern beside the bed and lay back on her pillow, her hand absently picking at a stray thread on the covers. "Maria has been playing it more frequently, I understand. Lady Lucas has been commanding it, you see, as Maria is out in society now with Lydia, so there is an expectation that she ought to be able to perform."

Jane sighed. "And Charlotte claims Maria is better than she is, does she not?"

"You know our friend too well. Yes, she was lamenting that very thing to me." Elizabeth's voice shifted into a tone that mimicked her friend's most petulant tone. "Why should I practice when no matter how hard I may try, Maria will always be accounted prettier, livelier, and more pleasing?"

Elizabeth gave up playing with the loose thread and scooted further under the covers, casting her head back on the pillow. "She's right, you know."

Jane lifted her head in the darkness. "Lizzy, what a horrid thing to say!"

"I do not mean that I agree with it. But you must acknowledge that Charlotte speaks rightly. There really is nothing she can do to please Lady Lucas with her accomplishments or the beaux she might attract. I do not say that Lady Lucas slights poor Charlotte, but you know as well as I that our mother has never let her hear the end of your beauty compared to Charlotte's, or my liveliness compared to hers, or Mary's playing..."

"Oh, Lizzy, stop. I hate it when Mama compares us like that."

"So does Charlotte, though she will not say it. And who can blame Lady Lucas for doting on the daughter, who is more likely to bring her maternal pride? Certainly, none of her friends." Elizabeth growled at the darkness and twisted her fists in the blankets.

Jane was silent for a moment. "Do you think that is the root of Charlotte's unhappiness?"

Elizabeth shook her head. "I do not know. It seemed to worsen when the weather changed, but that could be my imagination. I think..." She chewed her lip. "No, I am sure of it. It is much more than feeling overlooked by her family. There is something else. I wish I knew what it was."

Jane rolled over, tucking her feet up and accidentally pulling at the covers like always. Elizabeth fought to keep her share as Jane yawned, unaware that she was a blanket thief. "You did not ask her? Why would she keep that from you?"

"Because she does not know herself."

"That makes no sense at all, but I do not understand half what you say, anyway." Jane's voice drifted into drowsiness. "You never did explain how you came back all covered in mud with a sore ankle. Did you really walk all the way from Netherfield?"

Elizabeth drummed her fingers on the covers. "Yes, well... I had some help. From the horse," she amended hastily.

"You hate that horse," Jane replied groggily.

"'Hate' is such a strong word," Elizabeth mumbled, but Jane's deepening breaths yielded no sense of any reply forthcoming.

Just as well. It would not do at all to tell anyone that she had, through her own foolishness, soiled the inside of some strange gentleman's carriage. And it certainly would not do to think about that other strange gentleman's dark brown eyes and strong arm.

Not at all.

LONDON

"No, Bingley, I do not think we should return to Hertfordshire. What are you hoping to accomplish by it? The property is already leased to another, there are no other eligible houses in the area, and there is nothing to be gained by tormenting yourself."

Charles Bingley stretched his boots before the fire grate, swirling a glass of Darcy's brandy before his unfocused eyes. "Oh, right you are, of course, of course," he slurred. "I only thought... well, you are quite right, Darcy. Nothing remains to be done. 'Tis only..."

"What?"

Bingley shifted upon his elbows to sit a little straighter in his chair. "This is an excellent brandy."

Darcy raised an eyebrow. "I should hope so. I certainly paid an excellent price for it."

"And this chair," Bingley continued, his words garbling somewhat. "Fine leather. Truly the finest."

"Poor leather is uncomfortable and does not last," Darcy returned mildly. "Your point?"

Bingley shifted again, a frown turning his ruddy features. "Why, it is only that since we first met, you have been playing host to me. Never once have I been able to offer you a comfortable chair by the fire and a warm brandy."

Darcy had been in the act of tugging his pocket watch from his waistcoat, but his hand stilled on the fob. "That is not true. You paid for our meals and travel expenses today, for example. And when we are at the club together, we take turns buying rounds."

Bingley scoffed and waved a hand. "Bother that. I mean in my own home! When was the last time you called at my flat?"

Darcy's brow crunched in thought. "A fortnight ago. You asked me to look over a new rug you had purchased."

"And did you stay for tea? Drinks? No, no, for we both know your drawing room is vastly more comfortable. Even Hurst's townhouse would be something, do you know?"

Bingley squirmed a little and downed another slosh of brandy. "We both know he bought that with Louisa's dowry."

"Come, come, now." Darcy replaced the watch in his pocket after glancing at the time. Well after eleven—little wonder Bingley was in his cups. They had been at it for three hours. "You enjoy an evening with Hurst as well as I do—that is to say, not at all. 'Tis one thing to offer fine spirits. 'Tis quite another for the host to imbibe them so freely that he slithers under the table before his guests have taken their leave."

"Indeed." Bingley sighed and pinched his eyes. "Oh, you little know how I was looking forward to an evening in the drawing room, for once master of my own house and able to offer you the same courtesies you have always extended to me!"

Darcy smiled and eased forward in his chair to stand, replacing his empty glass on the sideboard. "It is a commendable sentiment. Never fear, for I have no doubt that honour will be yours soon enough. Perhaps in the spring, something will present itself."

"Spring! One minor setback, and you speak of waiting for months?"

Darcy strode to the fire and drew the poker from its rack to tease the embers. "You say you have surveyed nearly every suitable property through half of England, yes? It is nearly Michaelmas already. How many gentry find themselves in a mood to retrench and offer their properties to let in November or December? Do you truly think any new opportunities will present themselves before the seasons change more favourably once more?"

"Some old fellow might die. I do not think death is seasonal."

Darcy made a wry face. "And you think the odds are high that his heir will immediately let the property to another, do you?

"Oh, perhaps not." Bingley swiped a hand down his face with a sigh of resignation and kicked to his feet. "Then I shall hie me home and wait for another opportunity, shall I?"

Darcy fingered the wrought handle of the fire poker. "Your carriage will have been sent back to the mews hours ago. No doubt by now, your coachman is in little better state than you are. Come, Bingley, take your usual room and sleep off the nightcap. You will be thinking more clearly in the morning."

Bingley paused and, with a lazy, reluctant smile, tossed a jaunty salute. "Very good, sir. Yes, sir, I quite like that. No, sir, I do not require any assistance. I shall..." Bingley's careless chatter broke off as he tripped over the edge of the rug, sending his arms pinwheeling. He righted himself before Darcy could react to assist him, then turned around with an insouciant grin. "I thank you again for your hospitality, Darcy."

Darcy regarded him cautiously. "Are you quite certain you need nothing? Shall I call a footman for you?"

"No, no, keep your footman. Do you know, I believe I shall rise early on the morrow, Darcy. I might even drive back to Hertfordshire without you if I must. There was something rather canny about that whole affair."

"I think you mean 'uncanny.'"

Bingley squinted. "No, I am quite certain I meant 'canny.' Or was it 'cagey'?" He frowned. "Whatever it was, it bears insti… investi… looking into."

Darcy smiled thinly. He would much rather do without another head-jarring ride in Bingley's carriage. He was still paying for that journey today and was not eager to repeat it. "You are welcome to return on your own if you feel compelled. I believe I must call on my sister tomorrow."

"Oh. Cheerio, then." Bingley nodded tiredly, then turned around and wandered out of the study. Darcy watched him go, then resumed poking absently at the fire.

Perhaps he *ought* to go with Bingley tomorrow. Why the man was so possessed by this Netherfield estate was beyond him, but if he went, he might be able to prevent Bingley from making some impassioned mistake, like tracking down the new lessor and offering more money to buy him out of the lease. Or finding some other nearby house that was not nearly suitable for his station, merely so he could look upon the one that got away.

But keeping Bingley from making a foolish mistake could not be his first concern. Guarding his sister… and keeping himself far away from muddy damsels with eyes like the sunrise and a laugh like a bubbling brook… yes, that was much wiser.

ELIZABETH ENTERED HER AUNT Philips' drawing room, seeking out Charlotte's familiar figure amongst the smattering of early arrivals. She spotted her friend hovering near the window, back turned, tension evident in the line of her shoulders.

"Charlotte." Elizabeth approached, laying a hand on her arm. "I worried you might not come."

Charlotte mustered a half-hearted smile. "Mother insisted I could not miss the party."

Elizabeth scrutinised Charlotte's drawn features, the lacklustre eyes that belied her brave front. "Forgive me, but you seem out of spirits. Are you quite well?"

"The same as usual, Lizzy. Mother is so determined that socialising will lift my melancholy, but..." She trailed off, gaze distant.

"But you are not convinced?" Elizabeth finished gently, guiding Charlotte to a sofa in the corner.

As they sat, Charlotte sighed. "In truth, I often feel ill-suited to society's expectations. The pressure to be ever charming and secure an advantageous match—it can be so wearying."

Elizabeth nodded slowly, but a playful notion struck her—something that might make Charlotte smile a little more and pity herself a little less. "But if you think it bothersome for us, just imagine how dreary it must be for the gentlemen. They have not the luxury of retiring to a corner to watch the room go round. They must make themselves agreeable to simply *everyone*, regardless of their feelings. Now, how many of them do you think must find themselves obliged to put on some sort of false face in company?"

Charlotte shifted in her chair. "Quite several, I suppose."

"Just so! And I daresay they are far more hunted for their 'assets' than we ladies are and only think of the poor man whose fortune is *just* short of what everyone is seeking after?"

Charlotte looped a hand over her knee and twisted to level a significant glance across the room at Mary King. "Is it any less fair than those who are barely agreeable at all being pursued relentlessly for the one 'asset' they do have?"

"Oh, I quite agree. Why, only yesterday, Mama was singing praises of a dreadfully dull and pompous gentleman purely because he is rumoured to have two thousand a year. As if that alone were sufficient inducement to make one of us fall in love with him!"

That coaxed a chuckle from Charlotte. "Ah, Lizzy. Only a man of true wit and depth could hold your interest, regardless of fortune."

Elizabeth affected a playful pout. "Indeed, my standards may be too exacting. If I cannot find one to match my imagination, I may end up a spinster with only my books for company."

"What a pair we shall be—two confirmed old maids together." The smile reached Charlotte's eyes this time.

Elizabeth patted her hand. "Never that, my dear. Not when any sensible man should be falling over himself to win your hand."

"Sensible men seem in short supply, I fear." But Charlotte's tone had lightened perceptibly.

Sounds at the door heralded new arrivals. Elizabeth glanced over, then turned back to Charlotte with an impish grin. "More guests—your mother will want to see you circulating. But if the inanity grows too tiresome, I shall concoct a scheme to rescue you."

Elizabeth and Charlotte moved to stand near the edge of the room, where the air was fairly crackling with anticipation. The new tenant of Netherfield, Mr Wickham, was expected to make an appearance at the Philipses' party, and everyone was eagerly awaiting their first glimpse of the mysterious gentleman.

"I heard he is quite handsome," Mrs Long was saying to anyone who would listen. "And so charming, too! Mr Philips said he was absolutely delightful, and of course, he must know Mr Wickham rather well after managing the lease for him."

Mrs Bennet nodded eagerly, her handkerchief clutched in her fingers. "Oh, I do hope he takes a liking to one of our girls! Wouldn't that be something to have a daughter married to the master of Netherfield?"

Elizabeth rolled her eyes, turning to Charlotte with a wry smile. "Mama is already planning weddings, and she has not even met the man yet."

Charlotte chuckled softly. "At least *your* mother thinks you have a hope and a prayer of catching the man's interest."

Elizabeth turned sharply to admonish Charlotte for such a petulant speech, but she cut herself short when a sudden hush fell over the room. She strained up to her toes to watch Mr Wickham making his entrance, and even she had to admit that the reports of his good looks had not been exaggerated.

And it seemed that her appraisal was not unique among the female occupants of the room. All eyes were drawn to his striking figure. He was tall and well-built, with dark, curling hair that fell in a becoming manner across his brow. His eyes, a piercing blue, seemed to take in the room with a keen intelligence and a touch of mirth.

He approached Mr and Mrs Philips with a smile that was at once easy and confident, his manner polished and genteel. "Mr Philips, Mrs Philips," he greeted them warmly, bowing over Mrs Philips' hand. "Thank you so much for your kind invitation. I have been looking forward to this evening immensely."

Mrs Philips flushed with pleasure, her eyes bright. "Oh, Mr Wickham, the pleasure is all ours! We are so delighted to welcome you to our little community."

"Indeed," Mr Philips chimed in, shaking Wickham's hand heartily. "It is not every day we have the honour of welcoming such a distinguished gentleman to Meryton."

The gentleman laughed, the sound rich and warm. "You are too kind, Mr Philips. I assure you, the honour is mine. I have heard such wonderful things about the warmth and hospitality of Meryton's residents."

As he moved further into the room, Elizabeth found herself observing him more closely, fascinated by the way he interacted with the other guests. He seemed to have a knack for putting people at ease, his charm and wit soaking into every conversation.

To Mrs Long, who was notorious for her long-winded tales, he listened with every appearance of rapt attention, his eyes never straying, his smile never faltering. When she finally paused for breath, he interjected smoothly, "What a remarkable story, Mrs Long. You have a gift for narrative, truly."

Mrs Long preened under his praise, her cheeks pink with pleasure. "Oh, Mr Wickham, you are too kind. I do love a good story, it's true, but I do have a dreadful habit of running on so, and Mr Long claims I tell the same tales over again."

"Then your tales have fallen on the right ears, for they are all fresh to me, and I covet every word you have to say about this dear little town."

To Sir William Lucas, who was known for his somewhat pompous manner, Wickham was all respectful attentiveness, listening gravely to his pronouncements on the state of the nation. "I quite agree, Sir William," he said seriously. "The responsibility of the landed gentry is a weighty one indeed. I can only hope to discharge my duties at Netherfield with half the diligence and wisdom you display."

Sir William puffed up visibly, his chest swelling with importance. "Well said, Mr Wickham, well said, indeed. If you ever find yourself in need of advice, you need only call upon me. Why, when I was presented at St. James's Court, I found the advice of..." he paused for a wink and a theatrical whisper, "*certain* gentlemen... noblemen, to be sure, of course... to be valuable beyond compare."

"As do I, sir! My mentor, a fine gentleman in his own right, would applaud such a speech. I shall not hesitate to call on you for the minutest question."

And so it went; with each interaction, Mr Wickham seemed to know just the right thing to say, the right tone to strike, to make each person feel appreciated, respected, and heard. It was a fascinating skill, Elizabeth reflected, watching him work the room.

A social grace that went beyond mere charm or good looks. There was a warmth to him, a genuine interest in others that shone through in every exchange. He asked questions, listened attentively to the answers, and always seemed to find some point of connection, some shared interest or experience.

Even the most reserved guests seemed to blossom under his attention. Mr Harrison, the rector, who was known for his shyness, found himself drawn into an animated discussion of his favourite theological texts, for apparently, there was once a time when Mr Wickham had been destined for the church.

Mrs Goulding, who rarely spoke above a whisper, was soon laughing merrily at some witticism, for the man "dearly loved to laugh."

Midway through the evening, Mrs Philips' voice cut through the general hubbub. "Mr Wickham! We are so delighted to have you here in Meryton. Such a surprise, Netherfield being let so suddenly!"

Mr Philips tried to hush his wife, but she barreled on, oblivious, as she waved about her glass. "Poor Mr Bingley was quite disappointed, I hear, but his loss is our gain!"

At the mention of Mr Bingley, Elizabeth's ears perked up, a flicker of recognition sparking in her mind. What could Mr Bingley's disappointment have to do with Meryton's good fortune?

But that was all there was to be heard from her aunt Philips, for her uncle had drawn her away, obviously trying to prevent her from making a scene at their party. It would not be the first time... Elizabeth dabbed her mouth with her handkerchief to hide the irreverent smirk that overtook her features when she recalled one particularly memorable episode at Longbourn involving Aunt Philips, a bit too much of her Papa's brandy and Mama's new hat...

Yes, perhaps it was better that Mrs Philips took a moment to compose herself. What would Mr Wickham think of his new neighbours if they all slurred when in their cups? But it truly did set her curiosity awhirl.

Had Mr Bingley been inquiring about the same property just after Mr Wickham took the lease? The timing would have been about right, as well as the place she had encountered the gentlemen. Why, it made perfect sense. A pity, that.

A pity because there were not houses enough for both gentlemen, for both would have made for... interesting neighbours. But it *was* strange because Netherfield had sat vacant for over a year, and now two handsome, single men wanted it at almost the same moment? Uncanny.

Chapter Four

ELIZABETH SAT IDLY BESIDE Charlotte, toying with a funny little flaw in the fabric of her skirt and trying to look like she was *not* watching Mr Wickham charming the room. She could hardly help making mental comparisons between the two men who both wanted Netherfield. While Mr Wickham was undeniably charismatic and engaging, there was something about Mr Bingley's simple, honest kindness that stuck with her.

For herself, she could not help but fancy that, perhaps even more than Mr Wickham's polished charm. But charm could be useful, and it appeared that the gentleman did, indeed, know how to employ it well.

Lost in these thoughts, Elizabeth was startled when Lady Lucas descended upon them, her face alight with excitement. "Charlotte, my dear! You must come and meet Mr Wickham. Such a charming gentleman! Why, you look as though you do not even know which gentleman I speak of! Lizzy, tell her she must come at once."

"Of course, I know who he is, Mama. The whole room is talking of nothing else."

Lady Lucas tutted, waving her fan. "Then what are you waiting for, my dear? Your father must introduce you! Such a genteel man, he will appreciate your... kindness. Mr Wickham is quite the catch, you know. Five thousand a year!"

"Mama, Mr Wickham has already been enchanted by half the county," Charlotte protested. "What reason would he have for noticing me?"

"But you can speak, can you not? You are... well, you are eminently sensible." Lady Lucas sniffed slightly, and Elizabeth caught a slip of the lady's eye as she darted a glance at Lydia and Kitty, squealing with laughter in the corner. "If you will not speak to him for yourself, my dear, then consider Maria. A gentleman likes to think that he would find himself in possession of agreeable relations when he marries." Another swift glance at Elizabeth's family.

Elizabeth suppressed a smile. "Indeed, Lady Lucas."

Lady Lucas glanced around the room and clucked her tongue faintly. "Oh, and where *did* Maria go off to? I made her promise to wait for me by the Ficus plant, but she has gone off somewhere—no doubt giggling with her friends. I shall fetch her. Make haste, girls! We shall all be presented together."

Charlotte's eyes flickered with uncertainty as her mother tripped away. Elizabeth stepped closer. "Shall we go together? Or perhaps we could make our excuses to the gentleman and haunt the retiring room?"

Charlotte's smile was weak. "Lizzy, you know I am not unwell. But truly, I cannot present myself to Mr Wickham. Look at him, so charming and popular. What interest could he possibly have in someone like me?"

"A great deal, if he values good conversation, and by all appearances, he does."

"Then it is *you* who ought to meet him, Lizzy, not I."

Elizabeth shrugged. "A pity I have no interest in speaking to him without you at my side. Truly, how could I be presented to such an amiable gentleman without having my dear friend at hand to laugh at his foibles with me afterwards?"

Charlotte's smile was more genuine this time. "What would I do without you, Lizzy?"

"Let us hope you never have to find out," Elizabeth teased, linking her arm with Charlotte's.

Lady Lucas met them without Maria, but she seemed no less determined in her quest. "That silly girl has gone off who knows where, but we shan't miss *our* opportunity to meet the gentleman." She seized Elizabeth and Charlotte's arms, steering them across the room. "Come, girls. Mr Philips has promised to introduce us to Mr Wickham at once!"

Elizabeth caught Charlotte's eye, seeing her friend's resignation and trepidation. As they approached, Mr Philips turned from his conversation with Mr Wickham to greet them.

"Ah, Lady Lucas! And Miss Lucas and Miss Elizabeth, too. Just the ladies I was hoping to see." He gestured to Mr Wickham. "Allow me to introduce Mr George Wickham, the new tenant of Netherfield. Mr Wickham, this is Lady Lucas, her daughter Miss Charlotte Lucas, and Miss Elizabeth Bennet of Longbourn."

Mr Wickham bowed, his smile warm. "Lady Lucas, Miss Lucas, Miss Bennet. It is a true pleasure. I have been looking forward to meeting more of Meryton's most charming residents."

Lady Lucas beamed at Mr Wickham. "The pleasure is all ours, Mr Wickham. We are *so* delighted to welcome you to our community. Are we not, girls?"

Charlotte managed a shy smile and a polite curtsy. "Indeed, sir. Welcome to Meryton."

Elizabeth dipped a curtsy of her own. "A pleasure, Mr Wickham. We have heard so much about you already."

"All good things, I hope," Mr Wickham said with a droll smile.

"The very best," Lady Lucas assured him. "Why, you are quite the talk of the town, Mr Wickham!"

Mr Wickham laughed. "I am flattered, Lady Lucas. But I assure you, I am quite an ordinary fellow. I simply had the good fortune to take a liking to Netherfield."

His gaze drifted to Elizabeth, a flicker of interest in his eyes. But to her surprise and approval, he tore his eyes immediately back to Charlotte with a warmth that seemed perfectly genuine. "Miss Lucas, if I may say so, that is a lovely gown. The colour suits you tremendously."

Charlotte blushed. "Thank you, Mr Wickham. That is very kind of you to say."

"Not at all. I only speak the truth." He leaned forward with a conspiratorial whisper. "I daresay if the room were larger, I would have asked you to dance a reel. Would you have accepted, Miss Lucas?"

Charlotte's lips parted slightly, but her look was no less astonished than her mother's. "I… I expect I would, sir," she stammered.

"Then I shall look forward to another day," the gentleman assured her. "I mean to solicit your hand for a dance at the earliest opportunity. "And yours, Miss Elizabeth," he added, dipping a slight bow toward Elizabeth.

Elizabeth inclined her head. "I hope I will have a dance free, but I make no promises, sir."

Mr Wickham's brows jumped, and he laughed. "I've some competition, I see! I quite like that. Fear not, Miss Elizabeth, for I know when I am being teased, and I am patient enough to permit a lady to have her fun. Oh! And I daresay I am about to be stolen away." He lifted his glass with an apologetic smile to each of them as Mr Philips gestured to him from the corner. "Duty calls, I fear. More new neighbours to meet, but I shall look forward to speaking with both of you again."

Throughout the rest of the evening, Elizabeth could not help but remain acutely aware of Mr Wickham's presence. Wherever she turned, he appeared to be there, charming the local matrons or sharing a joke with the younger gentlemen, who laughed heartily at his witticisms. But he did appear to hold himself somewhat apart from the unmarried ladies of the room unless he could not escape the introduction. Curious.

Elizabeth had become separated from Charlotte, who was now in conversation with Lady Lucas and Maria. That purchased her the dubious pleasure of watching her younger sisters' antics without distraction. Lydia and Kitty flitted about the room, their giggles and shrill laughter drawing disapproving glances. Mary, on the other hand, was deeply engrossed in a lengthy and earnest conversation about morality with the new vicar's wife.

Elizabeth sighed, contemplating crossing the room to speak with Jane, who, so far, had been doing an admirable job of keeping their mother distracted. Just as she resolved to make her way over, a warm voice at her elbow startled her.

"Miss Elizabeth, you seem to be lost in thought." Mr Wickham appeared beside her, two glasses of punch in his hands. He offered one to her with a smile.

Elizabeth accepted it, returning his smile. "I am, thank you. And yourself? Is Meryton society living up to your expectations?"

"Exceeding them, I would say," he replied, his gaze intent on her face. "Particularly in terms of the charming company."

"You flatter us, Mr Wickham. I am starting to think you are quite the silver-tongued devil."

He chuckled softly. "Not at all, Miss Bennet. I simply have an appreciation for wit and beauty, both of which the area possesses in abundance... particularly *some* of its residents."

Elizabeth raised an eyebrow, trying to ignore the quickening of her heart at his bold words. "You are very forward, Mr Wickham."

"Forgive me," he said, his smile turning rueful. "I do not mean to overstep, but I am afraid your good uncle's spirits have quite overcome my senses. Or perhaps it is something else, entirely." He followed this cryptic statement with a friendly nod and a raising of his glass toward Elizabeth.

She studied him for a long moment, trying to read the intentions behind his words. He seemed sincere, his gaze open and earnest.

"Well, Mr Wickham," she replied slowly, "We are always happy to make new friends in Meryton, and no one could be more pleased than I with a witty new companion."

"Indeed? Then if you will be so good, tell me about your other 'witty companions,' for you strike me as a lady whose tastes in company run akin to my own. Pray, start by telling me the character of the town for some context."

Elizabeth hesitated for a moment, trying to think of how best to phrase her thoughts. "Meryton is a small, close-knit community," she began. "Everyone knows everyone else's business, for better or for worse. My own family, the Bennets, have lived here for five generations."

"And what of the other families? The Lucases, perhaps?"

"The Lucases," Elizabeth echoed with a wry smile. "Sir William Lucas is a respectable man who made his fortune in trade. He and Lady Lucas have several children, the eldest being my dear friend Charlotte. They are a pleasant family, though Lady Lucas has a rather singular focus on marrying off her daughters."

Wickham chuckled. "That is hardly unique to Lady Lucas, I believe."

"True enough," Elizabeth conceded. "Then there are the Gouldings, who are known for their excellent dinner parties, and the Philipses, my aunt and uncle. My aunt Philips is always ready with the latest gossip."

Wickham leaned in slightly, his tone conspiratorial. "And what of the young ladies of the area? Are there any I particularly ought to meet?"

Elizabeth raised an eyebrow, her lips curving into a teasing smile. "Why, Mr Wickham, are you asking me for recommendations? Hoping to make a match already?"

He laughed, shaking his head. "Merely curious, Miss Elizabeth. I value your judgment."

"Now, there is a pretty notion. You have known me less than half an evening, yet you seem to think I possess some insights worth hearing? You *do* know how to stroke my vanity, sir."

"Vanity? I've no interest in a lady's vanity," he protested. "But I know a lady of uncommon cleverness when I meet her. Moreover, I feel quite safe confiding in you, for I think you are not the lady to lead a gentleman astray for her own ends. So? Am I mistaken in my judgments?"

Her brows edged upward. "I like to think I am both honest and sensible, particularly in my dealings with gentlemen."

"Then we are agreed," he laughed. "Care to divulge your thoughts on all the local ladies? Ah, that one for instance. I met her earlier, but I confess, I cannot recall her name."

Elizabeth followed the direction of his gaze. "Miss King."

"King! Quite right. It was just there on my tongue before you said it. What can you tell me of her?"

"Oh, she is quite an... eligible young lady. An orphan, sadly, but she has a fine guardian in her uncle. She has a number of friends in town, though she is rumoured to be soon sent away to London."

"Dreadful shame! And... ah, that one? The younger Miss Lucas?"

"Maria. She is lively and a delightful dancer. I am more particular friends with Charlotte, of course. And then there are the Long sisters, though their tastes run more to red coats."

Wickham's eyes gleamed with amusement. "I shall keep that in mind. And let us return to your own family, Miss Elizabeth. You mentioned you have several sisters."

"I am the second of five daughters. Jane, the eldest, is the sweetest and most beautiful of us all. Mary, our middle sister, is very studious and, she fancies, pious. Then there are the two youngest, Kitty and Lydia, who are quite... ah... spirited."

"Spirited?" Wickham repeated, clearly intrigued.

"Yes," Elizabeth confirmed with a sigh. "Lydia, in particular, has a knack for finding herself at the centre of attention. She is quite fearless, much to my mother's delight and my father's consternation."

Wickham nodded thoughtfully. "It sounds as though your family keeps life interesting."

"Interesting might be one word for it. Chaotic is another. My sisters are quite a handful, each in their own unique way."

"From what I have seen, I would call it a delightful sort of mayhem. How does your mother manage to keep order?"

Elizabeth laughed softly. "Oh, there is very little order to keep. We mostly operate under the philosophy of controlled chaos. And occasionally, we manage to avoid catastrophe."

Wickham chuckled. "Controlled chaos sounds like quite the feat. Tell me, Miss Elizabeth, do you often find yourself in the role of peacemaker among your sisters?"

"More often than I would like to admit," Elizabeth replied, smiling. "But I do enjoy the challenge. And it does make for lively dinner conversations."

"I can only imagine," Wickham said. "I must admit, I envy you. I have no siblings, so I am fascinated by the dynamics of larger families."

"None at all, Mr Wickham? Have you any family to speak of?"

"Not as lively as yours, I am afraid," Wickham replied with a faint sigh. "I am an only child. My mother passed away when I was young, and my father followed ten years later. I had some distant relations I never met, and I had a very fine mentor who, I regret to say, has also passed on now. So, you see, Miss Elizabeth, I am almost entirely alone in the world."

"Well, it sounds as though you have done quite well for yourself despite that. Taking up residence at Netherfield is an accomplishment sure to win you universal approval."

"Ah, but I must confess, it was not entirely my doing," Wickham said with a grin. "I have been quite fortunate in my circumstances. And now, I find myself in the company of such charming new acquaintances."

Elizabeth raised an eyebrow, a smile playing at her lips. "You are very practised in flattery, Mr Wickham."

"I only speak the truth, Miss Elizabeth," Wickham replied, his tone earnest. "I have every hope of finding happiness here in Meryton."

"Well, I shall echo that hope for you, and I shall add to that hope my very warmest wishes that you may find a lady of worth here in Meryton. Though I must warn you, my sisters can be quite... overwhelming."

"I look forward to the challenge," Wickham laughed. "I am sure I shall manage."

Just as Elizabeth opened her mouth to reply, Lydia's voice rang out from across the room. "Mr Wickham! There you are! You must come and meet Kitty's new friend!" She bounded over, her eyes wide with excitement.

"Lydia, I am sure whatever it is can wait," Elizabeth began, but Lydia was already pulling Mr Wickham away.

"Come along, Mr Wickham! Kitty insists you meet him immediately!" Lydia insisted, practically dragging him across the room.

Wickham laughed, following obligingly. "Lead the way, Miss Lydia."

Elizabeth threw an apologetic glance back at him. "Forgive my sister. She is... very young."

"Think nothing of it," Wickham said, offering her a friendly wink over his shoulder. "I look forward to our next conversation, Miss Elizabeth."

Chapter Five

"Darcy! Now, there is a surprise."

Darcy inclined his head as his aunt, Lady Matlock, rose from the writing desk in her morning room. "Thank you for seeing me, Lady Matlock. I hope I am not troubling you by calling so early."

"Trouble?" She came to greet him, presenting her hand for him to bow over. "If there is any trouble, it is that I was expecting you last evening."

"Were you?" Darcy escorted her to the sofa, as she indicated. "I sent over a note that I expected to be in Hertfordshire some days, yet here I am already returned. What cause had you to expect me last evening?"

"Your cousin, of course."

"Richard? But I have not seen him."

Lady Matlock gave an elegant snort. "Do you imagine he does not know your comings and goings better than your own coachman? He had word that your carriage was seen in Mayfair late yesterday afternoon."

Darcy raised a brow as he accepted the seat Lady Matlock offered. "I see my cousin's talents extend into espionage. I shall have to guard myself more carefully if I wish to slip back to my own home unobserved."

"You may jest all you please, but Georgiana was quite expectant of seeing you when we heard." Lady Matlock fixed him with a knowing gaze. "I trust you are here to inquire about our dear girl's progress?"

"Indeed, Aunt. I have been concerned about her since her return from Ramsgate. Pray, how has she been faring?"

Lady Matlock waved her hand dismissively. "Oh, she is as she always is, Fitzwilliam. Quiet, reserved, far too shy for her own good. I had hoped that her time here with her cousins and myself would help draw her out of her shell, but I fear she remains as reticent as ever."

Darcy's brow furrowed slightly. "I see. And has she expressed any… discomfort with social engagements?"

"Discomfort?" Lady Matlock chuckled. "My dear nephew, Georgiana is always uncomfortable in society. It is high time she overcame this excessive timidity. She must learn to navigate the *ton* with confidence if she is to make a suitable match."

Darcy tensed. "Aunt, while I appreciate your concern, I believe we must be cautious in our approach. Georgiana is still young, and I would not wish to overwhelm her."

Lady Matlock's eyes narrowed. "Fitzwilliam, you cannot coddle the girl forever. She is of an age to be out in society. What of her debut? Surely you do not mean to keep her hidden away?"

"I have given the matter much thought," Darcy replied carefully. "While I understand the importance of Georgiana's introduction to society, I believe a more gradual approach might be beneficial."

"Gradual?" Lady Matlock echoed with a cynical laugh. "My dear boy, there is nothing gradual about a London season. Georgiana must learn to swim, or she will surely sink."

Darcy leaned forward, his voice low but firm. "Aunt, I must insist on a more measured approach. Perhaps we might begin with small gatherings, intimate soirées where Georgiana can gain her confidence?"

Lady Matlock sighed, but there was a glimmer of understanding in her eyes. "I suppose there is some wisdom in your suggestion. But Fitzwilliam, you must not let your protective nature stifle Georgiana's growth. She needs to spread her wings."

"I assure you, Aunt, that is my dearest wish. But we pressed her into her own establishment too quickly this summer, and…" He hesitated. "I should say that instead of permitting her to grow, it rather… terrified her. I would have her venture forth again at her own pace, with proper support and guidance."

"Very well," Lady Matlock conceded. "We shall try it your way, for now. But I warn you, Fitzwilliam, society waits for no one. We cannot delay Georgiana's debut indefinitely."

"I understand, Aunt. Thank you."

Lady Matlock leaned forward. "Now, then, let us set the matter of Georgiana aside for more pleasant gossip. You are quite behind all the talk this season."

"Aunt, truly, I—"

"None of that high-minded nonsense. You cannot afford not to be in the know when you come to my dinner party next week. Only think if you put your foot in your mouth!

Did you hear that Lord Ashbury's youngest son has been caught in a compromising position with Lady Worthington?"

Darcy offered a tight expression. "I had not."

"Well, it is quite true. Can you imagine? And she, a newly married woman!" Lady Matlock shook her head in mock disapproval, though her tone betrayed her delight in the scandal.

"Indeed, Aunt. How... unfortunate," Darcy replied, struggling to muster appropriate concern.

Lady Matlock barely paused for breath before continuing. "Oh, and you must have heard about the Barclays? Rumor has it they are on the brink of financial ruin. Such a shame. And after Lady Barclay just hosted the most splendid ball! They say Sir Randall lost all his fortune speculating on the Continent, but—"

"But there is no profit in speaking of it. What am I to do on the occasion?"

She sighed. "Honestly, Darcy, you are so tiresome. What harm can there be in a little talk? Besides, I wager you have not heard of Lord Wexfield. Oh! Your uncle speaks of nothing else. I've no head for politics, but it certainly seems like something *you* might be interested in."

Darcy shifted in his chair, his eyes flicking to the clock on the mantel. Blast, there was that twinge behind his left eye again. The megrim was looming, and he had best return home before other symptoms followed. "I dabble very little in politics, save where it directly concerns my interests."

"And how are you so certain this does not? Your uncle speaks of nothing but reforming constituencies and pocket boroughs, and... oh! I know not what else."

Darcy thinned his lips into an approximation of a smile. "Perhaps I will have a drink with him some evening and speak with him more on the matter."

"Well, I care nothing for any of it, anyway," Lady Matlock said, waving her hand dismissively. "What you *really* ought to know about are the lovely young ladies making their debut this season. The Honorable Miss Amelia Fairfax, for instance. Such a beauty, and her dowry is said to be substantial."

Darcy's attention snapped back to his aunt. "Aunt, I—"

"Oh, and Miss Clara Winthrop! A true diamond of the first water, and so accomplished. I hear she plays the pianoforte divinely." Lady Matlock's eyes twinkled meaningfully. "Perhaps you might call on her when next you have a free morning?"

Darcy cleared his throat uncomfortably. "Aunt, while I am sure Miss Winthrop is a charming young lady, I have no intention of—"

"And let us not forget Lady Penelope Rutherford. Such a sweet girl, and from an excellent family. Her connections alone would make her a most advantageous match."

"Aunt, I appreciate your... concern for my marital prospects. However, I assure you, I am quite content at present."

Lady Matlock tutted disapprovingly. "Fitzwilliam, you cannot remain a bachelor forever. It is high time you settled down and provided an heir for Pemberley."

"I am well aware of my responsibilities, Aunt," Darcy replied, his tone growing firmer. "And I have decided against seeking a bride this season. Not until..." He allowed a faint smile. This little notion would do the trick. "Not until Georgiana has been presented at court, and we see which way the wind is blowing. My remaining single could prove... advantageous in forming the right connections."

Her eyes narrowed, and she tapped a finger on the arm of the sofa. "Very clever, Fitzwilliam. But I still say the greatest danger is in losing opportunities to others." Lady Matlock frowned and looked as though she would have liked to argue further but was mercifully interrupted by the opening of the door. Georgiana entered, and Darcy had never been so relieved to see his sister.

Georgiana's eyes, wary at first, lit up upon seeing Darcy. She curtseyed to Lady Matlock before turning to her brother, her face breaking into a warm smile. "Brother! What a wonderful surprise. I had no idea you were coming today."

Darcy rose, embracing his sister briefly. He noted the way she clung to him, just a moment too long. "Georgiana, my dear. I wanted to see how you were faring."

As Georgiana pulled back, Darcy caught a flicker of apprehension in her eyes as she glanced at Lady Matlock. His aunt would likely interpret Georgiana's effusive greeting as a sign of confidence, not the neediness it truly was.

"I am well, Brother," Georgiana said, her voice slightly too bright. "Aunt has been most kind."

Lady Matlock beamed. "You see, Fitzwilliam? Our Georgiana is thriving. Perhaps your concerns were unfounded."

Darcy placed a gentle hand on Georgiana's shoulder, squeezing lightly—a silent signal to temper her enthusiasm. "Indeed, Aunt. Tell me, Georgiana, are you enjoying your stay?"

Georgiana's brow creased. "Very much. Though, I do fear I am little credit to our aunt. I..." She winced faintly. "I am afraid I do not perform well to strangers."

Lady Matlock waved a dismissive hand. "Nonsense, my dear. You simply need more practice. Now, shall we take tea and discuss plans for your debut?"

As they moved towards the tea table, Darcy caught Georgiana's eye. He gave her a small, encouraging nod. She returned it with a grateful smile, her posture relaxing slightly. She maintained a brave face for Lady Matlock, engaging in polite conversation and expressing her gratitude for her aunt's hospitality. However, Darcy could sense the underlying turmoil that she carefully concealed.

Some ten minutes later, Lady Matlock excused herself to attend to a household matter, and Georgiana's calm facade faded as soon as the door closed. She sank onto the settee, her shoulders drooping slightly.

"Oh, Fitzwilliam," she moaned, "I am trying so hard to be what Lady Matlock expects me to be. But I feel... confused."

Darcy sat beside her, taking her hands in his. "Tell me, dearest. What troubles you most?"

"I... How can I trust anything or anyone when I was apparently so wrong before? I simply cannot credit what you tell me of Mr Wickham."

Darcy bit back a sigh. And there it was again—that wave of dizziness. He ought to call for his carriage soon. "This again? Georgiana, we have spoken of this a dozen times. How can you still doubt my words?"

She shook her head. "But you were not *there*, Fitzwilliam. You maintain that he only meant to take advantage of me, but there was never one inappropriate word or gesture."

"His very presence there was inappropriate!"

"It was a coincidence," she insisted. "I saw the man he had come to Ramsgate to meet—a Mr Billings, that was his name. Mr Wickham was to become his steward."

"Steward! How terribly convenient, then, that my arrival disrupted his chances at honest employment," Darcy retorted, his voice dripping in sarcasm.

"He did not leave Ramsgate because he heard you were in town. I told you, he had a letter... Brother? Are you well?"

Darcy was wincing, squeezing his eyes shut against a sudden crashing sense of nausea. No, no, not now! He did not have time for this! He sucked air between his gritted teeth and tried to continue in a steady voice.

"Georgiana, you must understand that Mr Wickham could not possibly have had honorable intentions toward you. He knows better than most what expectations you were brought up to, and he knows equally well that he is not a suitable match. He meant to exploit you."

"He meant no such thing! I am sure of it, Fitzwilliam. He was only ever a faithful friend."

"Indeed. Tell me, was this 'faithful friend' ever entertained in your sitting room?"

She blinked. "Well, yes. With Mrs Younge present. She thought he was a remarkably polite guest, and she complimented you on having such a friend."

"That is not..." He bit his lips together. Dear heaven, it was too late, for he tasted bile. Another moment, and he would humiliate himself in front of his sister! His eyes darted to a decorative basin Lady Matlock kept on a side table. If needs must, he could employ that...

"Brother, are you listening? I feel as though you hardly hear a word I have said, and you do not care, anyway." Georgiana crossed her arms, but her eyes were brimming with tears.

Darcy worked his mouth. That bitter tang was starting to subside, but there was a strange new sensation travelling down the right side of his neck. He drew what he hoped was a calming breath and forged ahead.

"Did Wickham ever ask you for anything? Speak of his 'reduced circumstances,' lament a 'broken heart,' or try to get you to reminisce about your fondest childhood memories at Pemberley?"

Georgiana's gaze grew unfocused in thought. "Well... yes, I suppose... all those things..."

"There you have it, then. He was working upon your sympathies, Georgiana. And he would have succeeded, too, if I had not arrived when I did."

Georgiana's brow furrowed. "But, Brother, he said that he meant to leave Ramsgate a full day before you arrived. He told me the afternoon previous that he had an urgent letter from a distant relation and had to go to London on short notice."

"And he offered to escort you with him, no doubt," Darcy snorted.

And that was when his right hand spasmed. Horrified, he tucked it behind the arm of the chair, so Georgiana saw nothing. But it seemed to have acquired a life of its own, twitching and contracting like a coiling snake. And he had no control of it whatsoever.

"Not at all!" Georgiana was protesting. "He... Oh, what is the use? No matter how innocent it was at the time, you will only see the worst in whatever I say."

Shooting tingles were now spearing the length of his arm. He had to end this conversation, and quickly! "Georgiana, you have been deceived," Darcy grunted. "Wickham never had any such relatives. His sudden departure upon hearing of my arrival is evidence enough of his ill intent."

Georgiana scowled and stared out the window for a full minute, her jaw clenched and her eyes glittering with unshed tears.

Darcy used the moment to collect himself. His hand had gone entirely rigid, the muscles of his forearms contracted and the arm stiff. Angels in heaven, *what* was wrong with him? But he could not leave his sister yet… not when she finally looked as if she might be willing to hear something from him. "Forgive me, dearest, but… I am afraid men are not such tame, civilised creatures as most ladies expect them to be. Pray, trust me in this. I do know that of which I speak."

She kept staring out the window, her creamy throat bobbing in a frustrated sob. "I *do* trust your wisdom, Fitzwilliam. Truly, I do. But I was *so* sure of his regard. He was so sincere, and how could anyone who learned at our father's knee be anything but good?"

Egad… his face was frozen. Darcy tried to smile, or frown, or… or something, God help him, but the right side of his face seemed suddenly afflicted with the same palsy that had overcome his hand. He forced his tongue and the left side to work, but if Georgiana were paying attention—which she was not—he could not have hidden the trouble.

"Georgiana, Wickham is… well, in my experience, he is not the man our father hoped for him to become."

Was… was that *drool* he felt on the side of his mouth? He swiped at it with his left hand, and it came away wet. And Darcy could only stare in horrified awe. Oh, this was *so* much worse than it had ever been! The vomiting and dizziness that often accompanied his worst megrims would have been far more welcome than… whatever this was.

"But you do not *know* that. You have not seen him in five years, since the reading of the will."

That was enough talk of George Wickham for the day. Darcy's body was rebelling in every way possible, and yet his sister persisted in talking of that miscreant? This was no longer to be borne. "While that is true, I have experienced enough of him to believe my opinions are altogether too accurate. No, it is for the best that you came back from Ramsgate with me when you did. I am sorry to cause you any pain, but I am sure that you will reflect on the matter and discover that I am right."

She pouted, her gaze falling to the cold tea in her cup. "Why is it always *I* who will someday have to admit that I was wrong? Just once, I want to hear someone else admit that to *me*."

She was still a Darcy, after all—as proud and stubborn as any of them had ever been, and she despised being wrong. Darcy wanted to chuckle, but now the nausea came sweeping back with an almighty force. His eyes crossed, and he clutched his stomach. "Perhaps someday, but... good Lord, call for my carriage at once!"

He heard her start to ask why, but in the next instant, he had snatched that priceless basin from Lady Matlock's side table and buried his head in it.

"Surely, it is only a mild fever. I was travelling just recently, and—"

"Mr Darcy, with all due respect." Dr Westing frowned and shook his head, waiting for Darcy to subside with his excuses. "You have been experiencing these megrims for what... a few months now? Nearly a year?"

He quieted. "Better than six months."

"And you've still no notion of what might have caused them, do you?"

Darcy's brow furrowed. "Not as such." He puckered his mouth and cleared his throat. Surely, there was something... if only he could remember. "I had a fall from a young horse I was trying last winter."

Doctor Westing frowned thoughtfully. "And did the megrims begin after that?"

"Yes, but... not immediately. I walked away from the fall with only a scrape on my shoulder and a slight bruise to my temple that subsided in less than two days. I doubt it was causative at all."

"Indeed. And how long after that would you say that you began experiencing these megrims?"

Darcy started to shake his head but stopped himself when a stabbing pain in his eye reminded him of why he had permitted a doctor to see him in the first place. "I... I think April, so... a handful of months. I cannot recall exactly."

"That is the third time since my arrival that you said you could not recall something," Westing noted, scratching down something on a piece of paper beside him.

"Well, it was hardly something I thought to record," Darcy replied testily.

Westing thinned his lips. "Tell me more about your hand. What happened this afternoon?"

"I wish I knew. I was speaking with my sister when it seemed that my body was determined to carry on without me. My muscles locked, my face felt numb, and I was even starting to drool as I was speaking. Now, surely, that is some new fever. Something brought across the Channel by some deviant sailors on leave, no doubt. You have seen it before, yes?"

Westing shook his head with a weary sigh. "I have, but not in fever patients. There are... a few possible causes, though."

"Well? Tell me what must be done."

Westing got up from the chair and paced to the window. "Mr Darcy, I expect you have been experiencing symptoms far more frequently and with greater severity than you have confessed. In fact, were it not for Lady Matlock's insistence that I pay a call to her 'favourite' nephew, I doubt we would be speaking this afternoon."

"That is not true. I would have sent for you if I had suffered a repetition of today's... anomaly."

Westing turned. "Mr Darcy, the truth, if you please."

Darcy sagged, rubbing his temple. "Oh, very well. Indeed, I have been enduring these confounded headaches almost daily of late. Most days, I can carry on as though little is amiss."

"And the other days?"

He scowled. "I cannot endure light of any sort. My valet must draw the drapes and shield the fire grate, and I can hardly sit up in my bed."

"I see. And how long does that last?"

"Sometimes, it is days before I am right again." Darcy's shoulders rounded in a heavy exhale. "But that is rare. Once a month, perhaps. Only yesterday, I travelled to Hertfordshire with a friend. We intended to remain in the area for a day or two but were obliged to return the same afternoon. I suppose the travel fatigue is what has me so undone."

Westing tutted a little, clasping his hands behind his back as he paced. "Stress and fatigue may certainly trigger a megrim, but Mr Darcy, by my own examination of you—as well as what little you will confess—I believe your condition is worsening."

"'Condition?'" Darcy scoffed. "Many people suffer headaches."

"Fit, healthy men of seven and twenty do not usually experience almost daily megrims that frequently escalate into dizziness and vomiting. They do not usually have to spend a day or two a month in their beds in darkened rooms. They do not suffer sudden palsies, and they do not..." Westing paced before Darcy and leaned forward for emphasis... "show signs of memory loss."

Darcy's forehead pinched as the halo of the room cooled and faded, its spin slowing about him. "I exhibit no such thing."

Westing resumed pacing. "I took the liberty of speaking with Lady Matlock and Colonel Fitzwilliam before I came. You forgot the anniversary of your own father's death."

He stiffened. "Why should I mark the anniversary every year? Seems a morbid habit."

"The colonel said you forgot the date entirely, and when reminded, you looked pale and shaken."

"Do *you* like being reminded of such things?" Darcy shot back. "I have forgot nothing of import."

Westing smiled thinly—a patient smile, but Darcy felt no comfort in it. "I also spoke with your butler, sir."

Darcy blinked. "How dare..."

"You have begun neglecting your correspondence until he reminds you. You also forgot the name of two callers only recently—people well known to you, and had to be reminded by your footman."

"You would try to forget Mrs Woodrow Fairfax and her daughter if you knew them, too," Darcy grumbled.

"Mr Darcy." Westing returned to his chair. "I am afraid the time is come to face certain realities. There is something very much the matter."

Darcy blew out a breath. "Very well. Fetch your leeches or your drill. Extract a perfectly good tooth, change the humours in my room, saw off an arm. Whatever you must do, get on about the business, for I am blasted weary, and my head still feels as if some fool is banging a gong inside."

"I am afraid it is not a matter for either sarcasm or the barber-surgeon, sir."

"Then, what?" Darcy dug his fingers into the bridge of his nose, pinching as if it might numb the throb.

"Sir, I… I do not like to propose this, but… there is a strong possibility that you may have a tumour."

Darcy's hand dropped. "A what?"

"A growth, sir, inside your head. Malignant."

"I *know* what a tumour is, curse you! What makes you think I have one?"

"Well, naturally, I do not *know*. But the history speaks for itself—ah, increasing frequency and severity of localized headaches, the, ah, the dizziness, the vomiting, the forgetfulnes, and finally the palsy…"

"So, what? You can cut it out, naturally."

Westing's mouth fell open. "Mr Darcy, sir! No one… that is to say, there is not a surgeon in the world who could manage it. Not on a living patient, at least."

A peculiar thing, gravity. Most of the time, one existed with it without being entirely aware… but just now, Darcy's bones each sank into his chair with the weight of lead, and his heart was labouring just to permit him to draw breath. He made no sounds—heard no sounds—for a solid minute, and when he finally did hear something, it was a distant, fragile voice that spoke.

"How long?"

Westing's mouth worked as he bit his lips together. "As I said, sir, there is no way to even be sure. Why, the only knowledge we even have of such tumours is gained from post-mortem examinations, and—"

"How long?"

Westing's face faltered. "I cannot say. A few wee… ahem. Months, perhaps. Or it could even be years. Then again, it may be something else entirely."

"I've no patience with prevarication, Westing. The truth."

Westing swallowed. "We could watch the progression of your symptoms. That may tell us more, but… I am sorry, sir but it may be wise to put your affairs in order."

Chapter Six

"Forgive me, sir, but you have a visi—"

The butler never even got the word out before Charles Bingley burst into the foyer. "Darcy! Thank heaven you're back. I've been waiting for hours."

Darcy suppressed a sigh, forcing a polite smile. His head still throbbed, and the news from Dr Westing had left him so shaken he could hardly stand. "Bingley. I was not expecting you today."

"I know, I know," Bingley said, running a hand through his hair. "And it was dashed rude of me to simply invite myself in, but—"

"Come now. Giles would not have permitted you if I had not given standing instructions for you to be welcomed at any time."

Bingley's posture eased somewhat. "Very kind. I am at my wit's end, Darcy. This property search is driving me to distraction."

"I thought we settled the matter last night. You intended to wait until spring."

"Nooo..." Bingley's brow furrowed. "That was *your* advice, and I conceded the wisdom in it, but my mind could not let the matter go so easily."

"I see." Darcy's shoulders sagged. He was in no mood for Bingley's whims tonight. His head pounded with every heartbeat, and his vision blurred slightly at the edges, but... well, it did take his mind off his own troubles. "Very well. Shall we retire to the study?"

Once settled, Bingley spread a sheaf of papers across Darcy's desk. "Look here. My man of business has suggested a dozen properties, but none seem quite right."

Darcy picked up the nearest document, skimming it without much interest. His hand trembled slightly, a residual effect of the spasms earlier. "You have already considered and rejected this one."

"Yes, yes, but perhaps I was mistaken. What do you think? I know there is no ballroom, and you found the farmlands vastly disappointing, but it did have a fair view of the valley."

"It had a view because it was perched on a rocky hillside. The property cannot possibly sustain itself in farm rents."

"Well, what about this one? You recall, the one situated near the New Forest in Hampshire."

"How could I forget? The western wing was sinking into a peat bog." Darcy leafed through a few more pages, then impatiently tossed them back together in a stack. His fingers felt stiff, and he struggled to keep his composure. "What precisely are you looking for, Bingley?"

"That is just it!" Bingley exclaimed. "I thought I knew, but now... I want something grand enough to impress, you see, but not so large as to be overwhelming. Good hunting, of course, and a decent neighbourhood. But not too close to town. I want to establish myself as a country gentleman, after all."

Darcy raised an eyebrow, suppressing another wave of nausea. "That is quite a list of requirements."

Bingley deflated slightly. "I know. Perhaps I am being too particular?"

"Not at all." Privately, he thought Bingley might benefit from being *more* particular, not less so. "It is a significant investment. You should be satisfied with your choice."

"Indeed. And the more I think on it, the more disappointed I am that I could not get Netherfield." Bingley poured himself into his chair, his face dropping into dejection.

Oh, this would not do. Darcy straightened the pile of papers and pressed them back toward his friend in a dignified stack. His vision twisted again, and he blinked rapidly, trying to clear it. "I suggest speaking with my solicitor instead of yours. Perhaps he knows of something on offer."

"If it is *your* solicitor, he will try to lease me an earl's estate," Bingley groaned. "My income is not *that* comfortable."

"I will clarify your requirements. Are we agreed? Let us speak of this again when we have something new to speak of."

Bingley looked crestfallen. "You are right, of course. I am sorry to have imposed on you like this, especially when you clearly have affairs of your own to attend."

"It is no imposition. I am merely suggesting a fresh start might yield better results."

Bingley was just leaning forward in his chair to gather his papers when the door to Darcy's study swung open with a bang, startling both men. Colonel Richard Fitzwilliam strode in, his military bearing evident even in his casual attire.

"Well, well! What have we here? A war council?"

Darcy rose to greet his cousin, his legs feeling unsteady. Just when he wanted nothing more than to retire to his chambers... "Richard," Darcy greeted wearily. "What brings you here this evening?"

"Oh, this and that," Richard said airily, helping himself to a glass of brandy at the sideboard. "Mostly escaping the tedium of the barracks or my mother's drawing room. And you, gentlemen? Planning the invasion of France?"

Bingley chuckled. "Nothing so exciting, I am afraid. Just trying to find a suitable property to let."

"Ah, the great estate hunt!" Richard exclaimed, dropping into a nearby chair. "I had forgot all about that. A noble pursuit, to be sure. But surely not one to occupy all your time? Come now, you both look as if you've been poring over those papers for days."

Darcy sighed, his headache throbbing more persistently. "It has been... a challenge."

Richard's eyebrows shot up. "A challenge? For the great Fitzwilliam Darcy? Surely not." He leaned forward, a conspiratorial grin on his face. "Gentlemen, what you need is a diversion. Something to clear the cobwebs and sharpen your senses."

Bingley glanced at Darcy, then back at Fitzwilliam. "What did you have in mind?"

"A shooting party!" Richard declared. "In Derbyshire. I expect to have a month's leave. The weather is fine, the birds at Pemberley are always plentiful, and it would do us all good to escape London for a spell."

Bingley's eyes lit up. "Capital idea! Darcy, what do you say?"

Darcy hesitated. His vision swam again, and he felt a wave of dizziness. "It does sound diverting. But to leave Georgiana alone in London..."

Richard's expression sobered immediately. "Ah, of course. I should have thought. Mother has been trotting the poor lass out nearly every day."

"And I could not be so far away as Derbyshire. Perhaps another time," Darcy said apologetically.

Richard nodded, then snapped his fingers. "Wait! Why not bring Georgiana along? The country air would do her good, and she could stay at Pemberley while we are out shooting."

Darcy considered this. His head pounded, and his thoughts were sluggish. "Lady Matlock would be most seriously displeased."

"Oh, Mother will find some other young debutante to torment. Who knows? She might even happen upon one who enjoys all her attentions while Georgiana slips off to happier pursuits in Derbyshire. Come, Darcy, what say you?"

"That... might actually be beneficial. A change of scenery could lift her spirits."

"Excellent!" Richard clapped his hands together. "It's settled then. Bingley, you will accompany us, of course?"

Bingley nodded enthusiastically. "Absolutely! Why, it is the very thing."

"Splendid!" Richard drained his glass and stood. "When shall we leave? Three days' time—Friday? Darcy, you'll see to Georgiana?"

Darcy nodded, a small smile tugging at his lips despite the persistent pain. "Yes, I will speak with her tomorrow."

"Perfect." Richard strode towards the door, pausing only to clap both men on the shoulder. "Friday it is!"

As Richard turned to leave, he paused, giving Darcy a long, searching look. "Darcy, how are you faring? Mother mentioned you were... unwell earlier."

Darcy straightened, forcing his expression to remain calm and composed. "I am perfectly well, Richard. Just a bit of travel fatigue, nothing more."

Richard's eyes narrowed slightly, but he nodded. "Very well, if you say so. But take care of yourself, cousin."

Darcy nodded again, the tightness in his chest easing slightly as Richard finally exited the room. He closed his eyes briefly, willing the headache to subside and his strength to return.

ELIZABETH STEPPED CAREFULLY AROUND a particularly treacherous puddle as she made her way through Meryton's main street with her sisters. Jane walked beside her while Mary trailed behind, her nose buried in a small book of verse she had brought along specifically to read in case they should happen to pass any males with whom she did not wish to make eye contact. Kitty and Lydia bounced ahead, their excited chatter about ribbons and lace floating back to Elizabeth's ears.

"Lizzy, do mind where you're walking," Jane gently admonished as Elizabeth's foot squelched into another muddy patch.

Elizabeth grimaced, lifting her skirt to inspect the damage. "I am beginning to think we should have brought a boat rather than trying to wade. This flooding is getting quite out of hand. Even the streets of Meryton are scarcely passable!"

"They are not so bad if you keep to the edges," Jane commented drily. "You *would* insist on crossing every time you see someone you want to talk to."

"That is my entire purpose for coming to town." Elizabeth waved airily. "I am hardly in need of more ribbon, and I did not offer to chaperon Kitty and Lydia merely for the pleasure of seeing their purchases."

"Then, I suppose you will have to put up with a bit of mud on your hems. Oh, look, there is Mrs Goulding."

As they approached the milliner's shop, Elizabeth rushed forward when she saw how her neighbour was struggling with her parcels. "Oh, Mrs Goulding, let me help you with those," Elizabeth offered, reaching for a precariously balanced package.

Mrs Goulding smiled gratefully. "Thank you, Miss Elizabeth. I thought I was going to slip the moment my foot left the doorstep! This dreadful mud makes everything so much more difficult."

"Indeed, it does. I was just saying to Jane that the flooding seems to be worsening. Have you heard any reasons why it might be so bad this year?"

Mrs Goulding shook her head. "I'm afraid not. Mr Goulding says the farmers are at their wits' end. Some claim it is the water from Netherfield's stream, but Mr Hopper, the steward, claims the bank is holding as well as it ever did."

Elizabeth's brow furrowed. "Odd. I thought it was worse toward... well, never mind. I am sure Mr Hopper knows his business."

"Oh, one would hope. But I certainly hope we have no more rain for a while, for the parishioners claim the water is overflowing into their fields, and they fear for their crops."

"That's terrible," Jane interjected, her face creased with concern. "Surely something can be done?"

Elizabeth sighed. "If only it were that simple. The problem is the main waterway branching off from the River Mery, which runs right through Netherfield. If Mr Hopper says the dikes are all holding, then something more must be done. It would require a substantial undertaking to modify or control the water's course. What landlord would authorize that to save someone else's property when the flooding is likely to be only seasonal?"

"Well, perhaps this new tenant, Mr Wickham, will be more amenable to helping than the previous one," Mrs Goulding suggested hopefully.

Elizabeth was about to respond when the sound of hooves pulling out of sucking mud drew Elizabeth's attention. A handsome bay slogged through the mire nearby, with his legs and belly splashed with muck but his step bright and eager. Mr Wickham sat astride, his tall figure and fashionable top hat cutting a dashing silhouette against the morning sun.

Elizabeth's breath caught for a moment as Mr Wickham's eyes met hers. He dismounted and approached with a warm smile, bowing gracefully to the small group.

"Miss Elizabeth, Miss Bennet, Mrs Goulding. What a delightful surprise to encounter you on this fine morning."

Elizabeth dipped into a small curtsy, acutely aware of the mud clinging to her hem. "Mr Wickham, how do you do?"

"Very well, thank you, Miss Elizabeth," he replied. "Though I must say, the state of our roads leaves much to be desired. I hope you have not found the mud too troublesome?"

Elizabeth laughed lightly. "I fear my petticoats may never recover."

Mr Wickham's expression turned sympathetic. "A tragedy, indeed. Perhaps we should petition for a fleet of boats so the ladies in town may navigate the streets without ruining their hems."

"What an excellent notion. However, I am not certain how we would manage to steer them between the shops. I doubt many ladies have had experience rowing."

"A fair point," Mr Wickham conceded with a chuckle. "We shall have to put our heads together and devise a more practical solution."

Jane, who had been listening to their exchange with a gentle smile, interjected, "Mr Wickham, we hope you are settling in well at Netherfield."

"Most kind of you to inquire, Miss Bennet," he replied warmly. "I am indeed. The house is splendid, and the grounds are beyond compare. I look forward to exploring them more thoroughly once I have put more pressing concerns behind me."

"Oh, the grounds at Netherfield are lovely," Elizabeth agreed. "Especially the walk along the stream. Though..." She hesitated. "I imagine it is rather swollen at present." That comment earned her a nudge in the back from Jane, who likely felt that such talk was not the purview of ladies, but Elizabeth was rewarded when a shadow of concern flickered across Mr Wickham's face.

"Yes, I have noticed that. It is something I intend to look into further. But come, let us speak of more cheerful matters. How fares your family, Miss Elizabeth? Your father is well, I hope?"

As Elizabeth began to reply, she was interrupted by the shop door opening behind them, and Lydia tumbled out, followed closely by Kitty and Mary. Lydia's eyes widened with delight upon seeing Mr Wickham.

"Oh! Mr Wickham!" she exclaimed, her voice pitched higher than usual. "How fortunate we are to meet you here!"

Elizabeth opened her mouth to chastise her sister's exuberance, but Mr Wickham smoothly interceded.

"Indeed, the fortune is all mine, Miss Lydia," he said, his tone kind but not overly familiar. "I see you have made some purchases. Might I be permitted to admire your selections?"

Lydia thrust her package forward eagerly. "Oh yes! Look at this lovely ribbon. Isn't it divine?"

Mr Wickham examined the ribbon with what appeared to be genuine interest. "A very fine choice. The colour will suit you admirably, I'm sure."

He then turned to Kitty and Mary, giving each of them his full attention as they shyly displayed their own purchases. Elizabeth watched, impressed by his ability to make each of her sisters feel valued without further encouraging impropriety. If only Papa had mastered that talent, perhaps his daughters would not so readily make spectacles of themselves in their quest for male attention.

When he complimented Mary on the new sheet music she was clutching with her other parcels, suggesting that he would be delighted to hear her play someday, Elizabeth felt a warmth spread through her chest. That was probably the first time any gentleman had paid her sister such an honour.

It was hard to tear her eyes from him. The way the morning light caught his profile, the gentle timbre of his laugh, the grace with which he held himself - all of it combined to create an image of gallantry that was hard to resist. When he finally took his leave, bowing once more to the ladies, she felt an inexplicable pang of disappointment. She could not help but watch until he was out of sight, his tall figure cutting through the bustling street with easy confidence.

"Well!" Lydia sighed. "Isn't he just the most handsome man you've ever seen?"

Elizabeth turned to admonish her sister but found herself unable to entirely disagree. Instead, she simply said, "Come along, girls. We should be getting home."

"DID YOU SEE THE way Mr Wickham looked at me when I showed him my new ribbon?" Lydia gushed, twirling a strand of hair around her finger.

Kitty sighed dreamily. "He's so handsome. And *such* a fine figure on horseback!"

"Kitty, Lydia, please," Jane gently admonished. "It is not proper to discuss a gentleman so."

"I wonder if Mr Wickham might teach me to ride," Lydia mused. "Wouldn't that be thrilling?"

"What are you going to ride? That miscreant of Papa's?" Elizabeth asked. "That *would* be thrilling. We should sell tickets, Jane."

"Not everyone hates horses, Lizzy," Jane chuckled.

"And I don't hate them, either. I just know well enough to keep my distance. And speaking of which..." She spun round when the sound of hoofbeats approached from behind, her heart quickening as she recognized the rider.

Mr Wickham, once again astride his magnificent bay horse, drew up beside them. The animal pranced beneath him, its coat gleaming in the afternoon sun as Mr Wickham held him in with a feather touch on the reins. Elizabeth couldn't help but admire the picture they made—man and beast in perfect harmony, a vision of strength and grace.

Lydia let out a small whimper of delight, quickly hushed by Jane's firm touch on her arm. Kitty's eyes widened, and even Mary glanced up from her book, a flicker of interest crossing her usually stoic features.

Elizabeth couldn't help swiping a hand over her mud-spattered hem and wind-tousled hair. Goodness, why did she always have to look a fright when she met handsome gentlemen?

"We meet again, ladies!" Mr Wickham called out. "I hope I am not intruding, but I could not bear to pass by without offering my company for your walk home." With fluid grace, he dismounted, his boots hitting the ground with a soft thud. He gathered the reins in one hand and bowed slightly to the group.

"Mr Wickham," Elizabeth greeted him, trying to ignore the flutter in her stomach. "How kind of you to offer. But surely you did not plan to walk your horse all the way to Longbourn? We could not dream of imposing on you so."

"No imposition at all, Miss Elizabeth. A short walk would do us both good, I think. Ambrose here has been cooped up in the stables far too long. Duty, you know, coupled with a spate of foul weather. I have had little leisure of late and we are both growing a bit restless. Are you not, my good fellow?" Mr Wickham patted his horse's neck affectionately.

Elizabeth eyed the horse warily. "I'm afraid I must keep my distance, Mr Wickham. The last horse I encountered saw fit to unseat me most unceremoniously into a mud puddle. I have developed a healthy suspicion of the entire species since then."

Wickham's eyes danced with amusement. "Is that so, Miss Elizabeth? And here I thought you were a fearless adventurer. Shall I protect you from the terrifying beast?"

"Oh, yes," Elizabeth replied, her tone mock-serious. "One can never be too careful. These four-legged fiends are notoriously unpredictable."

"I assure you, this particular fiend is a perfect gentleman. Purchased from the Duke of Sterling's stables and gifted to me by a dear friend. He is as trustworthy a mount as I have ever had the pleasure of knowing. Perhaps he might even convince you to give horsemanship another try someday."

Elizabeth laughed. "We shall see, Mr Wickham. For now, I think I shall stick to my own two feet. Which are, I regret to say, rather sodden at this moment."

"Indeed. I am afraid my valet will give me rather a long look when he sees my boots. In all seriousness, Miss Elizabeth, is it always so muddy in September? If so, I shudder to think what another month or two of winter weather might bring."

Lydia giggled, twirling around to face Mr Wickham. "Oh, bother the weather, Mr Wickham. Don't you know, winter is when all the best parties happen! Do you think we might have skating parties if it floods and freezes? Wouldn't that be delightful?"

"Lydia," Elizabeth admonished, sending an appealing look to Mary, who liked being embarrassed even less than Elizabeth. Mary looked away, but not without giving Lydia a hard bump in the shoulder as if she had stumbled, thus causing Lydia to divert her attention back to the path.

Elizabeth thinned her lips in some satisfaction before turning back to Mr Wickham. "I am surprised my Uncle Philips has not already apprised you. No, this is quite unusual, and no one can account for it. It is as if the embankments were all suddenly gone, and the River Mery spilling over its confines."

"Well, that must be the case, then. Perhaps I will ride out with my steward on the morrow to inspect the weir."

"Weir? I was not aware there was one."

"Oh, yes! That is, I was told there was one upriver, but the property is large, of course, and I have not seen everything yet. Perhaps it will be a simple matter of a repair. But no matter, Miss Elizabeth, whatever it is, I shall see it attended immediately."

Kitty chimed in, "Mr Wickham, might we come along on your ride? We could have a picnic by the river!"

Elizabeth sighed, "Kitty, Mr Wickham has important matters to attend to. We should not impose."

Mr Wickham smiled kindly at Kitty. "Perhaps next spring, Miss Kitty. When the weather improves, I would be delighted to host a picnic for all my neighbours."

"That is most agreeable to hear, Mr Wickham. I know it will set many neighbours at ease for their crops next year," Elizabeth said.

"But of course. What is the duty of a landlord but to tend to his land?"

Elizabeth smiled. "It seems you quite grasp the undertaking, sir."

"I should hope I do. I was taught at the knee of the very best man ever to draw breath, Miss Elizabeth. Sadly, he is passed on these five years, but I revere his memory."

"Who was he, Mr Wickham?" Lydia asked. "Was he very grand? Oh! I bet he had ever so many carriages."

"Lydia, please," Elizabeth hissed between her teeth. "Mr Wickham, I apologise for my sisters' forwardness."

Mr Wickham waved off her apology. "Not at all, Miss Elizabeth. Youthful enthusiasm is to be cherished. He was like a father to me, Miss Lydia, and he was, indeed a very great man. Perhaps I will tell you more about him another time. Miss Elizabeth, I think you would have admired him as greatly as I did."

"I am sure he was a very good man, indeed. I hope you will not think me too forward, but what brought you to Meryton? Surely a man of your talents and connections—for, certainly, this fatherly figure did not leave you without some friends in the world—it seems you could have settled anywhere."

Wickham's expression turned wistful, a faraway look entering his eyes. "Ah, Miss Elizabeth, that is quite a tale. One perhaps best saved for a less muddy day." He chuckled softly. "Let me simply say that life has a way of leading us where we are meant to be. Meryton, it seems, is where I am meant to make a difference."

Elizabeth nodded, respecting his discretion while her curiosity only grew. "You know," she began, her voice thoughtful, "there was another gentleman interested in Netherfield before you—a Mr Bingley. I met him briefly and thought him quite kind. But I must say, I am glad it was you who took the property. Your intentions to help our community will prove invaluable."

Wickham's smile was warm, but Elizabeth caught a flicker of something—curiosity? concern? —in his eyes. "Mr Bingley, you say?" he replied, his tone careful. "I was not aware there had been another contender for Netherfield. How... interesting."

He seemed about to say more when Lydia's voice cut through their conversation. "Oh, look! We're almost home. Mr Wickham, won't you come in for tea?"

Elizabeth opened her mouth to chastise Lydia for the improper invitation, but Mr Wickham smoothly intervened.

"I am afraid I must decline, Miss Lydia. I have pressing matters to attend to at Netherfield. But I thank you for your hospitality."

As they reached the gate of Longbourn, Mr Wickham turned privately to Elizabeth. "Miss Elizabeth, it has been a pleasure. I look forward to our next encounter." With a final bow to the ladies, he mounted his horse with fluid grace and rode away.

Chapter Seven

Darcy stood before the mirror in his dressing room, his gaze fixed but unfocused. Thompson, his valet, adjusted his cravat with practised precision. The doctor's words echoed in his thoughts, the possibility of a tumour gnawing at him with a dread he could not dispel.

Thompson's deft movements blurred in the background as Darcy's mind wandered to the implications of such an ailment. *A tumour*. It explained so much—his headaches, the nausea, the spasms. The fear it instilled in him was unlike anything he had ever faced.

The thought of leaving Georgiana alone, unprotected, filled him with a paralyzing dread. She depended on him! He had so much to teach her, so much to shield her from. And Pemberley! Who would manage the estate? Who would carry on the Darcy legacy if he succumbed to this affliction?

His heart was galloping, a cold sweat breaking out on his forehead all over again. The thought of something growing inside his head, slowly taking away his faculties, was a nightmare he could scarcely bear. How bad would it get? Would he forget who he was? Become unable to care for himself?

Every time he closed his eyes, he saw the faces of his ancestors, each one a steward of Pemberley, each one trusting him to uphold their legacy. What if he failed them? What if he left everything unfinished?

"Is the knot to your liking, sir?" Thompson's inquiry broke through his reverie.

Darcy's eyes refocused on the reflection, noting the flawlessly tied cravat. "Yes, Thompson. Well done."

Thompson stepped back, and Darcy took in his appearance. Immaculate as ever, yet far from composed. He felt like a hollow shell, maintaining an exterior of strength while inside, fear and doubt churned incessantly.

This shooting party could not be more poorly timed. Initially, it seemed like a good idea—an escape. But even above whatever was happening with him, he wondered if the trip might be counterproductive for Georgiana. Returning to Pemberley, where she had previously known George Wickham as a child, might reignite fond memories better left to rot. In London, at least she had Lady Matlock's pragmatic influence to anchor her to reality and her duties as the daughter of George Darcy.

And yet, the prospect of spending time at Pemberley, his sanctuary, brought him no comfort. Every familiar room, every corner of the estate would be tainted by the shadow of his mortality. He had always envisioned growing old there, watching over the estate and guiding Georgiana until she married. The thought of leaving it all behind, unfinished and uncertain, was unbearable.

But... if his time was to be limited, then he had little of it to waste. He had things to finish at Pemberley, and the truth was, travelling by himself, in this condition, might not be wise. Going north with Richard and Bingley might be his best chance.

"That will be all, Thompson," he said, his voice steadier than he felt.

Thompson bowed and exited, leaving Darcy alone with his thoughts. He straightened his posture and, with a final glance in the mirror, turned and strode out of the room. Each step felt heavier than the last, his mind awash with the enormity of what he faced. He had to keep this hidden from everyone—especially Georgiana. The last thing she needed was more uncertainty and fear.

He tried to focus on the practicalities, on the tasks that awaited him, but his thoughts kept circling back to the same dreadful conclusion. *A tumour*. It was as if voicing it had suddenly made it grow, become more ominous. He could feel it, a dark cloud hanging over his mind, sapping his strength and will.

He could not let anyone see his fear. Not yet. Not until he knew for certain. But the doubt gnawed at him, a relentless, insidious presence that threatened to unravel him from within.

Darcy entered the drawing room at Matlock House, his eyes immediately seeking out Georgiana. She sat by the window, her embroidery hoop in her lap, though her hands were idle.

"Georgiana," he greeted her warmly, though his heart pounded with an anxious thrum that made his voice sound strained.

She looked up, offering a smile that was surprisingly bright. "Fitzwilliam. Good morning."

Darcy took a seat beside her, his head already beginning to pound. Good heavens, not again. "You are looking better today."

Her eyes lit up with pleasure. "Thank you, Brother. So are you. Do you like the new style for my hair? Lady Matlock's maid suggested it."

"Very fetching," he agreed, then added with a ghost of a smile, "Very ladylike."

She touched a tendril that the maid had left to curl down her cheekbone. "Do you think? I was hoping she could teach Catherine before we go to Pemberley. What day are we to leave? I am so looking forward to it."

Darcy held his breath as he studied her eager expression, his mind reeling with the fear and uncertainty that had plagued him since his conversation with Dr Westing. The possibilities gnawed at him incessantly, making it hard to focus. Stalling would do no good, so he might as well out with it.

"That is what I came to speak to you of today. I am concerned that revisiting Pemberley might stir up old memories of Wickham."

Georgiana frowned slightly. "But Fitzwilliam, I want to see Pemberley again. I have missed it terribly. And I am looking forward to spending time with Cousin Richard. And I like Mr Bingley very well, too. Is that it? You do not want me spending time with your friend?"

Darcy shook his head, and he could swear it felt like his brain was jangling around inside. "Not at all. Bingley is a fine enough fellow, but he and Richard and I will be occupied with the shooting party. We will not be good company for you."

Her enthusiasm wavered, replaced by confusion. "But I enjoy watching you all shoot. And I can spend time with you in the evenings."

Darcy leaned forward, his tone more insistent as the pain behind his eyes grew sharper. "Georgiana, I think it would be best if you remained here in London with Aunt and Uncle. There is more for you to look forward to here. Moreover, Lady Matlock's guidance will be beneficial for you as you prepare for your come out."

Her expression turned to one of frustration. "But why? I do not come out for another year. Surely!" She gave a short laugh. "A month or two at Pemberley could do no harm to my prospects. I want to be with you and Richard."

"You need to focus on your duties here," Darcy asserted, struggling to keep his voice steady. "You cannot let yourself get lost in the past."

Georgiana bolted to her feet, her fists clenched. "I am not lost in the past, Fitzwilliam. I just want to go home."

Darcy's voice hardened, more from the pain and frustration he felt than any real anger. "You are not going to Pemberley. I am making this decision for your own good."

Her jaw tightened. "Why are you treating me like a child? I am perfectly capable of deciding where I want to be!"

Darcy stood as well, his patience thinning and his head pounding. "Because you do not see the danger in indulging those memories. I think it is better for old attachments to weaken and new ones to grow in their place. Here in London—"

Georgiana's eyes flashed. "I have no friends in London! How am I supposed to create an attachment to anything?"

Darcy snorted, wincing at the sudden sharpness of his headache. "You have not been listening, either to our aunt or to me. I am sorry, Georgiana, but I do not think it best for you to come to Pemberley with us."

Her eyes shimmered with unshed tears, but she held his gaze as her lip trembled with a melodramatic promise. "You cannot keep me away from Pemberley forever. I will go back someday."

Darcy placed a hand on her shoulder, feeling the weakness in his arm and hating the new terror of wondering when his body was going to fail him next. "Of course you will, but not now. Please hear me, sweetling. It is not that I do not want you near. I simply think this will be the best choice for you right now."

She looked away, her voice cracking. "Very well, Brother. I will stay in London."

Darcy nodded and sighed. "Thank you, Georgiana. I will not be away for long, and I trust you will find vastly more amusements here than there."

Georgiana scowled, still staring at the floor. "I doubt that."

Darcy's head throbbed mercilessly, and he knew he had to leave before his sister saw just how unwell he was. "I… I should go now, Georgiana. Rest assured, we will discuss this further upon my return."

Her gaze softened slightly, worry replacing her frustration. "Are you well, Fitzwilliam? You *look* well enough, but you do not quite seem yourself and after the other day..."

Darcy hesitated. He wanted to reassure her, to tell her he was perfectly well, but the words stuck in his throat. "I... I am just a bit fatigued, Georgiana. The journey and recent exertions have taken their toll. It is nothing to worry about."

She frowned, her concern evident. "You must take care of yourself, Brother. Promise me you will rest."

Darcy managed a faint smile. "I promise. Now, you focus on your lessons with Aunt. I will be back before you know it."

SEVERAL HOURS LATER, DARCY was at his desk, poring over the intricate details of his father's will. He could have sworn there was a note in there about Wickh... well, no matter, for it seemed he was remembering it incorrectly, or it was never there at all. The afternoon sun cast a warm glow across the study, making him feel groggy and sluggish. His eyelids were beginning to sink, and his senses slowing so much that he barely registered the knock at the door.

"Mr Bingley to see you, sir," his butler announced.

That snapped him to. Darcy glanced up and gave his head a quick shake. "Bingley? Show him in, Jenkins."

Charles Bingley burst into the room, his face alight with excitement. "Darcy! The most extraordinary thing has happened!"

Darcy set down his quill, then blinked heavily when he looked up a little too quickly. The headache, which had dulled somewhat, was now roaring back to life. "What is it, Bingley?"

"I've received an invitation from the fellow who leased Netherfield. Can you believe it?" Bingley's words tumbled out in a rush. "A conciliatory gesture, I suppose. He said he heard my name from the neighbours—Mr Philips, I expect—and felt so terrible on my account that he wished to make amends. He has extended an invitation for a shooting party!"

"But we are to leave for Pemberley in two days," Darcy protested, trying to keep his voice steady despite the throbbing in his temples. "If I recall, the idea was largely yours."

"I know, I know. Darcy, would you despise me very much if I begged off? I did fancy the coveys in Hertfordshire over any I had ever seen, and... well, to be truthful, you did not seem terribly enthralled with the idea."

Darcy sighed and leaned back in his chair, lacing his fingers over his stomach. "Not entirely, but I just spent the afternoon arguing with Miss Darcy about... conflicting plans thereto, and everything is arranged now."

"Oh." Bingley's face fell. "Oh, dear. She will be terribly disappointed, then." His expression hardened reluctantly. "Very well. I shall write this fellow and beg off."

"No, no, that will not be necessary. Fitzwilliam will still wish to accompany me. So, tell me, who is this fellow?"

Bingley opened his mouth, then closed it again, his face ashen. "Do you know? I am ashamed to say I've forgot the man's name. I *had* his letter, and I was going to show you, but then I had to change my coat before I went out and dash it if the letter was not in the other pocket."

Darcy sighed again, his patience fraying under the strain of his mounting headache. "How could you forget the name of a man who invited you to his home for... a month? What exactly does this invitation entail?"

"As I said, it is for a shooting party, about the first of the month. He said he meant to invite a few other friends; mostly names I did not recognize. I quite fancy he is new money, given the sound of his connections."

"Undoubtedly," Darcy murmured drily.

"But what does that matter to me? Am I any different? My father's money came from the woollen mills."

"But you received a gentleman's education from your infancy, and you have friends among the peerage. You are well-established socially. You can bring nothing to yourself by this connection."

"Oh, bother that. It is only a shooting party, Darcy, perfectly respectable. And besides, my host wrote in his letter about his desire to deepen his connections with the local gentry by inviting them to accompany us in our sport. There, you see? Everything proper."

"Hmm," Darcy mused, tapping his thumbs together. The pain behind his eyes was becoming unbearable. "And you have no qualms about accepting?"

"None at all, old chap. I mean to write back to him at once if it… well, of course, I would not wish to offend *you*, Darcy."

"We already dispensed with that. I am not in the least offended that I shall not be put out for a shooting party that was not originally in my plans. But why are you so eager to go?"

"Well, it would be an excellent opportunity to revisit Netherfield. I might discover what it was about the property that appealed so much to me so that I might learn to find another like it. Or perhaps I will even persuade myself that it never truly was the property for me. Better yet, I might just meet with some new face who can put me in the way of finding my own house."

Darcy's fingers tightened together, his headache now a relentless pounding. "Those all sound like excuses. Confess it—you had already made up your mind to go, and you are trying to justify yourself to me."

Bingley's face fell slightly, but his enthusiasm remained undimmed. "Perhaps, but surely it could do no harm to maintain the connection with this man? Who knows what opportunities might arise? And besides, it would be a chance to see the neighbourhood again. You remember how charming I found it."

"I remember. But this fixation on Netherfield…"

"It is not a fixation," Bingley protested. "It's… it's cultivating connections! Expanding my social circle. Is that not what you are always telling me I should do?"

Darcy sighed, recognizing the stubborn glint in his friend's eye. "There are other ways to go about it. Ways that do not involve revisiting a disappointment."

"But that is just it, Darcy," Bingley leaned forward, his voice earnest. "This could turn that disappointment into an opportunity. And if nothing else, it would be a pleasant diversion. You must admit, we could both use one of those. Perhaps I could secure an invitation for you, as well."

Darcy pinched the bridge of his nose, feeling the headache intensify. His mind kept drifting back to Dr Westing's words, the possibility of time running out. He had decided he needed to go back to Pemberley to begin the process of… things he did not relish… but how could he manage it when, even now, the room seemed to spin? "Bingley…"

"Just think about it, will you?" Bingley pressed. "In fact, the more I think on it, the surer I am that you would be welcome."

Darcy arched a brow. That was precisely the problem, the one that Bingley was failing to acknowledge. Darcy's name had been "welcomed" by many and exploited by several. And from the sound of this circumstance, Bingley was letting himself into a position where he also might be used for his money or his connections.

"I will politely decline."

"Oh. Well, suit yourself. You will still go to Pemberley, I suppose? It would do you good to get out of town for a while."

Darcy opened his mouth to redirect the conversation back to this peculiar invitation. Bingley was a blind fool just to accept it when he could not even remember the name of the host. But his friend's mind was made up—that much was evident in the brightness of his eyes and the set of his chin. Bingley could be indecisive at times, but when he did make his mind up, he could be remarkably mulish about it.

"I will speak to Fitzwilliam on the matter," was all Darcy would commit to saying. "And I still urge caution for you. You know nothing of this man."

"All the more reason for you to consider coming with me!" Bingley shot back with a grin.

Darcy scoffed and shook his head as he pushed out of his chair. "Some other time, perhaps."

ELIZABETH SET OUT ALONG the path to Lucas Lodge, savouring the crisp morning air. The sky was a bright blue, and the sun cast a golden glow over the dew-kissed fields, making the world seem fresh and full of promise. She hummed a little tune, her spirits lifted by the thought of the upcoming Assembly ball—music, dancing, and the lively hum of conversation. Ordinarily, she looked forward to the public Assemblies for the chance to sparkle over the dance floor and laugh with her friends, but this time... this time, she had new cause for excitement.

Mr George Wickham, the intriguing new neighbour at Netherfield Park, had certainly stirred excitement in Meryton. His charming smile, the easy way he spoke, and his light-hearted manner were refreshing compared to the more solemn dispositions she was accustomed to. She laughed as she recalled how he had teased her about her muddy hem and confessed his own struggle with unruly dogs at Netherfield. Would he be as graceful on the dance floor as he was in conversation? The thought made her smile even wider.

Picturing Mr Wickham navigating his new home, dealing with the quirks of the estate with his affable demeanour, amused her. His graciousness, even with her silliest sisters, had not gone unnoticed. How would he react to her mother's incessant matchmaking and Mary's ponderousness at the ball? She winced as she pictured the scene, but that cringing sensation was replaced almost immediately by the surety that Mr Wickham would overlook such trifles. After all, he had been nothing but polite so far, and there was a growing awareness that his interest seemed particularly focused on *her*, not the foibles of her family.

As she walked, the weather began to change. The sun slipped behind a thickening bank of clouds, and the breeze turned sharp and chill. Elizabeth wrapped her shawl more tightly around her shoulders, quickening her pace as the first raindrops began to fall. She glanced back toward Longbourn, contemplating whether to turn back, but she dismissed the idea almost as soon as it came. She was too stubborn to abandon her visit for something as trivial as a little rain, and she would not consider riding a horse again after the last incident, even if it would have got her there sooner. At least, she reflected, her ankle was no longer sore.

The drizzle soon turned to a steady downpour, soaking through her shawl and dampening her skirts, but Elizabeth pressed on, determined to keep her mood bright. The weather might have soured, but she would not let it dampen her spirits. After all, she was on her way to see Charlotte, and she had a firm resolve to bring some cheer to her friend.

As she approached the house, a movement caught her eye near the edge of the property. Turning her head, she was surprised to see Charlotte outside, standing in the mud by the garden, cutting away at the turnip patch with a hoe. Elizabeth frowned; this was no work for the daughter of the house, and certainly not in such unpleasant weather.

"Charlotte?" Elizabeth called out, her voice tinged with concern. She quickened her pace, her shoes sinking slightly into the wet ground.

Charlotte barely looked up, her hands occupied with pulling weeds that had no business being dealt with in such a manner. Her hair, usually neat, was damp and clinging to her face, while her skirts were streaked with mud.

"Charlotte, what on earth are you doing out here?" Elizabeth asked, hurrying to her side. She gently took the half-filled basket from Charlotte's hands. "This is not work you should be doing, and certainly not in this weather."

Charlotte's shoulders slumped, and she wiped her forehead with the back of her wrist, smudging her skin with dirt. "What does it matter, Lizzy?" she replied with a weary sigh. "No one else seems to notice or care what I do or do not do. I might as well be useful."

Elizabeth's heart clenched at the bitterness in her friend's tone. "But this is not like you, Charlotte. You have always been practical, sensible. Why are you out here? Your mother will have a fit if she sees you like this, especially during calling hours."

Charlotte shrugged, her gaze dropping to the muddy ground. "Mama shan't even notice. I simply grew tired of pretending, Lizzy. Tired of smiling and acting as if everything is well when it is not."

Elizabeth placed a hand on her friend's arm, trying to draw her attention. "Pretending to whom, Charlotte? To your family? To yourself?"

Charlotte looked up at Elizabeth, her eyes reflecting a deep weariness. "To everyone. I have spent so long pretending that I am content with my lot, that I have no objections to being overlooked, but it wears on a person after a time. And then Maria gets new gowns when there is no money for me, and I… I just feel as though I am sinking, Lizzy."

Elizabeth's heart ached for Charlotte. "Oh, Charlotte, you are not overlooked. You have a family who cares for you—"

"They did, when they thought I might marry well," Charlotte interrupted, her voice trembling. "But no one thinks that now, do they? I am the eldest daughter, and yet I am treated as though I am already past my prime and of no use to anyone. I do not know how to change it, and I… I just stopped trying."

Elizabeth shook her head firmly. "This is not the Charlotte Lucas I know. You are strong, and you have always faced the world with grace and resilience. Do not let yourself be defeated by these feelings."

Charlotte managed a weak smile, though it was tinged with sorrow. "Perhaps you are right, Lizzy. Perhaps I am not myself lately. But it is difficult when every day feels like a reminder of what I have not accomplished, of what I will never have."

Elizabeth squeezed Charlotte's arm. "You are too hard on yourself. You have so much to offer, and there are still opportunities for you. But this—" she gestured to the basket and the mud-splattered hem of Charlotte's dress "—this is not the way to cope with your feelings."

Charlotte glanced down at her gown as if only just realising how bedraggled she had become. "I suppose I look a sight," she admitted, a small laugh escaping her.

"A sight, indeed," Elizabeth agreed, her tone lightening in an effort to raise Charlotte's spirits. "Come, let us go inside and get you cleaned up. We can have a proper talk and perhaps a cup of tea."

Charlotte nodded, allowing Elizabeth to guide her back toward the house. "I am sorry, Lizzy. I did not mean to alarm you."

"Do not apologise," Elizabeth replied softly. "I am glad I found you when I did. Now, let us get you out of this cold."

As they entered the house, Elizabeth could see that the warmth and comfort of Lucas Lodge had little effect on Charlotte's mood. They were just reaching the hallway when Maria appeared, her eyes widening at the sight of her sister. "Lizzy, whatever happened? Charlotte, what did you do?"

"She just needs to get warm and dry," Elizabeth said, trying to keep her voice calm and steady. "Where is your mother, Maria? I think she ought to—"

"Mama is in the parlour," Maria replied quickly. "Shall I fetch her?"

"Yes, please do," Elizabeth urged. As Maria hurried away, Elizabeth turned back to Charlotte, gently helping her out of her damp shawl and guiding her to a chair. "Sit here for a moment while I fetch you a dry blanket."

But before she could move, Lady Lucas entered the hallway, her expression more annoyed than concerned. "Maria says you have brought Charlotte in from the rain. Charlotte, whatever were you doing outside in this weather?"

"She was feeling unwell, Lady Lucas," Elizabeth answered, trying to keep her tone respectful but firm. "She needs to be looked after, and perhaps it would be wise to call for Mr Jones."

Lady Lucas waved a dismissive hand. "Oh, Charlotte is just in one of her moods again. This is not the first time she has done something like this. There is no need for a doctor, Lizzy dear."

Elizabeth frowned, incredulous at the nonchalance in Lady Lucas's voice. "But this is not normal, madam. Charlotte should not be out in the cold, doing menial tasks that—"

"Nonsense, Lizzy," Lady Lucas interrupted, her tone growing more curt. "She just needs a bit of rest. Charlotte has been like this ever since Maria began attracting more notice. It will pass, as it always does."

Elizabeth could hardly believe what she was hearing. "Lady Lucas, I really must insist—"

But Lady Lucas was already turning away, directing Maria to help Charlotte upstairs. "Take her to her room, Maria. A warm bath will do her good."

Elizabeth stood rooted to the spot; her mouth dropped open in shock. Was Lady Lucas truly so blasé about her own daughter?

Something was terribly wrong with Charlotte, and it seemed Elizabeth was the only one who truly saw it. How could she get Charlotte the help she so clearly needed if her own mother refused to see the truth?

Chapter Eight

The documents on Darcy's desk seemed endless—financial reports, estate matters, letters from tenants. He rubbed his temple, pushing the papers away. Today, at least, the ache was absent. For the past two days, the relentless throbbing in his head and the waves of nausea had subsided. He was starting to think that Dr Westing was an overreactive fool and that he had made himself sick with worry over nothing.

That meant he had plenty of other matters to distract him.

He tried to focus, but Georgiana's face kept intruding, her passionate defence of a man she claimed had acted as no more than a faithful friend. How, how could she be so... so foolish? Her refusal to hear him wasn't just stubbornness; it was a wall he couldn't breach. She truly believed what she was saying and would not be swayed from it.

He should have called Wickham out. That was what he should have done, but...

Confronting George Wickham over Georgiana's heartbreak could do nothing to help his sister. If the man had harmed her, taken physical advantage of her, no force or boundary on earth could have prevented Darcy from serving justice. But all Darcy could realistically accuse Wickham of was being too... friendly. And Georgiana was simply too naive to send the man packing when she sensed... or thought she sensed... what Darcy could only describe as an improper interest.

Was she even right? Darcy had never told Georgiana this much, but Wickham had written a letter to him after the entire debacle, claiming there had been a "misunderstanding," and all he had been doing in Ramsgate was keeping other, mal-intentioned suitors away from her. And Mrs Younge had corroborated it, so all he truly had to accuse Wickham of was hurting Georgiana's feelings.

Was that truly all? She gave her young sentiments a bit too much free rein; therefore, it was George Wickham's fault?

He stood and paced the room, frustration mounting with each step. Lady Matlock was expecting him this evening, and he could think of few obligations more odious to him at present. He should have gone to Pemberley early, away from the suffocating social obligations and prying eyes. If he had, he wouldn't be forced to spend the evening at his aunt's party, enduring her unsubtle attempts to push eligible young ladies toward him.

The idea of mingling with Lady Matlock's friends, engaging in meaningless small talk, and pretending to enjoy the company of people who scarcely knew more of him than the size of his coffers felt unbearable. The prospect of facing Lady Matlock's well-meaning but relentless matchmaking efforts made him want to escape even more.

He would speak with Richard this evening about Pemberley and what he needed to do once they arrived… and it was not hunting. He had almost told Bingley… but perhaps there truly was nothing to tell. Perhaps it was all a false terror. Still, Richard ought to know because… because there might come a time, very soon, when Darcy would depend on him for everything. For tonight, however, he was trapped in a whirl of social expectations.

But there was nothing else for it. And it was time to dress. Darcy took a deep breath, attempting to steel himself for the evening ahead. The semblance of normalcy was a relief, and he clung to it, hoping it would last. He called for Thompson, ready to put on the facade of composure and grace that society demanded.

THE GRAND DRAWING ROOM at Matlock's London house buzzed with polite conversation and laughter. Crystal chandeliers cast a warm glow over the assembled guests, their light reflecting off the polished silver and crystal goblets. Darcy stood amidst the throng, his jaw tightening with each young lady his aunt directed his way. Still, he felt better than he had in days. The headache had receded, and for the moment, he was free from the oppressive nausea that had plagued him. Dr Westing must have been mistaken.

"Darcy! Now, there is a surprise," Richard's voice rang out as he approached, a glass of champagne in hand. Darcy inclined his head, relieved to see his cousin.

"Richard. I had begun to fear you might not come," Darcy replied, accepting the offered glass.

"My dear Darcy, have you ever known me to miss one of Mother's soirées? The very best in food and drink *and* companionship. Why would I not be here?" Richard's grin was infectious, and for a moment, Darcy felt a spark of genuine cheer.

But no sooner had he begun to enjoy the evening than Lady Matlock descended upon him, a young lady on her arm and her eyes alight with matchmaking intent. "Fitzwilliam, have you met Miss Catherine Fairchild? Such a delightful young lady."

"Good evening, Miss Fairchild," Darcy said, offering her a polite smile.

"Mr Darcy, how delightful to see you again!" Miss Fairchild gushed, her eyes sparkling with anticipation. "Are you looking forward to the upcoming season?"

"Indeed, Miss Fairchild. It promises to be quite eventful." The words felt hollow, his smile forced.

"Oh, Mr Darcy, you must tell me—have you heard about the latest soirées in London? They say Lady Wentworth's gatherings are simply the talk of the town! Shall you grace any of them with your presence this Season?"

"I have heard mention of them," Darcy replied, maintaining his polite facade. "Her soirées are indeed quite renowned."

"Absolutely! Just last week, she hosted a delightful evening where everyone was in attendance. Lord Bellamy was there, regaling everyone with tales of his travels. Have you met him?"

"Only in passing," Darcy said, his interest mildly piqued. "He does have quite the reputation for storytelling."

"Oh, and Lady Montague was simply dazzling in her wit. She had everyone in stitches with her clever repartees. Have you had the pleasure of her company?"

"On occasion," Darcy admitted. "She is indeed quite... engaging."

Miss Fairchild's face lit up. "And then there was Sir Hamilton, who always has the most intriguing insights on politics. Do you follow his opinions, Mr Darcy?"

"I have read some of his work," Darcy said, his mind already wandering so much that he hardly knew what he was saying. "His perspectives are certainly... thought-provoking."

"And Lady Whitcomb, with her sharp tongue and keen observations! She can cut through any pretence with just a glance. She must be someone you appreciate?" She fluttered her eyelashes, clearly expecting agreement.

"She is a formidable presence," Darcy agreed, his gaze scanning the room for Richard's face.

"And let us not forget Mr Hargrove, who is always so charming and well-spoken. Do you enjoy his company?" She leaned in, clearly eager for his response.

Darcy hesitated, seeking a neutral reply. "Mr Hargrove is indeed a notable conversationalist."

Miss Fairchild continued to prattle on about various social figures, her words blending into a blur of names and anecdotes. Darcy glanced occasionally at the clock on the far wall. Blast, where had Richard got to? His cousin ought to have saved him by now. How was he to extricate himself from this clingy conversation without seeming rude? So much for his head not hurting.

"Do you not agree, Mr Darcy?" Miss Fairchild's voice cut through his reverie.

"Indeed," he said automatically, hoping it was an appropriate response.

"Oh, I knew you would! You always have such impeccable taste," she gushed. "I shall be certain to look for you there, and as I recall, you prefer light blue?" She fluttered her fan, sending him a coquettish smile over the edge. "I hope you shall be able to recognize me in my costume."

Darcy squinted. What the devil had he just agreed to? Not some blasted masque. Surely not... "I am sure it will be... memorable, Miss Fairchild," Darcy said, his smile strained. *Oh, bollocks.* There went the pain behind his left eye again.

"Mr Darcy?" a new voice interrupted. Miss Emily Tolland curtsied, her gaze fixed on him with unnerving intensity. "What a happy coincidence to see you here this evening. I hope you remember our dance at the last ball?"

"Of course, Miss Tolland," he replied, though the memory was faint and unremarkable. "It was a pleasant evening."

"It was indeed," she said, her tone suggesting a shared intimacy that did not exist. "I look forward to dancing with you again this season."

Even as Miss Tolland and Miss Fairchild were sending one another faintly territorial glances—masked by smiles, of course—Miss Delilah Hill approached, her mother trailing closely behind. "Mr Darcy, it is always a pleasure," she simpered, batting her eyelashes.

"Miss Hill," he acknowledged. "And Mrs Hill. A pleasure to see you again."

"Likewise, Mr Darcy," Miss Hill assured him with a radiant smile and an elegant curtsy. "I do hope you received the invitation for our musicale next week. His Lordship is all anticipation, and I know how it would please him to hear your opinions on the cellist."

"I am afraid I have a previous engagement." Darcy's eyes caught something over the lady's shoulder just then, and he seized on that flash of red until its wearer turned around.

By heaven, there he was. Whatever wicked whim had made Richard abandon him to the mercy of a bevvy of debutantes, his little joke was over now.

He turned his attention briefly back to the gaggle of ladies now gathered around. "I beg you to excuse me, ladies, but I must speak with Colonel Fitzwilliam. It has been a pleasure." He clasped one hand behind his back, made a short bow, and cut through them in pursuit of his cousin.

But even as he made his way across the room, Miss Anne Morton intercepted him. Darcy stifled a groan and forced a smile. Blast it, smiling made his head pound even worse.

"Mr Darcy, how fortuitous to find you alone," she said sweetly as she stepped into his path. "I hope you are meaning to dance this evening?"

"I am not certain, Miss Morton."

"Oh, surely you can spare one dance?" she said, her tone light and courteous, though she remained firmly in his way. "It would be such a disappointment if you did not. Everyone speaks of your grace on the dance floor."

"Your words are kind, Miss Morton, but I—" No, no, dancing was not on the table for him tonight. Even that little side-step he affected to manoeuvre out of her way was enough to tighten the cords of his neck and send a flash of dizziness through him.

"'Kind' does not describe my praise of your talents, Mr Darcy, but rather your willingness to grace us all with your gifts. I did so admire the way you led the set last time."

Darcy took a small step back. "Miss Morton, I truly appreciate your generous words, but my evening is quite spoken for."

Her eyes showed a flicker of frustration, quickly masked by her practised smile. "Very well, Mr Darcy. Perhaps another time, then. I shall look forward to it."

"Good evening, Miss Morton," he said, with a final nod, turning away before she could prolong the conversation further.

Finally reaching Fitzwilliam, Darcy shot his cuffs and glared at his cousin, who merely smiled back with that insouciant grin of his. "Richard," he growled.

"Darcy," Richard laughed, extending to him a full glass of champagne. "You look like you are in need of rescue."

"Rescue indeed," Darcy muttered, glancing around at the sea of hopeful debutantes. "No help from you, I see."

Richard sipped innocently from his own glass. "What, and disappoint Mother? You know she invited each one of those ladies with you in mind. I had to let them each have their go at you, you know, or she would cut me out of her will."

Darcy scowled but felt somewhat less querulous now. Whether it was the champagne or simply the absence of ladies chasing him, he could not say. "She must have been eager to seize her chance before we go to Pemberley."

"About that." Richard twirled the stem of his glass between thumb and forefinger. "I am sorry to have to inform you that I shall not be at liberty to accompany you after all."

Darcy's brow furrowed. Not Richard, too! "What do you mean?"

"My leave has been rescinded, and I have been ordered to Chatham with my regiment. Some nonsense about munitions and supply—oh, I really cannot recall all that was said, but I shall surely winter there. I am sorry, Darcy."

Darcy's heart sank. He had been counting on Richard's support, especially given his own precarious health. The news hit him like a blow, but he forced himself to remain composed. "So, Pemberley will have to wait. It seems I am stuck in London. There goes my excuse for missing the musicale next week."

Fitzwilliam nodded sympathetically. "It is a shame, but such are the demands of duty. How are you faring with all of this?" He gestured subtly to the room, where Lady Matlock was pointing at him as she spoke animatedly with another young lady and her mother.

Darcy's head began to pulse again. "Lady Matlock's influence is strong," he said, a hint of frustration in his voice. "She means well, but her efforts are relentless. And Georgiana... I worry about her constantly."

"Mother's intentions are good," Fitzwilliam agreed, "but perhaps a lighter touch would be more beneficial for Georgiana. She needs time to mature, not pressure to perform."

"I could not agree more," Darcy replied, his gaze distant as the pain intensified. "We must ensure she is not pressed too much socially. It could do more harm than good."

Richard nodded thoughtfully. "Perhaps we can have a word with Mother together. Explain that while we appreciate her support, Georgiana's well-being must come first."

"Yes, that would be wise," Darcy agreed, though he could feel the pounding in his temples growing stronger.

Fitzwilliam glanced across the room and chuckled softly. "It seems you have quite an audience," he said, nodding towards two young ladies who were staring at Darcy and whispering to each other behind their fans.

Darcy followed his cousin's gaze and sighed. "Perhaps I should look for an opportunity to leave London after all."

Richard's eyes narrowed with concern as he studied Darcy's face. "You do not look well, cousin. Is something the matter?"

Darcy forced a smile, though the effort made his head throb even more. "I am perfectly well, Richard. Just a bit tired, that is all."

"Are you sure? You look pale."

Darcy swallowed the rising nausea and nodded. "Yes, quite sure. Let us speak more of this later. Now, if you will excuse me, I believe I need some fresh air."

He moved away before Richard could press further, heading for the balcony. The cool evening air provided some relief, but the fear and disappointment lingered. Without Richard, the prospect of facing his uncertain future alone loomed even larger. He clenched the railing, forcing himself to breathe steadily.

THE MERYTON MARKET WAS bustling today, with vendors loudly advertising their goods and townsfolk haggling over prices. Children darted between stalls, laughing and playing, while mothers scolded them half-heartedly. Elizabeth nodded to Mrs Jenkins, who was examining a bolt of cloth, and waved at Mr Harrison, the butcher, who was deep in conversation with a customer about the best cuts of meat.

Try as she might, she could hardly recall the purpose of her errand to town today. Everywhere she looked, she found herself searching for the face of Longbourn's new neighbour, Mr Wickham. His charm and attentiveness captivated her. His smile was easy, and he seemed genuinely interested in everything she said. There was a warmth about him that drew people in, making her think of him more often than she liked to admit.

But then, for no reason she could fathom, the face of another man appeared in her thoughts, and she could not help a little sigh. Mr Darcy, the man who had helped her when she hurt her ankle. Now, *there* was another face worth meditating on. A pity *he* had not also come to settle in their neighbourhood, for it would be most agreeable indeed to have two such handsome new neighbours.

But Mr Darcy was probably in London or wherever he lived. So why did she keep thinking of him? It was not as if wealthy men often drove through sodden country roads to rescue muddy damsels, nor did they tend to return for them. Still, his smile, though fleeting, was... nice. Not so nice as Mr Wickham's ready charisma, but... well, it was hardly worth comparing the two men.

They were not unalike, though. Were they from the same part of England? Their accents had a similar cadence, which made her wonder. But that was silly because many men came from the north, and not all of them were single and handsome.

"Good morning, Miss Elizabeth!" called Mrs Long, her arms laden with parcels.

Elizabeth blinked back to awareness with a smile for her neighbour. "Good morning, Mrs Long. You look as though you have been very successful today. Mr Long will be dining like a king this evening."

Mrs Long stepped close. "Oh, indeed he shall! And have you heard the latest news?"

"Do tell, Mrs Long."

"They say Mr Wickham is considering a ball at Netherfield!"

"A ball, you say? How delightful! I am sure it will be the event of the season."

"Yes, yes, quite so. He has promised to attend the upcoming Assembly as well. There is even a rumour that he might bring a guest, but no one knows who it could be."

Elizabeth raised an eyebrow. "A guest? How intriguing. Let us hope it is yet another handsome, single gentleman of large fortune in want of a wife, shall we?"

Mrs Long nodded vigorously. "Indeed! But best not to get your hopes up, Lizzy. As I told Mr Long, it is likely an older aunt and uncle, or some such relation. For you know perfectly well, as a single gentleman, it would be scandalous for him to plan a ball without a hostess."

Elizabeth laughed. "Surely, there must be some explanation. Perhaps he has a sister."

"Or, heaven forbid, a wife hidden away in London!" Mrs Long exclaimed, her eyes wide with dramatic flair.

Elizabeth chuckled. "Oh, Mrs Long, your imagination is quite vivid. I cannot believe Mr Wickham would keep such a secret from us. But it does make for an entertaining story."

"Well, I am certain your mother will wish to hear, so be certain to tell her. Now, I must be off, but do keep me informed if you hear anything new."

"I will, Mrs Long. Enjoy the rest of your shopping," Elizabeth replied, watching as the older woman bustled away.

A ball at Netherfield! She could already feel her feet tapping to the lively music, feel the swirl of her gown between her fingers, and hear the swell of excited conversation when Mr Wickham asked her for the first set. For surely, he *would* ask, and naturally, it would be rude of her to decline.

Her musings were suddenly interrupted by the sight of a familiar-looking carriage making its way down the street. Her feet stilled. Why, that... that looked like Mr Bingley's carriage! The thought was tantalizing. She swirled back and craned her neck to get a better look, but the throng of people obstructed her view. The carriage rolled past, its occupants hidden behind the closed curtains. Elizabeth huffed in frustration. That could not possibly be the same carriage, could it? But if it were... were *both* its former passengers present today?

"Lizzy! Over here!" called Kitty from across the street, waving enthusiastically. She was standing in front of the butcher shop where Elizabeth had been supposed to meet her. Elizabeth shook her head. Her mother wanted her to select some ham to send to Longbourn, but she had not even completed her errand yet. How could she have forgot?

Elizabeth waved back and made her way through the crowd to join her sister. Kitty's face lit up as she saw her. "Lizzy, you will not believe the bonnet I saw at the milliner's! It has the most beautiful ribbons, a delicate lace trim, and the loveliest shade of blue. I am certain it would look perfect with my new dress for the Assembly."

Elizabeth smiled and nodded, but her mind was elsewhere. She kept glancing back towards the street where the carriage had disappeared. Was it really him? Why was she so intrigued by the possibility?

Kitty continued, oblivious to her sister's distraction. "And the flowers! Oh, Lizzy, the flowers on the bonnet are so intricately crafted. I can just imagine wearing it and how it would complement my dress perfectly. Do you think Papa will let me buy it? After all, it was not *I* who spent all my pin money, but Lydia, on that stupid fabric that makes her look like a tomato."

Elizabeth gave a non-committal hum, her thoughts still preoccupied. What if it *was* Mr Bingley's carriage? What would he be doing in Meryton? She couldn't quite shake the curiosity that had gripped her.

"Lizzy, are you even listening?" Kitty demanded.

Elizabeth blinked and refocused on her sister. "I am sorry, Kitty. I thought I saw someone familiar, but it was too crowded to be sure."

Kitty's curiosity was piqued. "Who did you think it was?"

"I am not certain," Elizabeth replied, trying to brush it off. "Just someone I met briefly. It does not matter. Tell me more about this bonnet."

"Well, as I was saying, the ribbons are the prettiest shade of blue, and the lace trim is so delicate..."

Elizabeth glanced one last time in the direction the carriage had gone, then shook her head. "I am sure it was nothing," she muttered to herself.

Chapter Nine

"You look lovely tonight, Charlotte," Elizabeth said, hoping to lift her friend's spirits. "I am certain you will enjoy yourself."

"Thank you, Lizzy. I am trying, truly."

"We are here to have a wonderful time, Charlotte," Jane added. "The music is lively, and the company is delightful."

The assembly hall buzzed with excitement, laughter, and the shuffling of feet. Elizabeth stood beside Jane and Charlotte Lucas, their second-best gowns a splash of colour against the darker tones worn by the gentlemen in the room. Familiar faces animated with anticipation moved through the crowd. Elizabeth glanced at Charlotte, who wore an artificial smile. How dearly she wished she could do more to ease Charlotte's melancholy! The Assembly was meant to be a joyous occasion, yet the weight of Charlotte's sadness seemed to cast a shadow over the evening.

"Look, here comes your brother John," Elizabeth said, watching the young man approach. "I think he means to ask for a dance."

John Lucas, barely sixteen and awkward in his newly acquired evening attire, made his way toward them. He stopped in front of Elizabeth, his cheeks flushed. "Miss Lizzy, may I have the honour of this dance?"

Elizabeth smiled warmly. "John, I am flattered, but I mean to stay with your sister. Perhaps another time?"

John's shoulders slumped slightly, but he quickly rallied. "Miss Bennet, it is just one dance. Charlotte can manage for a few minutes. Please?"

"I appreciate your persistence, John, but I have quite made up my mind. Unless Charlotte has a partner, I shan't be dancing tonight."

John's brow furrowed in determination. "But, Miss Bennet, you cannot miss the chance to dance. You may not get another one, you know. I promise I am a very good dancer. I have been practising."

Elizabeth glanced at Charlotte, who was watching the exchange with growing embarrassment. "I do not doubt your skills, John, but another time. Tonight, I must decline."

John sighed dramatically, throwing his hands up in mock despair. "I shall *never* get a partner! Even Elizabeth Bennet turned me down!"

"Oh, did you hear that little scamp?" Elizabeth gasped in mock horror. "As if I were his third or fourth or fifth choice! The very nerve of that rascal!"

Charlotte managed a genuine laugh, but as soon as the laughter faded, the melancholy returned to her eyes like a cloud obscuring the sun. Elizabeth exchanged a worried glance with Jane, who responded with a subtle nod of understanding.

Determined to keep Charlotte's spirits up, Elizabeth and Jane engaged her in light-hearted conversation as the lively music and laughter filled the ballroom.

"Did you see Mrs Long's hat?" Elizabeth asked, grinning. "I believe it has grown even larger since last year."

Jane giggled. "I half expect it to have its own chair next time!"

Charlotte managed a small laugh, glancing around the room. "It is certainly something to behold. Perhaps it will start a new trend."

"I do hope not," Elizabeth said, mock-serious. "I fear we would all be lost beneath such creations."

They moved closer to the musicians, and Elizabeth pointed out the vibrant decorations. "Look at those garlands, Charlotte. They have outdone themselves this time. The flowers are so fresh and colorful."

Charlotte nodded, her eyes lingering on the decorations. "They are beautiful. I wonder how they managed to get such lovely blooms in this season."

Jane squeezed Charlotte's arm gently. "It is a bit of magic, I think. Just like this evening. Let us enjoy it together."

Charlotte smiled faintly. "You are right. It is a lovely night."

Elizabeth caught sight of Mrs Jenkins and leaned in conspiratorially. "Did you hear what Mrs Jenkins said to Mr Harrison at the market yesterday? She asked him if he had any 'reputable' ham, as if he might be selling the scandalous kind."

Charlotte laughed again, a more genuine sound this time. "Oh, Lizzy! Scandalous ham, indeed."

"And speaking of the market," Jane added, "did you see Mr Green trying to sell his 'miracle vegetables'? I do not think anyone believed his claims that they could cure all ailments."

"Yes, and he was so serious about it! I half-expected him to start performing miracles right there among the cabbages."

Charlotte's smile widened, and she began to relax a little. "Jane, I believe you made that up."

"Jane?" Elizabeth scoffed. "Jane could not tell even a little fib. Why, Jane looks guilty when she is telling the truth. Come, Charlotte, let us put her to the test."

Jane took a sip of her punch and raised a teasing brow. "Do not be unfair, Lizzy. If you do, I shall not defend you when Lydia teases you about Mr Wickham."

"Mr Wickham?" Charlotte roused a little. "Oh, is he coming tonight?"

Elizabeth opened her mouth, her cheeks flushing as she stared back at Jane. Then she smoothed it with a smile. "Indeed, he promised he would."

As if on cue, the doors to the assembly hall opened, and Mr Wickham entered. A ripple of excitement passed through the crowd, heads turning, and conversations pausing. Elizabeth watched as he moved gracefully through the throng, charming everyone he greeted. His smile seemed to light up the room, and the way people eagerly welcomed him showcased his popularity in Meryton. Elizabeth could almost hear the collective sighs of admiration.

"There he is, Charlotte. Mr Wickham has arrived." Elizabeth nudged her friend gently.

Charlotte looked over but then averted her eyes. "I do not think I am up for meeting new people tonight, Lizzy. I feel rather... dull."

"Nonsense, Charlotte. You are always delightful company. Come, let us go and greet Mr Wickham. He has such a charming presence; I am sure you will find him pleasant."

Charlotte shook her head, looking down at her gown. "I feel frumpy and uncomfortable. I would only be a burden to your enjoyment."

Elizabeth exchanged a concerned glance with Jane. "You are not a burden, Charlotte. But if you truly feel that way, let us go to the retiring room together. We can freshen up and then join the others."

Charlotte managed a small smile. "No, Lizzy. I insist that you and Jane go greet the gentlemen now. I will go to the retiring room alone. I promise to join you both soon."

Elizabeth hesitated, but Charlotte's resolute expression left little room for argument. "Very well, Charlotte. But do not be long. We shall be waiting for you."

As Charlotte turned to make her way to the retiring room, Elizabeth's eyes followed her, worry gnawing at her. Jane touched her arm gently, drawing her attention back to the approaching gentlemen. Elizabeth took a deep breath and put on a bright smile.

Mr Wickham was weaving through the room with effortless grace, charming everyone he greeted. As he neared, Elizabeth noticed a familiar face beside him. Her pulse quickened—it was Mr Bingley! So, it *had* been his carriage she had seen in the market two days ago.

Wickham finally reached them, his eyes alight with genuine pleasure. "Good evening, Miss Bennet, Miss Elizabeth. It is a delight to see you both."

They curtsied together. "Good evening, Mr Wickham. The pleasure is all ours."

Wickham gestured to the gentleman beside him. "And may I introduce my esteemed guest, Mr Charles Bingley?"

Elizabeth's pulse quickened as Mr Bingley's eyes locked onto hers, recognition dawning in his widening gaze. A flicker of warmth crossed his features, his lips parting as if to speak her name. But Elizabeth felt a sudden surge of alarm—what if he mentioned their first meeting? The memory of that day, bedraggled and limping, was something she would rather not have broadcast, especially not in front of Mr Wickham.

She met Bingley's gaze with a faint, urgent shake of her head, willing him to stay silent. For a moment, he hesitated, the words dying on his lips. Then, understanding her unspoken request, he offered her a subtle nod and stepped back, allowing Wickham to take the lead in the introductions.

"It is a pleasure to make your acquaintance, Miss Bennet, Miss Elizabeth," Bingley said, his warm smile not dimming in the least.

Before the conversation could progress, someone tapped Mr Wickham's sleeve, drawing him aside momentarily. Seizing the opportunity, Elizabeth turned to Jane with a quick explanation. "That is Mr Bingley, Jane—one of the gentlemen who helped me when I injured my ankle."

Jane's eyes widened with realisation. "The day you took the horse out in such terrible weather? You were so muddy when you returned home."

Elizabeth nodded, her cheeks colouring slightly at the memory. "Yes, and now I must thank him properly. Mr Bingley, it is very likely I would not have been on both my feet yet had you not stopped when you did. I am sure to have done myself a mischief by trying to manage two miles in that condition."

Her expression warm, Jane added, "Indeed, Mr Bingley, we are very grateful for your assistance."

Mr Bingley beamed back at them both. "It was nothing, truly. Well, Darcy's idea, really, but I am pleased to see you fully recovered and enjoying the evening, Miss Elizabeth."

"It might have been Mr Darcy's idea, but it was your carriage, so my gratitude must extend to you both," Elizabeth replied lightly, hoping to move past the subject before Wickham could overhear.

Mr Bingley looked abashed, but before he could respond, Mr Wickham clapped him on the shoulder with a hearty laugh. "What is this? Laughing with the ladies without me, Bingley? Why, you have hardly met them, yet I think Miss Elizabeth is smiling at you more warmly than ever she did at me. Should I be jealous, my friend?"

Elizabeth laughed. "Not at all, sir. It was only a happy coincidence of timing. If you like, you may turn around again, and I will make certain to be frowning when you turn back."

Mr Wickham bellowed with laughter. "You see, Bingley? I did warn you—Meryton's ladies are not to be underestimated. It seems you have a talent for being in the right place at the right time."

"Not entirely," Mr Bingley said with a modest lift of his shoulders. "For if that were true, I would be *your* host at Netherfield rather than the reverse."

Mr Wickham shook his head regretfully. "Alas, my one regret in securing the lease was that I inadvertently caused the disappointment of a very good man. Miss Bennet, Miss Elizabeth, I hope we can make it up to Mr Bingley by showing him the very best of Meryton's hospitality."

"Of course, Mr Bingley," Elizabeth agreed, linking her arm with Jane's. She noticed the way Bingley's gaze lingered on her sister and smiled inwardly. "I trust you will find ours the most agreeable town this side of London. Tell me, Mr Bingley, do you expect your friend Mr Darcy may also return to Meryton?"

Mr Bingley began to answer, his expression cheerful. Before he could, Wickham's brows shot up in surprise. "Darcy? Why, I had no idea you knew my old friend Mr Darcy."

Elizabeth's curiosity was piqued. Mr Wickham and Mr Darcy also knew each other? How intriguing!

Bingley's face brightened. "You know him as well? Darcy and I met at Cambridge. He is one of the finest men I know."

Wickham's smile broadened, a genuine warmth in his tone. "Indeed, I could not agree more. Darcy and I grew up together. We were practically inseparable as boys. He is the very best of men, as was his father—why, I was just telling Miss Elizabeth only a few days ago about the good and noble man who mentored me."

"Ah, I have heard much good of him. Alas, I never met George Darcy, God rest his soul, but Fitzwilliam Darcy has always been generous," Bingley said warmly. "He helped me settle in when I first arrived at Cambridge. His guidance was invaluable."

Wickham nodded, his expression turning thoughtful. "Yes, he has a way of looking out for those he cares about. Our history is a bit more... complicated, but there is no denying his loyalty. I trust he is well?"

"Oh, quite so. We intended a shooting party at Pemberley this autumn, but... well, circumstances being what they were..."

Mr Wickham shook his head and waved a hand. "Say no more. It seems I unwittingly ruined more than one plan of yours. And Darcy's, from the way it sounds. What do you say we invite Darcy to Netherfield as well? It would be a pleasure to have him join us."

"That is a capital idea! Absolutely. Darcy would enjoy the company, I am sure."

Mr Wickham chuckled deeply. "Are you certain you are speaking of the same Darcy? I never saw him at a party but that he was looking for an excuse to leave early."

"Well..." Bingley spread his hands in a self-deprecating gesture. "You are not wrong there, but I am sure he would welcome the chance to leave London."

"Then it is settled! We shall write to him first thing in the morning. But I fear, Mr Bingley, we are boring the ladies. Miss Elizabeth?" He bowed deeply. "May I have the honour of this dance?"

"Mr Wickham, you are quite the dancer. Have you always been so light on your feet?"

"You flatter me, Miss Bennet. I only hope I do not disappoint."

"Disappoint! Hardly. Why, I think nearly every lady in the room is jealous of me."

Mr Wickham laughed as he extended his hand to her to lead her down the set. "There is one, at least, who is much better pleased with her present partner." He nodded to his right, where Jane was blushing in Mr Bingley's arms. "They make quite the picture together, do they not?"

"Mr Bingley seems completely enchanted," Elizabeth observed. "He can hardly take his eyes off her."

"And your sister? Do you think she is equally charmed?"

She watched for a moment. "Jane is reserved, but she would not be smiling like that if she were not enjoying his company."

Wickham chuckled. "The beginnings of attraction are always fascinating, are they not? The stolen glances, the hesitant smiles."

"Much like a play," Elizabeth agreed. "You can almost see the thoughts racing through their minds. 'Does he like me?' 'Does she find me interesting?' It is all most diverting."

"Quite so." He pirouetted and offered her his other hand. "And what about you, Miss Elizabeth? Do you enjoy being an observer, or do you prefer to be in the midst of it all?"

"I suppose a bit of both. I think of myself as a student of characters—albeit an amateur one—and it is rather difficult to do that from the centre of the throng. But there are few things I love better than to laugh and dance."

"Well, I must say," Wickham said, a playful glint in his eye, "I find you quite captivating, whether you are observing or participating."

Elizabeth felt a blush rise to her cheeks. "You are very kind, Mr Wickham."

"Kind? Not a bit of it. I am fascinated, Miss Elizabeth, and I find myself eager to know more of you."

"Flattery, Mr Wickham? What would you say if I told you that I am..." She stepped close in the dance. "... quite immune?"

"I would call you a liar, Miss Elizabeth. But a rather fetching one."

"Well, then! I see I am had. Very well, Mr Wickham, what would you like to know?"

He frowned playfully. "Let us start with something safe. Ribbons—do you always prefer lavender and green? Or do you occasionally fancy a bit of scarlet?"

She puckered her lips. "You can do better than that, Mr Wickham."

Mr Wickham dipped his head in defeat. "Dispensing with pleasantries so soon, Miss Elizabeth? Very well, I shall think of a better question. Tell me, how do you know Mr Darcy?"

She tipped one shoulder. "I only met him the one time, when he and Mr Bingley helped me with a twisted ankle."

"Miss Elizabeth, I feel there is a juicy story there."

"Nothing of the sort, but as you have, by now, surmised, tonight was the second time I have met Mr Bingley. I shall confess that it did make me wonder whether his friend intended to follow."

"He must have made quite the impression, then. Darcy does have a way of doing that."

She laughed. "If I tell you something terribly scandalous, can you keep a secret?"

"I am silent as the grave, Miss Elizabeth," he assured her.

"Well, I must admit, I was covered in mud at the time. I fear I was quite the sight, so much so that I wonder how Mr Bingley even recognized me in fresh attire."

Mr Wickham gasped. "Perfectly shocking, Miss Elizabeth! And did Darcy ride on top of the carriage to avoid dirtying his breeches with your hems?"

"Not at all. In fact, Mr Darcy was nothing but gallant. But why would he be otherwise?"

He held up his hand. "I am in jest, Miss Elizabeth. I am sure he was the perfect gentleman, as he always is. Oh! And to my regret, it seems our dance is over." He stepped back, twirling away to bow to her. "Miss Elizabeth, it has been an immense pleasure."

She curtsied. "The pleasure was mine, Mr Wickham. Thank you for the dance."

As Mr Wickham moved away to find her sisters, Mr Bingley approached Elizabeth with a cheerful smile. "Miss Bennet, may I have the honour?"

Elizabeth gave him her hand. "Of course, Mr Bingley. I hope you are enjoying yourself tonight."

"Indeed, Miss Bennet. It is a delightful evening, made even more so by your company. In fact, all Meryton has proven to be quite lively."

Elizabeth nodded. "It certainly has its charms. And have you been settling in well at Netherfield?"

"Quite well, thank you. The countryside is beautiful, and the people have been very welcoming. Mr Wickham is a fortunate man in the securing of his home."

Elizabeth offered Mr Bingley a sympathetic smile. "I think you are right. Tell me, what do you enjoy doing in your leisure time, Mr Bingley?"

"I enjoy riding and the occasional game of billiards. But what I love most is social gatherings like these. There is something so invigorating about being surrounded by friends and music, do you not think?"

"Absolutely," Elizabeth agreed. "There is a certain energy that comes from being in good company. And what about reading? Do you enjoy books?"

Mr Bingley chuckled. "I must confess, I am not much of a reader. My friend Darcy has an impressive library, but I find it difficult to sit in one place for so long. What about you, Miss Bennet? Are you fond of reading?"

"Very much so. I enjoy walking, reading, and spending time with my family. There is a great deal of satisfaction in a good book or a long walk through the countryside. But I declare, there is no delight like dancing."

Mr Bingley laughed heartily. "I am glad to hear that."

They passed the half-hour in perfect delight. Mr Bingley was just as gentlemanly as she had found him to be on their first acquaintance, save that his gaze occasionally wandered to where Jane was dancing with Mr Wickham.

She could hardly blame his distraction, for her thoughts were more often chasing after Charlotte. How long had it been since she had even seen her? Guilt twisted inside her as she scanned the room. No sign of Charlotte. Mr Bingley returned her to the side of the room, and she excused herself, her worry mounting with each step as she wove through the crowd.

Where could she be? Elizabeth moved quickly, her eyes darting around the hall. Faces blurred together, none of them Charlotte's. Panic rising, she finally stepped outside the main hall and spotted a servant. "Have you seen Miss Lucas?"

The servant nodded. "She left the dance some time ago, Miss Bennet."

Charlotte had left. How could she have been so wrapped up in her own enjoyment and not noticed? Guilt gnawed at her, more insistent now. She should have been more attentive, more aware.

Tomorrow. She would visit Charlotte first thing. Tonight's emotions and revelations had been overwhelming, but she couldn't ignore her friend's sadness. The music and laughter from the hall felt distant, almost mocking. Elizabeth vowed she would not let Charlotte go unnoticed again.

Chapter Ten

Darcy's hand banged down on his desk in shock as his eyes scanned the letter before him. Bingley's familiar handwriting, usually a source of lighthearted correspondence, now delivered a blow that left Darcy momentarily breathless.

Wickham. Hosting Bingley at Netherfield! The words seemed to leap off the page, each one more bewildering than the last.

George Wickham, with enough wealth to lease Netherfield? It was unthinkable. Where had he come by such means? Wickham could mingle with the gentry, certainly, but he was never a man of substance, nor even prudence. Darcy doubted there was even a farthing left of the three thousand pounds he had signed over to him five years ago. The idea of Wickham playing the part of a gentleman of property was fantastical.

His hand trembled slightly as he set the letter down. What could Wickham possibly want with Bingley? Darcy couldn't fathom Wickham's intentions. Why extend such an invitation? They had not known each other at university, for Wickham had developed his own circle of friends, quite apart from Darcy's… and he rarely showed his face in lectures. But if Wickham wanted to find out who Darcy's friends were, it would have been the work of a moment.

First, he spent the summer charming Georgiana, and now Bingley…

But that was not the most baffling question. How had Wickham managed this sudden rise? His charm had always been impressive, able to win people over with ease. But to become the new master of an estate like Netherfield? Darcy had seen all Bingley's figures when he was considering the lease. It required substantial means, and apparently Wickham had offered to pay even more than Bingley had been prepared to do.

Darcy stood abruptly, the letter slipping from his grasp and fluttering to the floor. He began to pace the room, his head starting to feel tight again as his pulse bounded at his temple. What the devil did all this mean?

He paused by the window, staring out without really seeing. What if Wickham had changed? Georgiana's recent, muddled revelations about him suggested... what? She had spoken of misunderstandings, of feeling confused at the very worst. But that was not enough to accuse Wickham of any ill intentions, though Darcy's instincts advised him otherwise. Could Wickham be trusted?

An immediate impulse surged through him. He needed to act. Writing to Bingley, suggesting he reconsider his stay at Netherfield, seemed prudent. Bingley might not be aware of Wickham's history of irresponsibility, and he was sure to be taken in.

Darcy strode back to his desk and grabbed a sheet of paper, the quill poised in his hand. How should he phrase it? "Dear Bingley, I feel it necessary to advise caution regarding Mr Wickham. He may not be as reliable as he appears..."

He hesitated, the nib of the quill hovering over the paper. Would a letter suffice? He could hardly write of his concerns regarding Georgiana—in fact, there were few specifics he could dare put down at all. Would Bingley understand the gravity of the situation through mere words on a page? Bingley, with his open heart and trusting nature, might dismiss his warnings as unnecessary caution. Wickham's charm had always been considerable, and Bingley could easily fall under its spell.

But confronting Bingley directly... Was that too much interference? Bingley was his own man, after all.

He paced the room for a few moments, his fingers working into a knot behind his back, and stopped again, staring at the blank sheet. No, he needed more than just words on a page. He needed to understand what Wickham was about, not just for Bingley's sake but for his own peace of mind. There were simply too many unanswered questions after last summer, and then this? Perhaps he had been mistaken in his judgment, but that did not seem likely.

Bingley's letter had also spoken of Elizabeth Bennet. That name drew a curve of his lips as his finger found the paragraph again.

Bingley had danced with her.

Danced... Darcy's brow pinched as he tried to imagine that rather... interesting creature... dancing. Not covered in mud and making sardonic quips to mask her pain, but fresh and at her best... drawing her partner in with her sharp wit and those captivating eyes.

It was not difficult to sketch her face. Hardly a day had passed that she had not flitted through his mind and warmed his thoughts with the memory of her laughter. What would she look like in a ball gown, with her hair coiled up just so, her creamy décolletage bared to the dewy kiss of candlelight?

He shook himself, snapping his vision back to clarity, and Bingley's words scripted on the page. *That* was why he would do very well not to return to Meryton! He had no business letting his fancy run wild on a mud-splattered vixen from a small town and an unremarkable family. Particularly not now, with his own future seeming somewhat... precarious.

But... perhaps it might not do any harm to... well, to warn her. She had several sisters, did she not? Four... his memory on the matter was too exact for his liking, but there it was. Her family and the young ladies of Meryton—Wickham's charm would easily enchant them. It might not be harmful—had not Georgiana sworn that the tiger had changed his stripes? But it was worth a look, at least. Yes, that was only proper.

A letter would not suffice. He would do better to see the situation, to make sense of Wickham's sudden rise, and ensure that all was well with Bingley and his new friend.

After all... Darcy blinked and clenched his fist as that stabbing panic lanced through his mind again. Westing *might* not be wrong. And if not, then Darcy would do well to see that others were well. That they were warned, while he was still able to give the word of caution.

To Meryton, then.

"Charlotte," Elizabeth began as she pulled her gloves off in the entryway at Lucas Lodge. "You left the ball so suddenly last night. I was worried. Are you well?"

Charlotte looked up from her needlework, her smile faint but present. She was seated near the window, a bit of muslin poised easily in her hands. The morning light cast a soft halo around her, but it could not disguise the faint lines of unease etched on her face. "Good morning, Lizzy. There is no need for concern. I assure you, I am quite well."

Elizabeth's frown deepened as she moved closer, the worry in her eyes unmasked. "No need for concern? You looked so... troubled. What happened?"

With a sigh, Charlotte set down her needlework, the motion deliberate and slow. "Truly, I was only weary. The Assembly held little interest for me, so I decided to leave, and Papa obliged. There is nothing more to it."

"Weary? It looked like more than that. You seemed... downcast. Are you certain there is nothing else?"

Charlotte's gaze held steady, though her voice was gentle but firm. "Lizzy, you are imagining far more than there is. I appreciate your concern, but it really was just fatigue."

Elizabeth studied her friend's face intently, seeking any sign of hidden distress. "Charlotte, I know you well enough to see when something is amiss. Please, if there is anything bothering you, you can tell me."

Charlotte's response was a resolute shake of the head. "I promise, Lizzy, there is nothing more. I simply had no desire to stay at the ball."

Elizabeth frowned, but what was she to do? If Charlotte was determined not to speak, she could not force her to do so. "If you say so, Charlotte. But know that my concern remains."

"I know, and I am grateful. Now, tell me, how is everyone at Longbourn? Any news worth sharing?"

"Oh, the usual. Kitty and Lydia are comparing the lists of their conquests from last evening. Mary is still recovering—it will be two days before she utters more than a monosyllable—and Mama is already fretting over the next Assembly."

A soft laugh escaped Charlotte. "That sounds like them. And how are you, Lizzy? Did you enjoy the rest of your evening?"

"Quite well," Elizabeth replied, her tone brightening. "I must tell you about my dances with our new neighbours. Mr Bingley was most agreeable. We danced the fifth together, and he was all charm and smiles. I believe he means to stay some while in the neighbourhood, so we shall all have an opportunity to know him better."

"That is wonderful to hear. And what of Mr Wickham?"

"Ah, Mr Wickham, the sun around which most of the room revolved last night. He is a captivating dancer, full of wit and conversation. We spoke at length, and I must admit, I found him very agreeable."

Charlotte leaned in, her complexion warming. "Tell me more, Lizzy. What did you talk about? Did he show particular interest in anyone?"

Elizabeth's cheeks flushed slightly. "We spoke of many things—his experiences travelling in Europe, his admiration for the arts, and his thoughts on various authors. He has such a way with words, Charlotte. He made even the most mundane details sound fascinating. And he asked about my family with genuine interest, not just the polite inquiries one might expect. He seemed particularly amused by Lydia and Kitty's antics."

"Well! That is certainly generous of him. Did you say you danced with him twice?"

"Oh, yes, and it caused quite the stir, but he was so easy that it hardly seemed to be noteworthy until afterwards when I reflected on it. I was the only lady he favoured so."

Charlotte's eyes widened knowingly. "Indeed, he must be charming."

"Quite! At one point, I asked him about the latest novel by Maria Edgeworth. That was when he was forced to admit that he truly is *not* an extensive reader, though he knows so many authors from his travels that he is often able to fool people quite nicely. We had a good laugh about that. He said he preferred a juicy bit of gossip over some dusty old epic, and I told him he would get along famously with my younger sisters. But he said he rather liked talking to a lady who made him think, and so... yes, that was when he solicited my hand for a second set."

"It sounds like he left quite an impression on you, Lizzy. How wonderful to find someone who can amuse you as well as you amuse everyone else."

"Such stuff! Come now, you know as well as I do that *you* are the true wit between the two of us. Oh, Charlotte, I wish you had been there. Mr Wickham would have quite enjoyed your conversation."

Charlotte smiled lightly, her fingers returning to her needlework. "And Jane? How did she enjoy her evening?"

"Oh, you ought to have seen how Mr Bingley gazed at her! I have never seen such admiration in a gentleman's eyes. I quite fancy *she* is the reason he declared to Sir William that he meant to linger at Netherfield for as long as Mr Wickham would have him."

"Then I am happy for Jane. And for you too. It sounds like you had a delightful evening."

Before Elizabeth could respond, Lady Lucas's voice called from the doorway. "Charlotte, dear, could you help me with the baskets? I told Mrs Long I would tend to what remained after the ball, and Maria was to help me, but she has gone off to Longbourn."

Elizabeth blinked. She had intended to discuss Charlotte's well-being but had been led astray by her own excitement. Now, it seemed, she had missed her chance.

Charlotte set her needlework aside. "Coming, Mama."

Elizabeth rose with her. "May I help? Surely, Charlotte, if you were too weary to dance last evening, an afternoon assembling and delivering charity baskets would be too taxing."

"Not a bit of it," Charlotte insisted. "Go on, Lizzy. Shall I see you at church tomorrow? I think Mama would not mind if I joined the Bennets in their pew."

Elizabeth nodded. "Yes... yes, of course! I shall hold you to that promise, you know. Else I will be forced to come after you."

"I will try," Charlotte vowed as she saw Elizabeth to the door.

Elizabeth wrapped her cloak about her shoulders and turned back as she stepped outside. The door was already closed, and Charlotte had gone off to help her mother. How... odd.

"Foolish, selfish of you, Lizzy," she scolded herself. "All that prattling on... you sound like Lydia." She knotted her fingers inside her gloves and found the path back to the village. If she dared to take the shortcut, she could pass by Netherfield...

But no, had she not already spent enough time and breath on those gentlemen today? Nattering on about them when she should have been encouraging Charlotte! She simply would have to learn to keep her wits about her when Mr Wickham was present.

"MR WICKHAM!" ELIZABETH EXCLAIMED, unable to contain her surprise as she, Jane, and Mary rose and curtseyed in greeting. "And Mr Bingley, how lovely to see you both."

"Good afternoon, Miss Bennet," Wickham replied, flashing a smile that could have rivalled a full moon in all its brilliance. "Netherfield was rather dull this afternoon, so we thought we might seek some of the best company to be had."

"You are quite welcome here, but I am afraid we will have to send out for good company."

Mr Wickham laughed. "I cannot decide whether that is modesty or sarcasm, Miss Elizabeth, but I fancy it regardless. Ah, thank you," he said when Hill offered to take his hat and coat.

"Please, do be seated," Jane invited, gesturing for the gentlemen to follow them into the drawing room. "I am afraid Mama, Kitty, and Lydia have gone to town, but may we offer you some tea?"

"We would be grateful, Miss Bennet," Mr Wickham answered for both of them. "I trust all the Bennets are quite recovered from dancing unto the wee hours last Friday?"

"The thing was simple enough," Mary replied before Elizabeth could speak. "If one does not dance every set, there is ample time to rest one's feet."

Elizabeth caught the curious arch of Mr Wickham's brow, and she hastened to smooth over what might be perceived as a rather peevish speech. "I am sure what my sister means is that you gentlemen must have been put to some trouble, indeed, seeing that the number of ladies far exceeded the number of gentlemen present. It is to your credit that both your hearts and your feet never faltered in the face of all the ladies awaiting their turns."

"Ah, Miss Elizabeth, you credit us with valour, but I shall let you in on a little secret," Wickham replied, leaning forward with a wink. "The pleasure was *entirely* ours."

"Oh, now that is a wondrous thing to hear. I understand you are still finding the town to your liking, Mr Wickham?" Jane asked.

"Very much so. I was particularly impressed by how friendly everyone was. Bingley, do you not agree?"

Mr Bingley blinked—for he had been gazing raptly at Jane—and his grin widened. "Oh, very much so. Why, I have not gone anywhere or met anyone but that I fancied this was the pleasantest part of all England."

"We are so glad you find it so, Mr Bingley," Elizabeth answered warmly.

"Indeed! I do hope Meryton's tolerance for greeting new faces is not yet exhausted, for I had an interesting letter this morning." He glanced at Mr Wickham, who invited him to continue with a smile and a nod. Bingley cleared his throat. "I have some happy news. My friend Mr Darcy has accepted my... that is, *Mr* Wickham's invitation to come to Netherfield. He should be arriving by tomorrow."

Elizabeth's pulse quickened. "Mr Darcy? That is..." She blinked and swallowed. Oh, it would be a false step if she said too much. "Is... this Mr Darcy... is he a particular friend of yours?"

"Yes," Bingley said, his smile broadening though his gaze flicked uncertainly to her sisters. Good man, he somehow managed to refrain from letting on that she had already met the gentleman! "I… I think you will find him quite interesting."

"I am certain I shall. Any friend of yours, Mr Bingley, of course."

"Oh, he is not merely *my* friend. Mr Wickham here has known Darcy for years! You will surely recall my surprise, Miss Bennet, when I mentioned my friend to my host and found we shared the acquaintance. Of course, when we discovered that, we simply *had* to invite him."

Elizabeth's eyes widened. "Yes, I do recall, it was a happy coincidence. Is he… ah… an amiable man?" She shot another glance at Mr Bingley, hoping he would keep her little secret, but she found the gentleman blushing at Jane, and entirely ignorant of her look.

"Darcy is a remarkable man," Mr Wickham supplied. "I am sure you will find him quite… intriguing."

Elizabeth laughed. "'Intriguing?' That sounds like a challenge, Mr Wickham."

Bingley chuckled. "Darcy can be somewhat reserved. Some might even say 'aloof.' But I assure you, he is quite a dignified fellow, and he is as good a man as ever I knew—save, perhaps, for his father."

She leaned forward, folding her hands over her knee. "I look forward to meeting him, then. Perhaps we can draw the man out of his shell, eh?"

"Be gentle with him, Miss Bennet," Mr Wickham laughed. "We would not wish to frighten him off before he has a chance to let down his guard."

"Oh, a recluse. My specialty! I shall have to see if I can find the key to this locked-up fellow. All in good sport, of course! But enough about Mr Darcy, who is not even here. We have hardly done our duty to the two of you, seated in our drawing room. Look, here is Mrs Hill with the tea."

After the gentlemen had whiled away their quarter of an hour and taken their leave, Elizabeth resorted to pacing the drawing room. Mr Darcy, returning to Meryton! His would be a welcome face this autumn. *Exceedingly* welcome if her first impression of him was at all accurate. Was he truly as kind as she recalled? More than likely, he was spoken for by some insipid London heiress.

A pity, really. Such a kind and handsome gentleman, one blessed with that wry turn to his mouth that spoke of deeper understanding than he let on, ought to be the rightful property of a wife who could appreciate his cleverness. Well, Mr Bingley had spoken of no wife coming to Netherfield with Mr Darcy, had he? How very interesting…

Particularly if Mr Wickham made good on his promise to host a ball at Netherfield.

Chapter Eleven

THE CARRIAGE JOLTED ON the uneven road, each bump sending a jarring throb through Darcy's skull. He pressed a hand to his temple, willing the headache to subside. It had begun shortly after leaving London, a relentless pounding that made each mile feel like an eternity. By the time they reached Netherfield, the pain had dulled to a persistent ache, but it was still enough to make his patience thin and his mood irritable... particularly when *that* man met him the moment his carriage drew to a halt.

"Darcy, welcome to Netherfield!" Wickham greeted, bowing with that slight turn to his head that Darcy's father used to affect. How curious to see Wickham emulating it! Yet, he looked perfectly at ease and sincere.

"Wickham," Darcy acknowledged with a tight nod. "Thank you for receiving me." Those words tasted as bitter in his mouth as they had sounded in his head the past four hours.

"The pleasure is entirely mine, Darcy." Wickham's smile, so disarmingly genuine, made Darcy's suspicions waver. *After last summer, how dare he...* "Please, come inside. Bingley and I have been eagerly awaiting your arrival."

Darcy stepped into the house. High ceilings adorned with intricate mouldings loomed above, while sunlight filtered through large, elegantly draped windows. Polished wooden floors reflected the light, and tasteful paintings lined the walls. The grandeur spoke of good taste, an understated opulence. Not Wickham's taste, though... he had hardly been here long enough to effect any changes of his own.

Wickham strolled ahead, his steps unhurried, casually gesturing to a Reynolds painting of an English pointer and three children on the opposite wall. "You might appreciate this, Darcy. I have always admired it, but until recently, the owner was unwilling to part with it. It looks well there, does it not?"

Darcy blinked. The boys in the portrait looked of a similar age, each with dark hair, but their eyes were dissimilar. One looked serious, his dark eyes focused somewhere to the side as he reclined beside the dog with a book in his hand. The other stared directly at the observer with bright blue eyes and a roguish smile. But the younger girl posed with them looked… uncannily like Georgiana. Rage prickled over the back of his neck, and the piercing light in his head intensified. *Where the devil had that come from?*

"Darcy! At last, you have arrived!"

Darcy snapped himself back to the moment at the sound of Bingley's voice. Calm… He forced himself to draw a steadying breath before Bingley was grasping his hand in his usual, buoyant greeting. "Bingley," he said, straining to keep the crack out of his tones.

"I cannot tell you how delighted I was when I got your letter!" Bingley enthused. "Wickham is a terribly generous host, do you not say, letting me invite my own guest?"

"Oh, come, Bingley," Wickham broke in with a laugh. "Do you not think I would leap at the chance to welcome my old friend? Such a fine coincidence! Come, Darcy, you must wish to refresh yourself. You always look primped and pressed as if you just stepped out your own front door, but I know you well enough to know you would welcome a moment to yourself. Barclay here will show you up, and then we shall have tea in the drawing room."

Darcy offered a strained smile, nodding curtly as Barclay stepped forward to guide him. As he followed the butler through the hallway and ascended the grand staircase, Darcy's thoughts were far from appreciating the grandeur of the house, with its polished wood and elegant decorations. One question kept tumbling about inside his head. *How?*

Barclay opened the door to a spacious guest room, furnished tastefully with a large four-poster bed, a writing desk, and a fireplace already lit to chase away the October chill. "Your room, Mr Darcy," Barclay said with a bow. "If you need anything, please ring the bell, and I shall attend to you immediately."

"Thank you, Barclay," Darcy replied, his tone brusquer than intended. He waited until the butler closed the door before allowing himself a moment of vulnerability. Running a hand through his hair, he winced as a sharp pain lanced through his temple, making him curse under his breath. He began to pace the room, trying to regain his composure, each step sending reverberations of pain through his skull.

The sight of the painting still gnawed at him, adding to the pounding in his head. Could it truly be a coincidence, some prized painting of some other gentleman's children, or was Wickham toying with him in some new perverse manner? But… he didn't seem to be toying with him. He seemed rather… content. Proud, but not in any improper way.

Darcy splashed some water on his face from the basin, hoping the coolness might ease the ache behind his eyes. For a moment, the cold water provided a brief but much-needed clarity, numbing the persistent throbbing. He adjusted his cravat, ensuring it was impeccably tied despite his trembling fingers, and straightened his coat. The exertion made the pain spike again, but he forced himself to ignore it. Satisfied with his appearance, he took one final look in the mirror, his expression now resolute and composed, though his eyes betrayed the lingering discomfort.

Darcy left the room, his footsteps purposeful as he made his way back downstairs. As he approached the drawing room, he could hear the murmur of voices and the occasional laugh, Bingley's voice unmistakably louder than Wickham's. Darcy took a deep breath before entering, his face a mask of calm politeness.

Bingley was the first to notice his return. "Ah, Darcy! There you are. Come, join us. Tea has just arrived."

Wickham, lounging casually in a chair, gave him a smile that looked patient and welcoming. "Darcy, do help yourself. I've taken the liberty of ensuring your favourite blend is available."

"Thank you," Darcy replied evenly, taking a seat. He accepted a cup from the maid, who poured, then curtsied before she went out. She was... well, she was precisely as he might have expected a maid in Wickham's employ to look. Young and well-shaped, with shining hair and a fresh face. Darcy frowned as he addressed his cup.

"The countryside here is truly splendid, Darcy," Wickham was saying. "The land is fertile, and the views are quite picturesque. Not so breath-taking as Derbyshire, naturally, but the farmers have fewer rocks to contend with in their fields. I believe you will find much to admire."

Darcy glanced around, taking in the elegant furnishings and the warmth of the fire crackling in the hearth. "It seems you have settled well, Wickham. How do you find the management of the estate?"

There. Let him answer *that.* Estate management required diligence and strategic planning—things Wickham was not known for.

Wickham's eyes gleamed with satisfaction. "Ah, of course you would ask that question. I am not so experienced as you are, turning my hand to the affairs of the master, but I cannot say I find the duty disagreeable. Do you know, I wake up in a cold terror some nights, haunted by the spectre of your father's face and wondering what I might have left undone during the day!"

Darcy thinned his lips and looked back at his cup. "Father was diligent in all his ways. As well as generous and honest to a fault."

Wickham laughed. "Oh, Darcy, I know very well what you are doing! Let me simply assure you that I strive to live up to his example. No, no, I find myself quite content here at Netherfield. It is no Pemberley, but then, no other place on earth is. The tenants are hardworking, and the land, though full of potential, requires constant attention due to some local troubles. But Bingley has been of immense help. His enthusiasm and diligence are invaluable."

Bingley beamed at the compliment. "Thank you, Wickham. The truth is, I have learned much under your guidance. This region does indeed have much to offer. Dash it all, if you should change your mind at any moment, I would be more than happy to assume the lease from you."

Darcy shifted uncomfortably. Wickham and Bingley had certainly grown... companionable. "Indeed. It is no small task to oversee such a property. Have you encountered any significant challenges?"

"There have been a few issues, but nothing insurmountable. We are presently dealing with some flooding in the lower fields, but surely, it is nothing more than what is seasonable for the region."

Darcy glanced at Bingley. There had been flooding several weeks ago when he was here before. Elizabeth Bennet had been quite flustered by the matter, but Wickham seemed rather to dismiss it. Surely, it had not entirely abated, even as the weather grew worse for the season. "Any reports of similar problems among your neighbours?" he asked carefully.

"Some. I mean to speak with a few of them in the coming days to learn what I may, but, as you can imagine, I have been rather preoccupied. My steward has me caught up on all the estate business, however, and I intend to make a good neighbour of myself, so that shall receive my next attention."

Darcy listened carefully, watching for any facial tics or inflexions that might yield... anything. But there was nothing to be found—just the manner of a man who appeared to be everything he claimed. It was unsettling, yet Wickham's demeanour left little room for doubt. Perhaps Darcy had underestimated him.

The notion bore some examination... some other time when his head was working properly.

"And the local community? How have they received you, Wickham?"

Wickham's face lit up again. "They have been wonderfully hospitable. The neighbours here are quite charming, particularly the Philipses and the Lucases. Then there is the Bennet family. They have been the most welcoming."

Darcy's fingers twitched on his cup, and he dared not look up until he was master of his facial expressions. "The Bennets, you say?"

"Oh, yes. I daresay you will hear that name again," Wickham replied with a throaty chuckle. "They say Mr Bennet is a man of wit and intelligence, though I have yet to have the pleasure of an introduction. His daughters, however, are both plentiful and delightful, and you will never find a hostess more eager to please than Mrs Bennet."

At this, Darcy glanced quickly at Bingley. Had he told Wickham about their meeting with Miss Elizabeth? The matter had never arisen between them, for it did not seem pertinent. But now, having reinserted themselves into the social sphere of Meryton, it seemed prudent that, as gentlemen, they would keep the lady's secret and not risk compromising her dignity.

Bingley, bless him, caught the sudden shift in Darcy's gaze and, after a question and then an answering guess flashed in his eyes, shook his head subtly. Darcy gave a faint nod in return. The lady meant nothing to him, truly, but... well, hang it all, she did not deserve to be humiliated.

Besides, for so long as he was in the area, it would not do to cultivate the ire of one with such a sharp tongue. Despite the throbbing pain behind his eye, he could not help a smile at that thought.

"PAPA, YOU MISSED QUITE the spectacle. Mrs Long and Mrs Purvis were just here for tea, and I must say, they were in excellent spirits. You could have had your fill of lively company. Lace, ribbon, and shoe roses until you swooned from the splendour of it all!"

Mr Bennet glanced up, quirking an eyebrow over an exasperated scowl. "And that is why I remain firmly lodged in this seat."

"Oh, come, Papa! They did have some rather interesting conversation." Elizabeth sat in the chair facing her father's desk and picked up a paperweight to toy with.

"And what, pray to tell, did these fine ladies discuss that would have rivalled my current reading?"

Elizabeth rolled the weight from one hand to the other. "Oh, nothing of great importance. Just plans for another Assembly in a fortnight, but it might be cancelled if there truly is to be a ball at Netherfield. Imagine the horror of such frivolity!"

"A ball, you say? The very thought sends shivers down my spine. However will my purse survive your mother's plundering? Am I expected to drag myself from my comfortable house to stand around gossiping with half a dozen coxcombs and one or two blackguards?"

"Those are our neighbours you insult! Come, Papa, it cannot be so dreadful as that. Think of the opportunity to hear endless praise of your daughters' accomplishments."

"Yes, the relentless flattery might be my undoing. Perhaps I should wad some cotton for my ears."

"Oh, Papa!" she laughed. "You do amuse yourself. But truly, you would have enjoyed the company today. Mrs Purvis developed a rather unfortunate hiccough in the middle of tea. There, tell me you would not have found something to chuckle to yourself about later at that."

Mr Bennet smiled briefly as he conceded the point, but his smile faded as he returned his gaze to the papers on his desk. "I fear my mind is too preoccupied with matters less pleasant than dancing, Lizzy."

Elizabeth, sensing the shift in his mood, softened her voice. "Is something troubling you, Papa?"

Mr Bennet sighed, setting his notes aside. "More reports of rising winter floodwaters. Many of the fields have been destroyed. The damage to Longbourn's lands alone is substantial."

Elizabeth's brow furrowed as she picked up one of the reports. "How badly has it affected us?"

Mr Bennet leaned back in his chair, rubbing his temples. "The lower fields are nearly ruined. The tenants are digging ditches to drain it off where they can, but if the normal seasonal rains continue, we may face even greater losses."

Elizabeth sat down opposite her father. "What can be done? Have you spoken to the tenants?"

"I have, but there is little comfort I can offer them. We must find a way to aid them, but our resources are not endless."

Elizabeth thought for a moment. "Perhaps we could organise a relief effort. The community could come together to support those most affected."

Mr Bennet shook his head. "You have a generous heart, Lizzy, but such efforts require coordination and funding. We must be realistic."

Elizabeth frowned in thought. "What exactly is the situation, Father? Why is the damage so severe?"

Mr Bennet creaked about in his chair, looking weary. "The river has been rising steadily, and it is only going to get worse through the season."

"But it is so every year," she interrupted.

"You did not let me finish. A neighbour reported that a man-made weir upriver has been breached and looks as though it has been for some time."

Elizabeth's eyes widened. "A weir? How did we miss that?"

"It was in the woods. The leak was probably small at first, and the weir has never shown any signs of weakness before. Now, the breach has grown, and devil take me if it does not look as if some fool has done it intentionally."

"Intentionally! But who would do such a thing?'

He shook his head and pinched the bridge of his nose. "Do not repeat that last bit to anyone. After all, no one else thought the same, so surely, it is nothing more than my ill-tempered fancy at being dragged out in hip waders to survey the wreckage. Besides, the result is the same—fields and houses at risk of ruin."

Elizabeth tossed the paperweight more quickly between her hands, eventually resorting to just squeezing it between both until her knuckles were white. "We need manpower to fix the weir and support the affected families. What about organising the local farmers and labourers? They have the skills and the strength needed."

Mr Bennet nodded thoughtfully. "That would be ideal, but many of them are already dealing with damage to their own properties. You'll not get them away from their own fields without some inducement."

Elizabeth pressed her lips together, thinking. "Could we petition the local government for assistance? They might have resources we have not considered."

Mr Bennet shook his head. "Petitioning the government takes time, and we need immediate relief. The tenants cannot wait for bureaucratic processes."

"What about the church?" Elizabeth suggested. "Mr Harrison, the vicar, might be able to rally support and resources from the congregation."

Mr Bennet sighed. "Harrison has been here less than two months. His influence is not half what Mr Saunders' was. In fact, there are a few 'ladies' of the area who are so dead set against him that should he attempt anything of the sort, he would be sunk before he began."

Elizabeth paused, then ventured, "What if we set up a fund with contributions from many in the community? Surely, everyone would want to help their neighbours."

He snorted. "*We?* Lizzy, do be serious. I have done what I can, but no one man can command the comfort of the entire town when you are speaking of the amount of money. I would be called a cheat and an opportunist."

Elizabeth hesitated, then said, "Have you thought of speaking with Mr Wickham? He is well-regarded in the community and might have some ideas or connections that could help."

Mr Bennet raised an eyebrow. "Mr Wickham? What could he possibly offer that others cannot?"

Elizabeth leaned forward. "He is popular and has the ear of many influential people. He might know of resources or be able to rally additional support. It wouldn't hurt to ask."

Mr Bennet sighed, still sceptical. "Do you truly believe Mr Wickham can make a difference?"

"He has mentioned a willingness to be a good neighbour, and we cannot afford to overlook any potential help. If he has any connections or ideas, it would be worth exploring. Desperation calls for unconventional solutions, Papa."

Mr Bennet considered her words, his frustration giving way to reluctant acceptance. "Very well. I will speak with Mr Wickham, but I am not so optimistic as you are."

Elizabeth felt a small surge of hope. "Thank you, Papa. I hope Mr Wickham can be of some help."

Mr Bennet leaned back, closing his eyes for a moment. "We will also need to provide immediate support for the families affected. Food, shelter, and clothing."

Elizabeth nodded. "Perhaps we could organise a collection of goods. The women in the community might be willing to contribute supplies."

Mr Bennet opened his eyes. "Possibly. Perhaps your uncle will speak to the local merchants about providing materials at a reduced cost or on credit."

"Or, again, perhaps that might be a task Mr Wickham could assist with. He is so very well-liked. I say we exploit that."

"Very well, I will speak with him. But it will take more than a few conversations to remedy this."

Elizabeth stood, one idea after another tumbling through her mind. "I will ask Mama to speak with Mrs Lucas and Mrs Long about organising the women. They can gather supplies and help where needed."

Mr Bennet gave her a tired, appreciative look. "Very well, Lizzy. Do you know, I had it in my mind simply to stare at these notes a bit longer with a glass of brandy in my hand and then wash my hands of the affair. Leave it to you to force me to act on the matter."

"Now, I know that for a falsehood, Papa, for had you made your mind up to be useless, you would still have found a way to do so."

He snorted a chuckle. "You know me too well. Well, well, let us see what there is to be done, eh? Be a good lass and send Hill in, will you? I may as well get about the thing."

"Of course, Papa."

Chapter Twelve

THE FOLLOWING DAY DAWNED with a crispness that lent an invigorating edge to Darcy's resolve. His mind felt fresh once more—a very fine thing, for by the time he retired last evening, his brain felt like a throbbing pile of mush. He had need of all his faculties today. In fact, a bit of his father's wisdom would not go amiss just now, but lacking that, Darcy could at least try to affect his manner and employ what intelligence he possessed.

Wickham was seated alone when he entered, a cup of tea in hand and a newspaper spread before him. Bingley was conspicuously absent.

"Good morning, Darcy," Wickham greeted with an eagerness that seemed nothing but sincere, setting the paper aside. "Please, join me."

"Good morning, Wickham," Darcy replied, his voice cool and, he hoped, revealing nothing. He took a seat opposite Wickham, arranging his utensils with deliberate care.

Wickham signalled to a maid, who promptly poured Darcy a cup of tea before retreating, leaving the two men alone in a room bathed in the golden light of morning. "I trust you found your accommodations satisfactory?"

"Indeed. Netherfield is quite comfortable."

Wickham's smile broadened. "I am pleased to hear that, and from you, of all men! It is truly a fine thing to win the approval of a man I respect like no other."

Darcy blanched for a moment, his fingers still twisting his knife about beside the plate. Wickham... *respected* him? When did that happen? "I... I thank you."

"Of course. I am a firm believer in granting credit where it is due." Wickham paused, glancing down at his own plate before meeting Darcy's gaze. "I know we have had our differences. Lord knows my youth was peppered with wrongdoing, but all my father's prayers and, dare I say, your father's unfaltering faith have, I hoped, wrought some good in me after all. I should like to lay aside the past, Darcy, if you will be so good as to grant me some measure of your goodwill."

Darcy narrowed his eyes. "The past… even so recent a past as this summer?"

Wickham smiled. "I might have guessed my motives could be misconstrued. That was why I wrote you that little letter, but I knew you would not take my word for it. I trust Miss Darcy has assured you that when I encountered her in Ramsgate this summer, I was the perfect gentleman toward her. No less, I think, than you would have expected Bingley to be, had he found himself living but a few doors down from the sister of a dear friend."

Darcy took a measured sip of his tea, unblinking as he appraised the rascal opposite him. "She did make such assurances," he conceded.

"Good. I would not have you think me capable of deceiving or taking advantage of any lady, but most particularly not the daughter of the man who nearly raised me. Now that we have dispensed with that bit of unpleasantness, I was hoping to ask your advice."

Darcy raised his brow and set his cup aside. "In what matter?"

"Why, Netherfield! I am rather new to all this, of course, but I have taken a keen interest in ensuring the estate is in good order. Even you must confess that it is a fine property with much potential, and I should like to do it justice with my humble efforts."

Darcy glanced around the room, noting the tasteful decor and the warmth of the sun streaming through the windows. "It is evident that great care has already been taken. The house feels both grand and welcoming."

Wickham nodded. "Thank you. I have already made one or two improvements since taking up residence. The gardens have been a particular focus—being dormant just now, of course. My steward advised me that this was the ideal time of year to consider next spring. I have ordered more wildflowers, more lavender and violets and daisies, and fewer of those stuffy hedges. I did have to keep that rather stunning maze, though."

"I noticed the gardens upon my arrival. They should complement the landscape rather well next summer."

Wickham leaned back slightly; his expression relaxed yet contemplative. "That is the goal. A place that feels like home yet retains its grandeur. We have had some challenges, though."

"Challenges?"

Wickham's expression turned serious. "Yes, I was just reading my steward's latest reports on the flooding. It seems the situation is worsening."

"Bingley mentioned some troubles with the lower fields. Is it very widespread?"

"It is," Wickham agreed, his brow furrowing. "The economic strain on the local community is becoming significant. Many families will struggle to make ends meet if their fields cannot be planted in time. I even heard of three families who lost nearly everything in their root cellars."

Darcy's gaze sharpened, his thoughts aligning with the gravity of the situation. "In such times, one must be wary. Troubled areas can become political pawns for ambitious individuals."

"Trust you, Darcy, to look beyond the immediate. I thought only of what must be done to alleviate the concerns at hand, but you bring up yet another concern. I hope no such travesty occurs on my watch. The people here deserve stability and support, not exploitation."

Darcy studied Wickham closely. The man before him seemed a far cry from the irresponsible youth he remembered. Wickham's demeanour was earnest, respectable—truly, everything Darcy's father had ever hoped for him. How... curious.

"Have you found any support from local authorities?"

Wickham sighed. "Not as much as I would like. You know how it is—natural causes, so no one is truly at fault, and no one wishes to claim responsibility. As it so often does, it seems that those who need help the most are the last to receive it."

"Indeed, it is a common issue. The government is often slow to act, and by the time aid arrives, the damage is done."

Wickham nodded. "It is a delicate balance. Too much government intervention can stifle local efforts, yet too little leaves people vulnerable. It is a challenge to find the right approach. Tell me, for you ought to know better than I, what is your opinion on the current political climate?"

Darcy's mouth turned up on one side. "That is a rather wide topic. Perhaps you might be more specific?"

"Oh! I care little enough for Parliament, all those laws and debates, back-door dealings, and such. What have I to do with that? But people, you see, they care very much about the Prince Regent. That is the figure everyone knows, from the lowliest kitchen lad to the nobility. But from what I hear, there is much debate on his ability to lead effectively. After all that business in France, why, one likes to know whether the man on the throne is an asset or a liability to the rest of us."

Darcy considered this for a moment, his gaze distant. Naturally, this was a thing he and his friends had canvassed in the club. No one wanted the bloody sort of upheaval of a class war, and it seemed the only way to avoid that was to serve his tenants well, look after his business affairs with integrity rather than avarice, and maintain relationships between farmers, labourers, and gentry. But Wickham was right: there was only so much a gentleman such as himself could do when the crown's every action drew so much attention.

He settled on an answer that sounded diplomatic yet clear. "The Prince Regent is a controversial figure. His extravagance and the ongoing war with France have strained the nation's resources. Many people are disillusioned with the leadership, but it is a war we must win. Napoleon's ambitions are boundless, and the cost of failure... I do not wish to consider it."

Wickham's expression had grown serious. "True, but the cost of the war is felt deeply in rural areas like this. Families are losing sons and fathers, and the financial burden is immense."

Darcy observed Wickham's thoughtful responses, feeling a growing sense of respect. The man seemed knowledgeable and genuinely concerned about the welfare of the community. This was not the reckless youth he remembered. He drew another sip of tea, then, after resting his cup aside again, commented in a casual voice, "You seem to grasp the matter quite well. Father would be pleased."

"I like to think his efforts on my behalf were not wasted," Wickham replied lightly. "Admit it, Darcy. You thought I would be lodged in a debtor's prison by now."

Darcy could not help the tip of his head or the arch of his brows. "I confess myself... surprised, but pleasantly so. May I ask how you came into such a fortune so recently?"

Wickham chuckled. "Ah, I knew that question would come eventually. It is quite the story—simple enough in particulars, however long the odds. A third cousin of my father's had accumulated a great deal of wealth through trade in tea and spices. When the old man passed away, it was found that I was the only surviving relative."

Darcy thought carefully, trying to recall any details about Mr Wickham Senior's history that might disprove the story, but nothing came to mind. "Trade can be quite lucrative. It seems you were fortunate to have such a relative."

"Indeed," Wickham said with a smile. "It was quite unexpected. I had no idea of his wealth."

"Really?" Darcy raised an eyebrow, intrigued despite himself. "And when did you learn of this windfall?"

"It was in July," Wickham replied, his tone almost casual. "I did not even know of this relative's existence until then when the solicitor came looking for me at the inn where I was staying at the time. I thought he was putting me on at first—so much so that I bought him a drink for telling such an amusing story."

Darcy calculated in his head. Wickham must have already obtained his wealth by the time he met Georgiana in Ramsgate. That eliminated that suspicion, at least—if Wickham were already expecting a vast fortune, he would not need to take advantage of hers... Well, no more so than any other young buck in the *ton*. He listened silently as Wickham continued.

"The solicitors said they had the devil of a time tracking me down." Wickham said with a laugh. "I had been in Newcastle at the time, considering joining the regiment to earn a living."

"Newcastle? *You* a soldier? I can scarcely credit it."

"Well, my prospects were rather limited, but I had just enough left over from that..." he cleared his throat, "... *consideration* you so generously bestowed on me some years ago to purchase a commission. A low rank, to be sure, but I thought the army might offer some stability. Little did I know that fortune would find me in such an unexpected manner."

Darcy's thoughts tumbled over one another as he tried to reconcile this new information with what he knew of Wickham's past. Everything seemed to align, yet there was an unease he couldn't shake. His head began to ache slightly, a dull throb at his temples, probably his own prejudices surfacing. Wickham's story was plausible, and his demeanour seemed genuine, but the discomfort in Darcy's head only added to his lingering doubts.

"The solicitors must have been quite relieved to finally locate you," was all he could manage to say.

"Indeed. They were quite exasperated by the time they found me. But all's well that ends well, as they say."

Darcy nodded thoughtfully, absorbing the story. Despite his reservations, Wickham's account seemed consistent and believable. There was no immediate reason to doubt him, and yet... the memories of boyhood were impossible to erase so completely.

"Your fortune must have come as a great relief," Darcy said carefully. "It certainly changed your circumstances."

"Immensely," Wickham agreed. "I was able to settle my debts and establish myself comfortably. It was a blessing I never expected."

Darcy was silent for a few moments. If all these things were true, then perhaps he had misjudged Wickham. Fortune had favoured the man, to be sure, but the fellow Darcy remembered from his youth would never have put that inheritance to good use or spoken so warmly of hope for good relations with his neighbours.

No, he would have frittered it away in vice, whether the task took a month or ten years. This man who spoke of investing and improving... well, this was a stranger.

"You have said very little of Miss Georgiana," Wickham said. "All I know is that she left Ramsgate shortly after I did. I hope she is well."

Darcy's grip tightened on his fork at the mention of his sister, another faint twinge beginning to form behind his eyes, but he forced himself to relax. Perhaps he had been wrong about Wickham's intentions toward Georgiana. She had insisted that Wickham was only looking out for her during their time in Ramsgate last summer.

"She is flourishing under the care of Lady Matlock," Darcy replied slowly. "Preparing for her debut next year."

Wickham seemed genuinely pleased. "I am glad to hear it. She is a lovely and accomplished young lady. I have no doubt she will be a credit to the Darcy name."

At that moment, the breakfast room door opened, and Bingley entered, his face alight with cheer. "Good morning, gentlemen! I see you have started without me."

"Good morning, Bingley," Darcy said, managing a smile as he settled back into his seat, twisting his fork so he could eat with it rather than consider spearing his host.

Bingley helped himself to a plate of food and joined them at the table, quickly becoming the centre of the conversation. "Darcy, Wickham and I were discussing plans for some shooting later today. The pheasant population seems particularly abundant this season and 'left to themselves far too long,' as Mr Bennet says. We have permission to hunt on Longbourn's lands as well, you know."

Wickham straightened in interest. "Hold a moment. You have met Mr Bennet?"

Bingley blinked innocently, rolling a bit of his breakfast in his cheek until he could swallow it. "Me? No, no. But I spoke with Mrs Bennet at the Assembly, and she promised her husband would save all the best coveys for us. I believe it was Miss Elizabeth who quoted that line about the pheasants being left to themselves. Yes, it must have been she, for she seems to like a good joke."

Darcy's spine stiffened at this second mention of Miss Elizabeth's name. Drat it all, why did he care that Bingley had met the lady again? But an afternoon outside of Netherfield's walls... particularly if that outing took them near Longbourn... could not be entirely disagreeable.

Wickham nodded enthusiastically. "Then, to the northern woods, we shall go. We have yet to enjoy a proper hunt. How perfectly fitting, Darcy, that you are here for it!"

Oh... He winced at the thought of fowling pieces blasting off beside his head. He had not anticipated *that*... heaven have mercy, he might be locking himself in a dark room by mid-afternoon. Darcy smiled tightly. "That sounds like a fine idea."

Bingley beamed. "Excellent! It will be like old times. We could use your expertise, Darcy. I fear," he confided to Wickham, "that I am not the shot my friend is. I scare the birds away more often than I bring home dinner, but Darcy almost never misses."

"Of course he does not," Wickham laughed. "He rarely ever did. But you know, it was always Colonel Fitzwilliam who was the eagle eye. I do not suppose you know Fitzwilliam, do you?"

"By Jove, I do," Bingley vowed. "And you are right there. I've a hope of aspiring to Darcy's skill one day, but Fitzwilliam is another thing altogether."

Darcy pushed his plate back. "Your skill will only improve if you practice, Bingley."

"There, I knew you would say that. Well?" Bingley hastily scraped the rest of his egg onto his fork. "Let us away as soon as may be."

Bingley was still chewing his last bite when a footman entered the room and cleared his throat. "Excuse me, sir. There is a Mr Bennet at the door. He wishes a moment of your time."

Bingley swallowed and exclaimed with pleasure, "Mr Bennet! How wonderful that he has come."

Wickham rose, jerking the front of his jacket. "Well, well, this is, indeed, a surprise. Darcy, if all I have heard is true, this is a gentleman you will want to meet."

"GOOD MORNING, GENTLEMEN," Mr Bennet announced, his voice carrying the weight of a man interrupted from his preferred leisure. His steps were brisk, eyes sharp and slightly amused as he surveyed the room. "I suppose you already know, but

I may as well introduce myself. I am Bennet of Longbourn, here to discuss matters of less than joyful nature, I am afraid."

Wickham came forward, extending his hand with a practised air of authority. "Mr Bennet, welcome. George Wickham, at your service."

Mr Bennet accepted the handshake. "Ah, Mr Wickham, the master of Netherfield. I trust your stewardship is treating the estate well, though I hear the river has other ideas."

"Yes, I understand the same. Mr Bennet, sir, allow me to introduce my guests. You have probably heard of Mr Charles Bingley, I presume?"

Mr Bennet's gaze flickered to Bingley, who offered a polite nod. "Mr Bingley, a pleasure. I have heard your name mentioned with great frequency and enthusiasm by the younger members of my household. It seems you have made quite the impression."

Bingley's cheeks reddened slightly, and he gave a modest smile. "I am honoured to hear that, sir."

"And," Wickham said, extending a hand toward Darcy, "a very old friend, Fitzwilliam Darcy of Pemberley, Derbyshire. Darcy only arrived last evening and has yet to explore the delights of Hertfordshire."

Darcy bowed slightly as Bennet's eyes flicked over him. Interesting eyes...

He stiffened when he realised he was staring, just to sketch a resemblance to the man's daughter. A daughter, he reminded himself, to whom he was not supposed to have been introduced already.

"Pemberley, you say?" Mr Bennet's brow arched, his eyes narrowing with curiosity. "Never heard of it, but do not take that personally, sir. I have yet to visit Derbyshire, though my brother-in-law claims it the most breathtaking part of the world."

"I would be dishonest if I did not agree with him," Darcy replied.

"As would I," Wickham put in with a laugh as he extended an arm to welcome Mr Bennet into the study. "But I am also quite smitten by the charms of Hertfordshire. Please, Mr Bennet, do be seated and tell us what brings you here this morning."

Mr Bennet settled into a chair with an air of reluctant duty, his expression suggesting he would rather be anywhere else but here. He was a man of middling height, his once-dark hair now liberally salted with grey. His features were marked with the lines of long-standing contemplation and occasional wit, giving him an air of both intellect and benign neglect.

He glanced at each of them in turn until everyone else had settled. "The matter at hand, gentlemen, is a broken weir on the River Mery. I am afraid it is rather deep in the woods, and the original breech went undetected for far too long. The flooding it has caused since its rupture is quite severe."

Darcy leaned forward, his expression serious. "Yes, I have heard of the troubles. It is essential to restore the weir as swiftly as possible. Perhaps a temporary barrier could be constructed to divert the water until permanent repairs can be made?"

Mr Bennet regarded Darcy with a blank expression, his silence stretching uncomfortably. "Mr Darcy is... what was it... Pemberley currently underwater?"

Heat surged to his cheeks, his discomfort intensifying as he felt the eyes of the room upon him. "No, sir, it is not."

"Then, with all due respect, Mr Darcy, your advice, though undoubtedly sound, is somewhat lacking in immediate applicability to our current predicament." Mr Bennet's tone was pointed, and he turned back to Wickham, leaving Darcy feeling the sting of his dismissal.

Wickham met Darcy's eyes with a subtle, almost pitying smile. Darcy's face burned, his mortification complete as he realised the room had fallen silent, everyone witnessing his rebuke.

"My friend Darcy is a clever fellow," Wickham apologised. "He only wishes to be helpful, and I daresay, we will be asking his advice before we have had done. Now, Mr Bennet, my steward tells me that some farmers may be unable to replant their fields, and the economic strain is escalating. It seems that outside support is imperative."

Mr Bennet nodded approvingly. "Exactly, Mr Wickham. We need actionable solutions and the will to see them through. Sounds a bloody nuisance."

Wickham smiled indulgently. "Am I to understand that is why you are at my door, because you would prefer that someone else took the organisation of the matter in hand?"

"You are not so foppish as you look."

"Oh, more is the pity. I do try hard to look like an utter macaroni, but you have caught me out," Wickham laughed. "Now, then, have you a list of the affected properties? Any accounting of the economic damage thus far?"

Darcy would have added to the discussion, but after Mr Bennet's chastisement, his words died in his throat. His opinion was neither wanted nor, apparently... needed. Save by Wickham, but he could not quite stomach being defended again by George Wickham.

Mr Bennet produced a sheaf of paper, and the strategising began in earnest. At each new detail, Wickham's responses—articulate, measured—cut through the room like a blade. How had he not seen this before? Wickham, the scoundrel, suddenly cloaked in humility and intelligence. A façade?

No, it seemed genuine, blast it. Darcy's own advice now felt like cold ash, distant and theoretical, crumbling under the weight of Wickham's practicality. Skepticism gnawed at him, but there it was—a grudging respect. The man had changed. Or had he? Darcy's mind whirled, his confidence shrinking back, leaving him to grapple with this unsettling revelation.

"Well, then, we probably ought not dally," Mr Bennet sighed. "I suppose a direct inspection of the river and the surrounding damage is necessary."

Bingley stood. "Then let us forego the shooting and instead take my carriage. We can see for ourselves what must be done."

"Agreed," Wickham said, rising smoothly.

Darcy stood as well, his thoughts a tangled mess. Mr Bennet's blunt honesty hit like a hammer, and Wickham—competent, poised—who *was* this man? None of these fit with his expectations. Everything felt skewed and off-balance. The ground beneath him seemed to shift and... oh, egad, there went his equilibrium. Darcy clutched his stomach and prayed against the queasiness that would probably follow next.

Wickham started for the door, all his energies now fixed forward as he led them from the room. "Mr Bennet, I trust you would like to accompany us?"

"Not a bit of it," the older man grumbled, though there was a twist of satisfaction about his mouth. "But my Lizzy will never let me hear the end of it if I do not."

Darcy's skin prickled with fire again at the mention of the lady, even as his feet felt as though they were rooted to the ground, and his mouth felt like it was full of cotton. Dash it all, he would have to meet her again just so he was not stricken by these waves of guilty panic whenever someone said her name. A proper introduction with nothing for either of them to be embarrassed about—that would suffice.

But that would have to wait until after this present shock. Wickham, of all people, taking charge of a community concern? It was the most preposterous thing he had ever heard, but there was no escaping it. Difficult as it was to credit, he had no choice but to follow.

Perhaps he would learn something.

Chapter Thirteen

"CHARLOTTE, YOU REALLY MUST join us outside. The sun is out today, and I can think of nothing better to lift the spirits," Jane urged, her voice light and hopeful.

Slumped in her chair by the window, Charlotte glanced up with a half-hearted smile. "Oh, Jane, you and Elizabeth are wasting your time on me. You ought to go and amuse yourselves. Nobody cares what I do, so why should I?"

Elizabeth, standing with her arms crossed, exchanged a look with Jane. The air of resignation around Charlotte was wearing thin. "Perhaps just a short walk in the garden," she suggested, her tone sharpening slightly. "It is warmer today, and a bit of sunshine might remind you that life does not have to be endured from behind a window."

Charlotte huffed and turned her gaze back to the window. "And what good would it do? Whether I go outside or stay in, it makes no difference. No one would notice either way."

"Charlotte," Jane said gently, sitting beside her and trying to catch her eye, "we notice. We care. You know we do. We just want to see you happy again."

But Charlotte shook her head stubbornly. "You are kind, but I do not want to be paraded about. I just want to be left alone."

Elizabeth's patience finally evaporated. "That is enough, Charlotte. I have quite had my fill of you pitying yourself, and I will stand for it no longer." Her voice was firm, leaving no room for further argument. "We will not sit by and watch you wallow. Now, are you coming outside, or must we carry you?"

Charlotte looked up in surprise, her sulky demeanour faltering. She hesitated, then sighed heavily. "Very well, if it will stop your fussing. Perhaps a short drive in the country, but I will not walk."

Elizabeth gave a satisfied nod. "A drive it shall be, then. I will fetch the pony and cart." Jane offered Charlotte a warm smile, relieved to see her friend relenting, however grudgingly.

Half an hour later, the three of them were wedged rather snugly into Lady Lucas's pleasure cart. It was hardly suitable for this time of year, but it was the only vehicle to be had at Lucas Lodge at the moment. Therefore, they all bundled warmly against the November chill and piled hot bricks around their feet.

Jane took the reins with a practised ease as she guided the pony along the familiar path. Charlotte, seated between her friends, seemed to sink into the worn cushions, her eyes reflecting a distant melancholy.

Elizabeth glanced at Charlotte with quiet concern. Since their last outing in the cart the previous summer, it appeared Charlotte had "grown." The once roomy cart now felt decidedly cramped. Clearly, her friend's lack of energy had begun to take its toll. Elizabeth held her tongue, unwilling to add to Charlotte's burdens, but Charlotte herself broke the silence.

"I fear I am not the same as I was," Charlotte murmured self-consciously. "It seems I have added more than just a little weight over the winter months."

Elizabeth flushed with embarrassment but quickly masked it with a comforting smile. "Oh, Charlotte, we have all added a bit of padding during the winter. I daresay the gentlemen prefer a lady with some curves."

"You needn't say such things to protect my feelings."

"Protect your feelings, nonsense. I speak from experience—have you seen Lydia lately? And she has *no* trouble finding dance partners."

Even Charlotte had to snicker at that. "She does... ah... fill out her bodices nicely."

"Precisely! More of us to enjoy, that is what I say," Elizabeth declared.

Jane, who had been unusually silent, glanced over at Elizabeth, her cheeks reddening slightly. She offered a timid smile, clearly relieved by the lighter mood. "Where shall we drive today, Charlotte?"

Charlotte considered for a moment. "Perhaps we should keep to the higher roads, to avoid the worst of the mud."

Elizabeth nodded in agreement. "An excellent idea. The view is always better, too. Perhaps Oakham Mount?"

With a flick of the reins, Jane steered the pony towards the elevated path, the cart jostling gently over the uneven ground. Charlotte settled back, a trace of her former self peeking through as the familiar countryside unfolded before them. The only bother was that the wheels slipped three or four times on the muddy road, eliciting a gasp from Charlotte and a sharp intake of breath from Jane.

"Perhaps we should turn back," Jane said after they had slipped for a fifth time. "This cart is far too light to manage the roads in this condition."

"You are probably right," Charlotte agreed… but with such a heavy sigh that Elizabeth's heart squeezed. Oh, no, they could not take Charlotte back home so soon after such a meagre attempt at cheer! They had only barely got her out of the house as it was and were not likely to succeed again if met with "failure" this time.

"Jane, stop the cart," Elizabeth commanded.

Jane pulled the pony to the side of the road, where there remained a bit of spongy grass, and drew him to a halt. "What?"

Elizabeth hopped down, her boots sinking slightly into the muck. "Let me see if the ground is firm beneath the surface," she said, stomping her feet on the path. Mud splattered her hem, and Jane's eyebrows drew together in mild reproach.

"Elizabeth, now your gown is a mess!"

For the first time in what felt like an eternity, Charlotte's lips twitched into a tentative smile, slow and cautious, as if unsure whether she could permit anyone to see her happy. Elizabeth, grinning in return, stomped harder, sending more mud flying. "It is only a bit of surface slickness," she assured them. "Nothing to worry about. We may slide a little, but never more than a few inches before we are quite in control again."

Jane sighed. "Your muddy boots are going to soil the inside of the cart now."

Charlotte waved her hand dismissively. "It is no bother, Jane. It will force me to get outside and clean it up. Are you and Lizzy not always saying that having some occupation would raise my spirits?"

Elizabeth and Jane shared a dismayed glance. *Charlotte* would have to clean the cart? Or was she just saying that out of this recent petulance of hers? At Longbourn, Mr Hill and the stable boy ensured the carriage was always spotless, but the Lucases did not have as many servants, so… it was *possible* that the duty would fall to Charlotte.

"Do not worry, Charlotte," Elizabeth said quickly. "We will help you clean the cart before it is put away."

"Indeed," Jane added, "We shall have a merry time of it."

But Charlotte was shaking her head. "Oh, I do not require—"

Jane stilled her with a hand on her forearm. "Charlotte. The pleasure would be ours. Truly."

Charlotte's face betrayed a conflicting tapestry of feeling—unworthiness and doubt being the clearest on the surface. But there was also a strong flicker of pleasure at being noticed. "Very well," she sighed. "If you have nothing better to do."

"Better?" Elizabeth scoffed. "What do you imagine we do all day at Longbourn? Dance ourselves silly and host droves of interesting people to tea? I assure you, it will be the pleasantest way to pass the afternoon. Now, help me climb back in so I can set about the business of soiling this thing properly so we have a truly decent excuse to keep to ourselves in the stables for the rest of the day."

Charlotte actually chuckled at that and extended her hand. However, before Elizabeth could put her foot up on the step, another carriage came into view.

Elizabeth's heart leapt when she recognised Mr Bingley's carriage. As it rumbled closer, she squinted, her pulse quickening when she made out her father, Mr Wickham, and... and Mr Darcy inside. Jane's cheeks flushed a delicate pink at the sight of Mr Bingley, but Elizabeth's thoughts were spinning on quite another gentleman.

So, the rumours were true! Mr Darcy *was* here, and so soon! Did he remember her? That awkward, muddy encounter that had left her mortified and curious about him all at once. Had he thought of her at all since then? She ached to find out, to read something—anything—in his expression.

The carriage came to a stop, and all the gentlemen stepped out—well... all save for her father, who leaned out the window and shook his head when he beheld her gown. But her father's gaze could not hold her interest when there were three others in closer proximity.

Mr Wickham stepped out first, tipping his hat, followed by Mr Bingley, and then her stomach dropped as she locked eyes with Mr Darcy. He looked just as she remembered—tall and imposing, with those intense, dark eyes that seemed to see right through her. His features were as striking as she recalled, too, the sharp angles of his jaw softened slightly by the hint of a smile that tugged at his lips. His dark hair, impeccably styled, framed a face that was both handsome and severe.

His initial smile of recognition quickly gave way to a look of surprise as his gaze travelled down to her mud-splattered shoes. Elizabeth's cheeks heated to scalding. Naturally, she *had* to have fresh splatters on her gown! He raised an eyebrow, his expression a mix of amusement and curiosity. She started to explain, even as she saw him start to bow in greeting, his eyes never leaving hers, but then he checked himself.

Of course… they would have to wait upon a proper introduction—he could not politely greet her as if they had already been acquainted. Elizabeth's heart pounded as she forced a pleasant, disinterested smile onto her face and waited for one of the other gentlemen to do the honours. Surely, she could count on Mr Wickham to do the gallant thing… and, hopefully, overlook her state of dress.

Drat it all. Why did she have to go and stomp in the mud just to make Charlotte smile? Mr Darcy would think she did not even own a clean pair of boots! Elizabeth scowled inwardly, and her lips thinned by the instant. The knot in her stomach only sharpened as they stood there, silently staring at each other, the moment stretching out interminably until someone else stepped forward to bridge the gap.

Mr Wickham glanced over his shoulder towards the carriage, where Mr Bennet remained seated, clearly disinclined to get out. Wickham's eyes narrowed slightly, obviously wondering if Mr Bennet intended to do the honours and introduce his daughters. After a second of hesitation, he turned back to the ladies with a charming smile, deciding to proceed himself.

"Good afternoon, ladies! Such a pleasure to encounter you all today! You must allow me to introduce my friend and guest, Mr Fitzwilliam Darcy of Pemberley."

Darcy inclined his head slightly, his gaze still fixed on Elizabeth. Wickham continued, gesturing towards them each in turn, "Darcy, this is Miss Jane Bennet, and this is Miss Elizabeth Bennet, both daughters of our guest." Another fruitless glance toward the carriage. Elizabeth forced a pained smile as she flicked her eyes to her father, who sat watching from the carriage as if he knew none of them.

Mr Wickham cleared his throat and turned back. "And Miss Charlotte Lucas," he said with another gesture, "the daughter of the Sir William of Lucas Lodge—the fellow we were just speaking of."

Mr Darcy made bows to each of them, but his gaze returned quickly to hers. Elizabeth's heart gave a strange little trip as his brows slanted again at her appearance. The formalities were now out of the way, and his desire to speak was plain in his eyes, but also the silent acknowledgement that the sentiment must wait.

Well, perhaps she would grant him that wish. If they ever had another opportunity.

ELIZABETH BENNET. THERE SHE was again… and again, covered in mud. Uncanny!

The first time they met, she had been in a similar state, and it seemed time had done little to change her circumstances. Was she always so… indecorous? That faint glint of defiance in her eye suggested that, quite possibly, she was. What a jolly change that would be from the powdered belles who frequented his aunt's salon. He could hardly pay her any notice—not any real notice—but he would be a cad and a blackguard if he did not confess to a burning curiosity about this feral creature who lurked the muddy byways of Hertfordshire.

A scandalous thought struck him and then stuck in his mind to tickle his fancy for a moment before he could catch it and crush it down. Why, this was exactly the sort of woman who would make his aunt and half the *ton* throw up their hands in horror while the other half crowned her as the Season's bold Incomparable.

The absurdity of it almost made him want to laugh, but not in company, with others looking to him to make the proper courtesies to the ladies they were introducing to him.

But how could he look at either of the other two when *she* was scorching him with a gaze that was every bit as amused and *be*mused as his own? She was trying to gauge his thoughts, even as he would have liked to hear her unvarnished tongue loosed once more. If only they could speak freely, but propriety demanded otherwise.

"Forgive us for interrupting your outing," Wickham was saying to Elizabeth Bennet. "I fear we may be inconveniencing you and possibly even delaying your return so long that the weather may become unfavourable."

Her eyes snapped from Darcy's back to Wickham's… *blast the man…* and her face brightened with a laugh. "Oh, it is no interruption. You merely find me discomposed because I was testing the road for safe travel. Our cart was slipping a little, and we were trying to decide whether we ought to go on."

"I might urge you against continuing," Bingley said. "Even *our* horses were struggling a bit on the slope."

Jane Bennet pursed her lips with a look to her sister that suggested this statement had confirmed her own sentiments, but the latter frowned. "But surely, your horses are very heavy..."

"But far stronger than your pony," Bingley replied gently. "If even they are slipping, I fear your poor pony would not fare better."

"You may as well give it up, Mr Bingley," Mr Bennet called at last from the carriage window. "My Lizzy will go wherever she pleases, no matter my thoughts—or anyone else's—on the matter." He put his head back inside, and Darcy heard a distinct chuckle.

Elizabeth's cheeks were scarlet by this time, and she crossed her arms in frustration. Then, however, she seemed to cast off her discouragement in a moment. "Well, then, there we have it. It is not safe for us to continue, so we shall turn back. I thank you gentlemen for your timely advice."

"Shall we escort you?" Wickham offered.

"No, no, that will not be necessary. We were quite safe this far, and besides, how are we to gossip about handsome gentlemen if there is a carriage full of them right behind us?" Elizabeth tipped her head, picked up her skirts, and offered a deep curtsey. "Good day, gentlemen. And *Papa*," she added, with a pointed glance at the carriage.

Darcy was fairly certain he heard another chuckle from within the carriage.

"Miss Elizabeth," Darcy said, stepping forward before the others could, "may I offer my assistance in helping you into the cart?"

Elizabeth's eyes met his, a flicker of amusement and a blush colouring her cheeks. "Thank you, sir."

Her gloved fingers were warm in his grasp, and her grip quite firm. He steadied her as she climbed into the cart, all too aware of the way her gaze kept brushing against his. The proximity sent a jolt of pain through his head, making it throb more intensely. The dizziness followed quickly, a disorienting wave that he tried to attribute to her nearness, but deep down, he knew better.

This was not appropriate. She was interesting, certainly, but "interesting" was not among the qualifications he required in a woman to whom he paid notice. Elizabeth Bennet could never be a suitable bride for him, and never had he stooped to cultivate interest in any female who could not meet that measure... which was no one, so far.

Until now, he had never thought of Elizabeth Bennet as even a true lady in the traditional sense. She was just a curious memory of a strange girl he met in Hertfordshire.

But being this close to her again, he realised with a jolt that he *had* been thinking of her, and far too much.

And now he understood why.

He was fascinated by her, and that was not a good thing. His head throbbed again, reminding him sharply of his precarious health and the uncertainties that loomed over his future. With deliberate effort, he cooled his manner, his expression becoming distant as he released her hand.

Her face changed instantly in response, the warmth fading into a polite mask. Good heavens, had he already been so obvious that she had been blooming under his approving gaze, so much so that when he withdrew it, she froze?

"Thank you, Mr Darcy," she said, her voice measured and formal.

He blinked for a second, then inclined his head in a reserved nod before stepping back to stand beside Bingley. The effort sent a sharp pain through his temple, and he fought to keep his expression neutral as he struggled to suppress a wince.

"We were just returning from an errand of our own," Wickham explained. "I shall see that Mr Bennet is returned to his carriage and set on his way home before the afternoon grows too late. I hope we shall be in company again soon."

"Oh, but we shall be!" Bingley reminded him.

"Indeed, my friend is right," Wickham gestured as if he had entirely forgot. "I was delighted this morning when Mr Bennet brought a dinner invitation from Mrs Bennet, and I am pleased to inform you that we shall all be dining at Longbourn in two days' time."

Elizabeth and her sister exchanged glances. "Papa, you said nothing of this," Elizabeth said, her voice carrying a note of curiosity.

Mr Bennet, who had remained seated with an air of indifference, glanced up from his musings. "What was I to say? Your mother insisted upon it, and I saw no reason to refuse. We shall have all your sisters in attendance, of course."

"It sounds delightful," she said warmly. "We shall look forward to seeing you. Shall we not, Papa?"

Another heavy sigh. "Yes, yes. We shall be delighted, Mr Wickham," Mr Bennet responded with a resigned wave of his hand.

"It is settled then," Wickham declared. "Friday evening, it is."

With the pleasantries exchanged, the parties began to part ways. Darcy frowned as he returned to the carriage and sat beside Mr Bennet, who was, by all appearances, already dozing. Either the man really was the most indolent fellow alive, or he had contrived a means to avoid conversation when the mood was upon him.

Not an… entirely… poor scheme. Perhaps one Darcy ought to contemplate, for this fascination with Elizabeth Bennet could only lead him down a path he was not prepared to tread.

Chapter Fourteen

"Mr Wickham seems quite popular with everyone," Jane murmured, her voice barely above a whisper as the door to Longbourn opened, revealing Mr Wickham and his party from Netherfield. "I think Papa even likes him."

Elizabeth nodded. "I believe he does. It will be interesting to see how our guest manages—" she cleared her throat softly, glancing over at Lydia and Kitty, who were trading giggles, "—*everyone's* company tonight."

Mrs Bennet fluttered about near the door, her cheeks flushed and her voice a touch too loud as she greeted the gentlemen. "Oh, Mr Wickham, how delightful to see you! And what a charming party you have brought!"

Mr Bennet stood beside her, his expression one of mild disinterest as he offered a polite nod to each guest. Elizabeth and her sisters stood back a little, watching the guests enter and waiting their turn to offer their greetings.

Lydia covered her mouth and almost... not quite... concealed a squeal. "Mr Wickham brought a pineapple! Such a lavish gift!"

Elizabeth glanced at Mr Wickham, who was presenting the exotic fruit to her mother with a charming smile. "He certainly knows how to make an impression."

Mrs Bennet accepted the gift with awe, gasping in pleasure and calling for Mrs Hill to bring a tray to display it properly. "Oh, Mr Wickham, how generous of you! Wherever did you find such a thing?"

Wickham's smile widened. "It is but a small token, Mrs Bennet, to show my appreciation for your kind invitation."

Elizabeth pivoted her attention to Mr Darcy. The slight curl of disapproval in his lips caught her eye. His gaze swept over the room, lingering on Mrs Bennet's overzealous excitement and Lydia's giggles, then lightly flicking over herself before settling into that familiar mask of detached politeness.

A pang of discomfort twisted in her chest. He would never think well of her family—of that, she had no doubt. It was almost a relief; if she settled that fact with herself now, she would never have to be disappointed in him.

Yet, it still stung. Distant, aloof, probably critical. Why should it matter? It did not matter at all.

Mr Wickham, in stark contrast, seemed genuinely pleased to know them. He offered his most charming courtesies to each of the sisters in their turn, then finally spoke again to their mother with an amiable smile and a slight bow. "Mrs Bennet, if I may, I daresay we have not been so warmly received in any house in Hertfordshire, and that, madam, is an excessive compliment, indeed."

Mrs Bennet beamed. "Oh, such a flatterer you are! Shall we proceed to dinner? Mr Wickham, if you would be so kind as to lead the way." She took Mr Wickham's offered arm, her eyes shining with delight. "Simply wait until you have had one of my syllabubs!"

As the gentlemen began to pair off with the ladies, Mr Bingley offered his arms to Jane and Mary with a broad smile. Her father, however, chose to walk alone, leaving the remaining three daughters unescorted.

Elizabeth sighed. How typically *Papa* of him.

The confusion on Mr Darcy's face almost made up for her father's disappointing performance. The gentleman was glancing after Mr Bennet, then his eyes bounced about the room as if counting the remaining daughters again for himself, just to be certain he had not miscalculated. And then he repeated the pantomime, his eyes widening just a little more with each bounce.

Clearly, he could not escort all three sisters. He hesitated, starting to move, then stopping himself. It would be rude for him not to escort anyone, yet equally rude to leave one sister entirely alone. After a brief moment of indecision, he started towards Elizabeth, resolving the dilemma with a determined stride.

He extended his arm, and her chest gave the oddest squeezing sensation. He *looked* pleased for an instant, an inviting warmth in his usually stern eyes, but as he drew nearer, his expression became more guarded, almost stiff. "Miss Elizabeth, may I escort you?"

"Of course, Mr Darcy," Elizabeth replied, placing her hand lightly on his arm. She could feel the tension in his muscles, the subtle rigidity that spoke of his discomfort. It was not at all like that first time he had escorted her, when she had depended upon the strength of his arm to keep her from falling on her injured ankle. So gallant and helpful had he been before that he had imprinted himself in her mind as the perfect gentleman.

But this time, he... well, he looked like he would rather be anywhere else, and she was almost afraid to touch him.

Oh, this would not do. She had seen hints of humour in him before, had she not? The poor soul looked positively miserable this evening, almost as if he were in physical pain. Perhaps she could say something to lighten his mood. She began by tilting her head toward him with a small smile until he was obliged to return her look. "Where did Mr Wickham obtain that gift on such short notice? I know of no one around here who has had one this season, and it even looked fresh! He has bestowed a rare favour upon my mother."

"London is but half a day's ride," Darcy observed, looking straight ahead.

"Well, yes, but to go to such trouble!"

"It was little trouble." His head swung around for an instant, and his eyes bored into hers with a particular weight. "And the pleasure of a gift is all in the giving, is it not?"

She hesitated, then smiled. "Well! Now, I wonder how many favours he sought to effect that particular 'gift,' but you are quite right. He does seem terribly satisfied to have given my mother such pleasure."

"Indeed," Darcy replied after several seconds, his voice thick with a raw sort of huskiness. "He does have a certain... charm."

Elizabeth glanced up at him, noting the careful neutrality in his expression. "You speak as though charm is not a virtue you particularly value, Mr Darcy."

Darcy hesitated, his eyes meeting hers briefly before looking ahead. "Charm can be a double-edged sword, Miss Elizabeth. It can mask many things."

Before Elizabeth could respond, they entered the dining room, the long table gleaming with polished silver and fine China. Mr Wickham guided Mrs Bennet to her seat at the foot of the table with a flourish, then moved to claim the seat beside her. And then, by some odd happenstance, Elizabeth found herself seated between Mr Wickham and Mr Darcy.

Why, how fortuitous! She had been curious to compare the two gentlemen side-by-side, and what better opportunity than at dinner, when she would be expected to speak with first one, then the other?

But as the first course was served, Elizabeth found herself working a deal harder than she had expected just to extract a handful of words from the man on her left. They were all one-syllable responses until she was tapping her toe impatiently under the table. Time to ask him some more pointed questions that could not be answered with "Yes" or "No."

"Mr Darcy," she began softly, "How long do you intend to remain at Netherfield?"

He paused the motion of his spoon. "My plans are not fixed, Miss Elizabeth." He never even looked up as he said it.

Elizabeth frowned. "Not fixed? Why, that means one of two things."

His brow edged upward. "Care to enlighten me?"

"Oh, naturally. Either you have no other prospects at all to brighten the dull days of winter, or you have far too *many* invitations to make your decision in haste. So, what of it, Mr Darcy?" She lifted her wine glass to her lips, then continued after she had set it down. "Are you still debating on who shall have the honour of your company through Christmastide and Twelfth Night?"

His mouth tightened on one side, and his gaze returned to his plate. "I have not yet determined that."

She sighed and turned back to her own syllabub. Mr Darcy was certainly proving to be a disappointment over her expectations.

Suddenly, he stiffened, drawing in a breath, and turned to her. "But you are right about one thing, Miss Elizabeth."

"Oh?" She set her spoon aside. "And what is that?"

"I have more obligations and invitations than I care to count. None, unfortunately, particularly appealing."

She pursed her lips. "Then, have you no family with whom to pass the festive season?"

"A great deal too many of them, in fact."

"And are they all in London?"

"For the moment, save for one aunt in Kent."

"Kent? I would have thought you might have said Lancashire or Northumberland."

His brow creased, and he looked at her questioningly.

"The way you speak," she offered by way of explanation. "I assumed you hailed from one of those counties."

He shook his head, still looking away as much as possible. "No, Miss Elizabeth. My family hails from Derbyshire."

"Derbyshire," Elizabeth repeated, trying to keep the conversation flowing. "It must be a beautiful place. Do you visit often?"

"Whenever I can."

Gracious, but he was a reluctant conversationalist. Best to try a different approach. "Do you have any brothers or sisters, Mr Darcy?"

"Yes," he said, his voice softening slightly. "I have a younger sister, Georgiana."

"Tell me about her," she encouraged gently. "She must be a delightful young lady."

Darcy hesitated, his gaze flickering towards Mr Wickham before he responded. "Georgiana is very dear to me," he said, his voice low. "She is... an excellent musician and a kind soul."

Elizabeth sensed there was more he wished to say but was holding back. "It sounds as though you are quite fond of her," she prompted, hoping to draw him out further.

Darcy's eyes darkened slightly as he glanced again at Wickham. "Indeed," he replied, his tone now clipped. "But perhaps this is not the time for such discussions."

Well. So much for drawing the man out. "Of course. Another time, perhaps."

THIS WAS ALL BLASTED uncomfortable. Despite his best efforts to remain detached, Darcy was acutely aware of Elizabeth Bennet's every movement and word. His head throbbed with a dull ache that seemed to grow sharper with each passing moment.

He knew it was unwise to engage with her—his interest would betray him in a moment, and that was precisely the last complication he required at present. Fitzwilliam Darcy smitten by a countrified bewilderment! But a tempting bewilderment she was, with eyes that crackled like a hearth flame and a smile that concealed far more than it divulged.

No, no, he must put her off, if for no other reason than she distracted him too much. His object in coming here was to learn more about George Wickham, dash it all, not one Elizabeth Bennet. And so, he attempted to keep his responses clipped and practical. But each attempt to avoid her left him feeling colder, more distant, and he worried she would think him rude. Why he ought to care was a mystery that would require some introspection, but care, he did.

His discomfort grew as the tables turned, and he was forced to watch Elizabeth's easy conversation with Wickham. They spoke with such familiarity and warmth, a sharp contrast to his own stilted attempts to prevent any intimacy. He listened intently, catching snippets of their dialogue about Charlotte Lucas, though he was supposed to be conversing with Catherine Bennet. The girl was too intimidated to speak much, and he doubted she had any thoughts deeper than the flavour of the soup to share, anyway.

Wickham was fairly leaning over the table, all but pushing his elbows onto it in his interest in the lady. "Miss Elizabeth, I have by now had the pleasure of meeting several families in the area, but I realise my understanding of them is still quite limited. Could you perhaps provide me with some particulars?"

He could tell she was smiling by the sudden roundness of her cheek as she gazed back at the rogue. "Of course, Mr Wickham. Who would you like to know more about?"

Wickham appeared to consider, but that was probably an act. Wickham knew exactly what he was about. If only Darcy did, as well. "I have been introduced to Sir William and Lady Lucas. They seem quite agreeable."

"Yes, they are," Elizabeth replied. "Sir William is always ready with a kind word, and Lady Lucas is very..." She hesitated— "Practical." Another bunching of her cheek into a smile, though this one flashed more briefly. "She is a devoted mother, always looking out for her family."

"And the Gouldings?" Mr Wickham continued.

"Oh, I would advise you to caution there."

Wickham affected a surprised grin. "Indeed?"

"Unless you wish to hear 'facts' about yourself repeated to the neighbourhood that are rather less than factual. They are well-meaning but rather prone to gossip. Mrs Goulding is particularly fond of sharing news, whether it is true or not."

Wickham chuckled softly. "And Mr Long?"

"Mr Long is quite respectable and very generous to his nieces, Annabelle and Maryanne. They are often in Meryton, visiting their aunt and uncle," Elizabeth explained.

Mr Wickham then glanced towards Darcy before continuing. "I was quite charmed by the younger Miss Lucas. Maria, I believe? However, I have had few opportunities to speak with the elder Miss Lucas."

Elizabeth's posture softened at the mention of her friend. "Charlotte is a dear friend, Mr Wickham. She is wise and kind, though she has been rather low-spirited of late."

Wickham's brows knitted. Egad, how did the man alter his entire face like that? He almost looked... sincere. "Low-spirited? That is unfortunate. Has something specific troubled her?"

Elizabeth sighed, and her fingers toyed with the fork beside her plate. "She has been avoiding company at every opportunity. She often claims some malaise, though the only thing that appears to be wrong is a lack of enthusiasm for anything. Jane and I fairly had to drag her into the carriage the other day—that was why we were so unwilling to turn back, do you see. It was difficult enough to get her out that one time. She seemed happy for a little while, though she smiles but rarely anymore. I am worried for her."

Wickham leaned in slightly, his voice low and sympathetic, even as his gaze flicked to Darcy for an instant. "I am sorry to hear that, Miss Elizabeth. I once had a friend who suffered from low spirits."

Darcy's attention sharpened, the throbbing in his head intensifying. What friend could that be? Not himself, surely. Wickham could not accuse *him* of low spirits simply because he preferred dignity and more solitary pursuits. He still enjoyed life, hang it all—at least, he did when his eyes were not crossing from stabbing pain and he could walk without getting dizzy.

"What became of your friend, Mr Wickham?" Elizabeth asked. "What was done to help him?"

Wickham's expression darkened momentarily. "It is a sad tale. I tried my best to encourage him, to brighten his prospects, but in the end, he took his own life." Wickham paused, then added hastily, "But such outcomes are rare, especially for ladies. Your friend likely needs only good company and something to look forward to."

Elizabeth's spine had stiffened at the mention of the man—whoever it was—putting an end to himself, but he could see the forced lift of her shoulders as she nodded thoughtfully, clearly trying to take some comfort in Wickham's words. "I hope you are right."

Wickham raised his glass, his demeanour brightening as he raised his voice to be heard by all. "Speaking of something to look forward to, I have been wishing to host a ball at Netherfield. However, I face the dilemma of not having a hostess. Perhaps I may canvass the subject in friendly company. What are your thoughts on this matter?"

There were several murmurs of interest, but it was Kitty Bennet, unable to contain herself, who blurted the loudest. "Two years ago, Mr Northam—you know, the previous master of Netherfield—he did not have a hostess either. He asked Lady Lucas and Mrs Goulding to help plan a tenant's harvest party for the estate. Surely, if that was appropriate, Mr Wickham could ask some lady of the neighbourhood to help."

Mr Bennet wadded the corner of the tablecloth to dab his mouth, then dropped it, casting a deadpan look at his wife. But it seemed that Bennet's lack of support for the notion was unique, for everyone else spoke approvingly.

Wickham's eyes lit up at the suggestion. "An excellent point, Miss Kitty. Perhaps there is a well-respected lady in the area who could be prevailed upon to act as hostess for the ball. It must be the mistress of one of the principal estates, of course—a lady with an unimpeachable reputation in the community."

Mrs Bennet flushed with pride and half-rose from her seat. "Oh, Mr Wickham, I would be honoured!"

Darcy felt a wave of bonafide nausea as he observed Mrs Bennet's unabashed enthusiasm. Heavens, where was the basin in this dining room? Was there a door through which he could excuse himself if the need arose? He doubted his hostess would even notice his departure.

Wickham had not actually asked her, but the woman seemed to assume the request tendered and accepted. Her face shone with delight, her voice loud and eager. Darcy's head pounded, the noise of the room amplifying the pain. He placed a foot down in front of the chair leg and gave a slight push... only a little advantage, in case he needed to step behind Miss Elizabeth's chair for the nearest escape.

But in plotting his path, he glanced at Elizabeth, who was staring open-mouthed at her mother's audacity. To her credit, she forced her jaw closed and turned away, and her eyes blundered into his. The flash of pained humiliation there... that was something with which he could empathise. He offered her a slight tightening of his lips but dared risk no more.

"Thank you, Mrs Bennet," Wickham said warmly. "I could not think of a more suitable hostess. It would be an honour to have you assist in planning the ball."

Mrs Bennet's eyes sparkled with delight. "Oh, Mr Wickham, you are too kind! I shall ensure that everything is perfect."

Darcy's expression remained one of silent horror, his eyes wide with incredulity. The very idea of Mrs Bennet in charge of such an event was almost too much to bear, and yet he could not help but feel a grudging admiration for Wickham's deft handling of the situation. Wickham had managed to turn a potential embarrassment into a moment of triumph for Mrs Bennet and, in doing so, had ingratiated himself even further with the family.

Blast the man.

Chapter Fifteen

The weather had dawned fair and bright, the kind of day that promised productivity and progress. However, the November rains had recommenced by the time the Bennet ladies were dressed, breakfasted, and ready to step out the door. Wet and miserable was, therefore, to be the order of the day.

Yet, there was nothing else for it. Elizabeth adjusted her poke bonnet, tying the ribbons under her chin with a secure knot against whatever wind and rain might conspire to do. The Bennet ladies would join others from town and the surrounding country, all armed with baskets of provisions to observe the repairs at the weir.

The carriage bogged down twice, requiring them all to step out to lighten the horses' burden until they were through the heaviest of the mud. Lydia complained each time, but it seemed she was less distressed over having to walk than she was about the prospect of delay toward their goal... and seeing the gentlemen who would be there.

Upon arrival, the extent of the devastation was starkly evident. The weir was a hive of activity, with men scattered across the site, labouring under a steady drizzle to reinforce and repair the structure. Timber and stone lay in heaps, the air filled with the sharp sound of hammers and the steady rhythm of saws. Elizabeth's eyes traced the long riverbank line where the floodwaters had breached, the force of nature having carved a path of destruction that demanded immediate and significant intervention.

She alighted from the carriage, her feet sinking slightly into the soft ground. As she walked closer, she took in the scene with curiosity and concern. The scale of the work required was immense. The air was thick with misty rain and the scent of fresh-cut wood, mingling with the earthy smell of the river.

At the forefront of the activity was Mr Wickham, astride a fine chestnut horse. He cut a striking figure, his posture erect and commanding, his expression one of focused determination. Elizabeth watched as he directed the workmen in an easy manner, his confident instructions carrying over the noise of the labour. His presence was magnetic, drawing the attention and admiration of the gathered crowd, many of whom were local gentlemen and prominent businessmen. Wickham's ability to present himself as both capable and generous had evidently won him much favour.

As Elizabeth joined the group of ladies gathered under a tent erected for their comfort, she noticed a flurry of whispers and curious glances. Mrs Long, who had arrived before the Bennets, was at the centre of the group, her voice low but animated as she relayed some piece of news.

"Mrs Long, what is it?" Elizabeth asked as she approached.

Mrs Long turned to Elizabeth with a look of pleased importance. "Have you not heard? Mr Wickham has pledged to cover the entire cost of the repairs himself!"

Elizabeth's eyes widened in surprise. "Surely that cannot be true. It is a large expense that must be borne by the whole community."

Mrs Long nodded vigorously. "That is what I thought too, but Mr Wickham insisted. He declared it before all the gentlemen, saying he wished to restore the town to its former prosperity."

A murmur of admiration rippled through the crowd, the matrons of the town nodding approvingly, the younger girls whispering among themselves. Jane, who had been listening quietly, turned to Elizabeth with a look of concern. "It is indeed generous, but do you not think it strange that he would take on such a burden alone? The cost must be astronomical."

Elizabeth nodded. "Yes, it is strange. And while his generosity is commendable, I cannot help but wonder why he would not seek the community's support for such a significant expense. Surely, it is not the fault of the newest comer to the neighbourhood that an old structure has failed."

Mrs Long pursed her lips, glancing back towards the men who were still discussing the repairs with animated gestures. "He said it was his way of giving back to the community that has welcomed him so warmly. A noble sentiment, to be sure, but one cannot help but wonder at the timing."

"Timing? Whatever do you mean?"

"Why! Surely, you know your mother means to play hostess for the ball at Netherfield. A shocking thing, if I do say so."

"It is... surprising," Elizabeth conceded. "But why do you think one has anything to do with another? Surely, you do not think Mr Wickham is playing at anything indecent?"

"Of course not! Quite the opposite—I rather think he means to silence any whispers about the oddity of it by proving his generosity now. Why, if that be the case, he may consider himself well assured of my good opinion. It has been ages since we have had the pleasure of a ball at Netherfield, and why should the little matter that its present master is unmarried be any hindrance when we have among us any number of ladies who would happily do the honours?" Mrs Long sniffed. "I only wonder that he did not ask *me* to assist Mrs Bennet. I did, after all, help a great deal with the last Assembly."

"I am sure Mama would welcome your advice," Elizabeth assured her.

"That is what I told her, but she kept running on about the seating arrangements. I tell you, Lizzy, at least *you* will be assured of some pleasure that evening, seated beside Mr Wickham at dinner. My poor niece will be lucky if she gets stuck beside Mr Darcy."

Elizabeth's brows arched. "Mr Darcy is probably wealthier than Mr Wickham if the rumours about him are true."

"Yes, but what good is wealth if the man refuses to let a lady catch his eye? I wonder why Mr Wickham even invited him to Netherfield if all he means to do is stand about by himself and look cross."

Elizabeth glanced at a grouping of gentlemen, her father among them, and saw precisely what Mrs Long had said. Mr Darcy was standing a little apart from the rest, one fist on his hip and the other hand experimentally testing a bit of quarry stone as if he thought the quality of it in question.

"He is... peculiar," Elizabeth confessed. "But I do not think him a bad sort. Not everyone is garrulous, Mrs Long."

"Well, they ought to be. I ask you, what good is a guest who does nothing to recommend himself to one's neighbours?"

"I am sure I do not know, Mrs Long."

Darcy stood a little apart from the crowd, his eyes scanning the scene with frustration. The repairs at the weir were necessary, the damage extensive, but the sight of Wickham at the forefront, directing the labour with an air of authority, set his teeth on edge. Surely, Wickham was not the man to put his head to so much trouble. When had Wickham ever exerted more than the minimal effort required for any task? Yet today, he appeared to be the architect of the project, with many hours apparently spent in planning to pull off the affair.

His head pounded relentlessly, and his vision occasionally blurred. He had experienced another palsy on the right side of his body the night before—thankfully, he had been alone in his room when it came upon him. There was still a "dead" spot near the corner of his mouth, and his fingers were still stiffer than they ought to be.

As soon as the episode was over, he scrawled a letter to his doctor, detailing the worsening symptoms with a trembling hand. What remedy might exist? The thought of admitting that the diagnosis could be correct gnawed at him. Impossible!

He could not yet surrender to that grim reality, so he requested the name of some medication to alleviate his ceaseless headaches. With forced confidence, he wrote that, upon receiving the doctor's recommendations, he would consult a local apothecary to procure the necessary treatment. Hopefully, Westing's reply and the apothecary's remedy would come before his next bad spell.

Some yards away, Bingley had been speaking animatedly with Mr Bennet, but now he hurried towards Darcy, his face very full of something. "Darcy, have you heard? Wickham has pledged to cover the entire cost of the repairs! He is paying the workmen; he just reimbursed Mr Harris for the expense of the logs, and he is doing the same for any other materials required. Quite a gesture, is it not?"

Darcy's jaw tightened as a sharp pain stabbed through his temple. "Indeed, it is a significant expense. One must wonder at his motives."

"Motives! I should think not having the town underwater by spring would be motive enough."

"But he is not alone in that. Why should he bear the expense of repairing all the damage himself?"

"Well, I am sure I do not know, save that he is quite a generous chap. Good heavens, Darcy, why such a dark look? You, of all people, ought to be proud."

Darcy narrowed his eyes, struggling to focus through the pain. "Proud? I do not follow."

"Why, everyone knows that you knew him as a lad, that your father paid for his education. He is not ashamed of that—rather, he speaks of it to anyone who will listen, that the Darcy family are responsible for any good that comes from him."

Darcy's jaw clenched. "He says that, does he?"

"That, and a deal more. Oh! You have not heard the splendid things he was just saying to Mrs Philips about Miss Darcy. He declares she will be next Season's Incomparable, sure to be courted by… why, Darcy, you do not look at all pleased. Something the matter?"

Darcy's mouth had screwed into a bitter scowl, his head throbbing more intensely. "What business has he in speaking of my sister? The cad!"

Bingley drew back. "Darcy? What is the matter? You are not… good heavens, no. I know you are not *jealous* of George Wickham, but I cannot understand this violent displeasure toward a man who speaks only well of you. Are you ill?"

Darcy blinked and forced a gulp of air into his lungs, fighting the nausea that threatened to overwhelm him. That excuse would do for the present. "Perhaps I am. Forgive me, Bingley. I ought to consider returning to Netherfield before I spoil anyone's pleasant afternoon, as I am clearly not required here."

"Well, hang on. Some of the gentlemen were talking, and you know, there is a question of petitioning for assistance from Parliament."

"Par…" Darcy squinted against the pain. "*Parliament?* Whatever for?"

Bingley winced and scratched his ear nervously. "I suppose it depends on how heavily the fields truly were damaged, of course, but Wickham and Bennet were just saying that if the topsoil is washed away, and it becomes a hardship…"

"Yes, yes, I see."

"So, you will come speak to them?"

"*I?*" Darcy sputtered. "Why would they ask for me?"

"They did not, but I suggested you might have some answers. Your uncle, the earl, is, of course…"

"An uncle in the House of Lords does not grant me any particular insight into the workings of politics. You ought to speak with one of the MPs from Hertfordshire."

"That is just the thing. You see, it seems that Meryton has its own MP. Sir William was just telling us a bit about it. Something to do with an old agreement with the Marquess of Hertford, and… oh, it would be better if you heard him explain it for yourself."

Darcy was rigid with interest now, despite the pounding in his skull. He narrowed his eyes, trying to mask his discomfort. "Indeed. Very well, Bingley. Lead the way."

AS THEY APPROACHED, MR Bennet was deep in conversation with Sir William Lucas and a few other gentlemen. Darcy and Bingley lingered at the back, listening attentively. Sir William was animatedly explaining to Mr Wickham the historical context of the borough's representation.

"You see, Mr Wickham," Sir William began, "the Marquess of Hertford managed to create a pocket borough here in 1703. Quite the thing it was, trading support on various issues to gain a representative for our borough."

Wickham nodded, and it was probably the first time Darcy had ever seen the man paying any mind to discussions of politics. "And how did he leverage his influence in the House of Lords?"

Sir William continued, "It all began with the great flood of 1701. The River Mery burst its banks, devastating the town and surrounding farmlands. The Marquess of Hertford, who held substantial estates in the area, saw an opportunity amidst the crisis. He understood that to rebuild and protect his interests, he needed more political influence."

"Ah!" Wickham laughed. "Gracious, but that is a familiar problem, is it not?"

"Indeed. The following January, the Marquess hosted a grand gathering at Hertford House. He invited the Earl of Salisbury, Viscount Grimston, and several other prominent figures. Over lavish feasts and prolonged discussions, he began to negotiate alliances. Hertford promised the Earl of Salisbury his support in a forthcoming bill concerning trade tariffs, which was of significant interest to Salisbury's holdings in the North. In return, Salisbury agreed to back Hertford's proposal for a new borough representative."

"Simultaneously, Hertford forged an understanding with Viscount Grimston, who was eager to secure military funding for a new regiment. Hertford pledged his votes in the House of Lords to support Grimston's cause, provided Grimston would advocate for the creation of the Meryton seat in the Commons."

Wickham's brow furrowed as he absorbed this information. "So, it was a series of quid pro quos, each man seeking his advantage."

"Precisely," Sir William affirmed. "The final and crucial move came in October 1702. Hertford utilized his influence in the House of Lords to apply pressure subtly but persistently. During the debates on the allocation of funds for coastal defences, he swayed key votes by promising to support their interests in exchange for their backing of his borough proposal. His timing was impeccable, aligning his request with the broader concerns of national security and local governance."

"By February 1703, Hertford's network of alliances was strong enough to present a united front. They submitted a petition, carefully crafted and supported by both the Lords and influential MPs in the Commons. The proposal highlighted the economic benefits and strategic importance of having a dedicated representative for the Meryton area."

"And we must presume it passed?"

"Oh, most assuredly," Sir William harrumphed, tugging at his lapels. "It was spring of 1703—forgive me, I quite forgot the date—the House of Commons passed the motion to include Meryton as a borough with its own representative, much thanks to Hertford's relentless lobbying. We have enjoyed particular attentions ever since."

Wickham laughed in astonished pleasure, even clapping his hands. "Why, there is our answer! A masterstroke of political strategy, indeed."

But Mr Bennet, who had been listening with keen interest, was shaking his head. "One might think as much, but I daresay if you plan to rely on Sir Harold Fenton, you had best accustom yourselves to mud that floods your Wellingtons and empty coffers."

Wickham's pleasure faded, and he turned to Mr Bennet in dismay. "Whatever for?"

Bennet chuckled. "Sir Harold has been our representative for nearly three decades. A good man for the most part, but his health has been in decline. Though he has served faithfully, his capacity to address our current needs is severely limited."

"Oh, dear. How dreadful for the poor man." Wickham sighed. "Well, what other options have we?"

"Wait a moment," Bingley put in, just as every other gentleman had begun to shake his head and look grave. "Darcy here read law at Cambridge. Darcy, surely there might be some alternative. Is there any chance of putting some more capable representative in the House of Commons?"

Darcy, who had been observing in silence, glanced reluctantly about the curious faces assembled before him. This was not his problem, and he had much rather stay out of the affair. But with everyone looking at him and the solution so obvious before him, it was a simple matter to speak the words.

"The appointment is for life, so I am afraid he cannot resign. However, if Sir Harold is willing, he could submit a request for the 'office of profit under the Crown.' This would allow him to take up another 'office,' if you will, making him no longer eligible to serve as MP and creating an opening for a special by-election."

Sir William's eyes lit up. "A sound plan, Mr Darcy. This could be the solution we need."

Wickham turned to Mr Bennet with a hopeful expression. "Mr Bennet, do you believe Sir Harold would consider such a resignation?"

Mr Bennet, who seemed to be the only one with personal knowledge of the MP, pondered for a moment. "I do know Sir Harold. He is quite elderly and may welcome the opportunity to step down gracefully. I will draft a letter immediately and see if he might be amenable to the suggestion."

"Oh, but before you ask the man to resign, you ought to at least put the question to him of our little local disaster," Wickham urged. "It may well be that we underestimate the man. I should hate to think we might put a good man out to pasture before his time."

"A capital notion," Sir William applauded. "Let goodness and fairness be our watchwords, gentlemen. Meanwhile, let us sample a bit of that luncheon our fair ladies have assembled before us, shall we?"

Chapter Sixteen

Elizabeth bustled under the tent, her hands deftly arranging the tray of biscuits as she prepared to serve the gentlemen. Rain still seeped through the fabric of the tent, creating running drips wherever some careless youth—Lydia, for example—had touched it, but there was also an odd blend of sun piercing through the clouds, casting a golden haze over the misty work site. She watched the faces of her father and her neighbours as they approached, each man's expression heavy with both inspiration and fatigue from the day's discussions.

Mr Bingley was the first to approach. He grinned as he walked into the tent, his gaze fixed solely on Jane, who stood nearby pouring tea. His admiration was obvious to anyone with eyes, his smile wide and genuine as he moved closer to her. Well, indeed! Perhaps her mother would have pleasure from that quarter, at least, for the man seemed only to increase his attentions to Jane the longer he stayed in town. But there was no point in staring at the couple now, so she continued her own task of serving biscuits to the others.

Mr Wickham walked with Sir William, both appearing quite pleased with something. Whatever their conversation was, it must have been an engrossing one, for Mr Wickham seemed to be oblivious to the fluttering attempts of the ladies around him to capture his attention. His allure was undeniable, yet he managed to maintain his focus on the discussion, only pausing to graciously acknowledge the ladies with a polite nod.

As Wickham approached, Elizabeth offered him a warm smile and a tray of biscuits. "Mr Wickham, would you care for some refreshment?"

He returned her smile, his eyes twinkling. "Thank you, Miss Bennet. You are most kind." He accepted the refreshment and quickly became involved in a conversation with Mr Long, their tones hushed and serious. Elizabeth would have very much liked to ask him what their discussion had been about, but they moved away too quickly for her to inquire.

The flow of gentlemen continued, each accepting Elizabeth's offering with varying degrees of gratitude and distraction. She moved with practised ease, ensuring everyone was attended to, yet her thoughts kept drifting back to the conversation between her father and Wickham. What could be so urgent and secretive?

Finally, Mr Darcy approached, looking decidedly unhappy about something. His usual stern demeanour was even more pronounced, and Elizabeth's curiosity fairly simmered over. Gone was her vexation with the man. He might be the only one willing to answer her questions. She met him with a bright smile, hoping to brighten his mood and goad him into a few rare words. "Mr Darcy, would you care for some refreshment?"

He looked around at the other gentlemen, who had mostly all wandered off or got snared into other conversations, before finally nodding and accepting a biscuit. "Thank you, Miss Elizabeth," he said curtly.

Elizabeth watched as he stood close, eating in silence. His brooding presence was almost a physical wall. Drawing him out might prove a challenge worth accepting. "Mr Darcy, I could not help but notice that there was a rather serious discussion taking place earlier. Might I ask what the gentlemen propose to do?"

Darcy hesitated, his eyes flickering with some internal conflict before he finally spoke. "We have been discussing the possibility of petitioning Parliament for aid. The damage to the fields is extensive, and without effective representation, our appeal may go unheard."

"And how do you plan to secure such representation?"

Darcy chewed in silence for a moment, and she thought he would not answer at all. Then, at last, he spoke. "It would seem that Meryton has its own representation in the House of Commons. However, your father informed us all that the current MP is quite elderly and may not be able to advocate effectively. They are considering asking him to resign to allow for a special by-election. If he agrees, the community could elect someone more capable."

Elizabeth nodded thoughtfully. "And who do you think might take on such a role?"

Darcy's gaze sharpened. "That remains to be seen. It must be someone who understands the gravity of the situation and is willing to act in the community's best interests."

"Well, was no name put forward?"

He dipped his head toward the others. "I believe that is the very subject being canvassed at the moment."

"And you are not among them to offer your wisdom and advice? Mr Darcy, I misjudged you."

His brow lifted. "I cannot tell whether that is an honest appraisal of my abilities or a sardonic jab at what you must perceive to be my officiousness."

She shrugged. "What if it is both?"

"Then I am afraid you will be disappointed on both counts. I am not among them because the affair is no business of mine. I have no property or claim in the region. Therefore, my input is not wanted."

Elizabeth was ready with a fresh tea plate the moment Mr Darcy finished the last of his biscuit. If he left, she might very well have no one else to ask, for surely, her father would not trouble himself to answer her questions so frankly. She tugged the empty plate from the gentleman's hands and traded it for a full one before he quite knew how to respond—he merely stared at her with an empty expression for an instant.

"If you think to bribe me with food in exchange for information," said he at last, "I am afraid I have little to offer."

"That is what you say, but I am willing to take my chances. Surely, you must have overheard something else. What are they meaning to do about the washed-out riverbed? What of the roads? I heard the North Road was hardly passable where it comes near the River Mery."

"I am sure Mr Wickham will pledge his assistance," the man said, but he looked quickly away as he said it.

"I am sure he will, but... why, Mr Darcy, whatever is the matter? Was that biscuit bad?"

"It is perfectly acceptable."

"Then it is the company," she declared, with a flick of her index finger toward herself.

"I assure you, it is not."

She set a hand on her hip. "Your assurances weigh little in comparison to that sour face you just made. What..." She glanced to her right, where her father and Mr Wickham were talking... or rather, her father was nodding, and Mr Wickham was sketching images in the sky with his hands.

"Is it Mr Wickham?" she guessed.

"I told you, Miss Elizabeth, there is nothing amiss." He finished the biscuit, then, not knowing what else to do, relinquished his plate to her with a brisk bow. "It has been a pleasure, Miss Elizabeth."

She watched him walk away, both empty tea plates stacked in her arms. "Well! At least Mr Wickham appears to be engaged in the matter, even if his friend is rather useless."

Chapter Sixteen

"Ah, nothing quite like the serenity of a peaceful morning," Mr Bennet mused aloud, peering over his newspaper. "Of course, it would be even more serene if one did not have to announce unexpected guests."

Mrs Bennet looked up, puzzled. "Unexpected guests? What are you talking about, Mr Bennet?"

Mr Bennet leaned back in his chair, a twinkle of mischief in his eyes. "Well, it appears my esteemed cousin Mr Collins will be arriving this afternoon. I do hope you all find the news as exhilarating as I do."

Mrs Bennet nearly dropped her teacup in shock. "Mr Collins? Arriving today? Whatever do you mean?"

"Indeed, I believe he is eager to grace us with his presence. I received a letter from him some days ago, and he is to arrive this very afternoon."

Elizabeth looked up from her plate, her curiosity piqued. "Today? And you thought now was the appropriate time to inform us?"

Mr Bennet shrugged, his eyes twinkling with amusement. "Well, better now than when you sit at table this evening with a stranger, my dear. Here, I shall read it to you."

He retrieved the letter from his coat pocket with an air of nonchalance as if the entire matter were a delightful joke. The room fell silent as he began to read aloud.

"Dear Sir,

The honour of being your heir has long been a source of pride for me, and it is with the utmost deference that I pen this letter to inform you of my forthcoming visit to Longbourn. My esteemed patroness, Lady Catherine de Bourgh, has most graciously granted me leave to make this journey, and I shall arrive at your residence by Wednesday afternoon. It is my sincere hope that this visit will afford me the opportunity to make the acquaintance of my fair cousins and to strengthen the bonds of familial affection.

Yours most respectfully,

William Collins"

Mrs Bennet clapped her hands together in delight, her face alight with excitement. "Oh, Mr Collins is coming! Do you know, I was quite certain we would have no notice at all from that man, but this is splendid news. Perhaps he means to do well by our girls, after all. Oh, girls! You shall put on your second-best gowns, and... oh, Lizzy, do not even think of disappearing off to Charlotte Lucas's this afternoon! I shall go distracted, I absolutely swear it, if you turn up bedraggled from some mishap again."

Elizabeth crossed her arms and sat back. "I doubt a parson would take a liking to me, anyway, Mama."

Mr Bennet leaned back in his chair with a sardonic smile. "Our cousin Collins' letters suggest he has a remarkable talent for obsequiousness and an impressive enthusiasm for flattery. I do wonder how well these qualities will serve him in person. It should be quite the performance to behold."

Lydia, who had been whispering with Kitty, now spoke up with a giggle. "I hope he is not too dull. A parson, how tiresome. Why can he not wear a red uniform?"

Kitty shrugged. "Even a parson can dance. We could invite him to the next assembly and see if he can keep up with the latest steps. Do you think he is tall?"

"What does it matter whether he is tall? He is a parson," Mary reminded her younger sisters. "Doubtless, he will have much better things to do than dancing."

"Oh, bother with his looks," their mother huffed. "He is to inherit this house, and that is good enough. Lizzy, be sure your hair is tidy, and your gown... oh, no there she goes, out the door again!"

"Ah! There you are, Darcy. I was starting to think you did not mean to join us," Wickham greeted with a genial wave of his hand as Darcy entered the breakfast room.

Darcy claimed a seat beside Bingley and forced a polite smile. "Good morning, Wickham." He hoped his response conveyed the appropriate warmth without betraying his discomfort. To think of him, happily eating at George Wickham's table... why, the whole thing still rankled. He simply did not know what to do about it.

Wickham settled back in his chair; his demeanour relaxed as he poured himself a cup of coffee. Bingley, after a thoughtful sip of tea, looked up with curiosity. "I was thinking a deal about this last night. Do you think the neighbourhood has a suggestion for someone to hold the office of MP if Sir Harold decides to step down?"

Wickham's eyes lit up, and he leaned forward slightly. "Actually, Sir Anthony Mortimer was suggested."

Darcy raised an eyebrow. "Sir Anthony Mortimer? I am not familiar with the name."

"Ah, not terribly surprising. He is not of the first circles but a most trustworthy and intelligent fellow. His father happens to be from just north of here, about fifteen miles. I happened to suggest him myself."

"You know him?" Bingley asked.

"Indeed, I met him in school."

"You did? I was at the same school as you were," Darcy reminded him.

"As was I," Bingley added.

Wickham chuckled. "And I hardly saw you, Darcy, and never met our good Mr Bingley here at all. Not everyone was in the chess club or the fencing club, you know. Come, Darcy, there were over one hundred eighty men in our class!"

Darcy frowned. "And the handful who escaped my notice probably did so for a reason. I am acquainted with all the good families and—"

"Oh, Darcy! You do amuse me," Wickham laughed. "A man must be born of the finest circles to be worth knowing."

"I did not say that."

"But it is in all your manners. Seriously, Darcy, he is an excellent chap. But do not take my word for it—Sir William knows him as well. He was quite pleased when I brought the man's name up, as were a number of others. They say Mortimer has implemented a dozen new farming practices at his estate and has also managed to secure an apothecary to serve his tenants."

Bingley smiled brightly. "Why, he sounds like a remarkable fellow! Having someone like him in London would certainly benefit Meryton."

Wickham continued modestly, "Indeed, and with the support of the community, I am confident he will be elected. But that is not ultimately up to me, so perhaps I will ask your opinions about the upcoming Ball. Tell me, Darcy, for you must have overseen many similar events. Ought we to serve white soup or oysters first?"

Darcy glanced up. "You are mistaken. I have never—"

"Oh, of course," Wickham chuckled. "I forgot, you are just as much of a bachelor as I am and have never played the host. Our situations are much the same. Well, save that you never enjoyed balls. But, quite seriously, most of the affair will be in the hands of Mrs Nicholls, and I've no doubt she knows what she is about. But Mrs Bennet has given me a guest list—rather extensive, I daresay. She tried to organise the seating, but I believe I shall make some alterations to that. You will thank me, Darcy, for she had you seated beside Miss Lydia."

Darcy's head snapped up with a swift look of horror. "Heaven have mercy," he breathed.

"Hah! I knew you would say that. I think we shall adhere to the usual protocol of the gentlemen escorting their most recent dance partner to dinner, so Darcy, I admonish you to choose well."

Darcy raised a brow and resumed moving his egg about his plate with his fork. "I expect I will be returned to London before then."

"Oh, Darcy!" Bingley protested. "You would not miss the fun. Truly, what can be so pressing in London?"

"My sister, of course," Darcy replied, not looking up from his plate.

"You spoke too quickly, Darcy," Wickham answered. "I was hoping Miss Darcy could be prevailed upon to come here. Why, think of all the lovely ladies she could meet and—"

Darcy stiffened. "I do not think that would be appropriate," he replied curtly, his voice strained.

Wickham's face softened apologetically. "Of course. Forgive me. I did not mean to suggest something that would be offensive to you. I had nearly forgot that Miss Darcy was not yet out. It was only the pleasure of good company that made me think of it, but you are quite right. Pray, forget I brought the matter up."

Darcy pushed back from the table, his breakfast quite forgotten. "I've no appetite this morning. I believe I require some exercise."

Chapter Seventeen

Elizabeth stormed out of the house, her mother's protests trailing behind her as she ran down the garden path, her breath coming in sharp bursts of frustration. "Capture his notice indeed!" she muttered. "As if I were a prize to be won." She swatted a hanging branch out of her way. "We have never even met the man!"

The crisp winter air stung her cheeks, but she welcomed the sensation, using it to clear the tangled mess of her thoughts. Her father's indifferent announcement about Mr Collins' arrival had been infuriating enough, but her mother's immediate scheming had sent her over the edge. She could still hear her mother's voice, her absolute surety, as she planned Elizabeth's future without a second thought for her feelings.

"Not even a word of warning," she grumbled, kicking a stray pebble off the path. "And now I am to be paraded like a broodmare for Mr Collins!"

She followed the familiar route, the one she often took when her thoughts were too loud to be silenced indoors. "Style my hair!" she grumbled. "Mend my fichu! And what could be so very wrong with my gown that some strange man would care about it? Balderdash!"

Lost in her mutterings, Elizabeth almost didn't notice the figure approaching on horseback until he was nearly upon her. Startled, she glanced up, her eyes widening in surprise to see Mr Darcy. He seemed equally taken aback, his pale countenance and the slight unsteadiness in his posture betraying an unease that went beyond mere surprise.

"M-Miss Elizabeth," he stammered. "I did not expect to encounter anyone at this early hour."

"Nor I, Mr Darcy." She hesitated, her eyes lingering on his face. His complexion was unusually greenish, the normal healthy glow replaced by a wan, almost sickly hue. Dark shadows underscored his eyes, suggesting many sleepless nights. His jaw was clenched tightly as though he were suppressing discomfort or pain.

Elizabeth's gaze shifted to his hands, which gripped the reins with a white-knuckled intensity. And there was a slight tremor in his fingers—the way they twitched with each movement of the horse. Even his posture seemed off; instead of his usual erect bearing, he sat with a stiffness that hinted at underlying strain.

Her concern deepened. Darcy was not a man to easily show weakness, yet it was clear that something was amiss. She doubted he would welcome her observation, but... well, it was not as if that was anything unusual of late.

"You appear somewhat out of sorts today," she said finally. "Are you quite well?"

Darcy stiffened, then forced a smile that did not reach his eyes. "Merely a lack of rest, I assure you. The fresh air seemed a suitable remedy."

Elizabeth was not convinced. The signs of his discomfort were too glaring to ignore. "Perhaps it would be best if you dismounted and walked for a while. The morning air is indeed refreshing, but it may be more beneficial if taken at a gentler pace. Would you care to join me?"

There was a moment of hesitation before Darcy acquiesced, dismounting with a grace that belied his obvious discomfort. He led his horse alongside as they walked, the rhythmic clopping of hooves on the path a steady counterpoint to their conversation—or lack thereof. He was walking beside her, to be sure, but the looks he kept casting her way were anything but easy. Elizabeth tried smiling tightly, but she could feel the heat of his eyes every time they slid towards her.

"Miss Bennet," he began after a moment, "If you will forgive me, I should say it is *you* who appear somewhat out of sorts this morning. Might I inquire if anything is amiss?"

Oh, that was simply unfair. She had asked first, had she not? Mr Darcy did not speak by the rules. She ought to simply deflect his question with another question, but upon glancing at him, her defensiveness softened at the genuine concern she saw in his eyes. Well... perhaps there was no harm in sharing... just a little.

"I have just learned we are to have a houseguest."

Darcy raised an eyebrow. "A houseguest? That seems hardly cause for such evident distress."

Elizabeth managed a wry grin. "Ordinarily, it would not be. But this particular guest is... well, let us say from what little I know of him, he is not one I would have chosen."

Darcy remained silent, clearly waiting for her to continue. Elizabeth sighed, glancing at the path ahead as if seeking guidance from its familiar turns.

"It is Mr Collins," she admitted finally. "He is a distant cousin and my father's heir, for the estate is entailed. That alone makes his visit awkward enough, but additionally, his arrival has been sprung upon us with little notice. My father, in his usual manner, mentioned it casually at breakfast as if it were of no consequence."

A flicker of something—understanding, perhaps—crossed Darcy's face. "And... your mother's reaction?"

Elizabeth could not help a laugh. "You are more perceptive than you look, Mr Darcy. She has already begun planning how best to secure his notice for me as if I were a bauble to be displayed. It is all rather tiresome."

"I imagine it must be."

Elizabeth glanced at him. "And you, Mr Darcy? What brings you out so early this morning?"

Darcy's gaze shifted, and for a moment, he seemed to weigh his words carefully. "The need for fresh air, as I mentioned. But also... I think you might understand the desire to escape one's own thoughts for a time."

Elizabeth studied him. The pallor of his skin and the tension in his posture were impossible to ignore. "It appears we both seek refuge in the morning air, then," she said softly.

His only response was a hum... more of a grunt, really. He stared at the ground as they walked, his horse's rein looped over his arm and his right hand clenched strangely.

"Sir, what..." She stopped herself.

"Yes, Miss Elizabeth?"

She tightened her jaw, then forged ahead. "You puzzle me exceedingly, sir. Upon our first meeting, you seemed so good-humoured—clever, even funny, and willing to be pleased."

"And you wonder what became of that genial fellow, Miss Elizabeth?"

She blanched. "Well, I... not in so many words, perhaps. But you do seem... altered."

"Come, now, Miss Elizabeth, you are nothing if not frank. What makes you think I was not simply euphoric from some illicit indulgence? I was, after all, a bachelor on a pleasure outing. It would not be such a shocking thing."

"From you? Indeed, it would be shocking. I believe I have the measure of your character, sir, and I declare, if you were indulging in snuff, I am Queen Charlotte."

A slight tug appeared at the left corner of his mouth. "Then perhaps you misjudged me, or I was putting you on that day."

"Try again."

Mr Darcy lifted his head back in a genuine laugh—the first, in fact, that she had heard from him since their first meeting. "Then what is your judgment, Miss Elizabeth? Why can you not simply presume I was in an exceedingly good mood?"

"Then I would beg to know why you have been so dour ever since." She stopped, forcing him to do the same and turn back toward her. "Or do you simply prefer being in a foul temper, unwilling to speak or make yourself agreeable in any fashion unless you can be the one in command of the situation?"

His eyes narrowed. "You make me sound rather petty, Miss Elizabeth."

She crossed her arms. "I speak as I find. Am I incorrect?"

Mr Darcy opened his mouth, but then there was a crease in his brow, and his words stilled. "You are, but..." He winced and shook his head, his brow pinching sharply as a hiss escaped his lips.

Elizabeth started forward, her hand extended. "Mr Darcy, truly, you look unwell. Forgive me if I gave offence, I—"

He put his fingers to his temple and sucked in a breath, then forced his eyes open. "It was not your words. It..." He shook his head again. "Never mind."

"You *are* unwell." She arched a brow and waited for his eyes to steady and focus on her face. "How long?"

ICE SHOT THROUGH DARCY's veins at her words. He dropped his hand—curse it, it was shaking again, twitching like a vile thing, even as his left eye felt like it was being stabbed with a hot blade. He tucked his hand behind his coat, and his voice cracked when he demanded, "What can you mean by that?"

Her eyes softened, and she gave him a strange look. "How many things can that question mean? How long have you been unwell? I assume you must have got some fever or something since our first meeting. That would explain—"

"Nothing at all. I have no fever, Miss Elizabeth."

She puckered her mouth. "Well, you *look* like you have a tremendous headache. That is exactly the face my aunt Gardiner makes when she has one of her megrims."

He blinked. "I..."

"There it is! I have it, for your face just confessed all." Her brow crumpled in sympathy. "These last few days, I thought you were merely unsociable, but you were in horrible pain!"

"Oh, I am entirely unsociable."

"Liar. Your friendships prove otherwise. Mr Bingley and Mr Wickham are perfectly amiable, and they have nothing but generous things to say of you."

There it was again—that stabbing throb, but this time, his stomach joined the rebellion. And he could not be sure that it was only this... malaise, whatever it was. It was hearing Miss Elizabeth speaking in such glowing terms about Wickham.

"I would caution you," he growled, "not to believe everything you hear, Miss Elizabeth."

"So, are you saying they are deceiving me about you? I should disbelieve them, should I? I thank you for the caution, sir."

That certainly blew up in his face. Darcy frowned and slid a long look to her but found her smirking and only waiting for him to meet her gaze. "I did not mean that, specifically, but..."

"But you meant something, sir, so out with it. Are you saying there is someone or something I ought not to trust? And, having given that caution, what proof do you have that I should trust *you?*"

Darcy's chest filled with air. Good heavens, how could he possibly keep ahead of Elizabeth Bennet when his head was trying to split in two? He would surely say something she would misinterpret or use against him. "I speak in generalities only, Miss Elizabeth," was his lame reply.

"Ah. So, you would caution me against insincerity in its most generic form. How helpful. Why, that is precisely how I shall proceed, Mr Darcy, when my father's cousin arrives in our drawing room and compliments my mother on her daughters and my father on the wonders of Longbourn—you see, I already have some little knowledge of him—then I shall..." She tilted her head, arching her brows in a question. "What? Not take him seriously? I think I have that much in hand."

"It is not necessary to tolerate insincerity, Miss Bennet. One must maintain their own integrity, even in the face of such... obsequiousness."

"Oh, now there is a fine word. Are you certain you have not met Mr Collins?"

Darcy smiled. "You paint a vivid picture of him."

"And you speak as though you have encountered many such characters, Mr Darcy."

His head panged again. If he only dared tell her... "More than I would care to admit. But it is not their opinions that matter, rather how one holds oneself amidst them."

"What a curious thing to say." Her forehead puckered in thought. "But I cannot disagree."

Darcy tried to nod, but a wave of dizziness washed over him, making it hard to keep his balance. He could not ignore Elizabeth's concerned glances, her unspoken thoughts clear in the crisp air between them. The biting winter breeze seeped through his coat, adding to his discomfort as they moved along the path. What the bloody devil had made him ride out today and subject himself to even more misery?

Oh, that was right. Wickham.

As they reached a small clearing, the sight of the bench nestled among a cluster of evergreen trees was a welcome relief. Darcy's stomach clenched, threatening to betray him. He paused, exhaling a breath that fogged in the cold air.

"Mr Darcy, please," Elizabeth's voice broke through his haze of exhaustion. "Let us rest for a moment."

He hesitated, pride warring with the undeniable need to pause. This had been one of his stupider ideas—riding out in a biting wind when he was barely managing to keep his two feet under him. "Perhaps just for a moment," he conceded, his voice strained.

He hooked his horse's reins over a branch of the evergreen and dropped to the bench. Not an instant too soon, either, for the earth spun around once or twice, taking his stomach with it.

Elizabeth seated herself beside him, her hands knotting in her lap, but her eyes fixed on him. "Mr Darcy, I cannot help but feel that there is more troubling you than just a lack of rest and a bit of a headache. Have you, perchance, tried willow bark tea? My aunt swears by it."

He pinched the bridge of his nose. "With negligible success."

Her eyes narrowed. "You speak as if this has been troubling you for some while."

"Indeed. Miss Elizabeth, if you do not mind, I would rather not discuss the matter."

She studied him for a moment, then nodded slowly. "Very well." Her lower lip pushed out in thought, and curse him, but if his head had not been about to fracture, he would have been tempted to kiss that plump lip.

No... ear-splitting headache or no, he was tempted, anyway.

Which meant it was a terrible idea for him to stay there, but, just for a moment, he did not possess the equilibrium to leave.

"Perhaps you would be happier discussing something else?" she suggested.

Darcy opened his eyes. "Such as?"

"Why, anything, really. You objected to the last subject, so it is for you to decide what to speak of next. The upcoming ball at Netherfield?"

He winced. "No."

"Your friends, then? Why are you riding alone today?"

"Because I wished to be alone."

"Ask an obvious question..." She cleared her throat, and he was fairly certain her eyes were rolling. "Very well, tell me about your sister. You said you would, sometime."

"I did. What do you wish to know?"

"Oh! What do I not wish to know? Is she in London? You need only nod, for I see that speaking is odious to you. Yes? So, is she staying with family? Is she to be presented at court?"

Darcy sighed. Despite himself, he was smiling. "She is staying with my aunt, Lady Matlock, who means to sponsor her for next Season."

"That is all very well. I am sure my mother would be delighted with such details, but now that I have got you talking again, tell me the important parts." She leaned forward. "She must depend upon you very much, I think."

He swallowed. "I... I expect she does."

"You are an attentive brother, I imagine. It is in all your looks when you speak of her. Tell me, do you write to her often?"

"Every other day, usually."

"And her replies to you? Are they full of the flummery that young ladies sometimes spout, or do they boast more substance?"

He hammered his thumb against a new throb at his temple but managed some approximation of a smile. "She speaks of our cousins and the people to whom my aunt has introduced her, mostly. Not to flaunt her list of acquaintances but rather to ask my advice regarding people I might know. Georgiana suffers from..." he winced again, more from the confession than the pain in his head. "A deal of self-doubt."

"Indeed? Does this stem from a timid personality? Surely not, if she is any sister of yours."

He grimaced. "She has been... misled, I think. But I suppose..." He scanned her expression as if he could pierce through the veil of her face and peer into her thoughts. "I suppose that is where my duty enters—to guide and advise her for as long as I may."

Elizabeth Bennet really did have astonishing eyes. They were fixed on him now, with a curious intensity that he had not seen in them before. She puckered her lips and leaned forward, and he almost thought she had a mind to compromise herself with him then and there... but she did nothing of the sort.

"One would think," she murmured, "that she will forever be your sister, even if she marries. Why would your time be limited?"

He swallowed. "I implied no such thing."

"Hmm." Elizabeth leaned back, smiling tightly. "My mistake. Well, if you are quite recovered from whatever was plaguing your head a moment ago, I think it best if we return home. Little as I like it, Mama will be terribly put out if I am rumpled and muddy from walking when Mr Collins arrives."

Darcy's mouth twitched. "Then the loss is entirely Mr Collins,' for I rather thought you made a memorable first impression that way."

Her laugh... well, it almost made suffering a megrim on a cold, windy hillside worth it.

"MR COLLINS! HOW DELIGHTFUL to see you!" Mrs Bennet exclaimed, rushing forward to greet him. "What lovely flowers! You are too kind."

Mr Collins stepped out of the carriage and bowed deeply, handing over the bouquet. "Mrs Bennet, it is my absolute pleasure. These flowers are but a small token of my appreciation for your warm hospitality."

"Hospitality, nonsense! Now, let me introduce you. This is Jane, my eldest, and Lizzy—I think you will agree that she is nearly as beautiful as Jane, do you not? Next is Mary, then Kitty and finally my dearest Lydia."

Elizabeth stifled a sigh and stepped forward to do her duty when it was her turn. "Welcome to Longbourn, Mr Collins," she said, forcing her voice to steady even as her thoughts ran wild. Wonderful. Another sycophant in the house.

"Ah, Miss Elizabeth, the pleasure is mine. I have heard much of your grace and beauty."

Her grace and beauty? From whom? Certainly not her father's letters. "You are very kind, Mr Collins," she replied, biting back the sort of remark she would have preferred to utter.

Mr Bennet, who had been standing back with his usual air of detached amusement, finally stepped forward. "Mr Collins, welcome. We trust your journey was pleasant?"

"Oh, indeed, Mr Bennet. It was most agreeable, and I cannot express how much I owe to the noble Lady Catherine de Bourgh for her generosity and guidance. Why, had she not recommended the proper bell posts and sent her *very own* driver, I daresay, my journey would not have been half so comfortable."

Elizabeth glanced at her father, whose eyes twinkled with barely suppressed mirth. "Indeed, Mr Collins, Lady Catherine's influence is unparalleled," he said, his tone dripping with sarcasm that Mr Collins seemed blissfully unaware of.

Mrs Bennet, beaming, ushered them all into the sitting room. "Come, come, Mr Collins. You must be tired after your journey. Let us sit and have some tea."

"Oh, yes, eminently fitting. Lady Catherine herself prefers a fine, stout blend after travelling, particularly in the winter. She always advises the most sensible course of action. I declare, there is no matter so great that she cannot offer her wisdom, nor too small for her notice."

Mr Bennet leaned back in his chair. "Tell me, Mr Collins, does Lady Catherine have strong opinions on... say, the proper care of house plants?"

Mr Collins perked up, nodding enthusiastically. "Oh, absolutely, Mr Bennet. Lady Catherine insists that ferns must always be placed in shaded areas, watered precisely at dawn, for it signifies both care and devotion to one's home."

"Fascinating," Mr Bennet mused. "And what of the ivy? I have had a devilish time with the one in my study. Does she have a preferred method for ensuring its growth?"

"Of course! Ivy must be trimmed regularly to maintain a dignified appearance, and it must never be allowed to climb too high, lest it appear unruly. Lady Catherine believes that such meticulous care reflects the owner's disciplined nature."

Elizabeth glanced at Jane, who leaned forward, eyes wide and attentive. She was too polite to do otherwise. Mary, on the other hand, stared blankly at the wall, clearly retreating into her own thoughts.

Mr Bennet continued to prod. "And I must know, what is Lady Catherine's stance on the correct arrangement of garden beds?"

"Oh, Lady Catherine is most particular about garden beds. She prefers geometric patterns for their sense of order and beauty, insisting that flowers be grouped by colour and height to create a harmonious display."

Elizabeth's feet were itching with impatience, and she squirmed in her seat. If only she could find a way to redirect the conversation, but Mr Collins seemed unstoppable, his words flowing like an unending river. She shot a look at her father, silently reproaching him for goading the man so, but he was enjoying himself far too much.

And, Elizabeth realised, he was keeping Collins from exploring Longbourn like it was his own. But it was only a matter of delay and amusement for her father. The humiliating inspection would take place eventually, so what was the point of listening to the man while they awaited the inevitable?

Just as Elizabeth thought she could bear no more of Mr Collins' inanities, there came a sudden, urgent knock on the front door. Everyone turned as Mr Hill entered the room, looking slightly flustered.

"Mr Bennet, sir," Mr Hill said, his voice steady despite the urgency in his eyes. "A tenant, Mr Harris, requests an audience. It appears to be quite urgent."

Mr Bennet rose from his seat, his amusement giving way to concern. "Show him in, Mr Hill."

A moment later, Mr Harris entered, his face flushed with worry. He bowed quickly to the assembled company before turning to Mr Bennet. "Mr Bennet, sir! Forgive the intrusion, but I need help. The river's rising fast, and my house is nearly washed away!"

Mr Bennet immediately stood, his expression turning serious. "Calm yourself, Mr Harris. We shall see what can be done. Come, let us go at once."

Turning to Mr Collins, Mr Bennet offered a quick, apologetic nod. "Mr Collins, I must attend to this matter immediately. I trust you will excuse me."

Mr Collins, his words run aground by the sudden interruption, managed a stiff nod. "Of... of course, Mr Bennet. Duty calls, as it must. Lady Catherine would see to the matter with utmost dispatch."

Mr Bennet stopped, looking back at his guest with a quizzical glance, then shook his head with a sigh. "My hat, please, Hill."

Chapter Eighteen

Not... again.

Darcy woke to a pounding in his skull, the megrim gripping his head with merciless intensity. Pain shot through his temples, each throb taunting him whenever he tried to blink. He groaned as waves of nausea rolled over him. Clenching his fists, he forced himself to sit up, the room spinning wildly around him.

The morning light filtered through the heavy drapes—too bright, too harsh. Darcy squeezed his eyes shut, willing the pain to subside. But it only deepened, relentlessly drilling into his brain. He pressed his palms against his temples as if he could physically push the agony away.

It had been ten days since Westing had uttered those hideous words. *A tumour.* The words haunted him, a grim reality he had tried to ignore or disprove. He could not be dying! He had too much left to do!

There was the new planting system he meant to implement at Pemberley and the east wing repairs he had ordered for spring after the weather improved. There was that shipping company he had just invested in and Georgiana's come-out to prepare for... not that *he* would be much material help there, but Georgie needed him, and he meant to frighten off any unworthy suitors with a firm glare. And there was still Bingley, with all the ventures for which he had sought Darcy's advice, and Richard... what if something happened to Richard? What if they were *both* just... gone? Who would there be to pick up the pieces?

Darcy curled himself into a ball, piling the pillows over his head to block out the light and muffle the sounds of his sobs. He, a grown man, reduced to tears over a headache!

But now, the unrelenting pain shattered his fragile illusions. He could no longer deny or claim that it was merely a passing pain. The agony was a living thing, a growing thing, that occasionally gave him glimpses of doubt, then roared back with all the certainty of promise.

He was dying.

The idea devoured him, a dark spectre he could neither escape nor fully confront. This thing, whatever it was inside his head, was stealing his future—moments snatched away in agony and moments never to be lived. How much was to be taken from him? All the things he would leave unfinished… and the one thing he had yet to even begin.

There would be no more Darcys at Pemberley after him.

That notion ought to have struck a chord of grief in him. The despair of knowing he could have, should have, if he had only not frittered away the time that was given him. His father had not led a long life, but his impact was still felt. How had *he* the right to do any less?

As it was, even if Darcy found a woman to marry this very day—and there *was* one he could not cease thinking of—there was no guarantee he would be able to produce an heir. In fact, the notion was laughable. The odds that he could get a wife with child, and that that child could be a son, and that the wife he would leave behind might have the wisdom and integrity to raise the next Darcy on her own…

No. There would be no last-minute wedding, no urgent attempts to get a child or desperate hope that all would carry on jolly well without him. There was just… not enough time. And frankly, not enough hope even to provoke sorrow. There was only this prevailing sense of numbness.

Darcy's breath hitched, and he rolled toward the edge of the bed. There was a smear of drool on the pillow, under where his cheek had been—and he had never even felt it. He groaned and staggered to his feet, clutching the bedpost for support.

His reflection in the mirror was a ghostly visage, pale and drawn, eyes shadowed with sleepless nights and ceaseless worry. The man staring back at him seemed a stranger, so far removed from the assured, commanding figure he had always known himself to be.

There were dark circles under his eyes every morning lately. Surely, someone would start to notice them and realise something was very much amiss. Heavens, Elizabeth Bennet already *had*, and she barely knew him! And when was the last time his valet had cut his hair? He scraped a hand through the unruly tangle, tugging at the unfamiliar length of it. Had Giles not recently suggested a bit of grooming? He usually did, for he kept a rather tight routine… but for the life of him, Darcy could not remember the last time the subject had come up.

This would not do. He stumbled to the window, pushing it open to let in the crisp morning air. It bit at his skin, a brief reprieve from the heat in his skull. Leaning heavily against the sill, Darcy closed his eyes, pressing his forehead against the cool glass.

It was precious little reprieve. The sounds of Netherfield, still strange to him, grated on his frayed nerves. The house—*Wickham's house*—felt stifling, its unfamiliar walls closing in with the weight of guilt and confusion. What was he even doing here?

He had told himself it was all about Bingley, seeing that his friend was not deceived. But now... what was it? He could probably think of it if that blasted gong stopped clanging inside his head.

Why should he care anymore about Wickham's activities? What did it matter to him that Wickham had somehow stumbled into a fortune? He ought to be pleased... his father would have wanted that for George... he might even be relieved and delighted himself if... oh, hang it all. What was the problem in the first place?

The money. That was right, the money. Odd, that. A swift fortune, to be sure, but Wickham would not be the first man to have his living made by the death of a stranger.

A soft knock interrupted his spiralling thoughts. Darcy turned, wincing at the movement, and saw his valet, Giles, standing at the door.

"Sir, are you well?" Giles asked.

Darcy tried to keep his face composed, his headache raging at the intrusion of light from the hallway. "Quite well, Giles," he lied, his voice strained. "The light... it is somewhat harsh this morning. A bit too much brandy last evening. Could you close the door, please?"

Giles quickly complied, stepping inside and gently shutting the door behind him. "Would you like a shave, sir?"

Darcy waved off the suggestion, his mind too clouded with pain to consider grooming. "No, Giles. Tell me, are Bingley and Wickham down at breakfast?"

Giles hesitated, clearing his throat. "They were called out early, sir. Some trouble in the village. They left their apologies and their direction in case you desired to join them later."

Relief washed over Darcy, a small respite from his larger torment. "Very well. I shall remain in my room for another hour. Do not alert the household."

Giles nodded and began to withdraw but then stopped, recalling something. "Sir, I have a letter for you. From Dr Westing in London."

Darcy's stomach tightened as he took the letter with trembling hands. "Thank you, Giles. You may go."

Left alone, Darcy stared at the page, his vision blurring with the effort. He sank onto the bed, ripping open the letter, his heart pounding. The words swam before his eyes, the pain making it impossible to focus. He let the letter slip from his fingers, collapsing back onto the bed, his mind and body too exhausted to fight any longer. He closed his eyes, hoping to sleep off more of the megrim, but knowing that rest was a fleeting comfort in the face of such relentless agony.

Darcy woke to the muted sounds of voices outside his door, the once quiet hallway now alive with the daily noises of the maids. Groggily, he pushed himself upright, the megrim still pounding mercilessly in his skull. He had no sense of time—hours could have passed or mere minutes. His body felt heavy, his mind sluggish, as he swung his legs over the side of the bed.

Giles was nowhere to be seen. Heavens, everyone would know he had been languishing abed all day! He struggled to his feet and gripped the bedpost until the room quit spinning. Perhaps it was not too late to salvage all appearances... He fumbled through the process of dressing himself, the simple act of finding his clothes feeling like a trek in the rocky Peaks. He tugged off his nightshirt, the cool air of the room biting at his bare skin and reached for his breeches.

As he tried to tug the fitted buckskin over his thighs and fasten the fall, his fingers trembled, his coordination failing him. In his haste, he noticed the letter he had dropped earlier, half-hidden beneath the edge of the bed. With a wince, he bent to retrieve it, the pain in his head surging with the movement. He sat back on the bed, the letter clutched in his hand, his breath shallow as he opened it once more.

This time, his eyes could focus, and he forced himself to read Doctor Westing's words.

My dear Mr Darcy,

It is with the deepest regret that I read of your continued symptoms. You asked for recommendations to provide some comfort, but I note nothing we have not already tried.

You may certainly speak with an apothecary to obtain morphine or laudanum, but I cannot promise any enduring relief. I fear you must indeed be afflicted with a tumour or perhaps another malignancy such as cerebral congestion.

Mr Darcy, I certainly advise you to seek a second or perhaps even a third opinion from someone learned enough to provide reliable counsel. However, I fear their diagnosis may be much the same. I entreat you to prepare yourself for the possibility that your time may be limited. Please know that I remain at your service and shall endeavour to provide whatever palliative care is within my power. My heartiest condolences, sir.

Yours most sincerely,

Dr Edward Westing

Darcy's hands shook, the stark finality of the words sinking into him. The diagnosis he had been denying now loomed undeniable, each word a nail sealing his fate. He closed his eyes, swallowing against the rising tide of despair. How could it have come to this? He, who had always prided himself on his strength and resilience, was now reduced to this frail, suffering shell.

The voices outside grew louder, a reminder that life continued beyond his private torment. With a deep breath, Darcy forced himself to stand, ignoring the dizziness that threatened to pull him back down. He needed to present a composed front, to hide his weakness until he could return to his own turf—London, at least, or preferably, Pemberley. Slowly, methodically, he finished dressing, each motion a small victory over the debilitating pain.

Fully clothed at last, he took a moment to steady himself, clutching the bedpost for support. He could not afford to let anyone see him falter. He straightened, folding the letter and tucking it into his coat pocket. It seemed that he would have to decide, rather quickly, how to spend what time remained to him.

ELIZABETH HAD PACED THE drawing room all evening as Jane sat rigidly on the sofa. The clock ticked loudly in the silence, each passing minute amplifying the tension of waiting. Mama and the rest of their sisters had long since gone to bed, but Jane and Elizabeth had been waiting for hours, the long shadows of their evening candles stretching across the floor.

Finally, the sound of the front door creaking open broke the stillness. Mr Bennet and Mr Collins stepped inside, their clothes muddied and their expressions weary.

"Mr Bennet, I must insist, had we only followed my suggestion to divert the stream—" Mr Collins began, his voice quivering, "—the matter might have been resolved in mere moments, and we would not have been so put out over the effort."

Mr Bennet rolled his eyes, a deep sigh escaping him. "Mr Collins, if you would kindly keep your suggestions to yourself. We did all that was possible under the circumstances."

"But Mr Bennet," Collins persisted, "if we had constructed a temporary dam or even used sandbags—"

"Mr Collins, your theories are endless, but none were practical today. The stream's force was beyond anything sandbags could contain."

"And what about my idea to reinforce the barn? Surely, that would have saved some of the hay and grain."

Elizabeth could see the weariness in her father's eyes and decided to intervene. "Mr Collins," she said gently, stepping forward, "Mrs Hill has seen to it that your room is made quite comfortable. A hot bath awaits you, as our honoured guest."

Mr Collins straightened, clearly pleased with the recognition. "Ah, Miss Elizabeth, your family's hospitality is unparalleled. I shall retire, then, to refresh myself after such a taxing day."

Elizabeth nodded, watching as he ascended the stairs. She turned back to her father, who sank into a chair, rubbing his temples.

"Papa," Elizabeth asked softly, "what happened?"

Mr Bennet leaned back, exhaustion cracking deep lines in his face. "The stream rose from last night's rain, washing out the foundations. The house is a total ruin. We've moved the family to the dower house for now."

Jane sat beside him and offered him a cup of tea. "And what of their livestock and possessions?"

Mr Bennet sighed heavily. "We managed to save the cows and pigs, but I am afraid they lost most of their hens. As to their possessions, we carried away what we could, but much was lost. We will have to support them through the winter until repairs can be made."

Elizabeth came to sit on her father's opposite side. "Perhaps we could arrange for some additional shelter for the livestock? The old stable might be made to suffice with a little work."

"That's a sound idea, Lizzy," Mr Bennet agreed. "And perhaps we can spare some of the winter feed from our stores."

Jane added, "We could also collect clothing and blankets from the village. I'm sure everyone would be willing to help."

"Let us hope."

"Oh, I cannot think there would be any doubt," Elizabeth insisted. "Surely Mr Wickham will be the first to offer some help. He has the means and influence."

Mr Bennet stared into his cup of tea, his expression darkening. "Wickham did offer help, but not in the manner you think. He proposed to buy the tenant's farm from Longbourn and make it part of Netherfield."

Elizabeth's mouth dropped open. "Buy the farm? But that would leave our tenants at the mercy of Netherfield."

Mr Bennet rubbed his eyes and set his teacup back on its saucer, passing it back to Jane. "Would that be such a terrible thing, Lizzy?"

"Well... Yes, I think..." She shook her head. "Mr Wickham is only the lessor, not the owner of Netherfield. How can he propose to do such a thing?"

Her father shook his head and leaned it on his fist. "I have no idea. But I am inclined to accept if he is able to find some means of making it work."

"But Papa!"

"Think, Lizzy. Longbourn itself is entailed, as well as most of the farmlands, but there is some liberty in the disposal of the tenant farms acquired in my father's lifetime—Harris' farm being one of them, and Rogers' being the other. They are currently held in fee simple and are, in fact, the only inheritance you can look forward to from your dear Papa. However, they are become something more of a liability than an asset, thanks to this sodden ruin of a winter. Mr Wickham has the means to invest in the properties to make them prosperous again. So long as there is no encumbrance—and that will be up to the men who keep books and read laws—if Netherfield can purchase the farm, then

Mr Wickham will bear the expense of the house repairs. And we..." He looked up with a weary attempt at a smirk. "We might burden Mr Collins somewhat the less, eh?"

Elizabeth swatted at her father's arm. "Papa! You are incorrigible."

Mr Bennet chuckled softly, but the weariness in his eyes did not fade. "Ah, but there is some truth in that, Lizzy. Now, if you will excuse me, I believe I shall retire for the night."

As he stood and made his way toward the stairs, Jane and Elizabeth exchanged a concerned glance. Once their father was out of earshot, Jane turned to her sister. "Lizzy, why do you think Mr Wickham would want just one tenant farm? What could he gain from it?"

Elizabeth frowned. "I am sure he is thinking of becoming a more permanent fixture at Netherfield. Perhaps he is trying to increase his rents, long term. Acquiring more land would certainly give him more standing."

Jane nodded thoughtfully. "That is possible. But do you think it is purely for that? Could there be another motive?"

Elizabeth sighed, shaking her head. "I cannot imagine Mr Wickham having any ulterior motives beyond that. He has always been kind and generous. Maybe he simply wishes to help in any way he can."

Jane's expression remained uncertain. "It seems such a strange proposition, though. To buy one farm when he could just offer assistance. Why go to such lengths?"

Elizabeth looked out the window, her thoughts a swirl of confusion and concern. "Perhaps he sees it as a way to ensure the tenant's security. If the farm becomes part of Netherfield, he might feel he can better protect them from future misfortune. Besides, if he buys it, then he can reap the benefits of his assistance in the long term."

"I think you must be right. There is nothing wrong with looking to one's own interests, so long as the needs of others are met first. I am sure he means to rebuild the farmhouse to something much finer than it was originally. It would be a noble act indeed."

"Yes, let us hope. Mr Wickham has always shown himself to be a good man. I choose to believe in his altruism."

Jane nodded, though her eyes remained clouded with doubt. "We shall see. For now, let us get some rest. I, for one, need a full night's sleep before hearing what Mama has to say about all this tomorrow."

"You worry about Mama, but I tell you, it is Mr Collins I do not look forward to hearing from."

Chapter Nineteen

"Gentlemen, I must inform you that I have decided to return to London immediately. There are... urgent matters that require my attention."

Darcy, Bingley, and Wickham were gathered in the drawing room for the afternoon, the fire crackling softly as Bingley and Wickham played at piquet. Darcy sat opposite them on the sofa with a book in his hand, the words running incomprehensibly across the page. By this point, he had no idea what book he was even holding, and he had been similarly unable to focus on Bingley and Wickham's swirling back-and-forth of conversation. There was no point in delaying his announcement any longer—the thing must be done.

Wickham spun around, and his face fell in disappointment. "Darcy, that is most unfortunate. Why, you only arrived a week ago."

"Indeed, but my mind is quite made up. I have asked Giles to make preparations to depart on the morrow."

Wickham turned his attention back to the cards in his hand, but his shoulders sagged. "Well! No one ever deterred you from your object, eh, Bingley? It is a pity, though, for you will miss the ball. I had also hoped to seek your advice on several matters."

Darcy raised an eyebrow, curiosity piqued despite his discomfort. "Which matters?"

Wickham twisted again in his chair, his face brightening with inspiration. "Do you remember last night when I told you about the Longbourn farm that was nearly washed away by the flooding?"

Darcy's forehead crunched. "I do not recall..." Surely, if it had to do with Longbourn and the Bennets, he would have paid attention... even if he did not wish to.

"Oh, you must remember. It was when I passed you in the hall last night. We were out rather late, as you recall. By the by, what were you doing yesterday?"

Darcy swallowed. "I had a deal of business to correspond."

"Ah, of course. Always was your way. Although the maids informed me you spent much of the day in your room, so I thought perhaps you might have found some 'other' amusements."

It was a few seconds before Darcy caught the implication. His neck crawled with heat. "Er... no."

"Ah. Well, no matter. Yes, anyway, I said something to you about that family who lost their house and the trouble of seeing all their livestock and possessions moved. 'Twill take a deal of money and no small amount of time to put it all right again. Anyway, I have been considering purchasing the land from Mr Bennet so that it might be held by Netherfield."

Darcy frowned, the audaciousness of the proposal striking him as more likely a figment of his addled brain than a real plan.

"*Buy* the farm?" Darcy repeated.

"Yes, that is what I said. Is that so shocking?"

"But you are not the owner of Netherfield. How do you intend to manage such a purchase?"

Wickham chuckled as he turned back to his cards. "Perhaps it does seem improbable, but I assure you, Darcy, I will see everything done through the proper channels. If an outright purchase is not permitted under my contract, perhaps I might sub-lease the property from Mr Bennet. I plan to speak to Mr Northam and Mr Philips on the matter, of course, and if necessary, I shall also address Sir Anthony Mortimer."

"Sir Anthony Mortimer? That was..." Darcy had to wedge the name from where it had lodged in his brain. "He was the man being put forward as a potential new MP for the area?"

Wickham nodded. "Precisely. I am sure he is the right man for the post."

Darcy pressed his fingers into his left eye socket as a sharp stab interrupted his line of thought. "What makes you so certain?"

"Oh, everyone around thinks well of him. At least, all those who matter, and I am certain the rest will be persuaded in time. And you remember Viscount Halstead, of course? He has always vouched for Mortimer."

Darcy hesitated, his mind stumping on the name as if he had just blundered into a tree. "Viscount Halstead? I know no such person."

Wickham laughed lightly, as if Darcy were making a jest. "Surely you remember, Darcy. We were all very good friends."

"I do not forget my friends."

"Well!" Wickham shook his head as he placed a card on the table. "I cannot think how you do not remember Halstead. Come, man, he visited Pemberley in our junior year! His father bought a horse from yours. Fine chestnut stallion, as I recall. We all used to go to the club together, and he even covered your debts once."

"That is not possible. I rarely gambled and never ran up debts."

Wickham snorted as he surveyed the table. "I assure you, you did, although you are not wrong that you *almost* never ended the night behind because you nearly always won. That was the beginning of my life in debt, as you recall, and my first great loss was to you. You were a devilish master at Whist."

"I enjoyed its stimulating challenges, but I never—"

"Oh, come, Darcy, no sense in trying to play the saint. We are all old friends here, are we not? Bingley, surely *you* recall Halstead."

Bingley, who had been listening quietly, paused with his hand over the stack of cards and blinked for a few seconds. "Y-yes, I do believe I recall the man. I think he had the highest marks in Latin, did he not?"

"Yes, that's the fellow." Wickham nodded. "Burned Darcy like you cannot imagine. Come, tell him. Egad, Darcy, what has become of your memory?"

"There is nothing the matter with my memory," Darcy snapped. And then he rubbed his throbbing temple, rather surreptitiously.

"Well, then surely you must recall Halstead, Darcy. Think back if you will. He was taller even than you, with sandy hair, and he hailed from Yorkshire."

A cold sweat broke out on his forehead. He searched his memory, but it was like grasping at shadows. He looked at Bingley, who seemed genuinely confused by his uncertainty.

Wickham pressed on. "Halstead had a lovely sister—I believe you fancied her for most of one evening—that is, until she spoke and dashed your illusions. Oh, and he was the only man who bested you at chess in your last year. Surely you cannot forget that."

Darcy's head pounded with the effort of trying to remember. Those all sounded very like things that might have been part of his experience, but they simply never happened! He would *remember* things like that. Would he not? His breath quickened, and it was as if the walls were closing in.

He glanced at Bingley, who was, by now, nodding in agreement with Wickham. "Yes, Darcy. I did not know him well, but I remember him clearly. I say, where is he now?"

Yes, where was this fellow now? For Darcy was well acquainted with the *ton*, and surely, even if he had somehow missed the man at university, he would have been introduced through Lord Matlock or at Almack's.

"Oh! Last I heard, he was in The States brokering some deal in cotton on behalf of his uncle, Lord Wexfield. Surely you remember *him*, at least?"

Darcy scratched his memory. That name he *did* recall. Lady Matlock had mentioned the man not long ago. But Halstead? Darcy was certain he had never heard of the man, but with both Wickham and Bingley swearing that Darcy must know him, how could he deny it?

The room spun, and Darcy gripped the arms of his chair. His memory, once so reliable, now seemed a traitor. He forced a smile, though it felt hollow. "Yes, of course. How could I forget Halstead?"

Wickham beamed, satisfied. "I knew you could not have forgot. With Halstead and Wexfield and many others vouching for Mortimer in London, it only strengthens Mortimer's position when the time comes."

Darcy nodded, though his confusion deepened as his voice faded. "Indeed... Indeed."

Wickham gathered the cards to shuffle and deal another round, and Bingley excused himself to pour a brandy on the opposite side of the room. Darcy shook his head when Bingley gestured, offering him a glass, and fell to fingering the pages of his book.

How could he have forgot a man he apparently knew so well as Halstead? But search though he might, Darcy had absolutely no memory of the man. His hand trembled, and his right eyelid began to twitch. This was all progressing faster than he could ever have imagined.

"I say, Darcy," Wickham said from the table where he was dealing cards, "one thing I had been meaning to ask you was what you thought of old Mrs Nicholls' cooking. Is she up to the task of cooking for a ball?"

Darcy shook his dazed head and tried to focus on Wickham's profile. "I have no way of knowing that, but everything I have tasted from her kitchen is more than adequate."

"You did not think her white soup was too salty?"

Darcy blinked. "I have not had the pleasure of sampling it."

Wickham turned to look at him fully, his face scrunched in half wonder. "Why, of course, you have. She made us a sample of it two days ago to see that I approved. Bingley was out, but you and I tasted it. I recall you made a rather peculiar face, and I wondered at it at the time, but I believe you had just got a letter from Fitzwilliam, so I presumed that might be the cause."

Dash it all, he was panting, and a cool sheen was breaking through his hairline and nearly trickling down his temple. "I… I did have a letter from Fitzwilliam the day before yesterday…"

"There, you see. You were probably distracted and entirely forgot what you were eating. Surely, you recall now. Was it too thick? Shall I have her use fewer eggs?"

"I… I do not…"

"Oh, no bother. I only thought you had such discriminating taste; you would have some opinions, but I suppose nearly every cook has their way, so I may as well let Nicholls do as she pleases. I shall have my hands full enough restraining Mrs Bennet, shall I not?" he laughed. "By the by, as you will not be here to open the ball with Miss Elizabeth Bennet, shall I offer to take your place with the lady?"

Darcy blinked. "What?"

Wickham stared at him as if Darcy had just kicked his hunting dogs. "Why… Miss Elizabeth! She is expecting you to dance the first with her, and I daresay, I believe you asked for the supper set as well."

Darcy's mouth was open, but only a vague gasp escaped. When did he ask Elizabeth Bennet to dance? And *twice* in one evening? That was not his usual form, particularly not so far in advance of the ball!

Then again… he had to confess that the notion *had*, indeed, occurred to him, and probably more than once. Elizabeth Bennet would be the one lady in all the room who would not be a punishment for him to stand up with. But when had he acted upon that sentiment?

Wickham turned back to his cards as Bingley rejoined him at the table. "I am sorry you shall miss the pleasure of dancing with the lady, Darcy. Egad, it looks as if you regret the loss more than I had realised. Well, no matter. I hope she will not be too disappointed if I offer to take your place. I confess I was a bit jealous when you engaged her first."

"I…" Darcy shook his head. "I did *not* ask Miss Elizabeth to dance at the ball," he stated bluntly. He was sure of that. He would *remember* that!

Wickham glanced over his shoulder, a peculiar look on his face. "Darcy, are you quite well this evening? You seem a bit off. Perhaps a bit of port will set you right."

Curse it, his cravat was choking him. Darcy gulped against the knot and felt a damp streak trickling down his throat. Blast, if that was more numbness from the side of his mouth, he would never recover from the mortification! He performed a quick swipe but found only nervous perspiration. "I..." He sucked in a breath to steady the quaking in his chest. "Excuse me, gentlemen, but I must return to my room to write some letters."

He stood, his legs unsteady beneath him. Wickham's voice followed him as he left the room, but the words were a blur. Each step was a battle against the pain and muddy confusion in his head, and a growing sense of dread dragged at him like an anchor. What was happening to him? *Why could he not remember?*

Reaching his room, he closed the door and leaned against it, trying to steady his racing thoughts. The headache roared, and he felt the world slipping away. He moved to his desk, the letter from Dr Westing still lying there. The words from the letter came back to him, chilling in their clarity: *"Your time may be limited."*

With trembling hands, Darcy sat and tried to compose himself. The faces of his friends, their voices insisting on memories he could not grasp, haunted him. He dipped his pen in ink, but the letters on the page blurred together. He set the pen down, his mind too fogged to write.

He needed rest, but more than that, he needed answers.

"Mama, with all the flooding and hardship round the area, are you sure a ball just now is in good taste?"

Mrs Bennet paused as she descended from the carriage to laugh at her daughter's preposterous suggestion. "Why, Lizzy, do you not know that times of hardship are when people *most* need a diversion?"

Elizabeth gripped the edge of her skirt to step down as the footman offered his hand. "Yes, but Mama, a ball is a rather extravagant expense. Ought we not be encouraging Mr Wickham to spend the money on repairing his own tenant farms and waterways? And what about us? You propose new gowns for Jane and... Mama!"

But Mrs Bennet was already prancing toward the steps of Netherfield, her bonnet ribbons fluttering behind her. "You shall see, Lizzy! Now, come along. The gentlemen are waiting!"

Elizabeth lodged her feet firmly in the gravel of the drive, her mouth screwed into a frustrated scowl. "Jane, she is going to make a spectacle of us all."

Jane, the last out of the carriage, inclined her head to thank the footman for his assistance and drew beside Elizabeth. "At least she permitted us to come today. We might be able to..." She cleared her throat.

"Restrain her? Good luck with that. You know she only permitted us to come today because there were three single gentlemen inside. No, I say the miracle was in you persuading her that Lydia and Kitty would do better to spend their time working over their gowns rather than coming with us. How *did* you manage that?"

Jane's mouth dimpled on one side in a shy chuckle. "Oh, I might have let a little 'spilt' candle wax spoil Lydia's lace."

Elizabeth let out an astonished laugh. "Jane Bennet! Why, I am impressed. That sounds very like something I would have done!"

"Where do you think I got the idea? Come, Lizzy, it will not be that horrid. The gentlemen are all generous, and it was Mr Wickham's idea to let Mama help."

"No, it was *her* idea. He was just too polite to refuse her." Elizabeth sighed and let Jane loop her arm to drag her into the house.

Jane was right in the reception they found inside. Mr Wickham and Mr Bingley were entirely welcoming and generous. Elizabeth sat beside Jane on the sofa, a cup of tea cooling in her hand as her eyes skated across the room. Where was Mr Darcy today? Perhaps he was occupied above stairs. Just as well—he would probably not view her mother so amiably.

She dragged her gaze back to the gentleman sitting opposite her mother and tried to keep her attention there, but the trouble was, details of things like dances and lavish suppers were so far removed from the top of her concerns that she could hardly believe they were even being discussed.

"... And the seventh shall be the supper set, of course," Mama was saying as she showed Mr Wickham a list. "I thought perhaps Sellenger's Round for that one. My Lydia dances that one particularly well. Have you spoken to your cook about the roast partridge? I think a roast venison would be much finer."

"Ah, but it would overpower the roast lamb, would it not?" Mr Wickham asked. "No, I think we shall keep the partridge, but Mrs Bennet, I have a daring suggestion about the dance order."

Mrs Bennet squinted at her list. "Why, there is nothing the matter with the order. I understand this is how it is done in London."

"Precisely my point, Mrs Bennet. We are a somewhat more relaxed gathering here, are we not? Now, I see that you have no waltzes planned. Shall we remedy that?"

Beside Elizabeth, Jane stiffened, and Elizabeth saw the quick flush rise to Mr Bingley's cheeks as his eye was drawn helplessly toward her sister.

"A waltz, Mr Wickham?" Mrs Bennet gasped. "Oh, why, to be sure, I understand they are becoming rather popular, but so scandalous!"

"Nothing of the sort, I assure you!" the gentleman laughed. "Yes, of course, the gentleman holds the lady somewhat closer, but with a fair space between them, and I daresay the steps are far easier to keep pace with than the reel. It is just what a gentleman prefers as a bit of a breather in an evening where there shall be, I fear, more ladies wanting a partner than willing gentlemen to provide one. Now, let us see. Shall we put it just after supper, where we might all ease into the rest of the evening with full bellies and a slower rhythm? Or shall it be just before, when we are all weary and beginning to need the rest?"

"Oh, by all means after," Mrs Bennet opined.

"I am afraid I shall beg to differ," Bingley spoke up. "Is not a faster dance just after supper to be preferred? Something like Mr Beveridge's Maggot to liven everyone up for the rest of the evening. I think I should vastly prefer the slower dance just before supper." He followed this with a significant look toward Jane.

"Very clever, my friend," Mr Wickham agreed. "Shall we change the sequence, Mrs Bennet?"

"Well, I..." Mrs Bennet giggled. "Oh, Mr Bennet shall go distracted if he has to dance with me that set! By all means, Mr Wickham. Oh, and I do hope you have not yet got a partner, for my girls are all splendid dancers, especially Lydia."

Mr Wickham smiled widely, and Elizabeth's face heated when his open gaze found her. "Oh, I am quite assured of that, Mrs Bennet. On that subject, Miss Elizabeth, I hope you will not be too disappointed if I beg your hand for that set. I know you had your heart set on another."

Elizabeth's throat tightened. "Whatever do you mean, sir?"

"Oh, why I thought the matter was settled between you and Darcy. Yes, I am sure he said something to me about it. Do you not recall, Bingley?"

Mr Bingley had been mouthing something to Jane—obviously, something rather inappropriate, by the red stain that rose on his cheeks when Mr Wickham caught him out—and he started when his friend spoke his name. "What? Darcy? Oh, yes, to be sure. A pity he has to return to London before the grand event."

Elizabeth felt as if she were a ball being bounced around in the street by a dozen children. "I... what? I do not follow."

"Why, no matter, Miss Elizabeth," Mr Wickham assured her. "One of us will see that you are properly engaged for the supper set, shall we not, Bingley? I would not wish for you to be disappointed."

She could only stare. "Disappointed in... what, precisely?"

"Oh, Lizzy, must you argue with everyone?" Mama huffed in exasperation. "The gentleman is offering to dance with you!"

She shook herself. "Ah, yes. I understand that, but what is this about Mr Darcy?"

"Some business or other," Mr Wickham replied with a wave of his hand. "Although I am sure he will be terribly disappointed to miss the chance to stand up with you, for I assure you, he was looking forward to it. But you know Darcy! He was never a man to neglect his duties."

Elizabeth swallowed. "I... I suppose not, Mr Wickham."

"Of course not. Now, then! We have the supper set and the one just after that settled. What did you propose for the ninth, Mrs Bennet?"

"Well! The quadrille, of course, but if you would prefer the reel..."

"Oh, the reel to be sure," Mr Wickham said, nodding over the page. "And then the quadrille next..."

Elizabeth set her saucer on the side table and merely leaned back, gripping the sofa cushion and trying to listen to it all. What had just happened? Mama was debating dances with the master of Netherfield, his guest was making mooning faces at a hotly blushing Jane, and Mr Darcy was leaving before any of it took place.

This... this was a very strange ball.

Chapter Twenty

Darcy leaned heavily against the desk in his room, the laudanum bottle still open beside him. He had taken a draught earlier, hoping for relief from the relentless pounding in his head. Instead, the room seemed to tilt and sway, the edges of his vision blurring. He rubbed his temples, wishing the pain to subside, but it continued to beat a merciless rhythm in his skull.

Through the haze of his headache and the disorienting effects of the laudanum, he could hear faint voices and laughter from outside. He staggered to the window, needing to focus on something, anything, to distract him from the agony.

Peering through the glass, he saw Elizabeth and Jane Bennet walking in the garden, escorted by Bingley. They moved slowly, admiring the dormant maze and shrubs, their voices drifting up to him in soft, indistinct murmurs. Elizabeth's presence drew his eye like a lodestone, her graceful movements and animated expressions focusing his attention as nothing else had done.

Darcy's heart pounded with a different kind of pain now, one that had nothing to do with his physical suffering. His mind, hazy from the laudanum, clung to the sight of Elizabeth like a lifeline. She looked radiant in the afternoon light, her laughter carrying up to him like a soothing balm, cutting through the fog in his head.

His thoughts, usually so sharp and controlled, had been drifting and tangled like a distant echo. But her image wavered before his eyes, a beacon in the blur. His legs felt like jelly, but he pushed away from the window, swaying slightly. His head would be clearer around *her*—somehow. The idea pulsed with his heartbeat, overriding any remaining logic.

He staggered toward the door, each step a battle against the spinning room. His chest tightened in desperation and longing. What could he have been thinking, planning to leave without seeing her again? Impossible. The laudanum blurred the lines between reason and impulse, leaving only a raw need to be close to her, to feel her presence steady him.

Everything around him felt unreal, his senses dulled yet heightened in bizarre ways. He stumbled down the stairs, gripping the bannister as his vision swam. He had to see her. Hear her voice. Each thought beat in time with the throbbing in his head, the laudanum stripping away his usual reserve, leaving him raw and exposed.

He stumbled to the door, gripping the frame for support. His vision was swimming, and the floor felt uncertain beneath his feet. He made his way down the stairs, the descent feeling like an eternity, each throb of his headache a reminder of his frailty.

As he reached the ground floor, he heard Wickham's voice from the drawing room, discussing the menu with Mrs Bennet and Mrs Nicholls. Darcy clenched his teeth, pushing forward. His head only ached more around Wickham, and Mrs Bennet was another thing altogether.

Outside, the cool air hit him like a shock, momentarily clearing some of the fog from his mind. Bingley was leading Jane Bennet, with Elizabeth following behind, along a path that would be bordered by roses in the spring. Darcy took a deep breath, steadying himself before he approached them.

Bingley noticed him first. "Darcy! We did not expect you to join us. I thought you had something like a hundred letters to write before your departure."

Elizabeth turned at Bingley's words, her eyes widening slightly at the sight of him. Darcy forced a smile, though it felt strained. "I... I needed some fresh air," he said, his voice sounding hollow even to his own ears.

Miss Bennet's hand was resting lightly on Bingley's arm, and she bobbed softly in greeting. "It is a lovely day for a walk. We were just admiring the garden while Mr Wickham and Mama finished with Mrs Nicholls. Would you care to join us?"

Darcy nodded, though the motion made his head throb even more. "I would like that very much," he replied, stepping forward to fall in beside Elizabeth.

She glanced at him, her eyes searching his face. "Are you certain you are well, Mr Darcy? You look... rather unsteady."

Darcy swallowed, his throat dry. "I have been... unwell, but the fresh air is helping. Please, do not let me interrupt your tour."

Elizabeth's brow remained furrowed, but she nodded and continued walking. She even took his arm, though he could not recall whether he had offered it or if she had merely grabbed it to help keep him on his feet. Likely, it was the latter. Darcy sucked in a manful gulp of air and mustered all his equilibrium so as not to fail in his task of escorting the lady properly.

"Mr Darcy, they turned to the left," Elizabeth murmured at his side.

He blinked, forcing his eyes to focus. "Yes, of course." He straightened his spine marginally and guided her after Bingley and Miss Bennet.

Her eyes were darting between his face and the path. "Truly, Mr Darcy, you look... rather worse than when I saw you the other day. Have you thought of seeing a doctor, sir?"

"It is just a megrim, Miss Elizabeth," he hissed, though he had meant to make his voice sound gentle.

"Yes, and apparently, it has not yet abated. Two days? That is not normal, sir."

"Thank you for noticing."

"I was only trying to... Mr Darcy, the path is more to the centre of the way. We are listing off to the right again." She stumbled slightly, for he had gone so far astray that he had somehow pushed her slippered feet into the muddy grass beside the walking path.

He cleared his throat and lifted his arm, and hers with it, as he pulled them back. Perhaps if he looked confident enough, she would think he was only admiring the naked tree branches.

"Sir, truly, you are quite unwell. Would you consider seeing Mr Jones? He is our local apothecary."

"I am afraid there is nothing Mr Jones can do." Darcy sighed and blinked until Bingley's back came into focus ahead of them. "And I mean to return to London tomorrow, anyway."

"Oh." Her voice was quieter now. "Yes, Mr Bingley said something of that. He... he said you regretted not being able to attend the ball."

Darcy whirled to look at her and immediately regretted the speed of the action. He swallowed as his brain sloshed to a dizzy halt inside his skull. "I fear I am... disappointing you, Miss Elizabeth?"

Her lashes shadowed her cheek for a moment, but then she lifted her face to him. "Are you, Mr Darcy?"

The knot that had been pounding behind his eye moved into his throat, and his mouth worked uselessly. "I understand I am. Forgive me, Miss Elizabeth, but it cannot be helped."

"Oh, there is nothing to forgive on my part. No, I should think it will be a tremendous relief for you, not having to play party to a ball which you are sure to despise when there are better amusements in London."

Drat, his voice still felt like it would squeak if he tried to use it, but he made the attempt, nonetheless... and indeed, it did squeak. "Noth..." He cleared his throat. "Nothing of the sort, I assure you. I only mean to attend to some personal matters."

"Is one of them to see a doctor about your headaches?"

"Why do you speak in plural, as if this is a common state for me?"

She paused on the path, her bonnet tilted up to him against a few light raindrops that were just beginning to fall. "I suppose I might be in error there. Very well, shall I guess at other reasons for your departure from Meryton less than a fortnight after your arrival? It cannot be that you do not enjoy your host, surely."

This time, he did not try to fight against the break in his voice. He simply stared at her for a few seconds, refusing to make an attempt at a reply, then resumed walking. As her hand was resting on his arm, she was obliged to either join him, or sever the contact, and walk away.

Naturally, she followed him, the vexing creature.

"Did you know there is to be a waltz at the ball?"

He stopped again. "That is something of a break from convention, but I am hardly surprised."

"You are not scandalised?"

"I have waltzed many times in London. I find nothing scandalous about it, but it is a particularly onerous dance if one does not enjoy one's partner."

"Too true. I suppose I ought to be glad that I shall not be obliged to stand up with Mr Collins for that."

Darcy's head was still floating from the laudanum, but he did manage to pick through his memory of those he had met in Meryton, and that name did not surface as familiar... which meant he was probably forgetting something again. "Ah... Mr Collins?" he asked hesitantly.

"Oh, you have not met him, but Mr Wickham and Mr Bingley did. He is Papa's cousin—his heir, actually, and he came to... I do not care to say *what* he came to do, but the short of it is that when he met Mr Wickham, of course, he was pressed with an invitation to the ball." She sighed.

Darcy pinched the bridge of his nose and held it tightly for a few seconds, hoping for either ample pain to break through the laudanum haze or sufficient numbness to deaden the piercing inside his head. At least in talking to Elizabeth Bennet, he felt like he could make sense of what she was saying, quick and whimsical though she was.

"I take it you do not relish the thought of dancing with your cousin."

"Oh, I shall have to dance with him, but at least it will not be *that* dance, for Mr Wickham has already offered."

Darcy tripped.

Hard.

"Mr Darcy, are you quite well?" Elizabeth ducked under his pinwheeling arms to safety, but then tugged at his hand as he was in the process of righting himself.

"I am..." He shook his head, which was a mistake, for his vision shuffled and jiggled about inside his skull. "Egad. What the devil was that rock doing in the path?"

Elizabeth bit her lip and looked back over their shoulders with a doubtful expression. "Yes... a rock," she said slowly. "How very unsporting. Mr Wickham should have words with his gardener."

"What was it you were saying about Wickham offering... was this the supper set, by any chance?"

She tilted her head. "Why, yes, it was. I understand I shall have to 'make do' with him as my partner since you will be returning to London."

Darcy secured her hand upon his arm once more, and only then did he discover they were nearly out of sight of Bingley and Miss Bennet. Fine chaperons they made. "I did not realise I would be causing you a hardship, Miss Elizabeth."

"It is not—"

"I should hate to disappoint a lady. You may count on my attendance at the ball."

Her mouth drew into a thoughtful bow, and she studied him as she walked, but Darcy looked swiftly away. Too much laudanum in his blood, and too little clarity in his head... if he looked at her for much longer, Bingley and Miss Bennet would be long gone, and Elizabeth Bennet's reputation in tatters by the time he returned her to the house.

"What about your important business in London, sir?" she asked softly.

His chest rose and fell. What was the use? A second surgeon's opinion? A third? His will was in order, save for a few details to update, Georgiana was cared for by Lady Matlock better than he could do. He would only cause distress to his family when he began making his preparations to die sooner than necessary.

And perhaps, just once, he could enjoy the company of a lady he admired on the dance floor. One last ball.

"It will wait, Miss Elizabeth."

"Mr Bennet is heedless and does not listen to me," Mr Collins declared as he trudged along behind Elizabeth and her sisters. "Had he only taken my advice, the flooding could have been mitigated by now. Lady Catherine would most certainly have supported my recommendations, I assure you."

Elizabeth traded a glance with Jane, who rolled her eyes in silent agreement. She suppressed a sigh, for there was little hope of deterring Mr Collins once he was on such a topic.

"Indeed, Mr Collins," Elizabeth said, trying to sound patient. "And what was it you suggested to my father?"

"I told him, quite plainly, that the stream should be diverted to avoid the lower fields," Mr Collins replied, puffing out his chest. "A simple matter of engineering, really. Lady Catherine would have had it done in no time."

Jane raised an eyebrow. "And how exactly would you divert the stream, Mr Collins?"

"With a series of trenches and embankments," he answered confidently. "A plan Lady Catherine herself would no doubt approve."

"Trenches and embankments?" Lydia chimed in, her tone incredulous. "But wouldn't that take ages to build?"

"Nonsense," Mr Collins replied. "With proper supervision, it could be completed efficiently. Lady Catherine once oversaw the construction of a new bridge at Rosings. Quite the feat of engineering, I assure you."

Elizabeth suppressed another sigh. "I see. And what did my father say to your suggestions?"

"He dismissed them, unfortunately," Mr Collins said, shaking his head. "But Lady Catherine would never allow such neglect."

"Perhaps my father has other priorities at the moment," Elizabeth suggested, her voice even.

"Other priorities, indeed," Mr Collins muttered. "Lady Catherine would understand the importance of immediate action."

"Mr Collins," Jane interjected gently, "could you tell us more about Lady Catherine's management of Rosings? I am curious to know how she handles such matters."

Elizabeth arched a brow at her sister. A curious tactic, that—hushing the man on a subject they found vexing while encouraging him to expound on a subject about which they cared almost nothing.

Mr Collins' eyes brightened. "Ah, Lady Catherine de Bourgh! I suppose I have had little opportunity to describe her to you, thanks to the troubles at hand, but I declare, she would have seen through them in a moment. Her wisdom is unparalleled. At Rosings, she oversees every detail with such precision. Her counsel on agricultural matters is particularly noteworthy."

Well… about what she expected, but it was better than listening to him criticising Papa.

"Indeed," she encouraged, "I recall you mentioned her extensive knowledge of estate management. Please, tell us more about her insights."

Mr Collins puffed up with pride, his chest swelling. "Lady Catherine believes in thorough drainage systems, you see. At Rosings, we have the most advanced irrigation channels. She always insists that the ditches be dug deeper and the embankments be reinforced regularly. Such foresight prevents any flooding issues."

"Oh, that will not do," Elizabeth declared. "We can easily surmise what Lady Catherine's advice might be, for it is perfectly reasonable and right. But what of the lady herself? Tell us more about her. Has she much family?"

Jane shot Elizabeth a grateful look, her eyes sparkling with relief at the change in topic. Elizabeth nodded subtly, her mind drifting even as she maintained an attentive expression.

"Oh, indeed!" Mr Collins exclaimed, his enthusiasm undimmed. "She has one daughter, Miss Anne de Bourgh, who is a lady of many talents. Though her health is delicate, she is the epitome of grace and refinement. Lady Catherine takes great pride in her daughter's accomplishments, particularly her proficiency on the pianoforte."

Elizabeth's mind wandered as Mr Collins droned on, her thoughts flitting to the upcoming ball and Darcy's unexpected decision to stay. Perhaps she would take particular care in the styling of her hair... more so than usual, for with both Darcy and Wickham in attendance...

"And then there are the gardens at Rosings. Lady Catherine herself supervises the planting and arrangement. Each season, the grounds are transformed into a veritable paradise of blooms," Mr Collins continued, oblivious to the inward sighs of his audience.

Kitty and Lydia had finally run on ahead, their patience clearly worn thin. Elizabeth caught Jane's eye. At least this conversation was harmless, if tedious.

"How fortunate you are, Mr Collins, to be in the service of such a remarkable lady," Elizabeth said, trying to keep her tone light. "Her attention to detail must be truly inspiring."

"Indeed, Miss Elizabeth, it is the highest honour. Lady Catherine's every word is a lesson in propriety and excellence. Why, she even advised on the correct arrangement of my furniture at the parsonage. Her taste is impeccable."

"Tell me, Mr Collins, is there aught of Rosings or Lady Catherine or even the Hunsford parsonage which you *cannot* laud with the greatest enthusiasm?"

He sobered. "One thing, my fair cousin, and one thing, only. My house wants nothing but a mistress to make it the most charming, most delightful situation on earth."

Elizabeth groaned inwardly, but an instant later, inspiration struck.

"And... ah... what, precisely, do you seek in such a mistress?" she asked carefully.

"Why, only what is fitting and proper. Lady Catherine advised me to seek a lady who was not brought up too high, so that she would not disdain her position in life, nor too low, so that she would be properly prepared for all her duties as the wife of a parson."

"And you would commend such a lady in public?"

"Oh, to be sure! Why, I can think of nothing finer than to boast of my good fortune, and I am quite certain that Lady Catherine could find no fault in such a creature. Indeed, happy will be the lady who accepts my hand, Cousin Elizabeth." He followed this with such a simpering, winsome look that Elizabeth's stomach flipped over inside her belly.

She smiled tightly. "That, I can believe, Mr Collins."

"I am afraid I cannot sit long with you today, Lizzy," Charlotte sighed, glancing at the clock on the mantel. "There are too many chores to be done—putting up herbs, dipping candles. Mama will be beside herself if they are not finished by evening."

Elizabeth shook her head, leaning forward. "Charlotte, you look exhausted as it is. You need rest, not a mountain of household work."

Charlotte looked about the room vaguely. "Oh. I rest a little too often, I daresay. That is usually the problem, for I cannot manage enough interest in anything to show any bit of keenness when I *am* about my tasks, so Mama assumes I have done nothing. And that only makes it worse," she finished with a little shrug.

"So... she gives you more to do? Charlotte! Here I thought you were only suffering from a lack of appreciation by those closest to you, but it is also exhaustion atop that? Little wonder you have been a petulant shadow of yourself!"

Charlotte's brow clouded. "Petulant shadow? Truly, Lizzy, I'd no idea I had become so tiresome. I had simply got to the end of my feelings and... no, I do not wish to talk about it."

"I think you must, if only so we know how to keep you from going there again," Elizabeth insisted, taking Charlotte's hand in hers. "I know I have been guilty of not seeing how you feel on occasion, so please tell me."

Charlotte frowned. "I just wanted it all to stop—the demands, the pity, the way I seem to be... invisible, but still so much of a burden that it seems no one can abide my presence."

Elizabeth leaned closer. "That is not true!"

"Is it not, Lizzy?" she asked softly.

Elizabeth swallowed. Good heavens, how many times lately had she been just as guilty of brushing off Charlotte as anyone in her family had been? She gritted her teeth. "Well, whatever has been before, something must change. You cannot be expected to simply bear up under everything without some little pleasantness for yourself. Are you doing *all* the chores of the household?"

Charlotte gave a tired smile. "It is the duty of the eldest daughter, is it not? Mama depends on me, and Maria and John... well, they are still learning."

"But surely, some of these tasks could wait. Or be shared? John is nearly grown."

Charlotte's smile faded. "You know how it is, Lizzy. Family is... well, it is my duty. I do not like to think of myself when..." She lifted her shoulders. "You know. I failed to find a husband, so I must make myself useful somehow."

Elizabeth frowned. Indeed, perhaps it was time to share that outlandish, wild notion that had struck her earlier. "Charlotte, there might be a way to change your circumstances."

Charlotte looked up from her hands, curiosity and a hint of wariness in her eyes. "What do you mean?"

Elizabeth took a deep breath, her heart pounding with the audacity of her suggestion. "You could catch Mr Collins' notice."

Charlotte's head snapped fully up, her hands stilling in her lap. "Mr Collins? Your *cousin* Mr Collins? But Lizzy, why on earth would I want to attract a man I have never met? A man *you* say you do not even like!"

"He is not to my taste, to be sure, but he is not a bad man. Not clever or handsome, but neither is he vicious or truly repugnant."

"That sounds like a winning combination," Charlotte replied dubiously.

"It is when you consider that he will be master of his own property someday."

Charlotte's brows raised. "Well. Be that as it may, I have never been skilled at attracting men."

Elizabeth leaned in with a wicked smile. "Mr Collins is not like most men. All that is required to win his favour is an attentive and rapt audience."

Charlotte frowned, clearly puzzled. "But how can that be enough? Surely there must be more to it."

Elizabeth shook her head slightly, choosing her words carefully. "Mr Collins is eager to please and seeks validation. If you show interest in his words and praise his connection to Lady Catherine, you will find him more than willing to return the interest."

"But Lizzy, I am not good at pretending," Charlotte protested. "What if I cannot make myself agreeable to him?"

Before Elizabeth could respond, Lady Lucas entered the room, her expression one of mild exasperation. "Charlotte, Maria needs your help to make over her gown for the ball. She is in a dreadful state."

Charlotte thinned her lips into a smile, even as she reached for the hem of her gown to stand. "Coming, Mama."

Elizabeth made a face as Lady Lucas left the room and quickly reached out, stopping her friend with a gentle hand on her arm.

"Wait, Charlotte," Elizabeth said. "Do you see, this is just what I was talking about. It is all about Maria, is it not?"

Charlotte blinked, staring at the floor as her throat worked. "Maria is younger and prettier, and—"

"And your mother has already thrown you over, has she? Who is helping *you* with *your* gown, Charlotte?"

Charlotte looked uncomfortable, her eyes avoiding Elizabeth's. "Ah… It is my gown that we are making over for Maria. She has grown, and it fits her better now. I have decided not to attend."

Elizabeth's eyes widened in shock. "Not attend? Charlotte, what do you mean?"

Charlotte shrugged lightly, a resigned smile on her lips. "Mama wishes for Maria to be seen. After all, I am eight and twenty years old and have more than had my chance. It is time for Maria to be noticed."

Elizabeth felt a surge of indignation. "That is exactly why I desired for you to make yourself agreeable to Mr Collins. He might not be the most attractive or intelligent man, but anything that belonged to him would only ever be praised. It seems you have had nothing but criticism."

Charlotte's eyes widened, her confusion turning to surprise. "Lizzy, you cannot be serious."

Elizabeth nodded vehemently. "I am entirely serious. Mr Collins is the heir to Longbourn. His standing is secure, and as his wife, yours would be too. No one could criticise you then."

Charlotte sat back down, looking thoughtful. "But what if I cannot make myself agreeable to him? What if he does not choose me?"

Elizabeth smiled gently. "Mr Collins is easily pleased. Just listen to him, nod in agreement, and show admiration for what he says of Lady Catherine. You have the perfect demeanour for it, and thank heaven, you are not half so impertinent as I am. And think of what it would mean for you, Charlotte. No more sharing gowns with Maria, no more being overlooked."

Charlotte sighed, her expression softening. "Perhaps you are right, Lizzy. It is worth considering."

Elizabeth squeezed her friend's hand. "I know it seems daunting, but you deserve happiness and security. Mr Collins can provide that, even if he is not the man of your dreams."

Charlotte nodded slowly, a glimmer of hope in her eyes. "Thank you, Lizzy. I will think on it."

Chapter Twenty-One

"LIZZY, LOOK! THE CHANDELIERS are even grander than the last time Mr Northam hosted a ball!" Lydia exclaimed, her voice bubbling with excitement as the Bennet family stepped into the entrance hall of Netherfield.

Elizabeth took in the scene before her, the room bathed in the warm glow of countless candles. The air was thick with the scent of fresh flowers, and elegant decorations adorned every surface. Why, it must have taken every waking moment of the last fortnight to perfect, and Elizabeth could hardly stop from turning around to try to take it all in. Mama had outdone herself... Well, and Mrs Nicholls.

Mr Wickham and Mr Bingley were standing at the door to greet them, but Mr Darcy was curiously absent. Elizabeth's eyes skipped up the long staircase until Mr Wickham stepped forward with a charming smile. "Mr and Mrs Bennet, Miss Bennet, Miss Elizabeth, Miss Mary, Miss Catherine, Miss Lydia, and Mr Collins—welcome. We are delighted to have you all here tonight."

Mrs Bennet, her eyes shining with excitement, immediately took her place beside Wickham, assuming the role of his *de facto* hostess for the evening. "Oh, Mr Wickham, everything looks splendid! I shall be happy to assist you in welcoming our guests."

Mr Bennet, who had been inching towards the refreshment table, was halted by his wife's stern call. "Mr Bennet! Do come and stand with me. It is only proper that we greet our friends together."

Wickham nodded in agreement, his smile never wavering. "Indeed, sir. Your presence would be most appreciated."

Grudgingly, Mr Bennet returned to stand beside them, offering a wry smile to Wickham. "Very well, very well. But I daresay you will have a livelier greeting line without my presence."

"You do yourself too little credit, sir," Wickham assured him. At that moment, the gentleman caught Elizabeth's eye and bowed to her with a charming, self-deprecating smile. "Miss Elizabeth, I hope you will not think me too forward, but would you object to opening the ball with me? I find myself in need of a most gracious partner."

Elizabeth's heart fluttered with relief and a touch of excitement. She had been hoping for this very invitation, particularly after her small fib to Mr Collins earlier when that gentleman asked for the same dance. "I would be honoured, Mr Wickham."

"Thank you," he said, his eyes sparkling with gratitude and mischief. "You have saved me from certain embarrassment."

Just then, Mr Darcy arrived downstairs, coming to stand a little behind the others with a slight bow towards the new arrivals. He looked distinctly pale, but his eyes were clearer than they had been in days. Wickham, noticing Darcy's arrival, moved to make the introductions.

"Well, we are not all introduced, I see," he said, extending his hand to encourage Darcy to come forward. "Mr Collins, allow me to present my friend, Mr Fitzwilliam Darcy of Derbyshire."

Mr Collins' eyes widened. "Mr Darcy? The same Fitzwilliam Darcy of Pemberley, nephew of Lady Catherine de Bourgh?"

Darcy's eyes edged toward Elizabeth, and his throat bobbed as he nodded. "Yes, I am."

Collins beamed, practically bouncing on his toes. "Why, what a connection! I am the clergyman to Lady Catherine de Bourgh at Rosings Park. She often speaks of you with the highest regard."

Darcy managed a tight smile. "Thank you, Mr Collins."

"Oh, the pleasure is *entirely* mine, I assure you! Why, I shall take care to write Her Ladyship the instant I—"

Before Collins could utter many more syllables along that line, the arrival of the Lucases drew everyone's attention, and poor Collins was shoved to the side. Undeterred, he hurried over to make their acquaintance, leaving Mr Darcy in a momentary respite. And, for the moment, Elizabeth was quite alone as well.

"Mr Darcy," she said, stepping closer, "you look better this evening. Are you quite well?"

Darcy's expression softened slightly, but there was a strange intensity in his gaze as he looked at her. "Thank you, Miss Elizabeth. I am... managing."

"That is well, sir. I should hate to think of you in discomfort this evening."

Rather than make a reply, Darcy continued to stare at her, almost as if he were searching for something within her expression. He almost seemed to list forward as he did so, and for an instant, Elizabeth was struck with how very rich and thick his eyelashes were. What a strange thing to notice about a man! But there it was—dark lashes hooding even darker eyes, with the most delicious little random locks of hair poking from behind his ears. It was when he drank in a breath, and his head tilted slightly, as if he were trying to study her face better, that she blinked and stepped back.

"Well, sir, I hope you will find it an enjoyable evening."

Darcy's chest rose, and he straightened again. "Indeed. If I may be so bold, Miss Elizabeth, I have no partner for the opening set. Would it be too much to ask for that, in addition to the supper waltz?"

She winced. "I am afraid Mr Wickham has just solicited my hand for that set, sir."

His look flared for an instant, then cooled into detachment. "I see. Well, then, I wish you a pleasant evening. Until our dance, Miss Elizabeth."

He dipped his head politely and walked toward the ballroom, leaving Elizabeth looking after him in bewilderment.

"Miss Elizabeth," Wickham said as he offered her his hand for the Grand March, "Shall we? I must admit, I have never had the honour of opening a ball before."

"Indeed? Neither have I, but it cannot be so very difficult, for the steps could not be easier. We simply walk, do you see?"

"Ah. You will have to forgive me, Miss Elizabeth, for you see, I have only been to one ball in my life—apart from that delightful Assembly some weeks ago—and I was but nineteen."

"Goodness! And were you never invited to any balls afterwards, even by the Darcy family?"

Wickham laughed. "I think you overestimate the Darcy temperament, Miss Elizabeth. Darcy only goes to a ball when he is dragged to one, as he was this evening."

Elizabeth cast a glance over her shoulder at the gentleman standing against the wall. Mr Darcy had sounded anything but reluctant last week when he spoke to her about attending this evening, but he certainly had the look now of a man who was only there because he had to be. His arms were crossed, and he was standing beside the Ficus plant where no one else could stand beside him. His eyes were unfocused but drifted faintly to the floor.

"There, Miss Elizabeth, I do believe we are doing exceedingly well, do not you? Ah, you are looking at Darcy to see if he approves."

She shook her head. "No, I was only—"

"You may as well give over that notion, for he approves of little. He will have opened a ball so many times that he almost certainly has perfected every step."

Elizabeth could not help one last glance at Darcy as they passed him again. This time, his eyes lifted just long enough to touch hers, then fell once more.

As they continued the procession, Wickham leaned in slightly. "Your mother has been invaluable in preparing for this ball. I must thank her for all her help."

Elizabeth laughed softly. "I am sure Mrs Nicholls deserves most of the credit. My mother can be quite enthusiastic, but the real work often falls to the servants."

"Enthusiasm is a valuable trait, Miss Elizabeth. Now, let us not disappoint our audience. I must say, Miss Elizabeth, you make this all look effortless. You must congratulate me, for I chose my partner exceedingly well."

"And here I thought I would have to guide you through the steps, Mr Wickham. You are quite the natural."

Wickham grinned. "Ah, but I have a capable partner. You see, I have always believed that dancing is much like conversation. A good partner makes all the difference."

"And do you often find yourself in need of a good conversational partner?"

"Only when I am fortunate enough to find someone who can keep up with my wit," Wickham replied with a playful wink.

Elizabeth shook her head, smiling. "I shall do my best to rise to the challenge, then."

As they proceeded down the set, Elizabeth's gaze caught on Charlotte, who stood near the refreshment table. At least she had come! She wore one of her older gowns, but it was a shade that flattered her skin. But the best part of her ensemble this evening was that faint flicker of hope that illuminated her face as she surveyed the room. That was a look that had been too long absent from her features.

Elizabeth had found only a moment to speak with her while other guests were still arriving and was relieved to hear that her friend was truly considering the scheme of attracting Mr Collins. She offered a faint smile as Elizabeth passed. But half a second later, she could not help but overhear Lady Lucas drawing to her daughter's side.

"Charlotte! You were to stand beside Maria."

"But Mama, I—"

"No, no, for I'll not have her chasing after that heedless Lydia Bennet. Come look sensible beside her so someone will ask her to dance."

Elizabeth sighed and cast a look over her shoulder... as Charlotte's head bowed in defeat.

Wickham followed her gaze and remarked, "Miss Lucas is looking radiant this evening."

Elizabeth nodded slightly. "Yes, she is. If only she would find a bit of kindness in the room."

"Oh, I should not be too concerned about that. I intended to ask for the honour of her company for the supper set, as I must surrender yours to Darcy."

Elizabeth snapped her gaze to him. "But she has already—" She closed her mouth. "That is to say, I... I believe my cousin Collins meant to ask her."

Wickham laughed. "Will he not step on her feet? Come, you would not condemn your friend to a lumbering partner for all that while, would you?"

"No, I... well, I suppose it is not for me to decide, is it?"

"My philosophy exactly, Miss Elizabeth. Why, if I had the arrangement of the evening to my liking, you would have a different partner as well."

She smirked faintly. "You object to my intended partner, sir?"

"Not at all. No, Darcy is a fine gentleman. It is only a pity he cannot appreciate your liveliness and charms as well as others might."

She narrowed her eyes at him. "Sir, I cannot know what you mean by that."

Mr Wickham chuckled as he turned her at the end of the set. "Ah, Darcy. Always the enigma. I fancy he thinks very little of admiring a lady's finer qualities, but then, he can afford to be overly choosy. You know, his presence here has disappointed quite a few ladies in London."

Elizabeth swallowed. "Disappointed? How so?"

"Oh, it is not that unusual. He merely has a habit of charming ladies and then withdrawing his interest. It is especially surprising given that he is supposedly engaged to Miss Anne de Bourgh."

Elizabeth's heart skipped a beat. "Engaged? I had no idea."

"Indeed," Wickham continued, as if sharing a secret. "It is a long-standing arrangement, though I doubt he will honour it. His popularity with the ladies is quite remarkable, despite this well-known engagement."

Elizabeth's thoughts churned with this new information. She glanced again at Mr Darcy, whose intense gaze seemed to pierce her across the room. "But surely my cousin Mr Collins would have mentioned such an engagement if it were true?"

"Oh, I am sure he will. It sounded as if he only learned of Mr Darcy's presence when he arrived." Wickham laughed. "I daresay you will hear far too *much* of the engagement when next you speak to the man! But whether Mr Darcy intends to fulfil that promise is another matter entirely. Many think he prefers to keep his options before him, and well, he might. As I said, he is quite sought after. But I should be surprised if Darcy dishonoured the lady, no matter what the gossip may be."

Elizabeth felt a pang of doubt. Wickham's words, though cloaked in admiration, cast a shadow over Darcy's character. She turned her attention back to the dance, but her mind was far from settled.

Darcy watched as Elizabeth's previous partner returned her to the side of the room. Her gaze flicked around, and for a moment, their eyes met. She looked guarded, but Darcy steeled himself, determined to claim this dance as they had agreed. His head had been relatively clear tonight, thanks to a day spent in a dark room swimming in laudanum. He approached her, his heart pounding.

"Miss Elizabeth," he said, bowing slightly as he reached her. "Shall we?"

She offered a polite smile, though there was a hint of reservation in her eyes. "Of course, Mr Darcy."

He took her hand, and a tremble of nerves travelled up the cords of his arm at the contact. "You said you have never waltzed before?"

She lifted her shoulder. "Neither have at least half the other people in this ballroom. But I daresay that will not prevent some rather valiant—and perhaps clumsy—efforts."

"It is simple enough. Just follow my lead. Start by placing your right foot behind your left," he instructed softly. "Then glide smoothly forward. One, two, three... Yes, that's it."

Elizabeth followed his guidance, her brow furrowed in concentration. "Like this?" she asked, her steps hesitant but graceful.

"Exactly. You are a quick learner, Miss Elizabeth."

She nodded her gratitude, but she was murmuring the count to herself and did not reply for a moment. Darcy studied her knit brow, the squint with which she stared fixedly at his chest as her head bobbed faintly in time with their steps. Any moment now, she would feel herself master of the art... and she would look up into his face.

He swallowed. *Please, heaven, let the nausea gnawing at him abate.* Just long enough to survive this dance and enjoy the supper afterwards. The waltz demanded precision, and he needed every ounce of his focus on the steps—and on Elizabeth. If the rest of life's pleasures were to be denied him, if his future were to be cut short, he would add this night to his bank of memories—things to pull out of the trove and smile over when that day came that he discovered his time was at an end.

But he would push that day back as long as he could. Tonight, he would lose himself in the making of that memory... in admiring a lady merely for herself, for once in his life, because his habitual standards—the duty of marriage to a society heiress and founding a new generation of Darcys to carry on after him... well, those were no longer considerations.

He showed her the next movement, his hand steadying her as they turned. "Now, step to the side and then forward again. One, two, three... Yes, very good." Her touch grounded him and sent shocks of pleasure rather than pain down his spine. Was it the lingering traces of laudanum, or was it the warmth of her body through the fabric of her gown that intoxicated him? He marvelled at how quickly she picked up the rhythm, her movements becoming more fluid with each step.

And that was when she looked up into his eyes, and his heart might well have stopped.

Egad, this was lunacy. What madness had persuaded him to think he would be satisfied with one dance? Perhaps... Perhaps there remained before him... *possibilities* he had not considered carefully enough.

Darcy's thoughts swirled, a chaotic blend of admiration and longing. Every graceful turn, every twirl brought them closer as Elizabeth eased into the dance. The scent of lavender in her hair, the soft rise and fall of her breath, the way her fingers rested lightly on his shoulder—all of it captivated him completely.

"You are doing wonderfully," he murmured.

Elizabeth's gaze faltered, and he realised he had been staring without blinking. "Thank you, Mr Darcy. It really is rather... ah..." She cleared her throat. "Engaging."

He could hardly think of anything to say, the words caught in his throat as he became more aware of the rising tension in her eyes—a blend of anxiety and something he dared to hope was confused desire. She certainly *looked*... well, she had not looked at anyone *else* the way she was looking at him. He had been watching her all evening—he knew all too well how she looked at other men. There was something there when she lifted her eyes to him that had been absent in other men's arms.

Perhaps... it was not lunacy, after all. Perhaps...

"Miss Elizabeth," he began, his voice low and halting. "I... must confess something. I have been considering... many things of late."

Her eyes flickered with confusion and curiosity. "Oh? And what matters occupy your thoughts so deeply, Mr Darcy?"

He hesitated, searching for the right words. "I find myself... considering the future, and what it holds. I thought I would not have the time for..." He stopped. How was she to understand that? He had told her nothing of his fears, but she was not entirely ignorant of the fact that he was unwell. Perhaps that was enough. He filled his lungs and tried again.

"I had thought certain pleasures would be denied me, and yet, I am... utterly tempted."

Elizabeth's brow furrowed slightly. "Tempted, sir? By what?"

"By the prospect of... securing my family's future," he replied, his eyes searching hers. "Of finding someone who might... partner me, who might..." He trailed off, his throat tight with unspoken words.

Her expression hardened slightly, a flicker of something cold passing through her eyes. "I see. You speak of Miss Anne de Bourgh, do you not? Everyone knows it has long been arranged."

Darcy blinked, startled by her assumption. How had she even heard of that? "No, Miss Elizabeth, you misunderstand—"

She interrupted, her tone becoming warmer yet defensive. "If there is any misunderstanding, it is my comprehension of your character. You would not, sir, be the man to withdraw from his commitments? No? I wondered when I first heard of it, but Mr Wickham speaks highly of your character, Mr Darcy. He believes you to be an honourable man, despite what others might say. I find his perspective… enlightening."

Darcy's chest tightened. "Wickham… he is not what he seems, Miss Elizabeth. There are things you do not know about him."

Her eyes flashed with indignation. "And what do I not know, Mr Darcy? That he is kind, charming, and considerate? That he has spoken of you with nothing but respect and admiration?"

"He is…" Darcy's head panged, and he closed his eyes against the shot of light across his vision. A hiss escaped him, and he felt Elizabeth stiffen in his arms.

"Are you well, sir?"

He forced a smile… or the closest expression he could approximate. "Well enough. Miss Elizabeth, I cannot say with any degree of certainty *what* Mr Wickham is at present, but the man I knew from my youth is not as honourable as you believe."

Elizabeth's brow furrowed, her steps faltering slightly. "Then, you believe people cannot change?"

"In my experience, they do not."

"But you have nothing specific of which to accuse him?"

Darcy's jaw tightened. "No. I can only say that your trust should not be lightly given."

Elizabeth lifted her chin. "You expect me to take your word over my own experience? When he has shown nothing but integrity since his arrival?"

Darcy's grip on her waist tightened slightly as they turned. "I have known Wickham for the whole of my life. His charm masks his true nature."

"And what, pray, is his true nature?" Elizabeth's voice was sharp, cutting through the music around them. "I have seen no evidence of deceit."

Darcy drew in a deep breath, struggling to convey the gravity of his words. "He squandered his inheritance, lied about his circumstances, and has a history of wild and reckless behaviour."

"Oh! And I am certain none of your other friends have a history of wild behaviour. I am not entirely ignorant of the way young gentlemen pass their university years, Mr Darcy. Have *you* any shadows upon *your* past that might smack as unsavoury now?"

"It is not merely that," he growled.

"Ah, yes, you claim he lied about his circumstances. Which, pray tell, are those? The same circumstances that allowed him the means to lease Netherfield? A man may *say* anything he chooses, but his bank balance must agree."

"A strange chance," Darcy gritted through his teeth. "But the whims of fortune aside, he was always a spendthrift."

"Why, how fortunate that he appears to have mended his ways! You saw, I am sure, sir, how he has 'squandered' his money since arriving here? Paying for repairs to a broken weir, helping our neighbours, hosting us all here tonight? Truly, the actions of a madman, sir."

Darcy bit back a rather unwise retort, choosing instead to stare over her head across the room—where George Wickham was making Charlotte Lucas laugh. And a spear of white, hot… *jealousy?* shot through his core.

He shook his head and ground his teeth against the tight jarring inside. "I only urge caution, Miss Elizabeth. A man does not change overnight, nor so drastically."

Elizabeth's steps grew more hesitant, and her movements became less fluid. "And yet, he speaks of you with such respect. Why would he do that if he did not admire you or desire to win your approval after a lifetime of being looked down upon?"

"I…" He swallowed. "I do not know."

Her expression softened for a moment, then steeled again. "And how do I know you are not simply trying to discredit him out of jealousy or spite?"

Darcy's jaw clenched, the frustration boiling beneath his calm exterior. "Because, Miss Elizabeth, I have nothing to gain from lying to you."

Elizabeth met his gaze, her eyes searching his face for any hint of falsehood. "You ask a great deal of me, Mr Darcy. To doubt the character of a man who has shown me only kindness, based on your word alone."

"Yes," Darcy admitted, his voice barely above a whisper. "I ask you to trust me."

For a moment, they moved in silence. Darcy's heart hammered with each step. He had intended to speak of his own feelings, to hint at the possibility of something more between them, but now everything seemed to be falling apart. He desperately wanted to bridge the gap, to change her mind. The thought of proposing had seemed so clear—it was the perfect answer for them both! Delight and hope for his remaining days and a comfortable future for her. He could give her that, even if there was no child born after him.

But now, any such notion felt impossibly distant. Conflict flickered in Elizabeth's eyes as she tried to reconcile the man she admired with Darcy's accusations, and unfortunately, most of the shadowed looks she gave were reserved for him.

He had not convinced her. He would have done better not to speak at all, but what was he to do when he tried to talk to her of marriage, and she flung Anne de Bourgh in his face? All he could think of was how very much he would like to make Wickham's headache and throb the way his was doing at that moment.

"Thank you for the dance, Mr Darcy," she said curtly as the final notes played. She stepped back, her polite facade firmly in place. "I believe supper is about to be served."

Darcy nodded stiffly, his chest aching with the unspoken inspiration that had somehow possessed him in the last half hour. "Indeed, Miss Elizabeth. Shall we go to supper?"

Elizabeth gave a brief, noncommittal smile as he offered her his arm to escort her to the dining room. "Indeed, sir."

Chapter Twenty-Two

Elizabeth sat at the long, polished table in the grand dining room of Netherfield, tapping her toes under the table as her eyes rolled around the room—taking in her mother near the head of the table, her father sitting as far away as possible, her sisters... She grimaced and looked away.

The room buzzed with the sounds of clinking silverware, low murmurs, and the occasional burst of laughter. She tried to focus on the food in front of her, but her eyes kept drifting to the people around her, particularly to Mr Darcy sitting beside her, looking as though he were battling his own private war.

Darcy's face was a mask of calm, but she could not ignore the subtle signs of strain. His complexion was growing pale again—the way his eyes squinted slightly as if the light pained him, the occasional press of his fingers to his temples when he thought no one was looking—all were familiar to her by now. She had seen the signs before, and whatever excuses he had offered this evening, he was clearly still suffering from that headache. Anyone could be forgiven for being a touch irritable under the circumstances.

But why he had suddenly decided to speak ill of Mr Wickham baffled her. Had the man suddenly gone dotty? Had something happened that Mr Darcy refused to disclose? Or was it just plain, ugly jealousy? He and Mr Wickham had seemed to be on such good terms. Why now? Why would Darcy choose this moment to try and tarnish Mr Wickham's reputation, especially when Wickham was his friend and host? It made no sense.

Her frustration gnawed at her, making it hard to focus on the conversations around her. Instead, she glanced across the room. Charlotte was sitting beside Mr Wickham, her face aglow with laughter for the first time in ages. Elizabeth had hoped Mr Collins might show some interest in Charlotte, perhaps offering her a chance at securing his attentions. And what better opportunity than the supper set, complete with the most intimate, half-scandalous dance any lady in Meryton had ever performed?

But Mr Wickham had stepped in, and now Charlotte seemed captivated by his charm, a smile lighting up her face. Elizabeth chided herself for her initial frustration. Charlotte was clearly enjoying herself, and for once, she was not overshadowed by her younger sister, Maria. Mr Wickham's easy manner only added to Charlotte's glow, and it warmed Elizabeth's heart to see her friend so happy, even if just for the evening.

But was Mr Wickham's interest in Charlotte anything more than the amusement of the evening? Elizabeth doubted it. He was undeniably charming, but... well, Mr Wickham could enjoy the company of any lady he liked. And gentlemen who were popular with the ladies usually did not request Charlotte's company. She couldn't see him offering marriage, and a marriage was probably her friend's best hope for happiness. Mr Collins, though pompous and absurd at times, offered stability and security—things Charlotte desperately needed.

Elizabeth sighed and tried to twist her thoughts away from Charlotte and back to the other conversations around her, for her own dinner partner was still stubbornly silent. Jane was speaking softly with Mr Bingley, their heads close together in a private exchange. Across the table, Lydia and Kitty were giggling with their partners over some jest, while Mary, who had no partner, sat with a group of other girls, her fingers drumming lightly on the tablecloth as she ignored their chatter. And then, there was Mama, seated at the foot of the table and holding court with her friends... Elizabeth groaned. Perhaps that was enough looking around the room.

She stole another glance at Darcy. He sat rigid and silent, picking at his food without interest. Vexed as she was at him at the moment, she would rather talk to him than dwell on her frustrations with everything else in the room. She could at least extend him some sympathy, some sign that she understood his discomfort, but the crowded dining room offered little privacy.

Elizabeth took a deep breath and leaned slightly towards him, her voice low to avoid drawing attention. "Mr Darcy, I trust the evening is not too taxing on you."

Darcy's eyes flicked to hers, and for a moment, something softened in his gaze. But then he looked away, his expression hardening. "I appreciate your concern, Miss Elizabeth. One manages as best one can."

She studied his profile, noting the intermittent clenching of his jaw, the unsteady flickering of his eyelids. "It must be challenging to navigate such an evening when one is not at one's best."

He glanced at her again, his brow furrowing slightly. "Indeed. But I find that expectations are rarely considerate of one's personal discomfort."

"I can imagine. Such occasions demand much of us, even when we feel we have little to give."

Darcy's lips pressed into a thin line, and he seemed to struggle with his thoughts as his eyes skipped across the room to rest vaguely near the head of the table, where Charlotte sat with Mr Wickham. "Yes, well, those who think happiness is within their grasp often find themselves disappointed."

Elizabeth blinked as the back of her neck prickled. "You speak as if from experience."

Darcy hesitated, his gaze searching hers. "Perhaps I do. Or perhaps it is merely an observation."

Elizabeth frowned, trying to understand his meaning. Given the direction of his gaze a moment ago, it seemed like another dig at Mr Wickham. Was he suggesting that Wickham had ruined his happiness, or perhaps that the man was leading Charlotte on? Either way, it annoyed her. She had her own frustrations with Mr Wickham's choice, but it didn't give Darcy the right to insult her friend in the process.

"Happiness is not freely given, Mr Darcy. One must seek after it."

He looked at her for a long moment, his eyes dark and unreadable. "Not everyone is deserving of happiness."

She blinked, taken aback by his candour. "I suppose it is not a matter of deserving but of striving for it."

Darcy's gaze remained intense, as if he were trying to discern her very thoughts. "Even those who strive may find it elusive, Miss Elizabeth. We cannot control… all our days, can we?"

Elizabeth hesitated, sensing a deeper meaning behind his words but unsure of what to say. She looked at him, trying to bridge the gap between their mutual misunderstandings. "It is true that life often thwarts our efforts," she began, choosing her words carefully. "But perhaps it is our response to these challenges that defines us."

"And what if our response is not enough? What if the choices we make, even with the best intentions, bring nothing but pain?"

"Then…" She cleared her throat. "While I cannot speak from deep experience, I can say that in principle, true happiness is a thing that does not derive from our circumstances, but rather in spite of them."

He stifled a bitter chuckle. "How charmingly naive. Some people have not the character to surmount troubles. And some troubles, Miss Elizabeth, are dark enough to overshadow any pursuit of happiness."

Her chest tightened at his earnestness, conflicting with the irritation she felt. "And some people believe they are entitled to it—that it is owed to them, regardless of the cost to others."

Darcy's eyes narrowed slightly, his expression unreadable as his eyes twitched toward the head of the table once more. "Yes, there *are* those who think only of their own desires."

Oh, good heavens, were they back on Mr Wickham again? How tiresome. Elizabeth glanced around the room, seeking a distraction, but found none. When she turned back to Darcy, his gaze was still fixed on her, intense and searching.

He took a breath, seeming to gather himself. "Miss Elizabeth, I—"

"Mr Darcy," she interrupted, her frustration spilling over, "it seems we are destined to misunderstand each other. Perhaps it is best if we leave our conversation here."

Darcy's face tightened, and he gave a curt nod. "As you wish, Miss Elizabeth."

The silence that followed was heavy, and Elizabeth felt a pang of regret. But before she could say anything more, Darcy stood abruptly, excusing himself from the table. She stared after him as he left, but within seconds, his figure was swallowed by the swirl of the room.

THE REST OF THE meal passed in a blur. Elizabeth ate mechanically, barely tasting the food. Her thoughts kept drifting back to Darcy, to the look in his eyes when he spoke of disappointment and happiness. Was he speaking of Anne de Bourgh? Was the engagement not to his liking, perhaps? The phrase "sowing wild oats" came suddenly to her mind, and the idea left a bitter taste in her mouth. She couldn't shake the feeling that there was more to his words, something he was not saying.

And then there was Mr Wickham. Elizabeth couldn't ignore the nagging doubt Darcy had planted. Could there be truth in his warnings? Was she being blinded by Wickham's charm? But he had shown nothing but kindness and respect since his arrival. Surely, Darcy was mistaken—or worse, deliberately trying to mislead her.

After what felt like an eternity, the meal ended, and the guests began to disperse. She wanted to join them, to lose herself in the movement and forget her worries, if only for a little while. But she felt rooted to her seat, the weight of her thoughts holding her back. Eventually, the need for fresh air and a quiet space to calm her thoughts pulled her out of the dining room after the others. She made her way to the terrace, longing for just a moment or two to herself before plunging back into the ballroom.

The stars twinkled overhead, a stark contrast to the turmoil within her. She leaned against the railing, closing her eyes and taking deep breaths. The events of the evening swirled in her mind—Darcy's cryptic words, Mr Wickham's charm, Charlotte's radiant smile.

"Miss Elizabeth?"

The voice startled her, and she turned to see Mr Wickham standing a few feet away, his expression concerned. "Are you quite all right?"

Elizabeth forced a smile. "Yes, thank you, Mr Wickham. I just needed some fresh air."

He stepped closer, his gaze warm and understanding. "It has been a glorious evening, hasn't it? I hope you have enjoyed yourself."

She nodded, but her mind was elsewhere. "Yes, it has been a lovely evening. Thank you for your hospitality."

Mr Wickham's smile widened. "It is my pleasure, Miss Elizabeth. If there is anything you need, please do not hesitate to ask."

There it was again—that charm, that easy manner that made it so difficult to doubt him. But Darcy's words lingered in her mind, casting a shadow over their interaction.

"Mr Wickham," she began hesitantly, "may I ask you something?"

"Of course, anything."

She hesitated, unsure how to phrase her question without sounding accusatory. "I have heard... some things. About you and Mr Darcy. He... he implied that you had not always... that is, you were not always the sort of man we know you to be now."

Wickham's expression sobered thoughtfully. "I see. Mr Darcy and I have... a complicated history. He has never forgiven me for certain youthful indiscretions."

"Indiscretions?"

Wickham nodded, his gaze distant. "Nothing, I fear, that I ought to tell a lady, Miss Elizabeth. I was young and foolish. I made mistakes. But I have tried to make amends—surely, you see my efforts, I hope?"

She smiled. "Naturally, sir. Why, I think there is no one in all Meryton who does not."

Mr Wickham shrugged. "Save for Darcy. He seems determined to hold my past against me, but you must forgive him. Darcy is not wrong in recalling his experience. But I hope I can rely on your generous nature to permit a man to prove he is no longer the youth that his companions remember."

Elizabeth studied his face, searching for any sign of deceit. But all she saw was a man trying to move on from his past, a man who had been judged too harshly. "I see," she said softly. "Thank you for your honesty, Mr Wickham."

He smiled again, but it was a sadder smile this time. "Thank you for listening, Miss Elizabeth. It means more than you know. May I ask, do you intend to dance again this evening?"

She tightened her lips into a smile and shook her head. "I am obliged to dance the last with Mr Collins, but I should like a few moments to myself first."

"Of course. I will ask a footman to bring you some refreshment if you like."

"I thank you, but no." She tilted her head. "Wait a moment. Would you try to encourage Mr Collins to ask Miss Lucas for a set?"

His grin widened. "With pleasure, Miss Elizabeth."

With that, he bowed and left her alone on the terrace. She watched him go, her heart aching with confusion. Both men seemed good. They seemed earnest. Could both be truthful but simply have conflicting views? Surely, that made the most sense.

The sound of laughter and music drifted from the ballroom. Elizabeth sighed, feeling more lost than ever. The night had raised more questions than answers, and she had no idea how to find her way through the maze of conflicting emotions and loyalties.

As she turned to rejoin the party, her gaze caught on a window a little above and to the side of the terrace. Mr Darcy stood in the shadows, his face half-hidden in the dim light. He watched her with an intensity that sent a shiver down her spine. Their eyes met for a brief moment, and she saw a flicker of something in his gaze—regret, perhaps, or longing. But then he turned away, disappearing into the darkness.

DARCY STOOD BY THE window of his room, his head aching and his heart heavy. The dim light of the room was a small reprieve from the brightness and noise of the ball. He had retreated here after the disastrous dinner, unable to endure the relentless throb of his headache in the overly illuminated rooms of Netherfield. He pressed his fingers to his temples, trying to will away the pain, but it was no use. The laudanum had dulled the edges of his agony but had not extinguished it.

As Darcy looked out over the terrace below, his gaze fell on Elizabeth. Of course, she would have to come back where he could see her once more. It was like she knew she was taunting him.

She was engaged in an intimate conversation with Wickham, her expression open and unguarded. Wickham, ever the charmer, seemed to be thoroughly enjoying her company. The sight triggered a tumult of emotions in Darcy—anger, jealousy, and a deep, aching longing. These feelings were unfamiliar to him, disorienting in their intensity.

He had tried to hold himself together in Elizabeth's presence, to maintain some semblance of composure despite the physical pain and the emotional turmoil. But it was clear she did not enjoy his company tonight. Her guarded expressions, the way she turned to Wickham for conversation, all spoke volumes. It stung more than he cared to admit.

Elizabeth smiled at something Wickham said—he could see the slight tilt of her head from where he stood, and he knew her mannerisms well enough by now to read her with precision. She seemed to trust Wickham, to genuinely like him. It was a bitter draught to swallow. How could she be so deceived by that man? Darcy knew Wickham's true nature... did he not?

Something still seemed off about all this, but perhaps it was more a product of Darcy's own incapacitation. His powers of observation were diminished, his own doubts and insecurities surely clouding whatever he might otherwise have observed. *Had* Wickham changed? Darcy could not allow that he had, but Elizabeth certainly seemed to think the man worthy of her regard. The jealousy flared hotter, fueled by his helplessness to intervene.

He had not realised until now how much he had pinned his hopes on this evening, or how wildly they had spun beyond his grasp when she was standing beside him. The idea of marrying Elizabeth, of spending his final days with someone who inspired and understood him, might have been a beacon in his darkening world.

He had lingered in Meryton for this chance, had endured the agony of his illness and the burden of his prognosis, just to have a beautiful evening with her. The sight of her in that evening gown, more resplendent than any of his imaginings, now seemed a cruel taunt.

Darcy leaned heavily against the window frame, his eyes never leaving Elizabeth. Wickham had gone now, and she stood alone for some minutes, letting him drink in the sight of her slim shoulders squared against the November cold. Delicate, but strong... Darcy's throat ached with longing.

He could have loved her.

That thought was a shard in the chest. Where had it come from? With a start, he recognised that the *feeling* had been simmering since their first meeting. The tenderness that bent his soul whenever he looked at her, the lightness that overtook his face when she spoke, and even the sense of peace and clarity she brought whenever she was near. Indeed, the sentiment of love, or at least the beginnings of that feeling, had long been making itself known.

But the *act* of loving... now, that was another thing altogether. The notion of caring for, holding, and cleaving and baring his most intimate thoughts—of sharing all of himself and what remained of his life with someone he could hold dear—that was something he might have found with Elizabeth Bennet, had George Wickham not somehow made a mockery of him.

She turned at last, and some impulse made her look up, directly into his window. He saw a flicker of something in her gaze—perhaps curiosity or confusion—but it quickly passed, cooling into a distant sort of curiosity. He was a puzzlement to her, no more.

The ache of loss in his chest deepened, a gnawing grief that threatened to consume him. The idea of proposing to Elizabeth had seemed so clear, so right. It had offered a semblance of hope. Not only a way to leave a meaningful legacy, but to have a friend beside him through the trials ahead—someone who saw him for himself. But tonight had shattered that hope. She was not interested in him; she was enamoured with Wickham. It was clear in every glance, every smile she bestowed upon him.

Darcy's fists clenched at his sides. The injustice of it all rankled. Wickham did not deserve her trust, her affection. Yet, Darcy was powerless to change her mind. His attempts to warn her had only driven a wedge between them. Indeed, he would have done better to simply smile and play along with whatever she believed because he had no proof that she was wrong.

Enough of this. He turned away from the window, his steps dragging with every inch. The room felt oppressive, the walls closing in on him. He needed to leave, to get away from this place where he could not trust even the truths of his own mind. To London, then, at last, where he ought to have gone more than a week ago. Time to focus on his affairs and prepare for the end.

Chapter Twenty-Three

Elizabeth woke with a dull, throbbing ache behind her eyes. She squinted against the pale morning light streaming through the window, her head pounding in time with her heartbeat. Too much punch last night. Too much dancing, too little sleep, and far too much happening. The last half of the evening had been a blur of emotions and confusion, and now she paid the price.

She rolled over, trying to find a more comfortable position, but images from the previous evening crowded her mind. Darcy's intense gaze, Wickham's charming smile, Charlotte's laughter... and Collins. *Ugh.*

Elizabeth groaned, pressing the heels of her hands into her eyes, trying to block out the memories. She had hoped to steer Mr Collins toward Charlotte, knowing how desperately her friend needed a secure future. Charlotte, however, was too distracted by Wickham to make an earnest attempt at catching Collins' notice when they finally danced. Elizabeth had watched in dismay as Collins hardly paid attention to her, deciding instead to fix his attention on Elizabeth's sisters.

A sudden knock on the door made her sit up, and she winced at the involuntary movement. "Lizzy? Are you awake?" Jane's voice called from the other side.

"Yes, come in," Elizabeth croaked, her voice rough with sleep and headache.

Jane entered, looking far too bright and alert for someone who had attended the same ball. "Mama wants us downstairs. There is something... well, something important happening."

Elizabeth frowned, swinging her legs over the side of the bed. "Important? What do you mean?"

Jane hesitated, a troubled look passing over her face. "It is Mr Collins. He is... he is proposing to Mary."

Elizabeth's heart sank. "Proposing to *Mary?* But... but he should be proposing to Charlotte!"

"I know," Jane said softly, sitting beside her. "But he was determined to 'settle the companion of his future life' this very morning, and Mama steered him away from both you and me."

"She did? I thought she *wanted* Collins to pursue me!"

"Yes, until she saw you and Mr Wickham dancing last evening. She quite has it fixed in her head that you will be the next mistress of Netherfield."

Elizabeth squinted. "But I danced with half a dozen others, too. What about Mr Darcy?"

"Oh, she was terribly put out over that. Did you not hear her? All through supper, she could only lament how you should have been with 'someone who could appreciate your wit, like Mr Wickham, not some prideful, dull fellow like Mr Darcy.'" Jane thinned her lips and rolled her eyes at Elizabeth.

Elizabeth sagged deeper into her mattress. "Mr Darcy is not dull. Prideful, perhaps, but not dull."

"Well, it matters little, anyway. Mama is entirely persuaded that she will have three daughters married before Christmas, and Mr Darcy is not one of the men she fancied for a son-in-law. She has already begun listing houses for Mr Bingley to consider leasing—after he proposes marriage, of course."

Elizabeth dropped her face into her hands. "Of course. Well, what of Mr Collins? Why is he suddenly pursuing Mary? I thought he scarcely noticed her."

Jane shrugged. "He danced the first with her but, to my knowledge, never spoke to her the rest of the night."

"Exactly! Why would she even consider accepting?"

Jane frowned. "Because he asked, and... well, Mary seems to think it's her duty."

"And Mama left Mary as the sacrificial lamb. I have to stop this," Elizabeth muttered, standing quickly and regretting it as her head spun. "Only think how pedantic and intolerable Mary will become if she marries a man like Collins! Charlotte might make him a sensible sort of fellow—at least, she will not be ruined by him—but Mary is—"

Jane reached out, gently gripping her arm. "Lizzy, it's too late. Mary has already accepted."

The weight of those words nearly crushed the air out of Elizabeth's lungs. Mary, dutiful and serious Mary, had accepted Collins's proposal. It was done. There was no undoing it now. Elizabeth felt tears prick at the corners of her eyes, a mixture of frustration, disappointment, and guilt for not intervening sooner. For being too distracted last night to help her friend.

"Come, Lizzy," Jane said gently, helping her to her feet. "We must go downstairs."

Elizabeth nodded, taking a deep breath and trying to steel herself. She dressed quickly and followed Jane down the stairs, each step sending a jolt of pain through her head. Her mother's voice floated up from the parlour, cheerful and triumphant.

"Oh, Mr Collins, this is such splendid news! I knew you would make the right choice. Mary will be a perfect wife for you."

Elizabeth felt a surge of anger. How could her mother be so blind? So selfish? This was a dreadful choice for Mary! She wanted to scream, to tell them all how wrong this was, but it would do no good. The decision had been made.

As they entered the parlour, Elizabeth saw Collins beaming with self-satisfaction and Mary sitting primly beside him, her hands folded neatly in her lap. She looked content, even satisfied. Elizabeth's heart ached for her sister, for Charlotte, for the future that might have been.

"Congratulations, Mr Collins," Elizabeth said, forcing a smile. "Mary, I hope you will be very happy."

Mary nodded, her eyes meeting Elizabeth's with a hint of gratitude. "Thank you, Lizzy. I... I believe this is the right path for me."

Elizabeth swallowed hard, unable to say anything more.

The rest of the morning was frantic oblivion. Congratulations were exchanged, plans were made, and all the while, Elizabeth felt a growing sense of despair. She had tried to do the right thing, to help her friend, but it had all gone so horribly wrong. Collins was now part of her family, and there was no escaping the reality of it.

When the initial excitement had settled, Elizabeth found a moment to slip away. She needed air, needed to clear her head. She wandered out into the garden, the crisp morning air a welcome relief from the stuffy parlour.

She found a quiet corner and sank onto a bench, burying her face in her hands. The headache throbbed mercilessly, a physical manifestation of the turmoil inside her. She thought of Darcy, of his own headaches and the strange, intense look he had given her at the ball. She had tried to extend sympathy, to understand his pain, but it had all gone so wrong. What had he meant by those cryptic words? Had he been trying to tell her something important, something she had missed? If that had been his intention, he had succeeded only in sounding petulant and hyperbolic.

She squeezed her eyes shut against the weak morning sunlight and the pounding reminder of the amount of punch she had consumed last evening. She could barely even manage to think, to say nothing of holding a conversation with anyone. If this was any fraction of how Mr Darcy's head must have been feeling, perhaps she could understand a little bit of petulance.

Elizabeth took a deep breath as she approached Lucas Lodge, her feet dragging down the familiar path. Charlotte had been fragile enough of late, and this would shatter her newfound hopes.

Charlotte greeted her at the door, her eyes bright and a smile lighting up her face. "Lizzy! I was just thinking of you. Come in, come in! We have so much to talk about."

Elizabeth forced a smile, her stomach knotting with dread. "Charlotte, you seem in good spirits."

"Oh, I am," Charlotte said, leading her into the cosy sitting room. "Last night was... well, it was wonderful, was it not? Mr Wickham was so attentive, and did you see how well Mr Collins danced with me? I really think your plan might work, Lizzy."

Elizabeth swallowed hard, the words feeling like stones in her throat. "Yes, the ball was... quite the event."

Charlotte bubbled on, her enthusiasm undiminished. "I have been thinking about ways to cross Mr Collins' path now that we have got to know each other a little. Perhaps if I come to 'call on you' this afternoon? And you could 'ask' me for help with some of your needlework—oh, say it is something for the charity basket for the parish. That might impress him and give me a reason to visit Longbourn more frequently."

Elizabeth's heart ached as she listened. She took a deep breath, steeling herself for what she had to say. "Charlotte, there is something I need to tell you."

Charlotte paused, her smile faltering slightly as she took in Elizabeth's serious tone. "What is it, Lizzy?"

"Mr Collins..." Elizabeth hesitated, searching for the right words. "Mr Collins has... ah... made his intentions known."

Charlotte's eyes widened. "His intentions? Oh, Lizzy, you were right! How wonderful! I can hardly believe—"

"Charlotte," Elizabeth interrupted gently, her voice breaking slightly. "He proposed to Mary this morning. And she accepted."

For a moment, Charlotte stood frozen, the colour draining from her face. The joyous light in her eyes flickered and went out, replaced by a look of stunned disbelief. "Mary?" she whispered. "But... I thought..."

Elizabeth stepped closer, reaching out to her friend. "I am so sorry, Charlotte. I truly am. I had hoped—"

Charlotte turned away, her stare glassy and unseeing as her hands drifted to the wall to guide her around the corners of the hallway.

Elizabeth's heart broke at the sight of Charlotte's defeated expression. She followed behind. "Charlotte, you deserve so much better. I should never have brokered hope when it was not mine to offer. I just wanted to help you find security and happiness."

Charlotte's weak smile wavered, and she shook her head, tears welling in her eyes. "Lizzy, it is not your fault. I allowed myself to think I might have a chance, and now... now it feels like a cruel joke."

Elizabeth's chest tightened with guilt. "I feel terrible for pressuring you. I thought—"

"You thought Mr Collins might see sense," Charlotte interrupted. "But he's chosen Mary. Mary, of all people! How could he..."

Elizabeth swallowed hard, trying to find the right words. "I am so sorry. I only wanted you to have the happiness you deserve."

Charlotte's tears spilled over, and she wiped them away angrily. "And what do I deserve, Lizzy? A life of being overlooked? Passed over for someone younger, prettier, more agreeable? Heavens, Mary is no prettier or livelier than I am! And I do not even deserve fair consideration there!"

Elizabeth reached out, taking Charlotte's hands in hers. "No, you deserve to be loved for who you are. You are intelligent, kind, capable... any man would be lucky to have you."

Charlotte pulled her hands back, her expression a mixture of hurt and resignation. "But that is not the world we live in, is it? We have to be practical. We have to make do with what we can get."

"I hate that you feel this way," Elizabeth said, her voice cracking. "I hate that I could not do more to help you."

Charlotte's shoulders slumped, and she let out a weary sigh. "You have done more than anyone, Lizzy. But we cannot change the way things are. We just have to accept it."

Elizabeth felt a surge of frustration and helplessness. "It is not fair. You deserve so much better than Mr Collins."

"Fairness doesn't come into it," Charlotte replied quietly. "I should have known better than to let myself hope. You may as well go home now, Lizzy."

Elizabeth opened her mouth to protest, but Charlotte held up a hand. "I am quite serious, Lizzy. Just go—let me alone."

Elizabeth thinned her lips. "Very well."

Elizabeth left Charlotte's house with a heavy heart. As she walked home, her head hung low, and her thoughts churned with guilt and frustration. The bright afternoon sunlight seemed incongruous with her dark mood, each cheerful chirp of a bird feeling like a personal affront.

As she turned a corner, she encountered Lydia and Kitty, walking arm-in-arm along the road. Their laughter rang out, and they seemed utterly absorbed in some juvenile joke. The sight of their carefree mirth made Elizabeth's heart ache even more. She wished she could share in their light-heartedness, but the events of the morning had left her too drained.

"Lizzy!" Lydia called out, her eyes sparkling with mischief. "Where have you been? You look as if you've lost your last shilling."

Kitty giggled, nudging Lydia. "She's probably been off having another serious talk with Charlotte. You know, if you were not so serious all the time, perhaps Charlotte would smile more often."

Elizabeth set her teeth into a grim line. "Where are you two going?"

Lydia skipped ahead, her curls bouncing. "We're off to see Maria Lucas. Come with us, Lizzy! We have all sorts of news."

Elizabeth shook her head. "I was just at Lucas Lodge, and I mean to return home."

Lydia pouted. "Oh, come now, Lizzy. You cannot be gloomy all the time. Have you not heard the latest?"

Elizabeth sighed, too tired to play along. "What news do you speak of, Lydia?"

"Oh, you will not credit it. At last, we shall be able to visit Netherfield without that grumpy Mr Darcy about!"

A chill ran through her. She stopped in her tracks, her heart pounding. "What do you mean?"

Lydia giggled again, clearly relishing the attention. "Mr Wickham and Mr Bingley came calling while you were out. They said that the ball was a smashing success. Everyone says Mama outdid herself, and not a thing was amiss, except that Mrs Long thought her nieces did not receive proper notice because she thinks Mama slighted them, but who cares about her? And Mrs Canterbury—you remember her, do you not? She said that Mrs Ellington said that—"

"Lydia, what is this about Mr Darcy?" she interrupted.

"Oh." Lydia shrugged. "Mr Wickham says that Mr Darcy has returned to London suddenly."

Elizabeth's heart sank. Mr Darcy gone? Whatever for? Her thoughts stumbled, recalling their strained conversation, his pained expressions, and the odd intensity in his eyes. She had sensed a connection, a glimmer of understanding between them, and now he had left without a word.

"Isn't it wonderful, Lizzy?" Kitty asked. "Now we can visit Netherfield and not have to worry about Mr Darcy looking down his nose at us. A pity he did not go before last night. Everyone was talking about it, how they were afraid to even approach the man. Better if he had gone before the ball, but at least he knows where he is not wanted."

Elizabeth barely heard her. She felt a deep sense of loss, an inexplicable feeling that she had failed Mr Darcy in some crucial way. He had been suffering, she knew that much. And he had wanted something from her, though she knew not what. She had been unable to reach him, to offer the comfort he so clearly needed.

"He... he left without saying goodbye?" she asked, more to herself than to her sisters.

Lydia shrugged. "Why would he? He's such a sour man. I'm glad he's gone. Now Mr Wickham need not be at such pains to entertain him."

Elizabeth's chest tightened. She had failed Charlotte, and somehow, she was quite sure that she had disappointed Mr Darcy too. Now she would never understand what he wanted from her, but she had sensed his need, his pain, and had done nothing to alleviate it. Had she pushed him away with her harsh words? Had she missed a chance to know a good man?

"Lizzy, are you entirely well?" Kitty asked, her tone more serious now as she noticed Elizabeth's distress. "Should we walk with you back to Longbourn?"

Elizabeth forced a nod, though her throat tightened. "Yes. You two go on ahead. I… I would like to be alone for a while."

Lydia and Kitty exchanged a glance, but Lydia shrugged and pulled Kitty along. "Suit yourself, Lizzy. Come, Kitty, let us race!"

As they dashed away, their laughter echoing down the lane, Elizabeth stood still, her mind awhirl with guilt and sorrow. She had thought herself strong, capable of helping those she cared about. But it was all ash. She felt powerless, her attempts at aid ending in failure and disappointment for people who would have done better not to listen to her.

Darcy sat at his desk, the letter trembling slightly in his grip. Richard's familiar handwriting flickered a faint smile on his lips. Chatham. Munitions. Supplies for the army. The words blurred as his mind wandered. Richard's second letter from his new post in Kent was something of an anchor to everything familiar, but now his cousin's cheerful presence felt achingly far away. The quiet of the room pressed in, broken only by the rustle of paper. He tightened his hold on the letter, wishing he could summon Richard's calm and clarity to dispel his own turmoil.

Darcy,

Chatham is a far cry from the battlefield—glory and honour and all that—but I daresay I am grateful for it. The endless shipments and inventorying of supplies keep me occupied. Just yesterday, a shipment of gunpowder arrived three days late, causing quite a stir. The quartermaster nearly lost his wig in frustration! It took all my persuasion to calm him down and assure him that we would manage without causing Wellington to lose the war. Though I sometimes yearn for more direct action, there is never a dull moment here.

You will be pleased to know that it is highly unlikely I will be sent to France. Our duties here have been deemed "critical to the war effort," and it seems my skills are more useful behind a desk than in a trench. I have become quite adept at navigating the bureaucracy, though I do miss the camaraderie of the field. The other officers here are a decent lot, but not one of them could fight his way out of a wet sackcloth. I am left to wonder whether I was assigned here because I was the only man with valuable battle experience or because I have been deemed as useless in the field as the rest of the lot. My own hubris requires it to be the former, and I shall thank you not to disabuse me of the notion.

I hope this news finds you in good spirits, dear cousin. I think often of the fine sport we missed this autumn at Pemberley, and I must solemnly charge you to keep my room ready for the moment I am granted leave. Until then, know that you are in my thoughts.

-Richard

Darcy sighed, his fingers tracing the edges of the paper. Richard's words brought a measure of relief, knowing his cousin was safe and not directly in harm's way.

He toyed with the idea of replying, of confiding in Richard about the tumour that plagued him, but the words would not come. What could he say? That he was dying? That he could not promise a waiting room at Pemberley because he had no way of knowing how much time he had left? It felt too soon, too raw. Richard had enough to worry about with his own responsibilities. And Georgiana... he could not bear to burden her with this news just yet.

His eyes wandered to the unopened letters on his desk, one from Lady Matlock and another from Georgiana. He had not yet informed them of his return to London three days earlier. What could he say? How could he explain his abrupt departure from Meryton or the secretive way he kept the knocker off his door? How could he reveal the truth of his condition without causing them undue distress?

Darcy stood and moved to the window, looking out over the bustling streets of London. He felt adrift, caught between the need to protect his family and the growing fear of this thing consuming him from the inside out.

"A second opinion," Doctor Westing had advised. "It is always wise to seek another perspective, particularly when the circumstances are so grave."

He could not continue in this state of limbo, waiting for the inevitable. He had to act, to seek answers. Darcy returned to his desk, pulled out a fresh sheet of paper, and began to write a note to Westing, requesting him to arrange an appointment with another physician. Perhaps this new doctor would offer some hope, some clarity.

As he sealed the letter, Darcy's thoughts drifted back to Elizabeth Bennet. Her image, her voice, haunted him still. He had left Meryton with a heavy heart, knowing he had not made amends, that he had left things unsaid to the one person he seemed to be able to speak to at all. If he had only managed to find the right words, he might even now have the right to go to her as a friend, a future partner for what remained of his days, and one with whom to share the depths of his pain and fears.

As the only one who could truly make him smile just now.

Did she think of him? How had she taken the news that he had gone? He snorted and kneaded his forehead. She probably scarcely noticed his absence, and if she did, she could have no possible inkling of the true conflict that had driven him away, or the regret with which he went.

But there was no time for such thoughts now. No time for anything, truly. He had to focus on the present, on the steps he needed to take. Darcy placed the letter on his desk, ready for his steward, and sank back into his chair.

Chapter Twenty-Four

THE PAST WEEK HAD been a blur of pain and despair, the echoes of Elizabeth's preference for Wickham reverberating through his mind with every stabbing reminder of his malady. He had convinced himself that his heartache was merely a byproduct of physical agony and the looming fear of his diagnosis. Determined to put his affairs in order, he sat at his desk, letters of business strewn about. The ink on his quill barely dried before he found his mind drifting back to the ball, to Elizabeth, and the pain that now seemed a permanent part of him.

He tried to focus on the letter to his steward at Pemberley detailing the maintenance of the estate's tenant houses. Each word seemed a struggle, as if the ink itself resisted his command. He paused, staring at the paper, and Elizabeth's face intruded on his thoughts. Her laughter, her eyes that sparkled with intelligence and fire, the way she had looked at him with a mixture of curiosity and something he dared not name. His heart twisted painfully.

Egad, somehow, he had convinced himself that he was truly in love with the woman. That *must* be it because nothing else could explain the way his heart floundered in his chest at the thought of her.

How and when had he managed to lose his senses over a woman he had known but mere weeks? And most of those encounters had been tainted with the nearly certain knowledge that he did not have the luxury of finding love nor the time left on this earth to make such a pursuit worthwhile. But there it was, all the same. Given no choice but to endure without her, he had to confess... it was the most exquisite torment he had ever known.

He forced himself to continue writing. There were so many things to finalize if his prognosis was as dire as he feared. Instructions about the estate's finances, provisions for Georgiana's future, arrangements for the care of his tenants—all these matters required his attention. Yet every line he wrote felt like an echo of futility. How could he think of the future when he would have no part in it?

The next letter concerned the estate's annual harvest. He needed to instruct his steward on how to handle the upcoming season, the distribution of profits, and the improvements needed in the granary.

But the details swam before his eyes. Elizabeth's voice, her mannerisms, the way she had captivated him with her wit and spirit, all conspired to distract him. How had he let himself hope for something more with her, as if she held some sort of magical cure in the power of a woman's caress? How had he thought, even for a moment, that he could escape his fate?

He shook his head, trying to clear the fog that seemed to settle over his thoughts. He needed to write to his solicitor about adjusting certain particular figures in his will. The disposition of his properties, the guardianship of Georgiana—these were matters of utmost importance. He had to ensure that everything was in order, that there would be no disputes, no uncertainties. Yet every stroke of the pen felt like a farewell, a step closer to accepting the end he had fought so hard to deny.

Elizabeth. Her name seemed to be written in the margins of every page, her image imprinted on his mind. He had stayed in Meryton, enduring the pain and the fear, just for a chance to be near her. And now, even as he tried to prepare for the worst, she occupied his every thought. He could not escape the longing, the regret, the hope that had so cruelly slipped through his fingers.

Darcy pressed a hand to his forehead, the familiar throb of his headache a reminder of his reality. He could not afford to lose himself in memories and what-ifs. He had to finalize these letters, to ensure that everything was taken care of. But the words refused to come. The prospect of seeing a new doctor, of perhaps finding some glimmer of hope, was his only solace.

He had scheduled another doctor to call today for a second opinion, and it was his last hope for any relief. If the diagnosis remained the same, he would have to consider telling his family, preparing them for the inevitable. The thought of facing them, of seeing their faces when they learned the truth, was almost more than he could bear. But he would do it. He would do his duty, for Georgiana, for Pemberley, for the legacy that he would leave behind.

And yet, through it all, Elizabeth lingered in his mind, a reminder of what might have been, of the happiness that had seemed just within reach before slipping away.

The knock at the door came swiftly, and Darcy called for his butler to let the physician in. Dr Merton, a man of middle age with a kind face, entered the room with a medical bag in hand. He greeted Darcy with a respectful bow before taking a seat opposite him.

"Mr Darcy, I trust you are managing as well as can be expected?" Dr Merton began.

Darcy managed a weak smile. "As well as can be, Doctor. I am hoping you might offer me some clearer answers than I have received thus far."

Dr Merton nodded, opening his bag, and taking out a few instruments. "Let us begin with an examination. I understand your symptoms have persisted for some time now?"

Darcy described the relentless headaches, the nausea, and the moments of dizziness that had plagued him for months. The doctor listened intently, his brow furrowing as he took notes.

After a thorough examination, Dr Merton sat back, his expression grave. "Mr Darcy, I must be honest with you. Based on your symptoms and the results of my examination, there are a handful of possible causes, but with the duration of the symptoms..."

"You may say it, sir."

Dr Merton sighed. "I am afraid, sir, that I must agree with Doctor Westing. It is almost certain that you have a tumour in your brain."

The words struck Darcy, leaving him breathless. His vision blurred momentarily, and he gripped the armrests of his chair, fighting the urge to collapse. The reality he had feared but never fully acknowledged was now undeniable, crushing any remnants of denial. His chest tightened, and his mouth went dry as he struggled to process the doctor's verdict. "Is there... any hope of treatment?" he asked, his voice barely above a whisper.

"There are some treatments, but they come with significant risks and limited success. However, there is a surgeon in Cambridge, Dr Pembroke, who has developed a reputation for his advanced work on cranial operations. He may be able to provide a more accurate diagnosis and discuss potential surgical interventions. Dr Pembroke's methods are unconventional, yet he has seen some success where others have not."

Darcy's grip tightened on the armrest, his voice tense. "Such as?"

The doctor cleared his throat, adjusting his spectacles. "Dr Pembroke has been experimenting with trepanation, which involves creating an opening in the skull to relieve pressure or remove damaged tissue. He has also had some success with resectioning certain types of tumours, though this is exceedingly rare and fraught with danger. The brain is delicate, and most tumours are unreachable without causing significant harm."

Darcy's face hardened as he absorbed the information. "So, you are telling me that he might not be able to help me at all?"

The doctor nodded solemnly. "Indeed, Mr Darcy. Dr Pembroke can only operate under very specific conditions. Most tumours, particularly those deeply embedded, remain untouchable. However, he may provide a diagnosis beyond any shadow of doubt, which could at least offer clarity on your condition and the options available to you."

Darcy's impatience flared, his voice sharp. "Why should I travel all the way to Cambridge merely to hear a third doctor confirm what I already know, especially if there is no treatment available?"

The doctor remained calm, his expression sympathetic. "Mr Darcy, I understand your frustration. However, Dr Pembroke's expertise goes beyond mere diagnosis. He has access to the latest research and techniques in pain relief. While the likelihood of a successful intervention is slim, he may be able to offer insights or recommendations that others cannot. It is also possible that he might identify a less dire explanation for your symptoms."

Darcy leaned back in his chair. The thought of undergoing yet another examination, of exposing his vulnerabilities once more, was almost unbearable. Yet, the promise of certainty—or even a glimmer of hope—well, he could not let that go without examination.

"And if he finds nothing new?" Darcy's voice was quieter now, the anger drained from it.

The doctor sighed. "If he finds nothing new, you will at least have the peace of mind that comes from knowing you have explored every possible avenue. You will have done everything within your power."

Darcy closed his eyes and pinched the bridge of his nose with a sighing hiss. The doctor was right; he could not leave any stone unturned. He owed it to himself, to Georgiana, and to the legacy of his family to seek out every possible chance of survival, no matter how slim.

Opening his eyes, he nodded curtly. "Very well. I will go to Cambridge."

The doctor inclined his head respectfully. "I shall make the necessary arrangements for you to see Dr Pembroke. And Mr Darcy, please remember—you do not face this alone. Inform your family. They will want to support you through this."

A pang of guilt and apprehension sliced through him at the thought of telling his family. He had shielded them from the truth for so long, out of hope that Westing might have been mistaken. But now, it seemed he had no choice. He would have to call on

Lord and Lady Matlock to bring them into his confidence. And eventually, he must tell Georgiana.

He stood, the decision made, and extended his hand to the doctor. "Thank you. I will make the necessary preparations."

As the doctor departed, Darcy remained in his study, the room feeling colder and more oppressive than before. He walked to the window, staring out at the bustling streets of London, feeling a profound sense of isolation despite the throngs of people below.

"Now, Mary, you must think of when you leave the church. Oh, pish-posh, do not look at me that way. This bonnet will set off your face—you know your cheeks need a little... setting off. Lizzy, what do you think of this lace at the edge?" The table before them was cluttered with fabric swatches, ribbons, and lists of wedding necessities, each item a reminder of the rapidly approaching nuptials of Mary and Mr Collins.

Elizabeth glanced at the bit of frippery her mother held up, her thoughts elsewhere. She forced a smile, her head nodding mechanically. "Yes, Mama, it is lovely."

"Indeed, it is. Just wait until Mrs Long sees you in this, Mary. Now, what do you think of this satin? Jane, you too—I should like to hear what you think as well, and Lizzy?"

Elizabeth examined the fabric, running her fingers over the smooth material. "It is quite lovely, Mama. I think it would suit Mary very well."

Mary smiled faintly, her posture prim and proper. "Thank you, Lizzy."

Mrs Bennet nodded, satisfied. "And the veil? Should it be lace or something simpler?"

Jane leaned in. "Lace, I think. It adds a touch of elegance."

"Yes, lace it is," Mrs Bennet agreed, smoothing the fabric with a satisfied nod. "We want everything to be perfect for Mary's special day. Mary's wedding is only the beginning, after all."

Jane tilted her head. "What do you mean, Mama?"

"I mean, my dear, that it is only natural for a mother to think of *all* her daughters being happily settled. Mary is the first, but you and Lizzy will soon follow in her footsteps."

Elizabeth's eyes widened. "Mama, you cannot be serious. Jane and I are not even engaged."

Mrs Bennet waved a hand dismissively. "Oh, but it is only a matter of time. You must also think of your own wedding attire. Of course, you, dear Jane, and especially you, Lizzy, must think of something grander than what is fitting for a parson's bride."

Jane blushed and looked down, her cheeks pink. "Mama, we should focus on Mary now."

"But we cannot leave these things for the last minute, my dear! After all, Mr Bingley may propose any day."

Lydia, sprawled in a chair with Kitty, scoffed. "Oh, Mama, Lizzy and Jane are not thinking of weddings. They are too busy pretending to be serious. Besides, have you heard the latest about the officers?"

Kitty sat up straighter. "Oh yes! Did you know that Captain Carter is to dine with us next week?"

Elizabeth sighed, trying to steer the conversation back. "Mama, what do you think of this lace for the bodice of the gown? It has a delicate pattern that would suit Mary perfectly."

Mrs Bennet barely glanced at the lace. "Yes, yes, that will do. But Lizzy, have you not noticed how often Mr Wickham looks your way? And Jane, Mr Bingley was practically glued to your side at the ball. You both must start thinking seriously about your own matches."

Jane shifted uncomfortably. "Mama, Mr Wickham and Mr Bingley have their own minds. We cannot assume anything."

Lydia burst into laughter. "Oh, Jane, you are too modest! And Lizzy, you are too distracted with your books to notice when a man admires you."

Elizabeth rolled her eyes. "Lydia, perhaps it is you who are too distracted with the officers to notice anything else."

Kitty giggled. "Well, at least they are interesting! Much more than discussing lace and silks."

Mary was glancing between them all, still sitting primly with her hands folded in her lap. She cleared her throat. "I think the lace is lovely, Jane. Thank you for suggesting it."

Mrs Bennet beamed at Mary. "There, you see? Mary appreciates the importance of these details. Now, Lizzy, do you think we should have satin or leather for her wedding shoes?"

Elizabeth exchanged a look with Jane, both of them feeling the pressure of their mother's expectations. "I think satin would be more elegant," she said finally.

"Satin it is, then!" Mrs Bennet declared, her eyes twinkling with satisfaction. "And remember, girls, this is the only time she shall have a wedding. Everything must be perfect for our Mary."

Mary sat somewhat straighter—no doubt delighted at being the centre of her mother's eager focus for once. Lydia and Kitty, however, could hardly focus on Mary for two minutes together, and sat elbowing each other and trading snickers over this officer or that. Elizabeth rolled her neck and sighed. This was going to be a long, dull afternoon.

Jane's foot shifted restlessly on the rug, and Elizabeth stifled a yawn as her attention wandered to the sounds filtering through the walls from her father's library. Mr Collins's voice droned on, a persistent murmur even over the lively din of the parlour. She could only imagine the trials her father was enduring, trapped with Mr Collins's endless self-congratulation.

"Mama, perhaps this lace would be more suitable for the veil," Jane suggested. Elizabeth sucked in a stale breath and pulled her attention back to the table.

Mrs Bennet ran the lace between her fingers, examining it with a critical eye. "Yes, you are right, Jane. It is exquisite. Mary, you will look like an angel."

Mary's smile widened, and she murmured her thanks, but Lydia's laughter from the opposite sofa interrupted anything else she might have said. "And can you believe it, Kitty? Mr Denny said that he once saw a duel! Imagine that!"

Kitty's eyes widened. "A duel? How thrilling! Who was it between?"

"Jane, what do you think of this trim for the pelisse?" Mrs Bennet asked, holding up a length of delicate satin.

Elizabeth's head snapped from one conversation to the other. Gracious, how was anybody to focus on a single thing? She was tempted to rub her temples again... and again, she wondered if this was how Mr Darcy had felt at the ball. Overwhelmed and lost in the middle of it all.

"Now, Lizzy, do pay attention," her mother chided gently, interrupting her thoughts. "What do you think of these flowers for the bouquet? Lilies, perhaps, or roses?"

She shook her head. "I beg you would excuse me, Mama. I... I just remembered something I meant to do."

"But the flowers! Now, if it were your wedding, I should say roses and lilies for Jane, beyond a doubt, but for Mary—"

Elizabeth stood to her feet and pointed. "Mary is right there. Perhaps you may ask her and stop considering this a 'rehearsal' of some sort for other weddings that are not yet planned. I am going upstairs."

Chapter Twenty-Five

Elizabeth passed by her father's study and couldn't resist the mischievous urge to poke her head in. Mr Collins was in the middle of an animated discussion, his voice carrying through the partially open door.

"And you see, sir, this new technique of crop rotation, championed by none other than Lord Cathcart, could greatly enhance the productivity of Longbourn's fields. The benefits are manifold, particularly for the root crops, which..."

Mr Bennet leaned back in his chair, trying to interject. "Mr Collins, that only works when—"

"No, no, I assure you, sir, the Four-Course Crop Rotation is infallible. It was developed in Norfolk—I shall familiarise you, sir. It involves a four-year cycle of different crops: wheat, turnips, barley, and clover. Each crop replenishes the soil in a unique way, reducing soil depletion and increasing productivity."

"Mr Collins, I have on these shelves three books on that very topic. While interesting, what you fail to account for is—"

"Then you have heard of it! Why, sir, I cannot help but wonder why it is not already implemented. Longbourn could be prospering much more handsomely. Perhaps you have not read Lord Cathcart's account. Lady Catherine has a copy in her possession, and I flatter myself, I doubt not that she would lend it to you to see that Longbourn's lands are improved as much as they can be before..." Collins cleared his throat and gestured modestly between them.

Elizabeth's father was drumming his fingers on the desk, a vein popping out on his forehead. "I am sure your readings are extensive, but you must understand that Hertfordshire's soil is—"

"Lord Cathcart's method has proven successful across various estates," Collins interrupted, his enthusiasm unabated. "Turnips and clover, in particular, improve soil fertility and provide excellent feed for livestock. Surely, adopting such a progressive system would benefit Longbourn immensely."

Mr Bennet sighed, rubbing his temples. "But Mr Collins, our soil is heavy clay, not the light, well-drained soil that turnips prefer. We have already considered this system and found it unsuitable for our conditions."

"But the introduction of barley and clover also enriches the soil, providing nutrients that wheat depletes. It is a brilliant cycle that—"

Elizabeth stepped into the room, thinking it was past time to rescue her father. "Excuse me, Mr Collins," she interrupted with a light knock on the door as she passed through. "A note was delivered from the local parson, Mr Harrison. He asks that you call on him at your earliest convenience."

Mr Collins's chest puffed with pride. "Mr Harrison has requested my presence? How flattering indeed! I shall make my apologies, Mr Bennet, and take my leave at once. It would be most impolite to keep a fellow clergyman waiting."

Mr Bennet leaned his forehead on his hand, one greying eyebrow arched. "Oh, no inconvenience on my part. I believe you have expressed yourself with sufficient eloquence for one afternoon."

"You flatter me, sir," Mr Collins declared, gathering his papers. "I shall return shortly, and we can continue this most enlightening discussion. Good day!"

Elizabeth lingered by the door, watching as Mr Collins bustled out of the room. She turned back to her father, who appeared as if the weight of the world had been momentarily lifted from his shoulders.

"Clever, Lizzy. But what will poor Mr Harrison say when you deliver to him an unexpected caller who expects him to set aside his afternoon to hear how he ought to be managing his parish?"

"He is a man of God. Perhaps he can pray for supernatural rescue. Papa, can I fetch you anything?" she asked, stepping further into the study.

"No, Lizzy, thank you. I only wish for a bit of peace and quiet. Things that appear to be in short supply in this house."

Elizabeth sat down in the seat Mr Collins had just vacated. "Are you certain that is all, Papa? You look rather troubled."

He sighed. "It is nothing, Lizzy. I simply want to read my book."

"And which book, pray, is that?"

Mr Bennet swallowed and blinked, his mouth half-open to respond, but then his brow furrowed. Eventually, he had to shuffle through his disorganised stack of letters to turn over the spine of the boxy tome buried on his desk. "*The History of Tom Jones*," he read.

Elizabeth frowned and crossed her arms. "I see you were terribly eager to get back to it. Papa, please, tell me what is truly on your mind."

Mr Bennet lowered his book with a resigned sigh. "Very well, if you must know, Sir William and I called on Sir Anthony Mortimer this morning."

Elizabeth's face brightened with recognition. "Sir Anthony Mortimer? The man who is being put forward as MP?"

Mr Bennet nodded reluctantly. "Yes, the very same."

"And does he have generous feelings toward the neighbours? Will he likely help us accomplish the necessary aid to restore property damaged by the floods?"

Her father thought for a moment, then nodded again. "Yes, Sir Anthony seems as though he will be active and effective in Parliament. He certainly gave that impression."

Elizabeth laughed lightly. "Then what is the matter, Papa? You do not look pleased."

Mr Bennet shook his head. "I cannot quite agree with Sir Anthony's politics. He spoke rather critically of Wellington."

Elizabeth puckered her brow and tilted her head. "He would not be the first man to do so."

"Nor the last, I daresay, but this was... no, never mind, Lizzy. I cannot quite describe my impression, for it went beyond mere words. Sir William, however, endorsed the man wholeheartedly. So, it seems there is nothing else to do but accept him as our choice."

Elizabeth hummed in thought. "Have you considered speaking to Mr Wickham about Sir Anthony? After all, it was Mr Wickham who suggested his name. Perhaps he would understand your concerns, and together, you could either discuss the matter until your concerns are allayed or consider other candidates to propose."

Mr Bennet nodded faintly. "Yes, I suppose that is a sensible course of action."

"Good," Elizabeth said with a smile. "I am sure he will be willing to listen and discuss it with you."

Mr Bennet sighed, picking up his book again. "I will go to speak with him. Just as soon as I finish this chapter."

"Good day, Mr Darcy," the butler intoned with a slight dip of his head. "Her ladyship is not at home, but Lord Matlock is in his study."

Darcy nodded, handing over his coat and hat. "Thank you, Perkins. Please ask if he will see me."

The butler bowed before he disappeared. Darcy waited in the entrance hall, his anxiety mounting with each passing moment. The words he had rehearsed had shattered like grains of sand the moment he walked in the door. What was he supposed to say? When the butler returned and motioned for him to follow, he knotted his hands behind his back and prayed they would not shake when he had to speak.

As he entered the study, the smell of tobacco wafted over him. His uncle, Lord Matlock, sat behind a massive oak desk, puffing on a cigar and tracing his meaty finger down a piece of paper. At first glance, the scene appeared tranquil, but the lines of strain etched on Matlock's face told a different story.

"Ah, Darcy," Matlock greeted gruffly, setting the cigar down. "Take a seat and tell me what brings you here."

Darcy hesitated at the sharpness in his uncle's tone. "Thank you, Uncle," he said, taking the offered chair. He studied his uncle's face, the agitated weariness in his eyes. This would not, in fact, be the time to say what he had come here to say. Matlock looked like an angry cur gnawing on a bone shank. "Is something the matter? You seem... preoccupied."

Matlock stubbed out his expensive cigar and waved his hand dismissively, though his expression remained tight. "Forgive me, Darcy. Nothing that ought to trouble you."

Darcy eased a little more deeply into his seat. "Then, I take it, it is not to do with Georgiana?"

"Georgiana? No, no. Saint of a girl, like her mother."

Darcy's brow edged upward. "I doubt many would call her a saint, but thank you. It is not Richard, is it?"

Matlock shook his head as he fished inside his desk drawer for a hidden bottle of Scotch. "Not at the moment. I am afraid I have been wrestling with political matters all day. There is some tomfoolery afoot in the House of Commons that has been costing me sleep and far too many hours at my desk."

"The House? And it concerns you? Might I ask what the trouble is?"

Matlock sighed as he pulled the stopper on the Scotch. He poured two glasses and handed one to Darcy. "It's a finance bill for military funding. Vital, really, given our current situation with France. But there are private interests—wealthy and powerful ones—who oppose it for their own personal gain."

Darcy took a sip of the Scotch and had to fight back a faint cough. Matlock somehow always found a stiffer whiskey than Darcy was accustomed to. "Who is behind this opposition?"

Matlock's eyes narrowed, and he stared into his glass for a long moment. Darcy watched his uncle's face, noting the deep lines of concern. The silence stretched—whatever troubled Matlock was significant.

"Uncle, you seem particularly burdened by this matter," Darcy ventured carefully. "If it is something where I might offer assistance or at least a sympathetic ear, you may count on my discretion."

Matlock sighed heavily, swirling the amber liquid in his glass. "Well do I know that, but it is... complex, Darcy. Sometimes, secrecy is necessary even within the family."

Darcy nodded. "I understand. I hope you have prudent counsel, then."

Another long pause followed. Matlock seemed to be wrestling with his thoughts, his fingers drumming lightly on the desk. Finally, he looked up, meeting Darcy's gaze. "It is Lord Wexfield. He is causing me all manner of bother."

Darcy sipped more of the Scotch. "Wexfield? From Lincolnshire?"

"The very one. Chairman of the Finance Committee and the Committee on Military Affairs. Also sits on the Committee of Public Expenditure and the Committee on Foreign Relations."

Darcy puckered his lips in thought. "Rather a powerful fellow."

"Powerful, and after his own interests."

Darcy scoffed. "Name a man in Parliament who is not."

The earl shook his head. "Wexfield is something altogether different. If he could, he would revoke financial support for the entire war effort and divert the gold into his own coffers. The devil take the hindmost."

"He is not a Napoleon sympathiser, is he?"

"I suspected that at first, but no. No, I think Wexfield is a Wexfield sympathiser."

Darcy straightened and set down his glass. "What, specifically, has he done to make you think that?"

Matlock sighed heavily and rubbed his temples before responding. "It is a matter of his actions, Darcy. He is the chairman of the Committee of Supply, and consistently he has argued against funding for critical war measures. He has used his influence to block bills that would send much-needed supplies to our troops on the Continent, arguing instead for domestic investments that conveniently benefit his own interests."

Darcy frowned. "Surely, there are legitimate reasons to argue for domestic investments during wartime."

"Legitimate reasons, perhaps," Matlock conceded, "but not when it comes at the cost of our soldiers' lives. Wexfield has been particularly insistent on reducing the budget for military provisions and reinforcements. Every time there is a discussion about fortifying our positions or sending additional troops, he is there to argue against it."

Darcy's eyes narrowed. "Is there more?"

The earl nodded, his face grim. "He has also been vocal in the Naval Affairs Committee, pushing for reductions in shipbuilding and naval maintenance. He claims it is to reduce the national debt, but our navy is our first line of defence. Weakening it now, of all times, is pure folly."

"Is that all?"

"No, he has taken it a step further by obstructing the passage of the Finance Bill, which would allocate funds for our ongoing campaigns. His opposition has delayed critical support and allowed our enemies to gain ground. But the worst..." Matlock shuffled in his seat, frowning and pouring himself more Scotch. "He has been gathering power in the lower House by 'buying' MPs. It is well known among those of us in certain circles, but no one has been able to prove it or do anything about it."

Darcy's frown deepened. "How?"

Matlock leaned back, his expression dark. "You know the lower House controls most financial legislation."

Darcy nodded.

"Wexfield has been rallying support there, and some of his backers are newly elected members with dubious backgrounds. There are whispers that he's using his wealth to sway votes, ensuring that any motion he opposes is defeated. But proving it? That is another matter entirely."

A chill shivered down his spine. The idea that someone could be actively working against the country's interests from within was deeply unsettling. "And this finance bill for military funding—how does Wexfield gain from diverting it?"

Matlock sighed, his fingers drumming on the armrest of his chair. "Wexfield has substantial investments in several industries that stand to benefit if the war effort is weakened. He owns shares in companies that supply goods to the French, and he has financial interests in neutral territories that profit from trade disruptions. By blocking military funding, he ensures that those investments remain profitable."

"He is deliberately weakening our position to line his own pockets?"

"Precisely," Matlock said, his voice heavy with anger. "But it is more than that. Wexfield is also rumoured to be involved in smuggling operations, moving goods across the Channel under cover of night. He's leveraging his political power to protect these illicit activities."

"And he's using his wealth to buy support in Parliament?" Darcy asked.

"I cannot prove it, but I've a letter here that puts one more nail in the coffin of my suspicions. He's been funnelling money into the campaigns of MPs who are sympathetic to his cause, ensuring they owe him their allegiance. He is effectively building a faction within the House of Commons that can block any legislation he opposes."

Darcy felt a surge of outrage that made the space behind his eye throb in pain. "Is there no way to expose him? To bring his actions to light?"

Matlock shook his head slowly. "Without concrete evidence, our hands are tied. The Prince Regent himself granted a request that removed a steadfast MP from some small borough in Hertfordshire from office, and it appears that the new man will be..." Matlock laughed darkly and sighed. "... rather useful to Wexfield. That was the one vote he needed to tip the balance, and it is all but done."

Darcy swallowed hard. *Hertfordshire?* Egad, *he* was the one who had suggested this! And every voice in Meryton had praised him for the notion. The queasiness from his head now spread throughout his core, and he was disturbingly close to besmirching the earl's desk.

"This is... indeed troubling." He laced his fingers in his lap, tapping his thumbs together as his pulse quickened. "Uncle, what do you know of Viscount Halstead? What involvement has he in this?"

Matlock frowned, his face creasing with concentration. "Halstead? The name is not familiar to me."

Darcy leaned forward. "Surely you must know him. He was said to have attended Cambridge and perhaps had connections with our family. I thought Richard might have known him."

Matlock shook his head again. "I am sure I have never heard of Lord Halstead. But why does he concern you? What is his connection to Wexfield?"

Darcy hesitated. The pieces of the puzzle were not fitting together. "Are you certain? He is supposed to be from Yorkshire. I understand he is currently in America, brokering a deal in cotton. Perhaps you might not have encountered him recently, but..."

"Darcy, I know the names and titles of every peer in the country. There is no title associated with that name, and every Halstead I ever heard of was from Essex."

The chair under Darcy was spinning. So, he had *not* simply forgot the man... he never existed! Wickham had him so persuaded that his mind had failed him, but the truth was that it was a fabrication all along! Darcy passed a trembling hand over his forehead.

"I... excuse me, Uncle, I..." Darcy cleared his throat, but it did no good. "I am afraid you have raised more questions for me than you have answered."

"How so?"

Darcy closed his eyes and pressed his fingers into his eye sockets. "Uncle, forgive me. I believe I must return home. I... there is something I need to search for."

Matlock drained the last of his glass. "Why the rush? You are not off to try to enact some sort of self-styled justice, are you?" He chuckled sarcastically. "Better men than you have already been foiled."

"No, Uncle. That would be far beyond my means and is not remotely within my thoughts. I only noted an... an inconsistency in what I recall. I think I should like to investigate something."

Matlock lifted his shoulders. "I probably ought not have told you all that, Darcy. You look as though a stiff breeze would knock you down. 'Tis only the way of politics, my boy. Next year, it will be a different villain altogether. By the by, what brought you in so urgently today?"

Darcy swallowed. "Nothing, Uncle. Nothing at all."

Chapter Twenty-Six

ELIZABETH WALKED BRISKLY UP the path to Lucas Lodge, her thoughts churning with the conversation she had anticipated having with Charlotte. The chill in the air bit her cheeks, but she hardly noticed as she made her way to the door. She had hoped to find Charlotte in good spirits, but recent events made her doubt that was likely.

She was shown into the drawing room by a maid, where she found Charlotte arranging flowers with a practised hand. The room was warm and inviting, but Elizabeth could not shake the sense of unease that had settled in her chest.

"Good morning, Charlotte," Elizabeth greeted, her voice light and cheerful. "I hope you are well today."

Charlotte looked up, her expression brightening. "Good morning, Lizzy! It is so good to see you." She set the flowers aside and motioned for Elizabeth to sit beside her. "How are the wedding preparations coming along?"

Elizabeth took a seat, smoothing her skirts as she did so. "As well as can be expected, I suppose. Mary is... content, and Mama is beside herself with excitement, as you can imagine."

Charlotte smiled, but it did not reach her eyes. "I am glad to hear it. Mary deserves all the happiness in the world, and Mr Collins... well, he will be a dutiful husband, I am sure."

Elizabeth watched her friend closely, noting the forced enthusiasm in her voice. "And you, Charlotte? How have you been?"

"Oh, I have been keeping busy," Charlotte replied, her tone bright but hollow. "There is always something to do, you know. And Mr Wickham has been such a cheerful visitor. He calls on Papa nearly every day to discuss politics."

Elizabeth's brow furrowed slightly. "Mr Wickham? I did not know he was so interested in politics."

Charlotte nodded, a small smile playing at her lips. "Yes, he seems quite passionate about it. But he always makes time to sit with me for a few minutes and take tea before he goes. It is... pleasant."

Elizabeth narrowed her eyes, her scepticism growing. "Any gentleman would likely do the same, Charlotte. It is only polite. Surely, your mother and Maria join you in hosting him."

"Oh, no. Maria keeps quite away—I think Papa told her to—and Mama always finds some convenient excuse for leaving the room. And still, he remains!"

"He..." Elizabeth cleared her throat delicately. "He can hardly leave in the middle of tea. It would be shockingly rude."

"But he stays much longer than a quarter-hour. He truly fancies my conversation," Charlotte insisted, her eyes shining with a fervent belief. "Did you not say yourself that he seemed like someone who valued good conversation over a pretty face when we first met him?"

Elizabeth hesitated, searching for the right words. She did not want to hurt Charlotte's feelings, but she could not help but feel uneasy about Mr Wickham's intentions. "I did say that, but..."

Charlotte's face fell, the brightness dimming. "But what, Lizzy? You think he could not possibly fancy someone plain and old like me?"

Elizabeth stiffened, her cheeks burning scarlet. "No, indeed! If anyone says such things about you, why I—"

"It is only the truth." Charlotte sighed. "I am plain. I always have been."

"But you are clever and honest."

Charlotte's brows arched. "I am also entirely on the shelf unless, by some miracle, there exists a gentleman tall enough to reach me."

Elizabeth made a tight smile. "And you think Mr Wickham might be that gentleman?"

Charlotte cast her eyes to the floor, then lifted her shoulders. "Do you think I am being foolish?"

Elizabeth forced a smile, shaking her head. "No, Charlotte. I do not think you are foolish. I just... I worry, that is all. I encouraged you to pursue Collins, and that was a foolish quest if there ever was one. Perhaps I ought to stay out of the matchmaking business."

Charlotte's expression softened, and she reached out to squeeze Elizabeth's hand. "Do you know, I wondered if you would try to warn me off for a different reason altogether."

"And what reason would that be?"

Charlotte's eyes flared, and she dipped her head forward in a conscious gesture. "You know."

"I am afraid I do not."

Charlotte widened her eyes again. "Him! I... well, Lizzy, everyone is talking about you and Mr Wickham as if the matter is settled."

Elizabeth sat back in her seat. "The matter is most assuredly not settled. And what do you mean, 'everyone'? The only person I ever heard make such assumptions was Mama, and you know as well as I do that she is delusional."

Charlotte's hand fell from Elizabeth's. "Well, I am sure it was Mrs Philips and Mrs Long too, but... there, I suppose they must be mistaken." She chewed her lip. "Lizzy, are you sure? I should hate to think I might be hurting my friend if... you know."

Elizabeth frowned. "I think we can safely say that I will not be hurt."

Mr Wickham, however... that man might deserve a bit of "hurting" if he wounded Charlotte.

Darcy was hunched over his desk, a pile of documents before him, the dim light from the lamp casting long shadows across the room. His study, usually a place of quiet contemplation and order, was now a chaotic mess. Papers were strewn everywhere, and Darcy's head throbbed with the intensity of his concentration and the ever-present pain that had become his unwelcome companion.

He rubbed his temples, trying to ease the relentless pounding, but it was no use. The headache was exacerbated by the stress and the strain of bending over the desk, his eyes squinting to read the small, faded print on the yellowed pages. Memories and suspicions surged through him, all centring on George Wickham and the intricate lies that seemed to be closing in on him.

Darcy's hands trembled as he rifled through the documents. He was certain there was something in his cabinet of documents, something that would shed light on Wickham's story and perhaps even his intentions. His blood was up, his heart pounding in his chest as he sifted through the papers, determined to find the elusive detail that would validate his suspicions.

A soft knock on the door barely registered in his consciousness. The door creaked open, and a footman entered, carrying a tray with a decanter of brandy and a glass. "Mr Darcy," the footman said hesitantly, "Mrs Hodges thought you might need some refreshment."

Darcy barely glanced up. "Thank you, but leave it and go," he muttered.

The footman hesitated, setting the tray down on a side table. "Sir, are you well? You look—"

"Nothing whatever is the matter," Darcy snapped, waving a hand dismissively. Then, he straightened with a sigh. "My apologies, Carson. I do not need distractions right now."

The footman bowed slightly, retreating from the room with a worried expression. The door closed softly behind him, and Darcy was alone once more with his thoughts and the mounting pressure in his head.

Hours passed in a dizzy fit of ink-stained fingers and rustling papers. Darcy's vision blurred and swam, his headache only worsening after he surrendered and sampled the brandy the housekeeper had sent.

"No, not this one…" he muttered to himself as he tossed one paper aside. "What is this? From Uncle… *'To my dearest sister'*… this ought to be with Mother's affects, not here."

He picked up another document, scanning it briefly. "Bills of sale for cattle… irrelevant." He tossed it aside and grabbed the next, reading aloud, "The tenant of Watkins Farm… compensation due… no, no."

A ledger book followed, and he thumbed through it impatiently. "Expenses for the spring planting… invoices from the blacksmith…" Darcy groaned and set it aside with more force than necessary. "This is all useless!"

His fingers fumbled through more papers, eyes straining to make out the script in the dim light of the study. "Mortgage agreements, land grants… curse it all."

At one point, he paused over a letter that looked like his father's hand, hoping it might hold some clue, but it turned out to be a missive from his great-aunt about a long-forgot feud. "Rubbish!" he exclaimed, flinging it onto the growing pile of discarded documents.

His frustration mounted with each futile discovery. "Why can I not find anything useful?" he growled, running a hand through his hair. He rubbed his temples, trying to alleviate the pressure building within his skull. It was all this dratted tumour. His memory might have been vindicated where "Halstead" was concerned, but he was by no means certain of it anymore. He might have dreamed this all up.

Another document caught his eye, and he quickly scanned it. "Arrangements for the annual harvest festival… how did this even get in here?" He shoved it aside, reaching for the next.

Pages from old account books, letters of correspondence, even a few poems penned by his mother—none of them held the information he sought. Each item was read in part, then discarded in frustration.

At last, his persistence was rewarded. It ought to have been the first place he looked—rather, it *was,* but he had not seen it before. Darcy had been so sure that he had looked thoroughly through the very depths of the drawer where he kept his father's documents that he had only opened it again now in sheer desperation.

And there it was. Surely, he could not have missed this the last time he searched for it, could he? *Had* he actually searched here? He rubbed absently at his forehead as he pulled out a thick sheaf of documents tied together with a faded ribbon.

It was his father's will—nothing he had not read a hundred times already. But within it, a separate bundle marked with Wickham's name that, at some point, Darcy must have stuck there and forgot about. His hands shook as he untied the ribbon and spread the papers out before him.

There, in the elegant script of his father's hand, was the will of Wickham's father, who had been the steward of Pemberley. Darcy scanned the document, his eyes narrowing as he reached the section detailing the elder Wickham's wishes for his son, George. As was to be expected, there was a list of all known family members, each meticulously noted, along with their circumstances and where they might be found, should the need ever arise.

Darcy's father had later penned notes beside each name, indicating the decease of nearly all of them. The remaining two—a widowed aunt in Leicester and a grandmother on his mother's side—Darcy himself had received notice of their demise.

According to this, Wickham had no remaining relatives. Darcy's breath caught in his throat as he read and reread the names, the annotations. Not one among them could match the description of this mysterious relative who supposedly left Wickham his fortune.

He had doubted his memory—for ample reason, as the pain and stress clouded his thoughts daily—but here was the proof. His father's meticulous record-keeping had vindicated him. Unless there was something that his father's solicitor had overlooked—and that was unlikely, for the Darcys paid the man to be thorough—Wickham had lied about his inheritance, about how he leased Netherfield, about everything.

Darcy slumped back in his chair, the tension in his body releasing in a wave of exhaustion. He had been right, at least about this. The truth was a small comfort, but a comfort, nonetheless.

The door creaked open again, and the footman reappeared, his expression cautious. "Sir, may I bring you anything else?"

Darcy shook his head, his eyes fixed on the papers before him. "No, thank you. I have what I need." He waved the footman away once more, his mind already turning to the next steps. He wanted nothing more than to piece together the rest of the puzzle, to confront Wickham and expose his lies.

For now, though, he allowed his poor head a moment of respite. The fire crackled in the hearth, the only sound in the otherwise silent room. Darcy closed his eyes, the pounding in his head dulling to a persistent ache as his mind wandered back to the conversations he had had with Wickham over the years, the lies woven into the fabric of their interactions. How had he missed the enormity of it? How had he allowed Wickham to manipulate him this autumn, to plant doubts and fears that had no basis in reality?

And then, there was Elizabeth Bennet. He winced, recalling the look in her eyes when she had defended Wickham. She had believed in the man's charm, just as everyone else did, including himself. And Wickham seemed to hold no little interest in *her*. There could be no doubt that Wickham intended to make a conquest of her.

That notion alone sent the blood coursing through Darcy's veins. Elizabeth Bennet might be beyond his reach—why would she wish to bind herself to a dying man? She was not the sort of woman who would be content to marry for a comfortable fortune. She expected—*demanded* more, and she deserved it. But she would not find it with Wickham if that was what she was hoping. Just like Georgiana...

Darcy sat bolt upright once more, a quill somehow finding its way into his hand. Was Elizabeth Bennet in just as much danger of being used as he himself had been? Why did Wickham seem so interested in her?

It had to be more than merely the attraction of a beautiful woman, because Darcy had seen the man dancing and flirting with nearly every woman in Meryton, some of whom were prettier by the common standards. But Darcy had never seen Wickham so gallant and accommodating as he appeared to be toward Elizabeth Bennet.

Then again, there were many things Darcy had not seen until lately.

What was he to do about any of it? He had already sent a letter to Doctor Pembroke at Cambridge, and the man was expecting him next week. Even that was too long to wait for Darcy's taste. Every day only heightened the agony inside his head and narrowed the chances that something might be done for his relief.

But... well, hang it all, Meryton was very nearly on the road to Cambridge. He could leave London tomorrow and break his journey at Netherfield. Whatever Wickham was about, he could not afford to send Darcy away after introducing him to everyone as his friend.

Still, what could he hope to accomplish? No one would believe him if he declared his suspicions—that Wickham was put into place by a powerful man to curry favour and sway votes. It seemed preposterous, even to his own ears. And it was probably the product of his addled head. A bloody shame Richard was not here to help him sound out the idea.

She might help him make sense of it. If she would listen to him.

The clock on the mantel chimed the hour, the sound reverberating through the quiet room. Darcy pushed the papers aside, his mind racing with plans and strategies.

But first, he needed to clear his head. The pain was becoming unbearable, the pressure in his skull relentless. Darcy stood, swaying slightly as a wave of dizziness washed over him. He needed fresh air, needed to escape the confines of the study and the memories that clung to every corner.

He crossed the room, his steps unsteady, and opened the window. The cool night air rushed in, a welcome relief against his fevered skin. Darcy leaned against the sill, breathing deeply, trying to clear the fog from his mind.

And that was where he found himself two hours later—collapsed at the threshold, his tongue bleeding, trousers rumpled, his cravat soaked, and the side table near the door knocked over in the apparent aftermath of a full-body convulsion.

Darcy put a shaking hand against the door frame, his eyes bleary as he tried to verify the time on the mantel clock. *Good Heavens.*

He swallowed and drew out his handkerchief to mop his face. Time, it seemed, was not his ally. His condition was surely worsening.

He crawled on his hands and knees to his desk, for he did not trust himself not to sway again and pulled himself up into his chair. Did he dare attempt the stairs tonight? Darcy surveyed the scattered disaster of his desk and found the footman's bell.

It served him right for snapping at poor Carson earlier, for no one had ventured to disturb him. But now, it seemed... well, he would have to ask for help just moving about his own house.

Bloody humiliating.

Chapter Twenty-Seven

THE STILL ROOM WAS filled with the earthy scent of drying herbs, the late afternoon sunlight filtering through the small windows, casting a warm glow over the room. Elizabeth and Jane worked quietly side by side, their hands deftly bundling sprigs of rosemary and thyme, securing them with twine to hang above the hearth.

"Did you know that Mr Bingley has two sisters?" Jane asked as she stretched for the nail in the beam above her head.

"I did not. Let me guess—they are each more beautiful than the other and so brimming with kindness and goodness that they have already undertaken to write to their brother to plead with him to secure for them a sister who is equally good and beautiful."

"Oh, Lizzy, stop," Jane scoffed as she reached for another spring of thyme. "That does not even make any sense."

Elizabeth chuckled, winding the twine around a bunch. "Well, then, what did he say about them?"

"Rather... I think the opposite. About the younger sister, that is. She has a terribly handsome dowry, but—"

"He told you how much her dowry is?"

"Not specifically, no, but he said she is in much demand because of it. I do not think he *meant* it to sound as if he were bragging, nor quite as if he meant to say that her dowry was the *only* thing her suitors found appealing, but..."

"But it sounds as though both are true, nonetheless?" Elizabeth guessed.

Jane hooked the last sprig of thyme on the nail and lifted her shoulders. "It did sound like that, yes. He was more than implying that I should not permit her to intimidate me... if I ever had occasion to meet her. Do you think he means... what I think he means by that?"

Elizabeth pursed her lips and raised an eyebrow. "You are only now noticing what everyone else has long seen. Mr Bingley hardly has eyes for anyone but you."

Jane blushed. "You are imagining things, Lizzy," she murmured, though the corner of her lips curled into a smile.

"Am I? You must admit, he is rather attentive to you, even when Mama is not hovering nearby to remind him how beautiful and accomplished you are."

Jane shook her head, though her smile remained. "Mr Bingley is kind to everyone. It is in his nature."

"Oh, indeed, he is kind," Elizabeth agreed. "But I do not see him offering to fetch punch for just anyone, nor do I see him seeking out every opportunity to stand beside them when he is not engaged in another dance."

Jane's blush deepened, but she could not suppress a soft laugh. "You are incorrigible, Lizzy. But truly, I do not believe he thinks of me in that way."

Elizabeth's smile grew wider, her eyes sparkling with affection for her sister. "Then you are the only one who thinks so, Jane. The rest of us are quite certain that Mr Bingley is very much taken with you."

"And what of Mr Wickham, Lizzy? He seems to have made quite an impression on you."

Elizabeth's own cheeks warmed slightly, though she gave a light shrug. "Mr Wickham is very amiable, and I find his company agreeable. But I believe it is you and Mr Bingley who are the subject of more speculation."

"Perhaps, but it is all just conjecture, Lizzy. Nothing more."

Elizabeth tilted her head. "Perhaps. However, conjecture has a way of leading to something more, especially when it comes to matters of the heart. There are simply too many knowing heads wagging whenever you and Mr Bingley are seen together."

Just as Elizabeth was reaching for another bundle of lavender, a shadow fell across the doorway. She looked up to see her father standing there, his expression unusually serious. Mr Bennet's brow was furrowed, and he seemed to be looking at something far beyond the confines of the room, his thoughts clearly elsewhere.

"Papa?" Jane asked. "Is something wrong?"

Elizabeth studied him carefully, her amusement fading as she noticed the slight twitch in his right hand, as though his fingers were moving of their own accord. His eyes were distant, and she could almost see the wheels turning in his mind as if he were carrying on a conversation with himself.

Mr Bennet blinked, his gaze finally settling on his daughters. He hesitated, his lips parting as if to speak, but no words came. Elizabeth and Jane exchanged concerned glances, the mood in the room shifting as they waited for him to say something.

"Nothing is wrong," he said at last, though his tone lacked conviction. He seemed to be considering his words carefully, his hesitation unusual and unsettling. "I simply thought... perhaps I might have a drink in my study."

Elizabeth straightened, wiping her hands on her apron. "Of course, Papa. I can bring it to you."

Mr Bennet nodded absently, his eyes already drifting away from hers. "Yes... yes, thank you, Lizzy." Without another word, he turned and walked slowly down the hall, his steps measured and deliberate.

Elizabeth watched him go, her heart sinking with unease. Something was clearly troubling her father, but what it could be, she could not guess. She exchanged another look with Jane, whose brow was now furrowed in worry.

"Jane, did you see—"

"I did," Jane murmured, cutting her off. "What do you think it means?"

"I do not know. But I intend to find out."

PAPA MIGHT HAVE GONE to the still room seeking a glass of small beer or mead, but Elizabeth thought the distress in his face called for something a touch stronger. She measured out a draught of scotch from the locked cabinet, then, thinking he might prefer something more substantial to sustain himself, stopped off at the larder for a small seed cake, some cheeses and cold meats. Balancing the tray in her hands, she walked through the hall toward her father's study.

Elizabeth approached the door to the study, her steps slowing as she noticed it was slightly ajar. She hesitated for a moment, peering inside.

Mr Bennet was seated at his desk, his posture slumped, one hand pressing against his forehead as though he could knead away whatever was troubling him. The sight tugged at Elizabeth's heart. She had seen her father irritated, exasperated, and even amused, but this level of distress was new and unsettling. She stepped into the room quietly, setting the tray on a side table before moving to leave. But before she could take more than a step back, her father spoke in a low, strained voice.

"Stay, Lizzy."

The words were heavy, laden with an unfamiliar gravity. Elizabeth turned back to face him, her heart tightening in her chest. She had known something was wrong, but the way he looked at her now made it clear that whatever it was, it was serious.

"I know you mean to ask, so let us not pretend."

Elizabeth moved cautiously to the chair across from his desk and sat down, her hands clasped tightly in her lap. "What is it, Papa?" she asked gently, searching his face for answers.

Without a word, he passed her a letter, the paper crinkled and worn from where he had read and re-read it. Elizabeth took it with trembling fingers, unfolding it carefully.

The letter was from Sir Harold, the longstanding MP for Meryton. Elizabeth recognised the name instantly; her father and Sir Harold had known each other since their youth, though they were not close friends, merely acquaintances who had crossed paths over the years. Mr Bennet had written to him recently, offering well wishes for his "retirement" and inquiring after his health. But the contents of Sir Harold's reply were far from what she had expected.

Elizabeth's eyes moved steadily over the page, absorbing the careful phrasing of each sentence. The letter was brief, but its tone was unmistakably weary.

My dear Mr Bennet,

I have suspected for some time that my tenure would not last much longer, whether by the will of the people or by less direct means. I do not place the blame at your door, nor at any one man's feet. However, I must admit that I have faced considerable pressure on my votes over the past two years—pressures that have worn me down more than I care to admit.

My health is not what it once was, and the demands of this position have become increasingly difficult to bear. What concerns me most, though, is the future of the office I leave behind. I urge you to carefully consider whoever is nominated for the by-election. There are interests at play that may not align with the best outcomes for our community. Take care to protect what we have built.

Elizabeth sucked in a breath as she finished reading. "This… this is not a letter of a man content with his departure."

"No," Mr Bennet murmured. "This does not sound like the Sir Harold I know."

"What does this mean, Papa? What could Sir Harold be warning you about?"

Mr Bennet's expression was grim as he leaned back in his chair. "I wish I knew, Lizzy. But I fear that whatever it is, it is more than just the usual political manoeuvrings. Sir Harold would not have written such a letter unless he believed the situation warranted it. It is not as though we were ever terribly close."

Elizabeth swallowed. The idea that someone might be manipulating the political process in Meryton was deeply unsettling. "Do you think Sir Harold is right? Is there someone behind this who should not be?"

Mr Bennet sighed again, rubbing his temples as though trying to relieve some of the tension that gripped him. "I do not know, Lizzy. I truly do not. But I intend to find out. Tomorrow evening, I am invited to Netherfield for drinks with a few others, and I expect Sir Anthony will be there. I mean to ask him whatever questions I can think of to prove his credentials."

Elizabeth watched the play of feeling over her father's face in silence. She could sense the worry and doubt in him, emotions he rarely showed so openly. This was the man who deliberately laughed at convention and provoked others for his own amusement. But he did not look amused now, and it frightened her.

He swirled the contents of the glass she had brought him, then downed the remnants in one go before heaving a long sigh. "Say nothing to Jane or the others. I ought not to have mentioned it to you, but I knew you would give me no peace unless I confessed."

Elizabeth smiled thinly. "Of course, Papa. I shall leave you to think of what to do."

He grunted, his temple leaning against his index finger as he rested his arm on the desk. But as she reached the door, her father's voice stopped her again. "Lizzy," he said, his tone hesitant, almost vulnerable. "If you think of any questions that might test the man, perhaps you could write them down for me. I find… I find I have begun to distrust my own senses lately, and I would appreciate your help."

Elizabeth turned back to him. "Papa," she began softly, "I have been wondering the same about myself. Whether I can trust what I see and hear. But I will try to think of something that might help."

Mr Bennet gave her a faint, weary smile, one that did little to alleviate the tension in his face. "Thank you, my dear."

DARCY COULD DELAY NO longer. He must see Georgiana, must ask her about Ramsgate—there was something there, some detail that either he had never credited, or had slipped through the cracks of his memory, and he could not rest until he had it. He signed the last document placed before him by his man of business and rose from his desk, though the movement sent a wave of dizziness crashing over him. He gripped the edge of the desk, willing the room to stop spinning.

When the world finally steadied, he made his way to his uncle's townhouse. As he arrived at the Matlock residence, he handed his coat and hat to the footman and inquired quietly, "Is Miss Darcy available?"

He did not want to speak with his aunt. Lady Matlock, though well-meaning, had a tendency to fuss, and Darcy was in no state to endure it. He needed to see Georgiana alone.

The footman returned with a nod. "Miss Darcy is in the music room, sir. Lady Matlock is presently occupied with guests."

Darcy breathed a sigh of relief, grateful to be spared an encounter with his aunt. He nodded his thanks to the footman and made his way to the music room, his steps slow and measured, every movement a reminder of the illness that was eating away at him.

When he reached the door, he paused, collecting himself before entering. He could hear the soft strains of the piano—Georgiana must have been practising. Steeling himself, he pushed open the door and stepped inside.

Georgiana sat at the piano, her back to him as her fingers danced lightly over the keys. The gentle melody filled the room, a stark contrast to the turmoil raging in Darcy's mind. For a moment, he simply watched her, trying to gather the strength to speak.

Sensing his presence, Georgiana turned, her eyes widening in alarm as she took in his appearance. "Fitzwilliam," she said, rising quickly from the bench. "You look unwell."

Darcy winced, though he managed a faint smile. "It is nothing for you to worry over, Georgiana. I have been unwell, it is true, but nothing serious. Come, sit with me." He gestured to the settee, his heart twisting at the lie. He was lying to the one person in the world he had sworn never to deceive.

Georgiana hesitated, her gaze flickering with uncertainty, but she did as he asked, seating herself beside him. For a moment, Darcy struggled to find the words, his mind a jumble of fragmented thoughts. He forced himself to focus, to push through the haze.

"Georgiana," he began, his voice low and controlled, "I need to ask you something about your time in Ramsgate. I know we have spoken of this before, but there are some details I must clarify. Please, indulge me one last time."

She looked at him, suspicion clouding her features. "Why are you asking me about it again? You did not believe me before, Fitzwilliam. What more can I tell you now?"

Guilt gnawed at Darcy, an ache deeper than the relentless throb in his head. He reached out, his hand trembling slightly as it closed over hers, the weight of his failure pressing down on him. How had he not seen it? How had he dismissed her so easily? "You are right," he murmured, his voice thick with remorse. "I should have listened to you—how could I not have? I failed you, Georgiana, and I cannot undo that. But please, I need you to trust me now. I need to understand. Start from the beginning... tell me everything you remember."

Georgiana bit her lip, uncertainty flashing in her eyes, but she nodded. "Very well, if it will help you. I first encountered Mr Wickham at the public rooms. It was a surprise—he seemed just as shocked to see me as I was to see him."

"He was alone?" Darcy asked sceptically.

"That day he was, but he told me that he was waiting for a friend to arrive in Ramsgate. He was not sure what day the man was to arrive, so he was simply amusing himself and biding his time."

Darcy's head throbbed with a pain that muddled his thoughts, each pulse drowning out the details of Georgiana's words. He struggled to find something—anything—coherent to ask, but the pain made it impossible to focus. Finally, desperate to keep the conversation going, he blurted out the first question that came to mind. "Can you describe Mr Billings? Do you remember anything specific about him?" It was a grasp at straws, and he knew it, but his mind could not conjure anything better.

"Mr Billings," she replied, her brow furrowed in concentration. "He did not say much about him at first, only that they were close and that Mr Billings would be joining him soon."

"Did he ever clarify what sort of friend this Mr Billings was?" Darcy pressed, trying to focus on her words despite the pounding in his skull.

Georgiana shook her head. "Not at first. But I did meet him about two weeks later when he arrived in town. They were at the public rooms together."

Darcy's vision blurred, the pain intensifying as he struggled to keep his thoughts in order. "So, you saw this Mr Billings? Could you describe him to me?"

She hesitated, then nodded. "Yes, I remember him. He was a shorter man, stocky, with very curly red-brown hair and eyes that were almost the same colour. He had the shoulders of a blacksmith but the hands of a gentleman. I thought he was striking in appearance, so I remembered him. He was only in Ramsgate for a few days before he left. Mr Wickham told me that Mr Billings had offered him an opportunity and that he had to return to London to arrange the details."

"What kind of opportunity?" Darcy asked, though his voice trembled slightly as he spoke.

Georgiana's memory faltered, and she looked down at her hands. "I do not remember exactly. I think it had something to do with being a steward for someone, but I am not sure. I wish I could remember more."

A steward? This was a dead end. Darcy's heart sank as he watched her struggle to recall the details. His own thoughts were slipping away from him, like water draining from a cracked vessel. He could not speak for a moment, the words refusing to form on his lips. He was barely able to concentrate, his mind swirling with blackness, threatening to engulf him.

"Fitzwilliam, you truly are unwell, are you not?" Georgiana asked, her voice trembling with concern. "Or is it my story that upsets you?"

Darcy forced himself to speak, though his voice was strained. "It is not your fault, Georgiana. Please, continue. How much longer did Wickham remain in Ramsgate?"

She hesitated, her eyes filling with worry, but she pressed on. "About a fortnight longer, waiting for a letter from Mr Billings to confirm the position. During that time, we encountered each other frequently in the public rooms, and he would introduce me to other ladies he had met on his morning outings. Really, Fitzwilliam, it all seemed entirely innocent at the time. Mrs Younge even permitted him to escort me back to our hired rooms, where we served him tea twice before he left."

Darcy's cheek twitched, his mind reeling as the implications of her words sank in. He could not speak; his throat was constricting with the effort. Georgiana was alarmed again, her voice filled with desperation as she continued.

"I know it was not proper to receive a gentleman, even though Mrs Younge was with me. But Mr Wickham was so friendly, so easy, just as though he were still a part of the family. I never meant to deceive you, Fitzwilliam. Please believe me."

Darcy closed his eyes, the darkness threatening to consume him. "I believe you, Georgiana. I truly do. I see now, in a way I did not credit before, how perfectly convincing Mr Wickham must have been."

Georgiana visibly relaxed, but her face clouded with confusion. "Why are you asking me all this now? What is happening?"

Darcy sighed, his heart heavy with the weight of the truth. "Because I was fooled, Georgiana. I was fooled, just as you were."

Her eyes widened in shock, her voice trembling with disbelief. "You? What do you mean? What has happened?"

Darcy hesitated, the truth almost too bitter to speak. "Mr Wickham has charmed an entire town, including some… very intelligent people… into believing he is the most benevolent man alive."

She puckered her mouth. "I… I do not understand."

"Neither do I," he sighed. "But there it is. He is living the life of a gentleman of means who is currently hailed as the saviour of Meryton in Hertfordshire."

Her face broke into a look of utter bemusement, and she shook her head. "A gentleman of means! How?"

"He has somehow stumbled into great wealth. Enough to lease an estate and essentially purchase the favour of all his neighbours by his magnanimity."

Georgiana shook her head in disbelief. "But that cannot be! He had almost no money when I saw him in Ramsgate. In fact…" She paused, her voice faltering. "I was embarrassed to tell you this before, but I gave him some of my spending money one day when Mrs Younge was not looking. He told me that his coin purse was stolen on the coach, and the bank where he kept his money was delaying on sending him more funds."

Darcy felt as though the ground had been ripped out from under him. His heart pounded in his chest, his mind reeling with the implications. "How much did you give him?"

"More than fifty pounds," Georgiana admitted, her voice small and filled with shame. "He promised to pay me back, and the day he left for London, he did return half the money to me. But I have not seen the rest."

Darcy's hands shook as he absorbed this new information. Wickham had lied about the timing of his supposed inheritance. Had he not told Darcy that he was already a wealthy man by the time he met Georgiana in Ramsgate? Or was he remembering that detail wrongly?

No, no, he was sure of it. The timing was wrong, and Wickham had used Georgiana's sympathies to live off of her until he could secure more money elsewhere. And undoubtedly, Wickham had known that Georgiana would be too embarrassed to tell Darcy about it.

Darcy took a deep breath, trying to steady himself. "Georgiana, I believe you. I should have listened to you before. You were right... George Wickham probably behaved every inch the gentleman, save for the part about taking money from a lady."

Georgiana straightened in her chair, her eyes filled with a mixture of relief and worry. "I am glad you believe me, Fitzwilliam. But I still do not understand why you are asking me all this. What is going on?"

"I wish I knew. Something is not right, and I wish I could think it through clearly, but I am struggling. It... it has been a trial of late to recollect and make sense of my own thoughts. I cannot even trust my own memory right now."

Georgiana scoffed. "What could you mean by that? You probably remember everything that ever happened in your whole life, even something silly, like... oh, like the name of Mrs Reynolds' favourite laying hen."

Darcy's face blanched as he realised the truth. "I..." He swallowed. "I do not remember," he whispered, his voice filled with a deep sense of loss. "What is her name?"

Georgiana's face paled in horror as she realised that Darcy was not jesting. "Henrietta," she whispered, her voice trembling with fear. "Her name is Henrietta."

Darcy closed his eyes and cupped his face in his hands, the realisation crashing down on him like a tidal wave. He was losing his grip on reality, on his memories, on everything he had once been. The sickness was taking more from him than he had ever imagined. Where would it end?

"There is something very wrong with me, Georgiana," he confessed, his voice barely audible. "I have been experiencing crippling megrims. The dizziness, the nausea… I have even experienced palsies, and… well, that explanation will suffice. The doctors do not know for sure what it is."

Georgiana's mouth dropped open, her eyes wide with fear. Her hands shook, and she reached out as if to steady herself. "How long before you recover, Fitzwilliam? You… you *will* recover, will you not?" The desperation in her voice matched the terror in her eyes, her fingers clutching the edge of the table as though it were the only thing keeping her grounded.

Darcy smiled tightly. "I do not know what will happen, Georgiana. But whatever happens, I want you to know that I am proud of you. You were right when I was wrong."

Georgiana's eyes filled with tears. "Oh, I care nothing for that! You must see another doctor, Fitzwilliam. You must!"

Darcy took a deep breath, trying to push through the pain and the fear. "I mean to see a specialist in Cambridge about my condition. He is the best in the country, and certainly, he will know what is to be done. All… all will be well. And I will write to you soon, I promise."

Chapter Twenty-Eight

Darcy stepped out of his carriage onto the gravel driveway of Netherfield, his limbs heavy with the fatigue of travel. The house loomed before him, its grand facade softened by the early afternoon light, yet something about it seemed slightly altered since his last visit. He could not place what it was—perhaps it was only his own state of mind, a mind fogged by pain and dulled by the effort to keep his thoughts in order.

As he stepped toward the house, his eye fell on a row of other carriages lined up in the stable yard. Only their tops were visible over the wall, but there were, indeed, at least seven other equipages all resting in the yard. Apparently, Wickham had company, and a great deal of it. His visit was rather poorly timed, after all.

Darcy paused, glancing back at his carriage. Ought he to go? Surely, he would learn nothing valuable of Wickham if the man was occupied in playing to the crowd. He had come here in hopes of securing a private conversation. But there was nothing else for it. He had already sent that letter, asking if he could break his journey on his way north, and he would lose face if he did not enter the house.

The butler, an older man with a severe countenance, greeted him at the door. "Good afternoon, Mr Darcy. We have been expecting you. Please, come in."

Darcy handed over his hat and gloves, his eyes scanning the entrance hall as he stepped inside. The air was cool and faintly scented with the polish used on the wooden panelling. No one was about, save for two of Wickham's unusually attractive "maids" bustling towards the drawing room at the far end of the hall with tea carts.

As the butler led him further into the hall, Darcy's gaze was drawn once again to the portrait that had unnerved him on his previous visit. The boys in the painting were still locked in their eternal poses, one serious, the other almost mocking. Perhaps their image *could* have been a mere chance—a strange coincidence that someone had commissioned years ago, perfectly innocent of how it might appear to Darcy. The girl, though—her resemblance to Georgiana remained disturbingly clear. The rage that had simmered beneath the surface on his last visit now flared again, prickling over the back of his neck. His head pounded with a familiar, piercing light, and for a moment, he wondered if he had made a mistake in coming here.

"Darcy," a voice called out, jolting him from his thoughts. Wickham appeared at the far end of the hall, approaching quickly with a look of polite contrition on his face. "I must apologise for not being here to greet you immediately. We have a number of guests this afternoon, and I was momentarily detained."

Darcy nodded stiffly, his mind still half-absorbed by the portrait. "No matter," he replied, a touch too formally. "I thank you for your hospitality."

"Could I do any less?" Wickham gestured with a smile. "Please, make yourself comfortable. If you wish to refresh yourself after your journey, your room has been prepared. I cannot tell you how pleased Bingley and I were to hear of your return so quickly. I imagine some urgent business at Pemberley calls you north?"

Darcy pulled his lips into a tight assent. "Business... yes. I see I have taken you from your guests, so I will—"

"Oh, no need to absent yourself, Darcy. These are all friends to you. Truly, I would be most honoured if you could join us in the drawing room as soon as you are refreshed after your journey."

Darcy's eyes narrowed faintly in the direction of the drawing room. "You have a rather large group of callers this afternoon. Something serious?"

"I should say so! The gentlemen of Meryton have gathered to formalize their choice of Sir Anthony Mortimer as their next MP. Mortimer himself is present, and we shall soon adjourn to a formal dinner. I have already ordered a place set for you at the table."

Darcy blinked, trying to process the information. The combination of travel and his worsening headache made it difficult to focus. Still, he managed to nod. "Thank you. I shall join you shortly."

Wickham's smile widened. "Excellent. I shall tell everyone we can look forward to your company, and I know I will be able to count on you, Darcy, for your clever head if any questions of a legal nature should arise."

With that, Wickham turned on his heel and departed, leaving Darcy alone with the footman, who waited patiently to escort him upstairs. Darcy followed him, each step sending a dull throb through his temples. The prospect of enduring a formal dinner in such company filled him with a sense of dread, yet he could not refuse the invitation without causing offence.

Once he was alone in his room, Darcy shut the door behind him and leaned heavily against it, his hand trembling slightly as he reached into his coat pocket for the small vial of laudanum he had brought with him. He uncorked it and measured a dose with practised efficiency, swallowing it down with the hope that it would ease the throbbing in his head.

He moved to the window, looking out over the grounds of Netherfield as he waited for the laudanum to take effect. A fresh snow was just beginning to fall over the formal gardens, coating the land in a pure, clean blanket. How could everything seem so serene when everything inside him felt so wrong? He closed his eyes, trying to focus on his breathing, on the rhythm of his heartbeat, anything to anchor himself in the present moment.

But the light behind his eyes still flickered, and the pain continued to gnaw at him, dulling his senses and clouding his thoughts. Somehow, he had to rally for the evening ahead, to maintain the appearance of composure and control. Wickham had been almost too eager to invite him to this gathering, to ensure his place at the table. The thought sent a shiver of suspicion through Darcy's already troubled mind.

He pushed himself away from the window and began to prepare for dinner, his movements slow and deliberate as he fought to keep the pain at bay. There would be time enough to ponder Wickham's intentions later—if his head allowed it. For now, all he could do was endure.

"Captain Carter is positively the most charming man in all of Meryton, do you not agree, Kitty?" Lydia's words were punctuated by giggles as she flounced onto the settee, fanning herself.

"Oh, indeed!" Kitty chimed in, barely able to contain her laughter. "And did you see the way he looked at me when we passed by the milliner's shop? I am certain he agrees about how fetching I looked in that new bonnet."

Elizabeth twisted a piece of embroidery thread between her fingers, trying to block out the shrill laughter that filled the room. Lydia's exaggerated tales of the officers grated on her nerves, jarring against the weightier thoughts that occupied her mind.

Mrs Bennet clapped her hands together. "My dear girls, how delightful it is to see you both so admired! But do remember to conduct yourselves with proper decorum—though, of course, a little charm never hurt anyone."

Mary, seated primly in the corner with a book balanced on her lap, looked up. "Charm is of little consequence when it comes to matters of true importance. A solid mind and good principles are the foundation of a respectable life. I do hope you will not be led astray by frivolous pursuits."

"Exactly so, my dear!" Mrs Bennet seconded. "After all, Lydia, you see how it came about for Mary. Perhaps it would do no harm to—"

"But she is only marrying Mr Collins," Kitty sighed. "I want to catch someone more exciting, like Captain Carter. You do not see Captain Carter lurking about the booksellers,' or reading Fordyce all the time, do you?"

Mary lifted her chin. "Booksellers and Fordyce are precisely what a gentleman should concern himself with, Kitty. A man's character is not built on mere excitement or frivolous pursuits but on his dedication to moral and intellectual improvement. Mr Collins may not be a captain, but he is a man of substance and duty, which is far more worthy of respect than the fleeting charms of an officer's uniform."

Elizabeth stifled a sigh as Mary's voice dripped with the smugness that had become all too familiar since her engagement to Mr Collins. It was insufferable, really, how Mary had transformed into a model of self-righteousness, as though her upcoming marriage elevated her to a higher moral plane.

"Do not be so dull, Mary," Lydia retorted, waving a dismissive hand. "We have plenty of time to think about serious matters when we are old and grey."

"Indeed, indeed!" Mrs Bennet agreed. "Youth is for enjoyment, my dear Mary. And your sisters are only having a bit of fun."

Jane sat beside Elizabeth, quietly stitching a handkerchief, her blank expression betraying no hint of anything like the vexation that Elizabeth was feeling. Elizabeth's mind still spun on that conversation with her father from the day before.

Her father and Mr Collins were at Netherfield even now, meeting with the gentlemen of Meryton. The selection of Sir Anthony Mortimer as their new MP should have brought some relief, but it did not. Her father's lack of enthusiasm about the man's qualifications had left her uneasy, but the fact that everyone else was so willing to endorse him with seemingly few questions asked only deepened her concerns.

Her thoughts were abruptly interrupted when Lydia's voice pierced through the fog in her mind. "Lizzy! Are you even listening? You have been sitting there with that sour look on your face for ages! Do stop being such a bore and tell us what you think of Captain Denny."

Elizabeth blinked, realising that she had been staring blankly at the wall, lost in her thoughts. "I think," she said, her voice clipped, "that it would do you some good, Lydia, to hold a serious thought in your head for more than a moment. You prattle on about these officers without a care in the world, but you might at least do others the courtesy of letting them think about something worthwhile!"

The words came out more sharply than she had intended, and the effect was immediate. Lydia's face fell, the hurt clear in her wide eyes. Kitty looked at Elizabeth in surprise, and even Mrs Bennet's cheerful expression dimmed. Jane's eyes flicked to Elizabeth, her mouth parting in silent concern.

"Lizzy!" Mrs Bennet's voice carried a note of reproach. "That was quite uncalled for."

Elizabeth's cheeks flushed with shame. "I... I am sorry, Lydia. I did not mean to speak so harshly."

But the damage was done. Lydia turned her face away, her lips quivering slightly as she tried to laugh it off. "Well, if you are going to be so grumpy, I suppose we shall just have to enjoy ourselves without you."

Elizabeth could hardly bear the sight of Lydia's wounded expression. "I did not mean it, truly," she stammered, rising quickly from her chair. "I... I think I shall go upstairs for a while."

As the drawing-room door swung closed behind her, she clutched her hands into fists and squeezed them over her face, standing momentarily in the hall. "Foolish, Elizabeth. How could you? Scolding Lydia like that. She may be frivolous, but you know better." The words felt heavy on her tongue, like stones she could not swallow.

She ought to go back and make a proper apology now, while the regret was most raw. But her blood was up, and so, no doubt, was Lydia's. There would be no sensible conversations had if she turned back now, so she pulled her hands from her face and made for the stairs. Perhaps after a good while muffling her frustrations with her pillow, she could be rational again.

Her pace quickened as she reached the hall, her only thought now to find solace in the privacy of her room. "Lydia is still young," she muttered to herself as she mounted the stairs. "You could recall yourself at fifteen. But no, you had to wound her pride instead. Always too quick to speak your mind..."

Her foot hit the stair awkwardly, and in her distraction, she misjudged the step. Her weak ankle buckled beneath her, and before she could catch herself, a sharp, searing pain shot through her leg. Elizabeth cried out, the sound muffled as she bit down on her hand, clinging desperately to the bannister to keep herself from collapsing.

Elizabeth cursed her carelessness, blinking back the tears that threatened to spill. "Stupid, stupid girl," she hissed under her breath, the ache in her ankle only amplifying her frustration. "This is what you get for rushing—no sense, no patience..."

"Lizzy?" Mrs Bennet's voice called from the parlour, tinged with irritation. "What have you done now?"

Elizabeth bit back tears, her breath hitching as she tried to compose herself. "Nothing, Mama," she called back, forcing her voice to remain steady. "I just... bruised my toe."

"For mercy's sake!" came her mother's exasperated reply. "It sounded as if you broke the stair!" Her voice shifted, and Elizabeth could tell that her mother was addressing her sisters, but still loudly enough for Elizabeth to hear every word. "Oh, I shall go distracted if Mr Wickham does not make his intentions known sooner and take her away. That girl, with her muddy hems and bruised shins! How shall I ever make a proper lady of her?"

Elizabeth's teeth sank into her lower lip as the tears streamed hotly down her cheeks. The pain was more than a mere bruise—it throbbed with each heartbeat, the strained muscle reminding her of her foolishness. She was still clinging to the bannister, the throbbing in her ankle making her feel faint. The idea of climbing the stairs to her room was too daunting now, and it would be easier to limp back down.

Hopefully, none of her sisters would think of coming out of the sitting room. She could endure only so much humility for one day.

Hobbling as best she could, Elizabeth made her way to the kitchen, each step sending fresh waves of pain through her ankle. When she reached the door, she knocked gently before pushing it open. Mrs Hill looked up from her work, her eyes widening with concern as she saw Elizabeth's pale face and the way she leaned heavily on the doorframe.

"Miss Elizabeth! Whatever has happened?"

"I twisted my ankle, Mrs Hill," Elizabeth replied. "Do you have a bucket of cold water? I think it would help if I soaked my foot."

Mrs Hill nodded quickly, setting aside her work. "Of course, Miss. Sit yourself down, and I'll have it ready in a moment."

Elizabeth limped to a nearby chair, sinking into it with a sigh of relief. As she waited for the water, she closed her eyes, trying to push away the embarrassment and the pain that seemed to swell with each passing minute. How had everything gone so wrong so quickly? The weight of her earlier outburst, the sting of Lydia's hurt, and now this—an injury caused by her own carelessness. She felt utterly wretched, her body and mind both aching as she sat there, waiting for the painful bite of the cold water and the brief numbness that might follow.

Darcy wiped the back of his hand across his mouth, the acrid taste of bile still lingering on his tongue as he sat back on his heels, the chamber pot beside him a miserable reminder of his condition. His stomach twisted again, but there was nothing left to bring up. He closed his eyes, trying to steady himself, but the room seemed to tilt and spin around him, the walls closing in like the jaws of some monstrous beast.

He dragged himself upright, using the edge of the bed for support, but as he stood, the world fractured into two, his vision doubling in a sickening blur. He swayed, his breath coming in shallow, ragged gasps, and for a moment, he considered calling for his valet. The man had just left, having seen to Darcy's dressing for dinner, and the thought of summoning him back, of admitting that he was not even capable of making it down to the dining room, filled him with a bitter sense of defeat.

But no. He would not give in to this... this weakness. He had been through worse. He would go down to dinner, would face whatever awaited him there, and would do so without the need for explanations or excuses. With a groan, he collapsed onto the bed, the mattress swallowing him up as the spinning in his head grew more intense. He lay there for a moment, his eyes closed, trying to will the world back into focus. The ceiling above him was an indistinct swirl of shadow and light, and he could barely make out the lines of the room, let alone the details.

Time ticked on, and Darcy knew he could not linger much longer. Dinner awaited him—no doubt Wickham and the others were already assembled downstairs, perhaps even wondering at his absence. The thought of Wickham, of the smug look that would cross his face if Darcy did not appear, was enough to push him into action.

With a trembling hand, he pulled out his handkerchief, dabbing at the sweat that had gathered on his brow. His skin was clammy, his fingers unsteady as they moved across his forehead, but at least the worst of the nausea seemed to have passed. He took a deep breath, trying to calm the rapid pounding of his heart, and forced himself to sit up.

The room swam before his eyes, but he gritted his teeth and swung his legs over the edge of the bed, planting his feet firmly on the floor. He stood slowly, testing his balance, and when the dizziness did not immediately overwhelm him, he began to make his way toward the door.

The hallway beyond was dimly lit, the light flickering uncertainly in his wavering vision. He reached out to the bannister, gripping it with all the strength he could muster. The wood was solid beneath his hand, a lifeline in the midst of the disorienting whirlpool that had become his reality.

Step by step, he descended the stairs, his eyes fixed on the bannister as though it were the only thing keeping him anchored to the earth. Each movement was deliberate and careful, his mind focused entirely on the task of placing one foot in front of the other. The stairs seemed to stretch on endlessly, an abyss that threatened to swallow him whole if he made one wrong move.

Devil take it, he was going to fall. He was going to fall, break his neck, and George Wickham was going to crow over him in triumph at last. Wickham, with that vile painting and all his convincing half-truths that even Darcy had nearly swallowed.

No! If all that was left to him was to call out the truth in the face of lies, then he would see the duty done before this thing in his head got the best of him. Darcy's grip tightened on the bannister, his knuckles white, and he forced his gaze forward, willing himself to continue until the ground levelled out beneath him.

Chapter Twenty-Nine

THE MURMUR OF VOICES quieted slightly as he entered the dining room, and the subtle rustle of fabric against wood signalled the room's attention shifting towards him. His vision swam for a moment, the faces blurring together, but he quickly forced his eyes to focus.

Wickham was the first to rise, a congenial smile plastered across his face. "Darcy! How good of you to join us. We were beginning to wonder if the rigours of travel had got the better of you."

Darcy managed a polite nod, though the effort to appear composed nearly cost him his balance. The room seemed to tilt slightly as he made his way toward the table, but he kept his steps measured and slow, gripping the back of his chair when he finally reached it. Bingley, seated to his right, offered him a concerned look as the footman pulled out his chair.

"My friends," Wickham said, gesturing around the table, "most of you already have had the pleasure of meeting my good friend, Mr Fitzwilliam Darcy of Pemberley, in Derbyshire."

Darcy paused before seating himself to incline his head toward the general assembly. Most of the faces were familiar—particularly Sir William Lucas on his left, Mr Philips across the table from him, and Mr Bennet just beyond.

Wickham extended a hand towards a new gentleman to his right. "Darcy, you have not met our guest of honour this evening. May I present to you our candidate, Sir Anthony Mortimer?"

Darcy hesitated, his gaze shifting to the far end of the table where Sir Anthony sat. He blinked, forcing his vision to clear, and saw that Sir Anthony was a full head shorter than Wickham, with auburn hair and a burly physique. His breath died in his chest. Sir Anthony's appearance matched perfectly with Georgiana's description of Wickham's "friend," Mr Billings.

Darcy shook his head... a thing he regretted almost instantly, but could he trust his memory on this point? Surely, he could not have remembered those details incorrectly. The shoulders of a blacksmith but the hands of a gentleman...

There could be no mistake. It *must* be the same man, for, as Georgiana had said, he had a rather distinctive look to him. Not a face anyone would forget easily, to be sure.

Darcy's hands began to tremble, and he quickly clasped them together to steady himself. With great effort, he inclined his head in a bow. "Sir Anthony," he greeted, his voice just loud enough to carry across the room.

"Mr Darcy," Sir Anthony replied, nodding in return, his gaze sharp and appraising. "I have heard much of you. We are pleased you could join us for this evening."

"The honour is mine." Darcy felt his stomach starting to squeeze and lurch again, but he forced himself to sit down, though his mind whirled with the implications of what he had just seen. The chair creaked under his weight as he lowered himself, and the room seemed to spin in slow, nauseating circles.

A moment later, a single file line of footmen began carrying in the soup course, and the room's focus on Darcy began to break up. That was when Bingley leaned toward him. "Darcy, are you quite well?" he asked quietly. "You look rather pale, old boy."

Darcy sighed, realising with a pang of resignation that if Bingley, the least observant man he had ever known, had finally noticed his distress, then surely everyone else must have as well. Including Wickham, who was now watching him with a faint, knowing smile. Darcy's grip on the edge of the table tightened.

"Merely a mild headache from travel," Darcy replied, doing his best to sound nonchalant. "Nothing more."

Bingley nodded, though his brow remained furrowed. "I hope an excellent meal will prove the only cure necessary."

Darcy managed a thin smile as he picked up his spoon, trying to steady his hand as he dipped it into the soup. The other gentlemen around the table began to engage in various conversations, most of them centred on politics. Darcy's gaze flickered to Sir Anthony again, then to Wickham, who was talking animatedly with Mr Bennet across the table.

At least Bennet appeared to be putting some real questions to the man. Darcy could not hear the specifics over the general hum of conversation, but Mr Bennet's manner was probing, his features guarded, and Sir Anthony was being forced to articulate himself about something.

That bore watching, to be sure. Perhaps the man who had sired such a cleverly irreverent daughter as Elizabeth Bennet might be the one man in the room who would not join lockstep with the going political tide.

As Darcy sipped his soup, a thought began to form in his mind. Bingley, intelligent though he was, had always been too easily influenced by those around him. Too willing to believe what he was told, and too eager to please to be confident in standing on his own two feet. Just how thoroughly had Wickham won Bingley over? Was there still any hope of convincing his friend of the truth? Perhaps he might test the waters a bit... discover precisely how strong the current was.

"Bingley," he said, keeping his tone casual, "do you think Viscount Halstead intends to lend his support for Sir Anthony's election?"

"Halstead...?" Bingley blinked, his expression briefly bemused as if he were struggling to recall the name. "Oh, yes," he said after a moment, his brow smoothing. "I am quite sure he will."

Darcy nodded, letting the comment rest for a moment before tilting his head slightly. "But wait," he said, pretending to puzzle it out, "I thought Halstead was in America."

Bingley's eyes widened as if surprised by the realisation. "Yes, indeed. You are correct, Darcy. Brokering that deal in cotton, was that right? Yes, I am sure I recall that."

Darcy's heart sank. Truly, Bingley had no real memory of Halstead but was simply going along with what others suggested and claiming the "memories" as his own. Darcy dipped his spoon into his soup again, his thoughts tangling together. What the devil was he to say now?

Between spoonfuls, he probed a bit farther. "Do you remember the time we all played cricket together? Halstead bested us both—though I must admit, it was a close match."

Bingley chuckled, his eyes lighting up. "Ah, yes! That was a grand time, indeed. Halstead was quite the player."

Darcy went quiet for a moment, his chest tightening with a sense of despair. Finally, in a voice so low that only Bingley could hear, he said, "There never was a Viscount Halstead."

Bingley looked at him blankly for a moment, then his brow furrowed in confusion. "But of course there was," he said, his tone almost defensive. "I remember him well. He bested you at chess once, and was quite the Latin scholar, as I recall."

Darcy shook his head slowly, his voice heavy with the weight of the truth. "No, Bingley. There was no such man. I can prove it."

Bingley stared at him, his expression troubled. He stirred the remnants of his soup thoughtfully as if trying to reconcile the contradiction in his memory. Then, after a long pause, he laughed lightly, though the sound was forced. "But you recalled him before. You said so yourself."

"I..." Darcy grimaced. "I was suffering a megrim, and I—"

"What, another headache? Darcy, you ought to see a doctor."

Darcy gritted his teeth. "I have, and it is... they are not... unmanageable."

"Gracious, how often has this been happening? Perhaps... egad, I hesitate to say it, but perhaps your memory is not what it was? Nothing to be ashamed of, to be sure. How could you be expected to think clearly when your head is splitting?"

Darcy's temper flared, and he clamped his jaw against the indignant outburst that was fore on his tongue. "Bingley, I am quite serious. You have been induced to believe you remember something that never happened simply because the events are hazy enough in your mind, and you refuse to disoblige someone. Viscount Halstead does not exist."

"No, no, Darcy, I am sure there is some simple explanation. An innocent misunderstanding, that is all. I think he went by Reginald when we knew him—perhaps he had not inherited the title yet. Egad, why are you so fixed on this? What matters it if Wickham and I remember a man that you do not recall? You act as if it was something of the greatest import." Bingley lifted his spoon to his mouth again, his forehead crumpling appreciatively. "I say, there is nothing to match Nicholls' white soup."

Darcy sighed, feeling the last shred of hope slip away. He had lost Bingley to Wickham's influence. As the servants began to clear the soup course, a crushing sense of defeat settled over him. How was he to convince anyone that they were being lied to if even Bingley would not listen to the truth?

ELIZABETH'S EYES ROVED AROUND the dimly lit kitchen as her fingers drummed on the work table. Her swollen ankle was still propped up on a stool, the tightness in her skin making every throb of pain feel like a knife twisting. She bit down on her lip, trying to hold back the tears that threatened to spill over. It seemed the ache in her ankle had only intensified as the evening wore on, the skin now flushed red and angry, the swelling so pronounced that even the slightest movement sent waves of agony shooting up her leg. How could she have been so foolish? The ankle had only just begun to mend, but in her rush to escape the embarrassment of the drawing room, she had managed to undo weeks of careful healing.

She gingerly touched the swollen joint, wincing at the tenderness there. To make matters worse, her knee was now sore as well, a dull ache that pulsed with every heartbeat. She must have banged it when she stumbled on the stairs earlier. A fresh wave of frustration welled up inside her, and she squeezed her eyes shut, willing herself to keep the tears at bay.

She had missed supper with her mother and sisters. Not that Mrs Hill let her go hungry, but she had tendered the excuse that she was in her room, not feeling well and wishing to be left alone. And now, it had grown so late that no one cared to ask where she was. The rest of the family had long since retired upstairs for the night, all probably assuming that she was in a temper or asleep.

That was just as well. Not that she did not wish to apologise—she owed Lydia that much—but she did not want anyone to worry, least of all Jane. If Jane discovered she had hurt herself again, she would insist on staying with her, fussing over her until she was tucked safely into bed. Elizabeth loved her sister dearly, but tonight, she could not bear the thought of being coddled. She had let them all go to bed, and now, it was probably safe to follow.

As she prepared to make the arduous journey upstairs, she heard the front door creak open. Her father had returned from Netherfield. Elizabeth turned to Mrs Hill, who had been quietly bustling about the kitchen, and asked in a low voice, "Mrs Hill, would you help me to the door? I should like to greet Papa."

Mrs Hill hesitated, her gaze flickering to Elizabeth's swollen ankle with concern. "Are you sure, Miss Lizzy? You're in no state to be moving about."

Elizabeth forced a small, strained smile. "It is nothing, really. I just want to see him for a moment."

With Mrs Hill's support, Elizabeth managed to shuffle to the door, biting down on the inside of her cheek to stifle a gasp of pain with every small hop. She was exhausted but could not resist the thought of seeing her father and perhaps gleaning some news of what had happened at Netherfield.

As Mr Bennet stepped into the house, Elizabeth could immediately see the weariness etched into his features. He greeted her with an indifferent nod, already lost in his own thoughts, but the shuffling sound she made as she approached him caught his attention. He paused, his tired eyes narrowing slightly as he took in the way she was leaning on Mrs Hill's shoulder and the awkward way she was moving.

"Lizzy," he sighed and shook his head, with the ghost of a smile playing at his lips, "what have you done to yourself this time?"

Elizabeth tried to brush it off with a wave of her hand. "Oh, truly nothing, Papa. Just my usual way of seeking attention, you know."

Mr Bennet chuckled softly, though the sound was heavy with exhaustion. He looked over at Mrs Hill and nodded his thanks. "That will be all, Mrs Hill. I shall take care of Lizzy from here. I know she means to corner me in my study before going to bed anyway."

Mrs Hill hesitated for a moment, her eyes lingering on Elizabeth with concern, but then she bobbed a quick curtsey and quietly excused herself, leaving them alone in the dimly lit hallway.

Elizabeth leaned heavily on her father's arm as he guided her into the drawing room, wincing with each step. Instead of leading her to the usual hard-backed chair in his study, Mr Bennet directed her toward the comfortable sofa by the window. With a soft groan of relief, Elizabeth sank into the cushions, easing her aching ankle onto a pillow.

"Thank you, Papa," she said with a teasing smirk as she adjusted the pillow. "You take great care to hide how considerate you can be when you choose."

Mr Bennet scoffed lightly. "Considerate? Lizzy, you mistake me. I have never found but that good, considerate people are taken advantage of. Put out and inconvenienced and occasionally even truly disadvantaged. No, no, I prefer to remain careless and indifferent, and I must say it has worked rather well these past twenty years."

Elizabeth sighed and shifted on the sofa, shaking her head. "You have not fooled as many people as you think you have."

"Hmm." He moved toward the fireplace, his movements slower than usual, and took up the poker to stoke the dying embers. The faint glow brightened under his efforts, sending a warm light flickering through the dim room. Elizabeth watched him, her eyes softening. Beneath his gruff exterior, her father had always been more caring than he let on.

But then, as he straightened and set the poker aside, she noticed the weariness in his expression. He sighed deeply, sinking into the chair opposite her, his shoulders sagging as he rubbed his forehead.

"I may have to reconsider that strategy," he murmured.

She shifted again, wincing as a sharp pain shot through her ankle. "Why do you say that? What happened at dinner?"

"Well, Sir Anthony Mortimer is a clever man, I will give him that. He answered all my questions with a certain eloquence, but..."

"But what?" Elizabeth pressed, her curiosity piqued. "What questions did you ask him?"

Mr Bennet sighed again. "I asked Sir Anthony about the allocation of funds for rural development, specifically for Meryton. I wanted to see if he was genuinely invested in our town's interests or if he would be more inclined to divert funds to the cities for larger, more prestigious projects."

Elizabeth nodded. "And how did he respond?"

Mr Bennet leaned back, his gaze growing distant as he recounted the conversation. "He said that rural development was indeed important and that he would make sure it was given due consideration. But he also emphasized the need to support urban growth, claiming it was essential for the overall prosperity of the nation. He talked a great deal about balance, about making sure that all regions benefited from government support, but... well, he provided no specifics."

Elizabeth frowned. "Did you ask him about how he plans to protect agricultural communities from the encroaching influence of industrialisation? Our tenants, and the farms—"

"I did," Mr Bennet confirmed, rubbing his chin thoughtfully. "His answer was similar. He spoke at length about the need to harmonise the old with the new, to ensure that traditional farming practices were not entirely overshadowed by industrial advances. He mentioned something about promoting technological innovation that could benefit agriculture. He went on for a long while about it. All very clever, naturally."

"What about your question regarding the upcoming legislation on land enclosures? The farmers are all deeply invested in the outcome of that."

Mr Bennet nodded slowly. "Ah, yes, I did ask about that. He gave what I suppose was a reassuring answer, saying he understood the concerns and that any legislation would be carefully considered to protect the interests of landowners and tenants alike. But when I pressed him on how he intended to vote on the issue, he said he would consult with his colleagues and weigh all perspectives before making a decision."

Elizabeth pursed her lips, absorbing the details. "It all sounds rather positive on the surface," she began slowly. "He sounds a… a prudent man. But, Papa, did he really answer your questions? It seems to me that he said a lot of words without actually giving you any clear answers."

Mr Bennet thinned his lips and nodded, a glimmer of approval in his eyes. "There, you have hit the nail on the head, Lizzy. Indeed, he had a great many fine words, but the more he spoke, the less he actually said."

Elizabeth snorted. "Well, surely, someone must think to make him commit to an answer. You cannot be the only one asking questions."

"No, in fact, it seems I am. The rest of the room was filled with nothing but praise for the man."

"But that is preposterous! He is not a pretty statue to be admired, but a man who proposes to represent us in Parliament! We must know how the man will act when he is not sitting at table with the community, when he is in London reading bills and voting on measures. Surely, someone else heard the conspicuous lack of any sort of decisiveness."

Her father crossed his legs. You would be the only other person to notice that. You, and I think, Mr Darcy, who looked rather nonplussed at dinner."

Elizabeth started, her heart flipping in her chest as she shifted too quickly on the sofa, sending a fresh wave of pain through her ankle. "Mr Darcy? What has he to do with this?"

Mr Bennet grunted, leaning forward slightly. "Darcy arrived while we were having drinks in the drawing room. He is breaking his journey at Netherfield on his way north."

Elizabeth blinked, trying to process this unexpected information. "How long does he intend to stay?" she asked, her voice wobbling just a little.

"I could not say. Darcy did not appear to be in a very conversational mood. I would not expect him to stay long."

Elizabeth's thoughts swirled. Her father was right about one thing—Mr Darcy was no admirer of Mr Wickham's, and that cynicism extended to Mr Wickham's "great friend" Sir Anthony. "Did you speak to him privately at all?" she asked, trying to sound casual.

Mr Bennet shook his head. "No, he was seated at the opposite end of the table and did not stay long for drinks after dinner. A pity, really. I think he would have asked Sir Anthony some pointed questions of his own, had he been so inclined. The man is intelligent, with a rather logical edge to his thinking that might have cut through Sir Anthony's smooth talk. I wonder if he plays chess," he mused.

Elizabeth fell silent, her thoughts racing. Mr Darcy... here, in Meryton again, and just when everything seemed to be falling apart. "Did he look... ill to you?" she asked after a moment, her concern slipping into her voice.

Her father paused, his gaze sharpening as his thoughts refocused. "Perhaps... now that you mention it. He did seem a bit off-colour. But then again, it could just be the strain of travel."

"Yes," she murmured. "Perhaps."

"Well, it is not for us to puzzle out, I suppose. Neither is Sir Anthony, who, I imagine, will run his election quite uncontested." Her father stood, moving toward the sideboard to pour himself a drink. As he passed back in front of her, he paused, his expression softening. "You ought to go to bed, Lizzy. You need the rest, and I shan't be good company tonight." He set his drink back on the side table, then extended a hand to help her up.

Elizabeth blinked out of a brief reverie, then nodded. "Yes, I think you are right."

As her father extended his arm, Elizabeth accepted it with a quiet nod, determined to hide the sharp pang in her ankle with every step. She found herself relying on his support more than she intended, the pain intensifying with each movement. The throb in her ankle deepened, and she bit down on the inside of her cheek to keep from wincing.

With every lift of her foot, the swelling in her ankle tightened uncomfortably against the confines of her stockings, the ache intensifying as she struggled to keep her balance. Her grip on her father's arm tightened, and she fought back a wince, her breath coming in shallow, uneven gasps. The stairs seemed to stretch on endlessly, and she focused on the bannister, trying to will herself up each step without faltering.

Her father glanced at her with concern, but Elizabeth kept her gaze down, not wanting him to see the strain etched on her face. She couldn't help but recall Mr Darcy's words from their conversation, the way he had mentioned his own pain, the throbbing in his head that had made him retreat from their company. How similar it felt now, this relentless pounding that seemed to consume her entire being, making each movement an ordeal.

Finally, they reached the landing. The last few steps to her room felt like a final trial, and by the time she sank onto the edge of her bed, her ankle was screaming in protest. She closed her eyes for a moment, trying to steady herself, and whispered a faint thanks to her father, her voice tight with exhaustion and lingering pain.

Her father lingered long enough to say, "Good night, Lizzy. Sleep well," before he closed the door. Elizabeth dropped backwards onto her pillow, hissing in pain as she lifted her ankle to lie on top of the bed.

Sleep was the last thing on her mind. All she could think of was Mr Darcy. What had brought him back to Meryton so soon, and why was he going north again so suddenly? Had his headaches improved? If so, what would it be like to talk to him once more when he was feeling himself, his personality not hidden beneath the dark shroud of chronic pain?

Would he smile at her again, with that warmth in those dark eyes that could make her stomach pool in her shoes? Understand her thoughts before she spoke the words, as he had done the very first day they met?

But more importantly, and much more urgently, she was aching to know what he thought of Sir Anthony. It was not an exaggeration to suggest that the welfare of their community might depend on clear heads and honest men. Mr Darcy was... well, he was one of those, at least.

And it would be good to see him again. But if he was leaving again soon, she would not have a chance before he went.

Not unless she did something desperate, and probably ill-advised.

Chapter Thirty

Darcy awoke to the now familiar fog of illness that had clouded his mornings for weeks. The pain in his head was a dull, insistent throb, pulsating behind his eyes and making every blink feel like an effort. He lay still for a moment, hoping that by some miracle, the heaviness in his limbs might lift and the world might stop spinning. But as his vision slowly cleared, the reality of his condition settled over him like a shroud.

With a weary sigh, he forced himself to sit up, his body protesting the movement with a wave of nausea. The room tilted slightly as he swung his legs over the side of the bed and planted his feet on the cold floor. For a moment, he simply sat there, gathering what little strength he could muster before standing and moving towards the mirror.

The man who stared back at him looked like a shadow of his former self. His skin was pale and drawn, dark circles etched beneath his eyes, and his hair, usually so meticulously kept, was dishevelled from tossing and turning all night. He looked as though he had one foot in the grave, and perhaps, he thought grimly, that was not far from the truth.

"What am I even doing here?" he muttered to his reflection, his voice raspy with the night's disuse. The question hung in the air, heavy with the weight of his own disillusionment. What had possessed him to stop at Netherfield, to involve himself in matters that were no longer his concern? He already knew the answers to the questions he had come to ask. Wickham was lying, as he always had. Nothing Darcy could do would change that. Bingley, ever the trusting soul, was taken in by him—just as Elizabeth Bennet had been.

The thought of Elizabeth brought a fresh pang of pain, one that had nothing to do with his physical ailment. She, who had seen him so clearly on so many occasions, had been so quick to believe him to be riddled with spiteful jealousy.

Well, perhaps he was.

But hang it all, she had been ready to trust every one of Wickham's lies! That she, of all people, had been deceived was a particularly galling realisation to accept. He had hoped...

No, he had been a fool to hope that she might see through Wickham's charm, that she might become that one person he could look to for a kindred mind and spirit. Those hopes had been dashed, and he had no one to blame but himself.

Still, there was one consolation in all of this mess: Georgiana. She was finally able to understand Wickham for what he truly was—a master deceiver who could make an honest man look like a fraud. With his last visit to Matlock House, the breach that had opened between them had been mended. That, at least, was something to hold on to, something that gave him a measure of peace amidst the chaos.

But what business did he have trying to mend what was not his to mend? The men of Meryton were happy to be swayed by Wickham, eager to vote for Sir Anthony Mortimer—or whoever he truly was. Darcy's head throbbed with the effort of trying to piece together the puzzle. It was all too much to think about.

He pressed a hand to his temple as if it could stop the agony. The best thing he could do—the only thing that made any sense—was to wash his hands of the whole affair and continue his journey to Cambridge. He might not find any answers there, but one thing he would not find was more doubt, confusion, and questions.

He heaved himself forward to reach for the bell for his valet. He would leave as soon as possible.

ELIZABETH'S EYES SHOT OPEN before the first light of dawn, snapping her upright in her bed as though something had struck her on the cheek. Sleep had been elusive, her mind restless, and her body sore. As she tried to shift her weight in the bed, a sharp pain shot through her ankle, a reminder of her ill-fated tumble the evening before. The throbbing had mercifully subsided, but the pain lingered, a dull ache that flared whenever she attempted to flex it.

She pulled the covers back and gingerly swung her legs over the side of the bed. Her ankle was still swollen, and the idea of forcing it into a stocking seemed impossible. The skin was an ugly mottling of purple and green, stretched and hot over the swelling. There was no possible way she could bend the joint enough to pull the wool stocking up over it. Wincing, she reached for one of her stockings and, with some effort, managed to stretch it enough to wrap around the tender joint as a makeshift bandage. To her surprise, the added support offered some relief, the pain less intense when she shifted her foot.

Ordinarily, she would have waited for the maid to arrive to help her dress and pin up her hair after tending to Jane, but Elizabeth could not bear the thought of waiting idly. A wild scheme had formed in her mind during the sleepless hours of the night, a plan so reckless that even in the light of day, it seemed half-mad. But her need to speak with Mr Darcy before he left—before it was too late to question him about Mr Wickham and Sir Anthony—overpowered her sense of caution.

Dressing herself quickly, Elizabeth clutched the bedpost for support as she tugged on her gown, the pain in her ankle sharp but bearable. She ran her fingers hastily through her hair, twisting it into a simple knot at the nape of her neck. Her heart pounded with anticipation as she made her way to the door, determined to carry out her plan despite the foolishness of it all.

She eased the door open and hobbled down the stairs as quietly as she could manage, each step a careful negotiation with her injured foot. By the time she reached the kitchen, her breath came in short gasps, and she clung to the doorframe for support.

Mrs Hill was already busying herself with the morning tasks, heating the fires and preparing the kitchen for the day. She turned, clearly surprised to see Elizabeth standing there, pale and dishevelled. "Miss Elizabeth! What on earth are you doing up so early, and in such a state? You ought to be resting, not hobbling about on that sore ankle of yours."

Elizabeth smiled weakly at the almost maternal concern in the housekeeper's tone. "I could not sleep, Mrs Hill, and thought a bit of fresh air might do me some good."

Mrs Hill's eyes narrowed with suspicion, but she said nothing at first. Instead, she motioned to a small pot simmering on the hearth. "I've made some willow bark tea for you. It will help with the pain and swelling."

Elizabeth sighed, knowing she could not refuse. Mrs Hill had been like a second mother to her, and there was no point in arguing with the woman when she took on such a tone. She lowered herself into a chair, accepting the steaming cup gratefully. The warmth seeped into her hands as she sipped the bitter liquid, trying not to make a face at the taste.

Mrs Hill stood over her, arms crossed, watching Elizabeth with a mixture of concern and exasperation. "Now, Miss Lizzy, what are you really about this morning? You've never been one to rise before the sun unless there was something on your mind."

Elizabeth set the cup down and looked up at Mrs Hill with a determined smile. "You know me too well, Mrs Hill. I need a favour. Could you ask Mr Hill to saddle my father's horse? I have a bit of business to attend to this morning."

The request left Mrs Hill momentarily speechless. She stared at Elizabeth, her brows knitted together in confusion. "Saddle a horse? Miss Elizabeth, surely you don't mean to go riding in your condition. And without your father's leave?"

Elizabeth's smile wavered, but she held her ground. "It is the first morning all week that the skies have not threatened snow or rain, and I am aching for a little fresh air."

"Fresh air, she says!" Mrs Hill shook her head as she turned back to her stove. "You will fall off that wretched horse again, and this time, you will catch your death out there in a snow drift."

"Nonsense! That horse and I came to a slight understanding, and I am certain the chill will do my ankle some good."

Mrs Hill looked over her shoulder at Elizabeth as if she had lost her senses. "I've no authority to question you, Miss, but this does seem rather unwise. You can hardly stand, let alone ride."

Elizabeth reached for her cup again, more to steady herself than anything else. "Please, Mrs Hill. It would mean a great deal to me. I shall be careful, I promise."

The housekeeper's stern expression softened, though she still looked doubtful. "I'll speak to Mr Hill, but only on the condition that you finish your tea and rest a while before you go gallivanting off. And if you fall and break your neck, I'll have you know I'll not be the one to explain it to your father."

Elizabeth laughed softly, touched by the woman's protectiveness. "Agreed, Mrs Hill. I will be as cautious as a mouse."

With a resigned sigh, Mrs Hill turned to the door. "Very well, I'll have Mr Hill see to it. But mark my words, Miss Elizabeth, this is a fool's errand if ever I've seen one."

Yes, yes, it probably was that. Elizabeth sipped her tea, the warmth spreading through her body, though it did little to ease the trepidation gnawing at her heart. This plan of hers was indeed foolish, but it was all she had left to grasp at before Mr Darcy slipped through her fingers once more.

DARCY DESCENDED THE STAIRS slowly, each step deliberate as he tried to steady himself with only one hand on the bannister. The headache from the night before had lessened to a dull throb, but his mind remained clouded, thoughts scattered like the mist that clung to the early morning air.

He ought to be able to function just well enough to take his leave. It was not the fact-seeking mission he had determined upon when he left London, but... well, a number of things were falling short of his expectations lately. He could hardly turn the entire world to his liking. If he could just keep his dignity intact long enough to thank his host, bid Bingley farewell and mount his carriage for Cambridge, he could...

But as he reached the bottom of the stairs, Wickham was there, waiting for him.

"Good morning, Darcy!" Wickham greeted him with a cheerful grin. He was impeccably dressed, his coat buttoned neatly and his cravat tied with precision. There was no trace of sleep in his expression; it was as if he had been waiting for this very moment. "I thought you might be up and about early. I hoped we could have a word before the others are stirring."

Darcy's scepticism flared instantly. Wickham's presence at such an hour, his overly affable demeanour—it all set Darcy on edge. He was well aware that he was not at his best, and the realisation was beginning to dawn on him that he had underestimated Wickham for far too long. The man before him was no longer the charming rogue Darcy had once known; he was something more dangerous.

Yet, to refuse Wickham's request would be to show weakness, and Darcy could not afford that. "Very well," he replied.

Wickham's smile widened as he gestured towards the study. "This way, then. I assure you, it will not take long."

The study was dimly lit, the curtains still drawn against the early morning light. Wickham moved behind the desk, the polished wood gleaming in the shadows. He gestured for

Darcy to take a seat, and Darcy complied, though the act of sitting felt like a concession—a ceding of power to the man who now stood before him.

Wickham positioned himself behind the desk, placing Darcy on the other side as though he were some sort of a supplicant. The humiliation of the moment prickled at Darcy's pride, but he kept his expression neutral, determined not to let Wickham see how deeply it unsettled him.

Wickham reached into a drawer and pulled out a small, elegant box, which he placed on the desk between them. With a flick of his wrist, he opened it to reveal a row of cigars, each meticulously rolled. He selected one and held it out to Darcy. "I know we've not even broken our fasts yet, but these are quite exceptional. A gift from a friend. I thought you might appreciate one before you go."

Darcy declined with a curt shake of his head, but his gaze lingered on the cigars. He recognized them instantly—these were the same Havanas that Lord Matlock favoured, rare and costly, difficult to obtain. Wickham's possession of them was a subtle but significant detail, one that spoke of connections Darcy had not fully accounted for. How had Wickham come by such luxuries? Who was this "friend" he spoke of, and what influence did he wield?

Darcy narrowed his eyes, the muscles in his jaw tightening as he waited for Wickham to reveal the purpose of this conversation. It was new and nerve-wracking to find himself on the defensive in a conversation with anyone.

Wickham chuckled as he lit the cigar for himself. "Yes, of course, a terrible vice, particularly so early in the morning. But one I indulge in from time to time, especially when the opportunity is too good to pass up. Now, to the matter at hand."

Darcy remained silent, his eyes fixed on Wickham as he exhaled a plume of smoke.

"I must say, Darcy," Wickham began, his tone suddenly warmer, almost deferential, "I have always admired your influence, your standing. Few men have managed to maintain such a sterling reputation, especially in our circles. I probably never said as much, but it is something I have always looked up to."

Our circles? So, Wickham truly thought them equals now, did he? And Darcy had not sufficient faculties at the moment to debate the man as he once might have. His head felt like someone had driven an ice pick into his eye socket, and the best strategy he could think of was to simply nod, keep his expression neutral, and listen to whatever Wickham wanted to say without giving anything away.

Wickham leaned forward slightly, his voice taking on a more earnest note. "I find myself in a position where your support could make a world of difference. You see, Sir Anthony's campaign is gaining momentum, but what we really need is an endorsement from someone of your calibre. Your name alone carries weight beyond Meryton—weight that could tip the scales in our favour."

Darcy's chest tightened. The request was not unexpected, but the directness of it still caught him off guard. He hesitated, choosing his words carefully. "I have never been one to involve myself in politics, Wickham. I prefer to leave such matters to those more inclined."

Wickham's smile faltered for a brief moment before he recovered, leaning back in his chair. "I understand your reluctance, Darcy; truly, I do. But this is about more than politics—it's about the future of this community. I have seen how much you care for Pemberley and its people. Meryton deserves the same consideration, don't you think?"

Darcy's temple throbbed as Wickham's words continued to flow, each one carefully crafted to appeal to Darcy's sense of duty. The blighter certainly knew how to make him do as he desired.

"I did not think the election was even contested." It was a costly effort, but Darcy had forced his tone to remain light and even, rather than accusatory.

"There is, in fact, a challenger, though he does not enjoy the same level of support as Sir Anthony."

Darcy frowned. "It still does not sound as though you have any need for concern."

"Oh, as to that, there are two or three sceptics—unfortunately, men of intelligence and influence. Mr Bennet, for one. I am sure you saw as much last night, and I daresay the fellow is twice as clever as his brother-in-law, so there is no help to be found from Philips in swaying him. I tell you, there is nothing like an intelligent man who fancies himself in the right. I doubt the Almighty Himself could change such a man's mind."

"Have you considered that there just might be a reason that such a 'clever' man would have withdrawn his support of your candidate?" Darcy asked... somewhat testily.

"I ask such things all the time, but in this case, I am sure of the cause. Bennet is old friends with the previous MP, and I've no doubt the fellow is sending bitter letters to anyone who will read them."

"Perhaps he knows something that he feels the residents of Meryton should be made aware of," Darcy retorted.

"And there, you have got it," Wickham agreed.

Darcy blinked. Now Wickham was... *agreeing* with him that something seemed wrong? "How so?"

"You see, people will say anything. And the more those things are said, the more they are believed, whether or not they have any basis in fact. You know this as well as anyone, I daresay."

Darcy arched a brow. "I had a prime example to observe for many years."

Wickham bellowed in laughter, his teeth clenched round that impressive Havana. "But I never could fool you for long!" He sighed and removed the cigar for a moment. "That is why I need *you*, Darcy. You can see through the nonsense to the facts."

"And what facts are those? Who *is* this Sir Anthony, and why are you so eager to support him?" Darcy shot back.

Wickham smiled. "Ah, Darcy, I thought you would have a little faith in me by now, but I see it is too early yet. Do you know," he chuckled between puffs of smoke, "I shall never forget what your father used to say. I can still hear his voice in my head, clear as a bell."

That was a peculiar topic shift. Darcy's hackles raised a little more. "My father said a great many things. To which of them are you referring?"

"Why, it was the 'Man of Principle' speech. Surely, you recall. We both heard it often enough."

Darcy frowned in thought. "There was no specific 'speech' of that nature."

"Indeed, there was. Egad, how could you have forgot? He was always saying how a man can have excellent principles, but if he follows them in pride and conceit, then his good qualities truly amount to nothing. You *must* remember that. He only said it every time he disciplined us."

Something caught and snagged in the dark recesses of Darcy's memory. That phrase, 'pride and conceit'... Good heavens, he *had* forgot!

It was true, his father had not found it necessary to discipline his heir nearly as often as he did his steward's son. But who could possibly treasure George Darcy's words more than himself? And that particular maxim had slipped his memory entirely.

He truly was losing his mind. He drove his fingers into his temple, trying for all his might to look as though it were simply a thoughtful mannerism, but in reality, he could not resist the urge to try to mend whatever was broken inside.

Chapter Thirty-One

Elizabeth gripped the reins tighter, her patience wearing thin as her horse resisted yet another attempt to steer it down the road to Netherfield. The morning air was crisp, the sky a dull grey that matched her blackening mood. The roads, still bearing the scars of the recent flooding, were rutted and uneven, but Elizabeth knew better than to think of cutting through the fields as she might have done in better weather.

She nudged the horse forward with her left leg, trying to compensate for the pain in her right ankle, but the creature baulked, its head jerking as if determined to return to the safety of Longbourn's stables.

"Come on, you obstinate beast," Elizabeth muttered through gritted teeth. "If you think I'll let you turn back now, you've got another thing coming."

The horse tossed its head as if in response, its ears flicking back defiantly. Elizabeth sighed, her patience fraying, and tried to soothe the creature with a gentle pat on its neck. "I'll have you know, I am reconsidering your future. Perhaps as a cart-horse? Or maybe pulling a dray? Keep this up, and we shall find out."

The horse, unimpressed, continued to resist, and Elizabeth's annoyance flared. She had left her riding crop behind, but now she regretted the decision. Without the crop, she had only her legs to guide the horse, and the weakness in her right ankle made that nearly impossible.

"Of all the days for you to grow a spine," Elizabeth grumbled, trying to nudge the horse forward again. "If you refuse to get moving, I'll sell you to the nearest farmer as a plough horse, and you can spend your days dragging iron blades through mud instead of taking pleasant little jaunts with me." The horse flicked its tail but otherwise ignored her threats.

She shifted her foot within the stirrup, and a sharp pain shot up her leg, making her wince. Biting back a groan, she lifted her foot out of the stirrup and let it dangle, hoping the relief from the pressure might ease the ache. And, of course, the horse took advantage of the weakness in her right leg to duck in that direction.

"Oh, no, do not concern yourself with me," she muttered, her irritation bubbling over as she tugged his head back toward Netherfield. "Just managing to stay in the saddle, no thanks to you."

The horse snorted, its ears twitching as it continued to resist her guidance. Elizabeth tightened her grip on the reins and forced herself to take a steadying breath. The last thing she needed was for the horse to pick up on her agitation and make a dash back toward Longbourn.

As she finally managed to guide the horse closer to Netherfield, Elizabeth's thoughts raced, panic rising in her chest as she realised she had no clear plan for what she was about to do. "Brilliant, Lizzy," she muttered to herself. "Ride out here with no plan, no crop, and no common sense. What could possibly go wrong?" The horse twitched its ears, as if mocking her self-recrimination.

In the past, she had often come across Mr Darcy during her walks, their encounters seeming almost serendipitous. But today, with the weather colder and the threat of rain in the air, there was no guarantee he would be out walking. His departure from Netherfield was imminent, and she had heard nothing to suggest he intended to linger any longer than necessary. Time was not on her side.

Elizabeth glanced up at the grey sky, her breath clouding in the chilly air. "If this turns into a wild goose chase, I'm blaming you," she told the horse, who seemed utterly unbothered by the accusation. The creature suddenly snorted, tugging on the reins in a clear attempt to turn around. "Oh no, you don't," Elizabeth snapped, pulling back and guiding the horse toward the driveway that led to Netherfield. "I'll drag you by the reins if I have to. You're getting me to that house, or so help me, I'll—" She cut herself off, realising she had no real threat to offer.

The horse, sensing her determination, seemed to relent a little, but Elizabeth knew better than to trust it. "Better," she muttered. "But don't think I'm above bribery. There is an extra apple in it for you if we make it there without incident."

As Netherfield finally came into view, Elizabeth's heart pounded with a mix of apprehension and determination. She needed to think, to find a way to approach Mr Darcy without drawing too much attention. But how?

"ARE YOU WELL, DARCY?"

Darcy dropped his hand, clearing his throat. "Perfectly."

Wickham's eyes narrowed faintly. "Indeed. Well, I am sure reflecting on such memories can still be painful. Your father was the very best of men."

Darcy thinned his lips in a forced smile.

"You always did have it easier, Darcy," Wickham continued, his voice softening. "Principled as a church deacon, even in your infancy, I declare. Whereas I..." He broke off with a chuckle and another puff of smoke. "Well, you might say that I had to take the harder way at every step. Though, I daresay I learned my fair share—more so, I fancy, than you, who never dreamed of straying from the path of rectitude."

Darcy bristled. "Are you saying that a youth squandered in vice and sloth could possibly be better preparation for assuming the mantle of duty later in life?"

Wickham laughed heartily as he removed the cigar from his mouth to flick off a bit of ash. "I see I have provoked you. I only meant that a man learns from his mistakes, but if he has never made any considerable missteps, why, he may well possess the same wisdom but perhaps lack the depth of understanding that a man only gains by dragging himself back to the straight and narrow inch by painful inch."

Darcy shifted in his chair. "What do you truly want, Wickham?"

Wickham half-smiled. "I am still learning, Darcy. Even now, at nearly thirty years of age, I find myself in need of your guidance—your approval. I am now navigating a world that is still new to me, and as valuable as some of the mistakes of my past have proved to be, I would rather not make them now while I have others who depend on me. I could use a steady hand like yours to help me see it through."

Darcy's unease solidified into something colder, more decisive. He might not have the ability to stop whatever was happening, but he had no intention of lending his support to Wickham's endeavours. The thought of being manipulated into doing so only hardened his resolve. "I appreciate your confidence in me, Wickham," he said, his voice carefully measured, "but I am not convinced that my involvement would be of any real benefit. For one thing, I harbour my own doubts about this candidate you ask me to support. And for another, there are far too many questions you yourself have left unanswered."

Wickham's eyes darkened, and for the first time, a flicker of irritation crossed his face. His tone hardened, losing some of its earlier warmth. "You know, Darcy, your pride is still as formidable as ever. I'd hoped that you might have seen beyond the past by now, that you might recognize when someone is trying to make amends, to build something better."

Darcy's jaw tightened at the accusation. He met Wickham's gaze evenly, refusing to be baited. "I am not opposed to change, Wickham, but I am cautious about where I place my trust. You ask for my support, yet this is not a cause I can fully endorse."

Wickham's expression soured, the mask of geniality slipping ever so slightly. He leaned forward, his voice dropping to a near-whisper. "You've always prided yourself on your principles, Darcy, on your sense of justice. But what good are those principles if they keep you isolated—if they prevent you from seeing what's right in front of you?"

"Oh, I see it." Darcy leaned forward in his chair, locking eyes with the man. "I see a candidate of no qualifications and murky history. I see a man who sidesteps every blunt question put to him, and I see fabrications presented as facts. I want nothing to do with any of it."

Wickham's eyes flashed with something akin to anger, but he quickly masked it with a tight smile. "I apologise if you misconstrued my words, Darcy. I have not deceived you, although we... ahem... appear to 'remember' things differently."

Darcy's expression had fractured—even he could feel the dead-white pallor seeping into his complexion, the shocked stare he could not seem to break. "What... what are you saying, Wickham?"

Wickham sighed. "Oh, come, Darcy. I have known you all your life, and something is altered about you. My money is on a woman—is that it?" He chuckled. "There is nothing like a pair of fine eyes to make a man forget even his father's favourite advice. I imagine you do not even recall the name of the first young lady you fancied."

He grinned, waited for a few seconds, and then when Darcy did not answer, he leaned forward and whispered, "It was Bridgette—that French maid."

"That is a lie. I never dabbled with the servants."

Wickham snorted. "Not at age seven, no. She was your mother's abigail, and... good heavens, we used to hide in Lady Anne's dressing room just so we could watch her shaking out the linens. Do you not remember? That satiny blonde hair she had, that smile, and that figure… Ah…" He sighed reverently and took another long draw on his cigar.

Darcy narrowed his eyes at the desk and clawed through his earlier recollections. There was… something… but he could have sworn his mother's abigail was named Elise, and had dark hair…

Egad… how much did he remember incorrectly? And if he could not remember, was he even capable of thinking clearly? Was there a chance, even the slimmest one, that Wickham was trying to make an honest man of himself and that Darcy's own faulty recollections and prejudices were barring the way?

Wickham flicked more ashes off his cigar. "Ah, well, no matter. Water under the bridge, eh? Look, Darcy, I apologise for setting upon you so. I would not dream of pressuring you into something beyond the scope of your comfort. I only hoped that you might see the value in what we are trying to achieve here."

Darcy swallowed and felt a trickle of perspiration slipping down his throat. But that was not all, for the muscles on the inside of his right arm suddenly went rigid, his fingers numb and spasming in almost an instant.

He *had* to get out of that study. Immediately, before something worse happened.

Wickham exhaled another plume of smoke, his gaze never leaving Darcy's face. "Nothing more to say, Darcy? Well, then," he said with forced cheer, "I know better than to argue with you. But know this, Darcy—I have never forgot what you and your father did for me. I have always looked up to you like a brother, and I will always treasure my connection to your family."

The words were meant to sting, to remind Darcy of the past, but Darcy was now too preoccupied with trying to remain upright in the chair to notice. The palsy had possessed his hand once more and was threatening to travel up the sinews of his neck. He could not afford even another second. Darcy rose from his chair, his movements jerky and rushed.

"I appreciate the sentiment, Wickham," he said. "I will be taking my leave now."

Wickham stood as well, his expression unreadable. "Of course. I shall have the servants prepare your things. Safe travels, Darcy."

Elizabeth's heart leapt into her throat as she caught sight of Mr Darcy's carriage being brought out from the shed. A moment more, and she passed into view of the stables, where two horses were standing to be harnessed. She had almost no time left.

She thumped her left leg on the horse's side, but not only did he not move in response, he jerked his head forward to snatch a mouthful of grass from beside the road, ripping the reins from her hands.

"Of course, you would choose this moment for that," Elizabeth muttered under her breath, glaring at the horse as it chewed in apparent indifference. She dove forward to reach the reins, then rocked back in the saddle again, trying to pull the horse where she wanted it to go. The horse, however, had other ideas, and rooted at the bit to grab another mouthful.

"Always helpful, aren't you?" Elizabeth snapped, her patience fraying at the edges. The horse's only response was to toss its head again, the reins slipping slightly through her fingers as it did. She tightened her grip, determined not to let the beast get the better of her.

She cast a quick glance toward the carriage being readied in the distance. There was no time to waste. Perhaps if she could slip around to the servant's entrance before she was seen... It was her best chance to get inside without causing a scandal or encountering the wrong gentleman.

What she meant to do next... well, that was as much a mystery as the strange panic that rose in her chest when she contemplated *not* seeing him before he left.

With a sharp tug on the reins, she tried to guide the horse around the side of the house. The beast reluctantly obeyed, its hooves dragging as if it could sense her urgency and was intentionally opposing it. Elizabeth's frustration grew, and she had to grit her teeth to keep from shouting at the stubborn creature.

"Must you fight me every step of the way?" she hissed, casting another wary glance around to make sure no one had seen her yet. The horse huffed in response, a puff of steam rising from its nostrils in the cold morning air. Elizabeth shook her head, wondering how on earth she was going to manage this. The animal seemed as intent on thwarting her plans as the universe itself.

As she neared the back of the house, her heart sank. A group of workmen was approaching, and she had to pull the horse back into the cover of the surrounding woods before they saw her. She held her breath as the workmen drew closer. As long as they were not coming in her direction, they would be gone in only a moment.

But to her dismay, they went to the back door of the house and waited for what seemed like an eternity until Mr Wickham himself emerged from the servant's door to meet them.

Elizabeth grumbled one or two highly unladylike things. Was the whole world conspiring against her? How was she to get to Mr Darcy now? Back to the front door, perhaps? But that would guarantee that she would be seen. There was nothing to do but wait where she was.

Mr Wickham seemed to be in no hurry to conclude his conversation. Rather, he seemed to be taking his time to give concise directions about something, and he was not pleased about it. His voice carried on the cold morning air, sounding uncharacteristically tense. Elizabeth strained to hear their conversation, though the words were too muffled to make out clearly. Whatever it was, it left Wickham looking agitated as he sent the men off with a curt nod.

"Brilliant. Just brilliant," she whispered to herself, her frustration mounting. It was odd, though—why would Mr Wickham come out through the servant's door? That was hardly the usual way to meet with workmen. Elizabeth's suspicions deepened, and she realised there was no way she could approach the house now without risking an encounter with him.

She tried to turn the horse away from the house, but her thoughts were racing too fast to settle on a clear plan. What was she supposed to do now? She barely had time to think before the horse, sensing her hesitation, decided to take matters into its own hooves. With a sudden jerk of its head, it pulled on the reins, and Elizabeth found herself in an unexpected tugging match.

"Oh, for heaven's sake, will you just—" She never got to finish her sentence. The horse yanked hard to the right, pulling her out of balance. With her injured ankle unable to brace her, she toppled off the saddle and into the mud with an undignified thud.

Pain shot through her ankle, and she bit back a scream, her gown now thoroughly ruined. "Well done," she muttered darkly, glaring up at the horse, who simply stared back with an air of indifference. "I hope you are proud of yourself."

Struggling to catch her breath and keep the tears of frustration at bay, Elizabeth tried to assess her situation. Her ankle was screaming in pain, and she was covered in mud. What was she to do now?

DARCY LEANED HEAVILY AGAINST the wall, his breath coming in shallow, panicked gasps. His right hand began to tremble uncontrollably, a cold shiver running down his spine as the familiar, dreaded sensation crept through his body. It had happened before—this harbinger of something worse, something that had left him on the floor, helpless and alone, with no recollection of how he had ended up there.

He could not allow that to happen again, not here, not under Wickham's roof. The very thought of it sent a wave of nausea crashing over him. He knew Wickham was a liar, a manipulator, but what if... No, he could not put himself at Wickham's mercy, not in this state. He needed to leave. *Now*. But his carriage would not be ready for nearly an hour, and he could not afford to wait.

Darcy's eyes darted around the halls and up the stairs, searching for any sign of Bingley. If he could just find his friend, perhaps Bingley could help him, could offer him the assistance he so desperately needed. But he knew, with a sinking heart, that Bingley was still abed, blissfully unaware of the agony that Darcy was enduring.

The spasms in his arm began to spread, crawling up his neck and down his spine, tightening like a vise around his rib cage. His eye twitched uncontrollably, and his vision blurred. Panic clawed at his throat as his breathing became more ragged, more desperate.

He had to get out, had to find somewhere—anywhere—he could go where he would not be seen, where he could ride out this storm in relative privacy. But the stairs seemed an insurmountable obstacle, and he knew he would never make it back to his room without collapsing.

Just then, out of the corner of his eye, he saw a maid passing through the door that led to the kitchen. In that moment, he knew he had no other choice. The servants—discreet and used to handling matters quietly—would be his only hope. He could trust them to hush up his troubles if he asked them to. While they might inform Wickham after the fact, at least he could pass through the horrors of the moment out of sight, away from prying eyes.

Darcy pushed himself off the wall, stumbling toward the door. His legs felt like lead, every step an agony. His arm jerked involuntarily, his hand twitching as though it had a mind of its own. He could feel the spasms intensifying, the muscles in his neck and chest tightening painfully.

He barely made it to the door, almost collapsing against the frame as he pushed it open with his good hand. The kitchen was bustling with activity, the warmth of the fires and the scent of freshly baked bread hitting him like a wave, but all he could focus on was finding a place to hide, a place where he could endure this torment in peace.

The maid looked up, startled to see him there, her eyes widening in concern. Darcy managed a weak, strained smile, trying to appear more composed than he felt.

"Please," he rasped, his voice barely above a whisper, "help me... somewhere private..."

The maid nodded quickly, her expression one of understanding and discretion. Without a word, she led him toward a small room off the main kitchen—a pantry, dark and cool, with a single chair against the wall. Darcy all but collapsed into it, his body trembling violently, as the door closed behind him.

He closed his eyes, his breath coming in ragged gasps, and prayed that whatever was about to happen would pass quickly—and that no one else would find him before it did.

Chapter Thirty-Two

Elizabeth watched in frustration as her horse, seemingly done with her struggles, yanked its head free of her grasp and wandered off, flicking its tail with a clear lack of concern. "Off with you then! Run off and get lost!" she fumed. "See if I care when you are turned into glue!"

She leaned heavily against a nearby tree, the bark rough against her palm, her ankle throbbing with each pulse of her heartbeat. The wetness from the mud clung to her gown, the cold seeping through the fabric and into her bones. She bit her lip to keep from crying out in sheer frustration. She had not come this far just to be stranded outside, muddy and helpless.

Elizabeth surveyed the area around the house, desperately trying to think of what to do next. The workmen who had been speaking with Mr Wickham were nowhere to be seen, and the house itself seemed quiet—too quiet for her to count on some other distraction. She needed to find a way inside, but she could not very well limp up to the front door in this state. What would she say? How could she even hope to find Mr Darcy without causing a scandal?

As she leaned against the tree, contemplating her increasingly dire situation, she caught sight of a young servant boy—no more than thirteen—making his way from the kitchen to the woodshed. It was a risky move, but Elizabeth saw no other option.

"Help!" she called out, her voice a hoarse yelp in the quiet of the morning. The boy stopped abruptly, dropping the wood in surprise as his eyes darted around in search of the source of the cry.

He hesitated, squinting into the trees, before cautiously stepping closer. As he approached, his eyes widened in recognition of her muddied gown and dishevelled appearance. "Miss? Are you... are you hurt?"

Elizabeth mustered a weary smile, grateful that he had come to her aid. "I need your help," she said, leaning more heavily on the tree. "I cannot walk on my own. Can you assist me to the house?"

The boy nodded, still wide-eyed, and quickly moved to her side. "Shall I fetch the master?"

"No!" Elizabeth's response was sharper than she intended, but she could not risk Mr Wickham discovering her. She softened her tone. "Please, no. Could you take me to Mrs Nicholls instead? I remember her to be a very clever woman, and she will know how to help me."

The boy looked uncertain but then nodded again, more firmly this time. "Of course, Miss. I can do that. Lean on me, and I'll get you inside."

Elizabeth gratefully accepted his offer, draping her arm around his shoulders as he carefully supported her weight. Together, they made their slow, painful way towards the house. Each step was a jarring reminder of how foolish her plan had been, but she clung to the hope that once inside, she might yet find a way to speak with Mr Darcy—if she could only avoid Wickham.

The boy led her through the servant's entrance, his brow furrowed with concentration as he carefully navigated the narrow passageways. Elizabeth focused on putting one foot in front of the other, her breath coming in short, laboured gasps as they neared the housekeeper's quarters.

When they finally reached the door to Mrs Nicholls' domain, the boy gently knocked, his voice still trembling slightly as he called out, "Mrs Nicholls, it's Tommy. There's a lady here who needs your help."

Elizabeth limped into the warmth of the kitchen. Her ankle throbbed with each step, the pain sharp and unrelenting, but she bit back any sound of discomfort. The last thing she needed was to collapse into a heap before even setting eyes on Mr Darcy.

And heaven help her, she was going to see him—somehow, some way—if it was the last thing she did today.

As soon as Mrs Nicholls appeared, her eyes widened in alarm at the sight of Elizabeth—muddy, dishevelled, and clearly in pain. Without a word, the housekeeper hurried forward, her hands gently but firmly guiding Elizabeth to a nearby chair. "Oh, Miss Bennet, you're hurt!" Mrs Nicholls quickly knelt beside Elizabeth, gently lifting her injured foot and propping it up on a nearby stool.

Elizabeth flushed with embarrassment, struggling to focus on anything other than the throbbing pain in her ankle and the dishevelled state of her appearance. The mud-caked hem of her gown, the sodden fabric clinging to her skin—everything about her screamed impropriety. "I am sorry, Mrs Nicholls," she rasped. "I am tracking mud all over your clean kitchen."

The housekeeper clucked her tongue, her sharp eyes taking in the full extent of Elizabeth's bedraggled state. "Never mind the floor, Miss," she said briskly, her gaze lingering on the front of Elizabeth's gown, where the snowy mud had created an embarrassing slush that made the garment cling to her like her own skin. "I'll send for an upstairs maid to see to your clothing, though I fear we have nothing suitable for a lady of your station. We shall have to wrap you in blankets until we can send for fresh clothing from Longbourn."

Elizabeth's face burned with a mix of discomfort and urgency. "I appreciate your care, Mrs Nicholls, truly, but..." She hesitated, glancing around the room to ensure they were alone. "I desperately need to speak with Mr Darcy before he departs."

Mrs Nicholls' eyes widened in surprise, and Elizabeth hastened to explain. "It is not... that is, I am not seeking an improper meeting. This is about the election of the new MP. I believe Mr Darcy may have information that could help my father, but my father did not have the chance to speak with him privately. I believe... that is, I think Mr Darcy might be willing to speak with me, but only if I can catch him without..." she cleared her throat. "I would rather not alert Mr Wickham of my presence... not yet."

The housekeeper's expression softened, but she shook her head. "Miss Bennet, Mr Darcy is not in a position to speak with you."

"Even if I make haste?" She tried to rise out of the chair. "I can make it to... oh, to the library if someone will help me. Surely, he is not already standing at the door, and—"

Mrs Nicholls shook her head. "I mean, Miss, Mr Darcy is in no condition to leave immediately. He... he is somewhat incapacitated."

A jolt of alarm shot through her. Mr Darcy incapacitated? "What do you mean?"

Mrs Nicholls' frown deepened as she deliberated on her response. Finally, she spoke, her tone cautious. "Mr Darcy is resting in my workroom, Miss Bennet. He is in some distress."

Without thinking, Elizabeth pushed herself upright, ignoring the sharp pain in her ankle. "Take me to him at once."

Mrs Nicholls raised her hand, shaking her head vehemently. "Miss Bennet, it's not proper. He asked for privacy. It is not for a lady's eyes."

Elizabeth hopped on her good foot, wobbling precariously. "Mr Darcy has been unwell for some time now. If he is in distress, I might be the only person in Hertfordshire he *would* accept help from. Please, Mrs Nicholls, take me to him—now."

The housekeeper hesitated for only a moment before nodding. She helped Elizabeth across the kitchen, down a narrow hallway, and to the door of her own quarters. Two footmen stood guard outside, their faces taut with worry and helplessness.

Elizabeth limped forward, bracing herself against the doorframe, and pushed into the room. What she saw made her heart lurch.

Mr Darcy lay on a makeshift pallet on the floor, his body convulsing in a terrifying rhythm. His eyes were rolled back, only the whites visible, and his limbs jerked uncontrollably. The room had been carefully arranged to keep the furniture out of his reach, and padding had been placed around his head to prevent further injury, but it was clear no one knew how to help him.

Without hesitation, Elizabeth moved to his side, grabbing hold of the nearest stable surface to support her weight. She dropped to her knees beside him, the pain in her ankle forgot in her urgency. She cradled his head in her hands, her fingers brushing against his clammy skin.

Elizabeth's breath caught in her throat as she watched the violent spasms wrack Darcy's body, her heart pounding with a fear she had never known before. Her hands trembled as she reached out, not knowing what to do, but unable to stand by without trying. "Mr Darcy," she whispered, her voice thick with panic as she cradled his head in her lap, gently brushing damp strands of hair from his forehead. "Please, stay with me. Please."

The convulsions showed no sign of stopping, and Elizabeth's desperation grew. She had no idea how to help, but she couldn't bear to see him suffer like this—couldn't bear the thought of losing him without ever understanding what it was that had drawn her to him so powerfully. "You cannot leave me now," she pleaded, her fingers tracing the lines of his face with a tenderness that surprised even her. "You must fight this, Mr Darcy. You must!"

As the seconds dragged on, each one feeling like a lifetime, Darcy's body finally began to still. Elizabeth held her breath, her hands hovering uncertainly over his chest, desperate to sense any sign of life. When he went limp, her heart seized with a terror so profound it nearly stole her own breath away. "No, no, no," she murmured, pressing her ear to his chest, her tears mingling with the sweat on his skin. She strained to hear, to feel, to find any indication that he was still with her.

And then, faint but undeniable, she caught the soft, fragile thump of his heartbeat. Elizabeth let out a shaky breath, her tears spilling freely now as she clung to him, the realisation crashing over her like a wave. She could not lose him—not now, not ever. The truth of her feelings, so long buried beneath layers of misunderstanding, surged to the surface, leaving her raw and exposed.

"Stay with me," she whispered, her voice breaking. "I cannot lose you, Fitzwilliam Darcy. Please… I cannot lose you." She held him tightly, refusing to let go, even as her own body trembled from the strain, from the enormity of what she had just discovered within herself.

Darcy's return to consciousness was slow and muddled, like swimming through thick fog. His mind struggled to grasp reality, his body sluggish and uncooperative. The first thing he became aware of was a dull ache radiating through his entire body, accompanied by a strange weight pressing down on him. His limbs felt heavy, his thoughts fragmented and disjointed.

Voices swirled around him, distant and tinny, as though muffled by layers of cotton. He could not make out the words, but the tone was gentle, concerned. He tried to focus, to pull himself out of the darkness, but his body refused to respond. The fog in his mind was suffocating, pressing down on him, making it nearly impossible to think clearly.

A sensation of warmth—comforting and familiar—stroked his face, the touch soft and soothing. His cheek rested against something warm, something that shifted slightly as though breathing beneath him. For a moment, he wondered if he was dreaming, the thought drifting in and out of his filmy consciousness.

"Mr Darcy... please, try to drink this." The voice was clear but distant, as if it were coming from the other end of a long tunnel. There was something familiar about it, something that made his heart leap, but the haze in his mind clouded his recognition.

Another voice, louder and more insistent. "Sit him up a bit, Miss. Are you certain we shan't send for Mr Jones? The gentleman looks nigh spent."

"No," the second voice countered, softer but firm. "Mr Darcy would prefer discretion, I am certain of it." There was an edge of protectiveness in the tone that sent a shiver of warmth through him.

The words were muffled, echoing in his head, but there was something in the way they were spoken—a gentleness, a familiarity—that tugged at the edges of his awareness. As he tried to make sense of the world around him, he became distantly aware of hands still stroking his face, a tender, rhythmic motion that soothed him even as it confused him.

His senses gradually sharpened, and he could feel the softness of a shawl draped over him, the scratch of wool against his skin. The fog in his mind began to lift, revealing the outlines of the room around him. He blinked, his vision clearing in fits and starts, until the world came into focus.

Elizabeth.

She was here. It really *was* Elizabeth Bennet, her face pale with worry, her eyes filled with something that looked dangerously close to tears. He felt the warmth of her legs beneath his cheek, the gentle rise and fall of her breath as she cradled his head. The realisation hit him like a bolt of lightning, sending a surge of mixed emotions through him—relief, confusion, and a deep, searing sense of embarrassment.

He tried to move, to sit up, but his body refused to cooperate. His limbs jerked awkwardly, and he could feel the tremor in his hands as he attempted to push himself up. "Miss Bennet..." he tried to say, but the words came out as an unintelligible mumble, thick and slurred. The humiliation burned through him, a flush of heat rising in his cheeks as he realised how helpless he must appear.

Elizabeth's eyes widened, her hands moving quickly to steady him, to offer comfort. "Shh... All is well, Mr Darcy," she murmured, her voice soothing. "You are safe. Just rest."

But there was no rest to be found in the humiliation that wrapped around him like a blanket. He had prided himself on control, on strength, and now he was reduced to this—a man who could not even speak without stumbling over his words. The feeling of helplessness threatened to overwhelm him, his mind reeling as he fought to regain some semblance of composure.

Darcy blinked hard, willing his vision to steady as he tried to focus on Elizabeth's face. The world around him still swam in and out of clarity, but gradually, he could make out the details—the muddied hem of her gown, the way the fabric clung to her form, and the shawl draped hastily over her shoulders. It did little to hide the state of her dress, and he could not help but notice how vulnerable she appeared, even as she tried to keep her composure.

Their eyes locked, and for a fleeting moment, the room seemed to stop spinning. His breathing steadied, and he managed to find his voice, though it was strained and tinged with an attempt at levity. "It seems, Miss Bennet... we are fated... to meet... when you are covered in mud."

Elizabeth's eyes widened, a hint of relief mingling with her concern. She looked helplessly at Mrs Nicholls, who hovered nearby, and then cleared her throat. "You do have a talent for stating the obvious, Mr Darcy," she replied softly, her tone caught between humour and worry.

Gently, she shifted her hands beneath his head, her touch careful and steady, as she nodded to the footman to place a pillow beneath him. As soon as the cushion was in place, Elizabeth began to rise, but Darcy shook his head, a stubborn resolve flickering in his eyes.

"No... I will not... lie here any longer," he muttered, the words coming with more force than before. He struggled to sit up, his pride pushing him to action even as his body resisted. The footman started to protest, his hand hovering uncertainly over Darcy's shoulder.

"Please, sir," the footman urged, "you must rest—"

"Enough!" Darcy's voice was low but firm, brooking no argument. "Give me your hand. I will not... remain here like a helpless invalid."

Reluctantly, the footman complied, offering his hand and helping Darcy to his feet. The room tilted alarmingly as Darcy swayed, the effort of standing far greater than he had anticipated. He clenched his jaw, determined not to show weakness, but before he could steady himself, Elizabeth was there—swift and sure, sweeping up under his arm on the opposite side, her small frame providing unexpected support.

"Easy now," she murmured, her voice a steady anchor in the chaos of his thoughts. Her presence—strong yet gentle—was both a balm to his pride and a reminder of how far he had fallen. Yet he could do nothing but lean into her, grateful for the strength she offered even as his heart ached at the thought of her seeing him like this.

Darcy took a tentative step forward, his legs trembling beneath him as if they might give way at any moment. Elizabeth, pressed close to his side, felt like both a lifeline and a fragile support. But as they took another step, Elizabeth's foot caught awkwardly beneath her, and she stumbled, hopping on her left foot to avoid putting weight on her injured ankle. She tumbled into his chest, and for a terrifying moment, Darcy feared they might both go down before anyone else could reach them.

But somehow, between the two of them, they struggled to stay upright, their breaths coming in uneven gasps as they leaned heavily on each other.

Darcy's pulse quickened, a jolt of fear snapping through his haze as he saw Elizabeth stumble. "Miss Elizabeth, you are hurt," he rasped, his voice taut with alarm. "You should sit... please."

Elizabeth pressed her lips together, her determination cutting through the pain that must be searing up her leg. "No, Mr Darcy," she insisted. "I must speak with you. I came all the way from Longbourn this morning on that wretched horse because it was too important to wait."

Her words hit him with an unexpected force, a warmth spreading through the cold dread that had gripped him all morning. Even through the fog clouding his mind, he grasped the weight of her determination, her loyalty, and the desperation that had driven her here. She had suffered to reach him.

"I know... how much you hate that horse," he managed. "I am honoured... truly honoured."

But Darcy knew he could not keep this up—his thoughts were slipping, his vision still a blur, and each word felt like it was dragged out of him. His gaze dropped, catching sight of her gown again—mud-streaked, clinging to her body, entirely too revealing. The sight sent a flush of embarrassment through him, mingling with his disorientation. "Miss Bennet..." he began, his voice strained, the words barely holding together. "Your... attire... it is not... suitable for... a proper conversation."

Elizabeth's cheeks flamed as she realised the truth of his words. She looked around, tugging the shawl more tightly around her shoulders, but it did little to cover her properly. Just then, Darcy's valet, Giles, hurried into the room, his face pale with worry.

"Sir, I only just heard that you needed me," Giles stammered, quickly moving to Darcy's side. "I came as quickly as possible."

Darcy was reluctant to be pulled away from Elizabeth, but he was in no state to hold this conversation here and now. The best course of action was to try to continue with his departure as planned, though he doubted he looked strong enough to take his leave without arousing Wickham's suspicion. Wickham would certainly expect to see him off.

Elizabeth leaned closer to Mrs Nicholls, her voice dropping to a whisper that Darcy could not quite catch. He watched as the housekeeper's expression shifted from concern to outright shock.

Mrs Nicholls straightened, clearly flustered, and responded in a tone that was just loud enough for Darcy to hear. "But Miss, as I've said, we've nothing here. Perhaps I could send to Longbourn for—"

Elizabeth quickly interrupted her with another hushed whisper, her eyes intense and pleading. Darcy strained to catch even a word, but Elizabeth was speaking too quickly, too low.

Mrs Nicholls looked deeply uncomfortable, her face etched with hesitation, but after a moment of consideration, she nodded slowly. "Very well, Miss Bennet," she said quietly, her reluctance evident in every word. "I will do as you ask."

Darcy wearily turned to Giles. "Help me... make myself more presentable. I need to... recover somewhat."

He turned back to Mrs Nicholls, who was still standing nearby, her expression conflicted. "Mrs Nicholls... I apologise for... the trouble I have caused. Thank you for your discretion in... keeping this from Mr Wickham. I would not ordinarily ask you to keep something from your master."

Mrs Nicholls gave Darcy a searching look, then sent the maids and the other footmen away, leaving only Giles in the room as Elizabeth hobbled out with a maid's assistance. Once they were alone, she spoke quietly. "Mr Darcy, I must confess... I would be very happy if Mr Wickham quit the region altogether. He is not an honest master."

Darcy's spirits plummeted as the reality of her words hit him with full force. Wickham had deceived everyone, not just in society, but within his own household, manipulating those who served him with the same calculating charm. The idea of abandoning these people to Wickham's mercies seared his conscience. He couldn't bear the thought of leaving them to suffer under such a man's control, not when he had the power—however limited—to make a difference.

"I will do something," he vowed, the words escaping before he had fully formed a plan. The promise hung in the air between them, a commitment he felt compelled to make, despite the uncertainty of how he might keep it.

Mrs Nicholls straightened her apron with a sniff, her eyes softening. "Thank you, sir, but, but you must first see yourself somewhere safe. And please, help Miss Elizabeth with whatever she is asking for. She is a good and honest girl, and I fear..." She hesitated, as if weighing her words, then continued in a low tone, "I feared that she might fall prey to my master's schemes."

Darcy smiled wryly, though the effort was exhausting. "There is probably little I can do in that regard... but I will try."

Chapter Thirty-Three

"Here you are, Miss," The maid said as she handed Elizabeth a fresh uniform. The garment was a simple, high-necked, ankle-length dress in a drab, dark fabric, accompanied by a crisp white apron with a full skirt.

Elizabeth pulled off her muddy gown with the maid's help, hopping the best she could on her good foot and slipping into the simple uniform. It was strange, disconcerting even, to be dressed as a maid, but she had little choice. She needed something dry and, more importantly, something decent, and this was all that was available.

The maid knelt before her, carefully unwrapping Elizabeth's injured ankle and replacing the makeshift bandage with a more substantial wrap of clean cotton. She had a clever way of wrapping it, bottom to top with a crisscross over the top of her foot and around the arch that was far better than Elizabeth's efforts. The sensation of her foot being more securely bound brought immediate relief, and Elizabeth sighed softly, grateful for the added support.

"Thank you," Elizabeth murmured, wiggling her toes experimentally within the new stocking. The pain had not vanished, but it was more manageable now. "Can you tell me where Mr Darcy went?"

The maid shook her head apologetically. "I'm not sure, Miss. But I'll ask one of the footmen for you."

Elizabeth waited in the laundry, the rough fabric of the maid's uniform brushing uncomfortably against her skin, reminding her of how far she had ventured from her usual comforts. The unfamiliar garment, hanging stiffly on her frame, made every movement feel foreign. The maid returned soon with a footman, who offered to guide her to Mr Darcy. She followed him through the winding corridors, her heart thudding more forcefully with each step.

Just as they reached the still room, the door creaked open, and Darcy emerged, his valet at his side. Elizabeth's breath caught at the sight of him. He was not fully recovered—the pallor of his skin still shone ghostly white, and there was a slight tremor in his movements—but there was a bit more steadiness in his posture. It was clear he was forcing himself to stand tall, to present the façade of the composed gentleman she knew him to be.

When his eyes met hers, something softened in his gaze, and a warmth spread across his features, causing an unexpected flutter in her stomach. It was a feeling that left her both exhilarated and terrified, and she could scarcely find her voice.

"Mr Darcy," she managed. "Are you... well?"

He glanced at his valet, then back at her, the ghost of a self-deprecating smile playing on his lips. "As well as might be expected, Miss Bennet," he replied, though the strain in his voice did little to mask the truth.

Elizabeth started to respond, but she became abruptly aware of the quiet attention of several servants lingering nearby, their eyes flicking between her and Darcy with poorly concealed curiosity. The moment felt far too intimate under their scrutiny. To make it worse, she probably had a foolish grin on her face. She sobered quickly and stammered, "Mr Darcy, could I trouble you for a moment of your time... before you leave?"

Darcy quirked an eyebrow, his gaze steady and questioning. "And how, pray, did you intend to see yourself home afterwards, Miss Bennet?"

Elizabeth's cheeks flushed. The truth was, she had not thought that far ahead. "I... I had not quite considered... I only hoped you could spare a moment."

Darcy's expression shifted to one of mild exasperation as he studied her. When he finally spoke, his words were gentle but firm. "I am sorry, Miss Elizabeth. I mean to depart Netherfield at once."

Elizabeth's heart sank, disappointment flooding her chest. Of course, he would want to leave quickly after everything that had happened. She opened her mouth to tell him she understood, that she would not expect him to linger under such circumstances, but before she could speak, his voice cut through her thoughts, softer now, yet carrying a warmth that sent a shiver through her.

"But not without you."

"Ensure the carriage is ready, Giles, and find out if Bingley is about," Darcy ordered, trying to inject some semblance of normalcy into his tone. The valet nodded, his eyes betraying a flicker of concern before he hurried off.

Pausing, Darcy forced himself to breathe, to steady the trembling in his hands. His gaze fell on Mrs Nicholls, who stood a few paces away, her brow furrowed in quiet concern. The lines of her face, etched with years of service and discretion, reminded him that even here, even now, there were those who saw far more than they let on.

"Mrs Nicholls," he said, "I owe you more than I can express. Your discretion has been... invaluable." The words felt inadequate, but they were all he could manage.

Mrs Nicholls gave a small nod, her lips pressing into a thin line as she met his gaze. "Mr Darcy, I only did what was necessary."

He inclined his head again, a gesture of respect and unspoken thanks. "I shall not forget your kindness."

Mrs Nicholls nodded, her expression softening with relief, and when Darcy caught a glimpse of Elizabeth, he saw a faint smile of approval on her lips. He wanted desperately to offer her his arm to the carriage, to treat her as the lady she was no matter what she wore, but doing so would draw too much attention. No, they would be obliged to sneak about and pray they were not discovered before they made their escape.

"This way, sir," the footman said, nodding toward a narrow door at the end of the corridor. "Go down this passage and take the first right. It'll lead you to the morning room—that room has been completely unused since the old master left, with the furnishings still covered. You'll pass through unnoticed and come out directly into the main hall."

Darcy nodded his thanks and moved toward the entrance, Elizabeth close behind. The passage was tight, the walls pressing in on either side, and he could feel Elizabeth's hand slip into the crook of his elbow as she steadied herself. The warmth of her touch, so delicate and firm at once, sent a shiver down his spine. The intimacy of the moment made him acutely aware of every breath she took, the soft rustle of her clothing brushing against his.

They rounded a corner, and for a moment, Darcy paused, unsure of the direction. The footman's instructions echoed in his mind, but the nearness of Elizabeth, her presence overwhelming, made him falter. He turned about for a few seconds, then, unaccountably, found himself staring at her, taking in the way the dim light softened her features, how her eyes, full of determination, held his gaze.

"Mr Darcy," she whispered softly, breaking the silence. "The footman said to take the first right."

Her voice snapped him out of his reverie. He blinked, shaking his head slightly to clear it. "Yes, of course," he murmured, chastising himself for the lapse. He tore his eyes away from her and led the way forward, taking the turn as instructed.

Darcy reached the end of the passage and paused at the discreet door that led into the morning room. He pressed his ear against the door, listening intently for any sign of activity beyond. The silence on the other side reassured him. Satisfied that it was clear, he slowly pushed the door open, the old hinges creaking slightly, and stepped through, holding it wide for Elizabeth as she followed close behind, her hand still resting on his arm.

The room was dim, the furniture draped in ghostly sheets, just as the footman had promised. Darcy hesitated only long enough to close the door behind them, then they were darting through the room to freedom. It was just then that a familiar voice drifted down the corridor outside, growing louder with every step. *Wickham.*

Panic surged through him. They were caught with no time to flee. If Wickham found them in this room, there would be no escaping the endless insinuations and probing questions that would follow. But no, how likely was that? The footman was quite right—no one used this room. Wickham would pass by in the outer hall, and they could leave once he had gone.

Darcy pulled Elizabeth deeper into the room, moving swiftly toward a spot partially concealed behind an arched beam. They were still in plain sight—there was no hope of hiding completely—but at least they were not directly in Wickham's line of sight on the off chance that he *did* happen to open the door for some reason. The shadows clung to them, but it was a fragile cover at best.

As Wickham's voice drew nearer, Darcy's pulse quickened with anxiety. Surely, Wickham would simply walk past the doorway—he never used this room! What were the odds that the *one* time he did was right now? Zero, or perhaps less! But to his dismay, the door handle turned, and indeed, Wickham began to enter the room. Panic surged through him—there was no time to hide, no time to think.

Wickham could not find them like this. No explanations for Elizabeth's attire, for why she was there with him in the first place. And he, why... he was supposed to be making his preparations to depart! Why would he be in an unused room with a woman who...

Well, there was *one* possible reason.

Inspired, he turned to Elizabeth, his hand already reaching out to pull her close, her back pressing against the wall behind them. "Do you trust me, Elizabeth?" he whispered.

She tilted her head. "I... of course. Why?"

He flinched as the door pushed open fully. There was not another instant to lose.

"Then forgive me."

Her eyes widened in shock, and before she could protest, he silenced her with a sudden, desperate kiss. She stiffened at first, a soft gasp escaping her. But the moment their lips touched, everything else faded. Her initial resistance dissolved, and Darcy felt her yield, a softness that mirrored the ache in his own chest. The world outside vanished, leaving only the heady press of his lips against hers, the raw need to keep her close.

Her breath hitched against his lips, and Darcy's heart pounded, the danger of the moment making every sensation sharper, more acute. The warmth of her body, the rapid rise and fall of her chest, the way her hands instinctively clutched at his coat—everything about her presence was a lifeline in the dark.

Wickham would see them any second. He was only a few steps away, his voice now joined by another—Sir Anthony Mortimer. Darcy forced himself to pull back just enough to see Elizabeth's face, her expression a portrait of confusion and... well, hopefully, that was desire, but he did not have the time to find out. He held her gaze, willing her to trust him just a little longer. She blinked, her breath catching, then her lips parted as she gave a faint nod.

Without hesitation, he leaned in and kissed her again, more deliberately this time, drawing her closer as if they had all the time in the world—hoping Wickham would see exactly what he wanted him to.

"Wexfield is impatient," Wickham began. "The vote is only a few days away, and we don't have enough support. How did we get here? What are you going to do about it, Mortimer?"

"It was *your* job to win their trust, Wickham. With all the money Wexfield handed over, how did you manage to fail so completely? They should have been eating out of your hand."

"They were! Especially after Bingley came. He always was a milksop, but for some reason, every mama with an unmarried daughter is falling at his feet. You've no idea the connections that softling has bought me."

Darcy must have pulled back from Elizabeth to listen. One of them must have, because they were blinking at each other again, and her head was shaking faintly. Was she trying to tell him something? But an instant later, her fingers were threaded through his hair, and she had pulled him back down to her again.

Perhaps there were better ways to hide in plain sight, but this one was... rather diverting. Darcy sighed and sank deeper into her arms.

"Then, what happened?" Mortimer demanded. "I thought you said this was locked up."

Wickham's voice, now sharp with frustration, cut through the darkened room. "Bennet. He's proving to be more troublesome than anticipated."

Elizabeth stiffened in Darcy's arms, breaking contact to hiss in a shocked breath. Darcy raised a hand to stroke her cheek, looking into her eyes with a grave expression that drew her focus back once more. She swallowed and leaned into him, her arms tight around his neck as she buried her face in his chest.

"Bennet," Mortimer replied. "You mean the white-haired eccentric I met last night? What the devil can he do?"

"You do not understand. Longbourn is the linchpin to this entire valley—geographically as well as socially. It is the largest estate for twenty miles around that has been in the same family for more than two generations. Bennet is the key to over half the gentlemen eligible to vote, and through his brother-in-law, he can sway all the businessmen in Meryton. I wager he is the only man in Hertfordshire who wields more influence than he cares to, and we have lost him."

"Then get him back," Mortimer replied indifferently. "Whatever you did before—"

"There lies the rub." Wickham paused, and they heard him pacing for a few steps. Darcy's muscles tensed, but strangely, his comfort was Elizabeth. She felt him go rigid, and she worked her fingers into the knots of his shoulders to ease him. And she kept kissing him, which... ah, that worked rather well.

"The key to Bennet," Wickham continued, "is his daughter. The clever one, Elizabeth. And I thought I had her sewn up as well, particularly when I set her off against Darcy—the chit loves an argument as well as he does—but something changed. I shall never win Bennet back if his daughter is against me, and she will turn Sir William through *his* daughter as well."

Darcy tightened his arms around Elizabeth as she smothered choked gasps into his neck. So, *that* had been Wickham's game! He stroked his thumb down the centre of her back, trying to soothe her for just another moment. Either they could remain unseen—doubtful—or they must maintain their little 'liaison' long enough to make it convincing. It did seem fairly convincing from where Darcy was standing, for Elizabeth hungrily plied his lips again as if their very lives depended on it.

"So, seduce the wench and have done with it," Mortimer said. "Marry her if you have to—come, Wickham, I do not need to tell you, of all people, how to get a woman to do what you want!"

Wickham was pacing again, hissing in frustration. "Not this one. Besides, it is too late. Did you know Bennet sent a letter to a certain member of the House of Lords, asking questions?"

Mortimer scoffed. "What contacts would a half-crazy, indolent old codger like Bennet have?"

"Apparently, Lord Matlock. The Meryton postmaster informed me this morning."

Darcy froze, his lips still brushing against Elizabeth's, but his focus shifted to the conversation unfolding just feet away. Elizabeth's breath faltered, and she started to pull back, her eyes wide with alarm. But Darcy gently coaxed her back into the kiss, his hand resting against her cheek with a tenderness that made her hesitate just long enough for him to hear more.

"Matlock? Preposterous."

"Not as much as you might think," Wickham retorted. "Collins is Bennet's future son-in-law, and Collins is a lapdog for Lady Catherine de Bourgh—Matlock's sister. No, I doubt there has been an introduction, but Bennet is the last old fool to care about that sort of formality. Regardless of how outside expectation it might be, Bennet did, in fact, write to the man."

Darcy swallowed, and his eyes found Elizabeth's. Her chest was rising in quick gasps now that probably had nothing to do with him, and fire had risen to her cheeks. If what

Wickham said was true, her father had just stepped into something larger than he could have imagined.

"You think Lord Matlock would even read something from an odd stranger who wrote on such a thin pretence of a connection about some little by-election in a town he never heard of?"

"I think Matlock would very much like to take any chance he could to meddle in the election, and I promise you, he has heard of Meryton. Besides, it's not just Bennet who is causing problems. Others are beginning to waver."

Mortimer's response was cold, his words barely masking his disdain. "You've botched this, Wickham. With the funds at your disposal, the town should be ours. What are you playing at?"

Wickham's frustration boiled over. "Me? I have done everything I was told to do, but we're running out of time! Wexfield will have my head if we don't secure these votes. You need to step up, Mortimer, or this entire election will be a complete waste."

Mortimer's reply was a low growl, but Darcy barely heard it over the pounding of his heart.

Elizabeth's fingers tightened against Darcy's chest, and when she pulled back slightly to catch her breath, Darcy didn't give her time to voice the fear he saw in her eyes. Instead, he kissed her again, this time with a purpose that sent a shiver through him. This kiss was slower, more deliberate, and Elizabeth, perhaps sensing their charade was about to be discovered, responded in kind, her lips softening against his. It was probably when she slipped her tongue over his that he groaned aloud, and that was the end of their temporary invisibility.

"What the devil?" Wickham's boots shuffled around the beam that concealed them, and Darcy's heart stopped, the kiss faltering as another pair of steps joined the first. Elizabeth's grip on him tightened, and he found himself holding his breath, waiting for the inevitable.

"Darcy?" Wickham's voice was suddenly loud, full of shock and unguarded amusement as he came closer. Darcy felt the shift in Elizabeth's posture, and that was it. No more excuses to keep kissing Elizabeth Bennet.

Wickham's laugh echoed in the room. "Well, well, well. Darcy, you old dog. I was not sure where you had got off to earlier—thought you were dressing for your journey, but I didn't expect this!"

Darcy slowly pulled back from the kiss, his heart pounding, and turned to face Wickham, making sure to keep Elizabeth shielded behind him as much as possible. Wickham's eyes gleamed with mischief as he took in the scene, and Darcy feigned a besotted smirk, hoping it would suffice.

Wickham glanced toward the partially hidden Elizabeth, still ducking her face. "I thought I recognized that dark hair," he chuckled, his voice dripping with insinuation. "Maria, eh? Always had a weakness for the dark-haired ones, didn't you, Darcy? But I didn't expect you to indulge yourself here, of all places."

Darcy narrowed his eyes. Had Wickham not accused him of lusting after his mother's abigail less than an hour ago? A woman Darcy was quite sure was brunette, but Wickham had declared that she was blonde. The inconsistency was like a sharp tack in his mind, but there was no time to dwell on it now. He made a split-second decision.

With a deliberate sway, he leaned slightly against the wall, feigning the effects of too much wine. He forced a lazy smile, letting his eyelids droop just enough to suggest inebriation.

"I was just… taking my leave," he slurred, his voice carrying the deliberate drawl of someone who had overindulged. He inclined his head slightly, hoping the gesture appeared more sluggish than stiff. "Bully of a girl, this maid of yours. If you'll… excuse me."

The subtle shift in his demeanour was calculated, every movement designed to project the image of a man who had lingered too long in his cups rather than one who had overheard a dangerous conversation. His heart pounded, but he maintained the veneer of nonchalance, praying that Wickham would buy the act and dismiss him without suspicion.

Wickham's smirk widened, but he made no move to stop them. Instead, he gestured to Sir Anthony, chuckling. "Egad, that would explain why you seemed a bit muzzy in the head when we spoke earlier. Hair of the dog? Well, Darcy, I am glad to find that Netherfield's 'hospitality' meets with your approval in some measure, at least. Come, Mortimer. We'll continue our conversation elsewhere while Darcy finishes his business."

Wickham turned and left the room, Sir Anthony following. As the door closed behind them, Darcy sagged, his entire body now limp.

He turned back to Elizabeth, who was still pressed against the wall, her breathing unsteady, her eyes wide with shock. The danger had passed, but the implications of what had just happened hung heavily in the air between them.

Elizabeth was the first to speak, her voice trembling. "Mr Darcy… you heard everything they said. They must know you have overheard them. You must leave at once."

"You overheard him, too."

"No. One of his maids overheard him—or so he thinks. Whoever Maria is, I would be concerned for her safety… or worse, if he now believes her to be a woman of easy virtue."

"More likely, he has already sampled that for himself," Darcy growled. "But I will send Mrs Nicholls a message to protect her maid. Come, we must hurry."

Elizabeth's eyes widened in alarm. "No! He knows we are in this room now. It would have been difficult before, but now it will be nearly impossible for me to get to your carriage without attracting his notice. I could sneak back through the servant's passage. Mrs Nicholls could get word to Longbourn, and I could—"

"No." Darcy's response was immediate, his grip tightening on her hand. "I will not leave you here at Wickham's mercy. We go together, even if I have to march you boldly out the door right under his nose."

Without waiting for her to argue, he pulled her toward the door, his heart pounding as they stepped out into the corridor. Like as not, Wickham had dragged Sir Anthony off to some other recess of the house to finish their conversation, but he would not be long. Unless he missed his guess, Wickham would rather quickly set about stopping Darcy from talking to anyone.

As they entered the main hall, Darcy's heart sank at the sight of Bingley standing at the bottom of the stairs. He turned, grinning broadly. "Darcy! I was waiting to see you off, but I thought you were still upstairs. What is…?"

Bingley's gaze shifted from Darcy to Elizabeth, his expression changing to confusion as he took in her maid's uniform. "Miss Elizabeth? And… Darcy? What is going on?

Darcy cursed inwardly. They could not wait another moment. "Bingley, there is no time to explain. You need to join us in my carriage—immediately."

"Well… of course, Darcy, but…" Bingley's brow furrowed as he glanced between them, clearly torn. "Where are we going? I should at least tell Wickham where I'm going. I cannot just disappear without—"

Elizabeth reached out, her hand gently touching Bingley's arm, her voice soft yet urgent. "Mr Bingley, if you care for my sister Jane… and I think you do… please. It would be wiser for you to come with us now."

Bingley's gaze flickered back to Darcy, searching his face for answers, but Darcy dared give him none. He could feel his headache flaring up, the familiar, ominous sensation of a spasm beginning on the right side of his face.

Elizabeth saw it instantly, the concern in her eyes sharp. "Mr Bingley, please help Mr Darcy to the carriage. *Now.*"

Bingley hesitated for only a moment longer before he sprang into action, rushing to Darcy's side. The urgency in Elizabeth's voice spurred him into motion, and together, they began to guide Darcy toward the door, the need to escape more pressing than ever.

Chapter Thirty-Four

THE CARRIAGE RUMBLED ALONG the uneven road toward Longbourn, each jolt sending a visible shock of pain through Darcy's already tortured body. Elizabeth sat across from him, her heart heavy with worry as she watched him suffer. Bingley was seated beside him and looked equally distraught, his hands wringing in his lap as he glanced between Darcy and Elizabeth, helpless to do anything more than offer his silent support. Darcy's head was clutched tightly in his hands, his face contorted in agony, the usually composed and formidable man now reduced to a broken figure hunched over in pain, trying desperately to endure the ride.

As the carriage hit another bump, Darcy let out a low, anguished moan. Elizabeth's breath caught in her throat, and she reached out instinctively, her hand hovering uncertainly over the space between them. She could see Bingley's gaze flicker to her, his own worry mirrored in her eyes. If only there was something, anything, she could do to ease Darcy's torment!

Finally, unable to bear it any longer, she leaned forward and called out to the driver to stop. Darcy's valet was riding on top of the coach. What was the man's name? Darcy had called him...

Elizabeth put her head out the door. "Giles! Is there nothing you can give him? Some medicine, anything to help?"

Giles leaned around the edge of the coach. "There is some laudanum, Miss Bennet, but—"

"No," Darcy growled through gritted teeth, his voice strained and hoarse. He roused himself just enough to look up at her, his eyes bloodshot and glassy. "No more. I will take no more of that cursed stuff." His hand shot out, grabbing her arm as if to anchor himself against the pain. "Just... just keep going. Get me to Longbourn. Please."

Elizabeth's heart twisted at the desperation in his voice. She looked back at Giles, who gave a helpless shrug, then nodded reluctantly. "Very well. But you must tell me if the pain becomes unbearable."

Darcy managed a faint, tight-lipped smile that was more of a grimace. "It already is, Miss Bennet."

The carriage lurched again, and Darcy let out another agonised groan, his body doubling over as if trying to shield himself from the relentless torment. Elizabeth bit her lip, her mind racing for a solution. Then, with sudden determination, she turned to Mr Bingley, whose face was ashen with worry.

"Mr Bingley, please... exchange places with me."

Bingley blinked in surprise but quickly complied. He helped Elizabeth switch seats, and as soon as she was beside Darcy, she gently pulled his trembling form toward her, guiding his head onto her lap.

"Shh," she whispered as she tenderly covered his eyes with her fingers, hoping to block out the light and ease at least a fraction of his suffering. With her other hand, she began to rub his temples in slow, soothing circles, her touch as gentle as she could make it.

Darcy sighed, a sound that was part relief, part exhaustion, as he relaxed just a little against her. Though his body remained tense, every muscle coiled with pain, the steady motion of her hand on his head seemed to bring him some small comfort.

The carriage rocked and swayed as it continued down the road, but Elizabeth hardly noticed. Her entire focus was on the man in her lap, on the way his breath hitched with each pulse of pain, on the way his fists clenched and unclenched as he fought to keep control. She wanted to tell him that everything would be well, that they were almost there, but such words would be meaningless in the face of his agony.

Instead, she simply held him, her fingers stroking his brow, her touch as calming as she could manage. Darcy's breathing gradually slowed, the tension in his body easing just a little under her care. Though the pain was still there, sharp and unyielding, he seemed to draw strength from her presence, from the soft, rhythmic motion of her hand.

"Now, just repeat that for me—clarify this story. What exactly are you telling me?" Mr Bennet leaned forward, propping his hands on his desk and squinting at Darcy. His hair was still mussed, he still wore his banyan, and he kept darting curious looks at Elizabeth.

"Forgive me, sir..." Darcy held up a hand, a breath hissing between his teeth as his eyes slammed closed. "A moment, pray."

Mr Bennet sighed and looked at Elizabeth. "Lizzy, what is your part in this? How did you find yourself at Netherfield with an injured ankle before the rest of us even broke our fast? Wearing a maid's uniform? And where the devil is my horse?"

Elizabeth blinked and cleared her throat. Bingley was frozen beside her, his face pale and stricken, as if the very ground had been pulled out from under him. Darcy sat slumped in the chair opposite her father, his eyes squeezed shut in pain, his knuckles white as they gripped the arms of the chair. He looked like he was barely holding on.

"Ah, that..." she began. "Yes, there is a simple explanation. Only..." She grimaced, tugging at one finger as she winced. "Perhaps it is not that simple. After what you said last night, I knew I needed to speak to Mr Darcy, and..."

Her father's deadpan look and raised brow stopped her. "I cannot think why you found it necessary to dabble in politics, child. Running off to speak with a gentleman, accost that man as he was about to step into his carriage?"

"Because it was personal, Papa. I..."

Darcy raised his hand, shaking his head. "I ought to explain. Mr Bennet, you and your daughter have been used, and your entire community set up like so many chess pawns."

Mr Bennet frowned. "The specifics, if you please, sir."

"The specifics..." Darcy thinned his lips in thought. "Perhaps I will first advise you that I am the nephew of Lord Matlock. I understand you are familiar with that name."

"I am." Mr Bennet crossed his arms and levelled a stern look at Darcy. "As is anyone who has ever met my cousin Collins, I imagine. I was aware of your connection to both

Lord Matlock *and* Lady Catherine de Bourgh." He followed this with a significant glare and a flick of his gaze at Elizabeth.

Elizabeth's heart pounded a frantic beat that echoed in her ears. Papa had heard too many half-truths and assumptions, and Darcy had no credit in his eyes yet. She had to be the one to speak. Besides, Darcy was hardly in any condition to do so. Her voice trembled, but she forced it out, the words tumbling over one another in her rush to explain. "Never mind that now. Papa, we overheard them this morning—Wickham and Sir Anthony. Wickham's job was to win the community's favour so that he could sway the vote for Sir Anthony. He was given money to do it. He has been manipulating everyone, playing us for fools."

Mr Bennet's eyes widened, a look of disbelief crossing his features before settling into something more weary, more resigned. His shoulders sagged slightly, and he was silent for some ten seconds as a battery of thoughts played over his face. "Well, that could explain it. I thought that weir looked like it had been intentionally damaged," he muttered, almost to himself. "I never imagined..."

Elizabeth's gaze snapped to Darcy, who was staring at the floor, his face ashen and drawn. Her heart clenched painfully in her chest as she watched him. He looked so small, so broken, and the urge to go to him, to wrap her arms around him and shield him from the world, was overwhelming. But she couldn't move, couldn't think beyond the terror that gripped her at seeing him like this.

Her father's voice cut through the haze again, sharper this time, more demanding. "Mr Darcy, what is the matter with you?"

Darcy's eyes flicked up, meeting hers for just a heartbeat before turning to her father. The pain in his gaze was almost unbearable to witness. "I... have been diagnosed with a brain tumour, Mr Bennet," he rasped out, each word seeming to cost him a great effort. "It is likely I have only a short while to live. I had hoped..." His voice cracked, and Elizabeth's breath caught in her throat, a sob threatening to break free.

Bingley gasped. "No, it cannot be true," he stammered, shaking his head in denial. "You cannot be ill! I would have noticed... I—"

Darcy's voice, strained but steady, cut through Bingley's frantic protest. "You did see it, Bingley, though perhaps not for what it was. All those times I disappeared into my room, the moments I was out of sorts, the megrims—did you think nothing of them?"

Bingley's face crumpled. "All those times... when you left the dinner table early, or took long walks alone, or seemed distant... How could I have missed it?" His voice wavered, thick with self-reproach. "How could I have been so blind?"

Elizabeth's chest felt as if it might cave in, and she was staring, gap-mouthed at Darcy. She had known something was the matter, but that it could be this! He could not be dying! Just when she had come to feel she could not exist without him... but everything made sense now. Some of the odd things he had said, his worsening symptoms, and that horrifying episode in the Netherfield servant's quarters...

Darcy met her gaze, and his eyes looked as though they might brim with tears. But then he blinked swiftly, and his attention drifted to Mr Bingley, who looked stricken anew. His complexion was mottled, and he was raking his hair with a shaking hand, his entire body trembling. "How could I have missed it?" he kept mumbling.

Elizabeth smiled gently at the mournful gentleman, trying to offer some comfort even as her own world crumbled around her. "Mr Darcy is... quite skilled at hiding his private troubles, Mr Bingley."

Darcy let out a bitter laugh, the sound raw and jagged. "Not skilled enough, it seems. She saw." His gaze found hers again, and this time, it lingered, filled with a mixture of pain and something deeper, something that made her chest tighten with emotion.

Then, Darcy suddenly drew himself up, a spark of clarity igniting in his eyes as if seized by a moment of inspiration. He let his hand fall from his temple and, with a steady breath, turned to face Mr Bennet. "Sir, I ask for your permission to marry your daughter."

The world tilted on its axis, and for a moment, Elizabeth couldn't breathe, couldn't think. Had she heard him correctly? He wanted... to *marry* her? *Now?* A fierce surge of hope welled up inside her, and she knew, even before her father glanced at her, what her answer would be.

Mr Bennet, however, did not appear surprised in the least. He looked at Elizabeth with a warm smirk, then shook his head with a chuckle. "I had been wondering what took you so long, Mr Darcy."

Elizabeth's heart pounded in her chest as Darcy turned to her, his expression softened by a vulnerability that she had never seen in him before. "I would have spoken sooner," he admitted, his voice low and thick with emotion. "But I thought I had little to offer you. Who would want a dying husband? But now... now I want to spend what time I have left with you... if you will have me. I promise, Elizabeth, you will be a rich widow when I am gone."

Widow. The word echoed in her mind, a dark shadow that threatened to snuff out the light that had sparked at his proposal. No! She would not accept that. She *could* not. Not after everything.

"No," she whispered, shaking her head. "Widow? How could you think I would be satisfied with that?"

He blew out his breath and tried to force a smile. "Well… I suppose I cannot be blamed for asking, after…" His smile broke, and then he lifted his shoulders, swallowed, and tried the smile again. "But perhaps I ought not… you deserve better than—"

"That is not what I meant." She slid forward and reached for his hand, caring not a bit that Mr Bingley was staring in pale astonishment or that her father was pouring himself a glass of brandy and watching with detached interest.

"No, I want nothing more than to belong to you." The words were a vow, a promise that came from the deepest part of her soul, and as she spoke them, she felt a strange calm settle over her, a certainty that this was right, that this was what she was meant to do.

Darcy's hand closed around hers, and she could feel the slight tremor in his fingers, the way his grip tightened as if he was afraid to let go. His eyes closed briefly, a shuddering breath escaping him as he murmured, "Thank you."

Elizabeth shook her head again, more firmly this time, her heart aching with a love so fierce it frightened her. "You had better not leave me, Fitzwilliam Darcy. I do not want your thanks—I want *you*. There must be something to be done, some doctor who can help…"

Darcy's face crumpled slightly, and he looked away, his voice rough with barely contained emotion. "There is a surgeon in Cambridge, a Doctor Pembroke, I was on my way to see, but I do not hold much hope. All I want is to know for sure… how much time I have left and if there is any relief for this pain. But…" He shook his head and attempted that fake smile again. "With everything here, and… well, I do not know if I can even endure the journey."

Elizabeth couldn't hold back the tears any longer. They slipped down her cheeks unchecked as she wiped his face, her fingers trembling with the fear of losing him. She didn't care that her father and Bingley were watching, didn't care that she was breaking down in front of them. None of it mattered. The only thing that mattered was him.

"We will go with you to Cambridge," Elizabeth's voice trembled, her heart hammering as she gripped his hand tighter. "We will find a way, Fitzwilliam. We will."

Chapter Thirty-Five

Darcy stood by the open window in Mr Bennet's study, watching as Bingley's carriage was prepared for departure to London. Bingley had sent word privately to the stables at Netherfield, being unwilling to return to that house himself, and his valet, carriage and horses were now no longer under Wickham's influence. His trunk of clothing... well, that was a loss, for now.

The morning air was cool, and it brought a faint measure of short-lived relief. In his hand, he held a letter addressed to Lord Matlock, a letter that contained the truth about Wickham, Wexfield, and the political machinations that had ensnared Meryton. It was his last hope of making things right, even as his own future grew increasingly uncertain.

Behind him, Bingley paced the length of the room, his steps uneven and filled with a nervous energy. Darcy could feel the weight of his friend's distress, the guilt that had settled over Bingley like a shroud ever since he had learned the truth of Darcy's condition.

Finally, Bingley stopped. "Darcy, are you certain you do not want me to accompany you to Cambridge? Surely, I could do more good by being there with you..."

Darcy turned from the window, meeting Bingley's anxious gaze. "Charles, you will do far more good in London," he replied with a gentle firmness. "You must take this letter to my uncle and ensure that he understands the full gravity of the situation. Matlock has been looking for a way to expose Wexfield's dealings for years. This letter—" he held it up briefly "—contains everything he needs to take action."

Bingley's brow furrowed with guilt, his hands clenching at his sides. "But Darcy... I should have seen it. I should have known something was wrong. You tried to warn me about Wickham, and I... I didn't listen. And now—" He broke off, his voice catching in his throat as he gestured vaguely toward Darcy.

Darcy felt a pang of sympathy, knowing how much Bingley had trusted him and how deeply their friendship ran. "You have nothing to reproach yourself for, Charles," he said softly. "Wickham is a master of deceit, and I... I kept my own troubles hidden from everyone, even from myself. But now, you can help me by doing what must be done in London."

Bingley's shoulders sagged, his expression filled with remorse. "I understand," he murmured, though it was clear he was not entirely at peace with the decision.

There was a moment of silence between them, heavy with unspoken fears and regrets. Then, almost hesitantly, Bingley looked up, his eyes clouded with confusion. "Darcy... I must ask... how did Miss Elizabeth see what those closest to you did not? When... when did this happen? I never saw—"

Darcy's chest tightened at the mention of Elizabeth. He had known the question was coming, but that did not make it any easier to answer. He took a steadying breath, searching for the right words. "Elizabeth... she has always had a keen perception, a way of seeing through to the heart of things. I suppose it was inevitable that she would see through me as well."

Bingley's confusion deepened. "But... when? How? I never saw any signs of..."

Darcy offered a faint, almost rueful smile. "That is because I did not wish for anyone to see. Least of all, her. It was only recently that... things became clearer. But Charles, you must believe me when I say that her regard for me has come as much of a surprise to me as it has to you."

Bingley stared at him, trying to reconcile this new information with what he had always believed. "Then... she truly cares for you?"

Darcy's smile softened, though there was a hint of sadness in his eyes. "Yes, she does. And that is why I must see this through. For her. For whatever time I have left."

Bingley nodded slowly, still looking troubled, but there was a new determination in his expression. "Then I will do as you ask, Darcy. I will take this letter to London and ensure that Lord Matlock does what needs to be done. And I must beg you to forgive me for being such a daft, blind fool."

Darcy smiled faintly. "It is I who was the fool, trying to manage on my own when the burdens might have been shared."

Before Bingley could respond, the door opened, and Mr Bennet entered the room, his hair still as dishevelled as it had been earlier, and his coat hastily thrown over his shoulders. "Now, before you depart, gentlemen, I need to clarify what you've just been telling me," he said, his voice more serious than Elizabeth had ever heard it. "You are certain of what you overheard?"

Darcy nodded gravely, his mind replaying the conversation between Wickham and Mortimer. "There is no doubt, sir. Wickham's task was to secure the community's favour for Sir Anthony, and he failed. They are desperate, and the measures they are willing to take to ensure victory are... disturbing."

Mr Bennet rubbed his chin thoughtfully, a dark look passing over his features. "And I shall take it upon myself to have a word with Sir Lewis and a few other gentlemen in the neighbourhood. They will not support Sir Anthony once they know the truth."

"Thank you, sir. Your word will carry weight with them."

As Bingley prepared to take his leave, he hesitated before turning to Mr Bennet. His usual cheerful demeanour was absent, replaced by an expression of deep contrition. "Mr Bennet," he began, his voice low and uncharacteristically sombre, "I owe you an apology. I have been... well, a dunderheaded ass, if you will pardon my language."

Mr Bennet raised an eyebrow. "An apology, Mr Bingley? And here I thought it was Darcy who deserved one, not I. What could you possibly have to apologise to me for?"

But Bingley shook his head, resolute. "No, sir. It is not just Darcy. I... I had hoped to prove myself worthy of more than just being an acquaintance."

Mr Bennet's eyes twinkled with amusement, and a small, wry smile played on his lips. "Worthy of more than just an acquaintance, eh? Well, I must say, Mr Bingley, I am quite fond of you. But while I would gladly welcome another pet about the house, I fear we are already overrun with females. My humble abode can hardly accommodate another mouth to feed."

Bingley flushed a deep crimson. "No, sir, that is not... I mean... you misunderstand me."

Mr Bennet chuckled softly, clearly enjoying the younger man's discomfort. "Oh, I understand perfectly, Mr Bingley. But come, speak your mind. I will not bite."

Bingley took a deep breath, his fists clenching at his sides as he glanced at Darcy, who was watching the exchange with quiet interest. "Sir," Bingley stammered, his voice growing firmer as he pressed on, "I would very much like to court Miss Bennet. But... I do not feel worthy of her. Not yet. Not until I have secured a house—a proper home to offer her. I could not ask for her hand without first providing that."

Mr Bennet listened quietly, his gaze occasionally shifting to Darcy, who had already made his intentions known regarding Elizabeth. Bingley's earnestness was clear, and there was a raw honesty in his words that must have struck a chord with the flippant Mr Bennet.

"Bingley," Darcy said, drawing Bingley's attention, "if there is one thing you can learn from me, it is that life is short. Do not wait."

Bingley's breath hitched as if he could scarcely believe what he had just heard. His colour rose. "Do you... do you truly mean that? *You*, Darcy?"

"I do. I have held you back, Bingley." Darcy frowned and swallowed, glancing away for a second. "You must do as you feel is right, without me... or anyone else... telling you how to manage your affairs."

Bingley blinked, his chest rising quickly.

Mr Bennet, who had been observing the interaction with quiet amusement, nodded thoughtfully. "Indeed, Mr Bingley. One ought to strike while the iron is hot."

Bingley's eyes widened in wild dismay and excitement, his gaze darting between Mr Bennet and Darcy. "But... sir," he stammered, "what do you mean? Is this some... some reference to Miss Bennet's feelings?"

Mr Bennet scratched his ear, chuckling. "No, Mr Bingley, it is not. Although the sentiment would certainly apply, I was actually referring to Mrs Bennet, who does not yet know that she has a second daughter engaged. You may as well give her a third."

Bingley blinked in confusion, and then understanding dawned on his face. His gaze flickered back to Darcy, who gave him a thin smile of encouragement. Mr Bennet leaned in conspiratorially, his tone light but laced with meaning. "If you wish to protect your friend from yet another pain in his head, Mr Bingley, you might consider declaring yourself at once. It would halve the burden of Mrs Bennet's joy, you see."

Bingley's face suddenly blossomed into hope. He glanced back and forth between Mr Bennet and Darcy, his eyes brightening with newfound determination. "Then, sir... if I may... may I speak with Miss Bennet immediately?"

Mr Bennet gave him a wry shrug as though the outcome were already certain. "By all means, Mr Bingley. I shall not stand in your way."

With that, Bingley bolted from the room. Mr Bennet watched him go, a chuckle rumbling in his chest. "Ah, to be young again," he mused aloud, his tone light and nostalgic. "Head over boots and all that. I felt like that once... and it was heaven for ten minutes."

Darcy allowed a soft laugh to escape, then sighed, a bittersweet note in his voice. "I rather hope the feeling will endure the rest of my life... however long that may be."

THE JOURNEY NORTH TO Cambridge had got off to a gruelling start. Every jolt of the carriage sent fresh waves of pain through Darcy's head, and the damp chill in the air seemed to seep into his very bones. The decision to leave Meryton so abruptly still felt too rushed. It was not that he lacked matters to attend to there—indeed, staying would have been the more sensible option, considering all that had transpired. Not least among his new concerns was his future mother-in-law—who had only consented to let him out the door after he gave her leave to begin planning a wedding for three weeks hence.

There was also Bingley and matters with Lord Matlock. Collins, his future... egad, his future brother-in-law, who was probably already penning an outraged letter to Lady Catherine. And whatever consequences might fall on the servants of Netherfield after his escape this morning...

But the sense of danger clung to him, an instinctual need to put distance between himself and Wickham, had driven him to insist on their departure.

Elizabeth would not hear of being left behind. Despite the oddity, the scandal even, of a lady travelling so intimately with a man who was not yet her husband, Darcy found himself deeply grateful for her presence. She truly did not mean to permit him out of her sight, whether out of protectiveness for his vulnerability or ardour for him as her future husband... either sentiment was welcome to him just now.

When it became clear that Elizabeth meant to lash herself to the back of the carriage if her father tried to prevent her from going, Mr Bennet joined them as well. His presence added a layer of safety to their journey, for Darcy had already been uncertain enough of his ability to manage on the road should another attack befall him. But, perhaps even more importantly, Bennet provided a buffer against the impropriety of Elizabeth and Darcy being alone together.

However, as they had all settled into the carriage, Mr Bennet had made an odd request. He asked for the rear-facing seat inside the carriage, all to himself. "Cannot abide the closeness," he announced. "Always had a morbid fear of being shut up in a confined space."

Elizabeth did not bother concealing the sceptical slant of her brows at her father's strange declaration, but the arrangement left Darcy facing forward in the carriage—which was far easier on his unsteady equilibrium—with Elizabeth beside him. The arrangement seemed intentional, a subtle manoeuvre by Mr Bennet to allow his daughter to be close to Darcy.

At first, the proximity of her body, with her father looking on, was hideously awkward. He was acutely aware of Elizabeth's presence, the warmth of her breath so close to his, the way her shoulder brushed against his arm with every lurch of the carriage. He had no choice but to lean on her when the pain became too much or when the dizziness nearly overwhelmed him. But Mr Bennet, true to form, buried his face in a book and seemed to take no notice of them, pointedly ignoring the pair as they sat side by side.

There was little to say that they could share before a chaperon, but also, little that needed to be said. She had always understood him from that first day, and he felt a deep, sinking relief in his chest. No more masks, no pretences, just... her. She was, perhaps, the only person he had ever felt that with since his father's death.

Her hand slid up the inside of his arm, her fingers tickling the sensitive skin under his wrists and then deftly lacing with his. The touch was gentle, intimate, and it sent a wave of warmth through him. She rested her chin on his shoulder, her smile soft and tender. It was a look that nearly undid him, and Darcy was seized by the nearly overwhelming urge to turn and kiss her, to lose himself in that simple, pure connection. But with her father mere feet away, Darcy clung to the last vestiges of his propriety, despite the longing that twisted his heart.

The carriage rocked along the muddy road, the scenery blurring past in a wash of grey and green. The rain had begun to fall in earnest now, the steady drumming on the carriage roof adding to the tension thrumming through Darcy's veins. His head throbbed mercilessly, and he found himself leaning more heavily on Elizabeth as they rolled into open country, putting Meryton behind them. Yet, there was a certain peace in the gentle sway of the carriage and Elizabeth's comforting presence by his side.

That peace was shattered as the carriage rounded a bend, and the driver abruptly reined in the horses. The vehicle lurched to a sudden stop, sending Darcy forward in his seat. The jolt sent a fresh stab of pain through his skull, and he gritted his teeth against the sensation.

"What is it?" Mr Bennet asked from behind his book, though his tone remained more curious than alarmed.

Darcy didn't answer. He motioned for Elizabeth to remain inside and dry as he pushed the door open and leaned out to assess the situation. The rain-soaked air hit him like a slap, sharp and cold, and he tilted his hat to better shield his face as he scanned the road ahead.

A tree lay across the road—a great thick trunk blocking their path entirely. Darcy's unease deepened as he took in the scene. This was no natural fall—the tree had been deliberately cut; its base sawn cleanly through. A sense of danger prickled at the back of his neck, and he found himself scanning the surroundings with a growing sense of dread.

There was no way to move the tree with any expediency, and going around was impossible as the sides of the road were marshy with flooding. Any attempt to manoeuvre around the obstruction was impossible. The only way out was back the way they had come.

Darcy had scarcely given the order to the driver to do just that, but as soon as the words were out of his mouth, the sound of approaching horses reached his ears. He glanced back down the road, and his blood ran cold as he saw them—Wickham on horseback, flanked by two workmen with axes.

"Darcy!" Wickham's voice rang out with a mockery that was unmistakable. He raised a hand in greeting as though they were old friends happening upon each other by chance.

They were trapped. Darcy's mind raced as he considered their options, but there was nowhere to go.

Elizabeth's face appeared through the curtain of the carriage window. "Mr Darcy? What is it?"

Darcy turned back to her, his expression grim. "Stay inside the carriage, Elizabeth," he ordered, his voice low and firm. "Do not come out, whatever happens. Mr Bennet..." Darcy waited until that gentleman's expression altered from bored to curious. "See that you *both* keep out of sight."

He stepped down to the road and shut the carriage door behind him with a decisive click.

Wickham had planned this. He had known Darcy would take this road, and apparently, Wickham had no intention of letting him go so easily.

"Well, Darcy, what a surprise to find you here," Wickham called out, his voice slick with false camaraderie.

Darcy did not answer, but from the corner of his eye, he saw Elizabeth's eyes widening through the carriage window. She shrank back, just enough for her father's quizzical face to appear beside her. Darcy had to resist the urge to give them any sort of signal. No need to inform Wickham that there was someone else in the carriage. Instead, he stepped away, walking to confront Wickham.

"What is the meaning of this?" he demanded.

Wickham just chuckled and rode his horse forward, stopping before Darcy and leaning down with an easy grin. "You seem to have run into a bit of trouble on the road. Nasty weather, isn't it? We were just out looking over the roads, and by thunder, look what we found? Wouldn't want anything to happen to honest people just trying to travel the roads. Especially a man of your standing."

Darcy's eyes narrowed. "What do you want, Wickham?"

Wickham's grin widened. "Oh, nothing much. Just thought I'd offer some assistance. The roads up north can be treacherous, full of bandits, you know. Especially when one is travelling alone."

"I am not interested in your help. Move aside."

"Now, now, Darcy. No need to be so hasty. I've heard some disturbing things about your friend Bingley. Did you know he left Netherfield in quite a rush? So much so that we were worried for his safety. My men intercepted his carriage on the way to London, just to be sure all was well."

Darcy's blood ran cold. Bingley? Intercepted? He had no way of knowing if Wickham was telling the truth, but the mere possibility was enough to make him hesitate.

Wickham reached into his coat pocket and withdrew a white handkerchief, monogrammed with Bingley's initials. A small, dark stain marked one corner, and Wickham held it up with a mocking smile. "He had a bit of a nosebleed, poor chap. But don't worry, he is back at Netherfield now, safe and sound."

Darcy's heart pounded in his chest as he stared at the handkerchief. Bingley had left so quickly that he hadn't even packed a trunk, taking only the clothes on his back. It was entirely possible that Wickham had intercepted him and that Bingley was now being held at Netherfield. But how could Darcy be sure?

Wickham's eyes gleamed with triumph, sensing Darcy's uncertainty. "I might suggest you turn back with us, Darcy. Let us go somewhere more comfortable, where we can discuss this like gentlemen. We would not want anything unfortunate to happen to Bingley, now, would we?"

Darcy's thoughts spun wildly, the urgency to flee clashing with the gnawing dread that Wickham's threats might be more than empty bluster. The possibility that Bingley's life could be at stake gnawed at him, tightening the knot of fear in his chest. But showing even the slightest hint of weakness... letting Wickham discover Elizabeth and her father in his carriage, even... was out of the question.

Wickham fed on fear, on hesitation, on any sign that his prey might falter. If Darcy faltered now, it would be like blood in the water to a shark. He had to keep his expression steady, his resolve unshaken, even as the reality of the trap they were in pressed down on him like a vise.

Darcy swallowed hard, his voice cold and measured. "If you have harmed him, Wickham—"

Wickham cut him off with a laugh. "Harmed him? Why, Darcy, I'm offended you'd think such a thing. Bingley is in excellent hands. But accidents can happen, you know, especially on these rough roads."

Darcy's breath quickened as he stared down the road, the fallen tree an ominous barrier between him and safety. The rain beat down in steady sheets, soaking through his clothing and chilling him to the bone. The cold was now seeping into his very core, the dampness aggravating the persistent ache in his head. But none of that mattered as much as the immediate danger.

Darcy's thoughts churned as he weighed the dangers to Elizabeth. He could not dare let her be seen, but what would she face if he left her here, with the carriage? Wickham had two workmen with axes—dangerous enough on their own—but they had no idea that there were passengers in the carriage. His own men were armed, their pistols loaded and ready, and Darcy knew they were capable of defending her. Mr Bennet would have overheard everything by now, and like many gentlemen, he kept two more pistols in the carriage. Darcy felt certain that Elizabeth and her father would have found them by now.

Even so, the thought of leaving Elizabeth behind twisted his gut. But if Wickham discovered her presence, the danger would escalate beyond control. To take her back to Netherfield, where Wickham could easily uncover her attachment to him, would be an even greater risk. Darcy's only hope was to negotiate carefully, to keep Wickham's attention on him while his men worked to protect Elizabeth.

Darcy had no choice. He would have to rely on the element of surprise and the resolve of those inside the carriage. Wickham had him cornered, and whether the threat to Bingley was real or a fabrication, Darcy could not afford to take any chances.

Taking a steadying breath, Darcy finally turned to face Wickham, his voice carefully measured. "If Bingley is truly at Netherfield, I will return with you at once. But I shall go on horseback. The coachman and your men can set to clearing this tree from the road in the meantime."

"Horseback?" Wickham scoffed, a derisive smile playing on his lips. "You are looking rather peaked, Darcy. I wonder why a man in your condition would be so eager to abandon a perfectly good carriage. Especially in this weather?"

Darcy kept his tone casual, refusing to rise to the bait. "It should not be so difficult to comprehend. As I said, I am eager to resume my journey, and it is not likely that any road menders will happen upon this 'accident' anytime soon. My men will stay with the carriage and see that the road is passable while I accompany you to clear up this matter with Bingley."

Wickham's eyes narrowed as he considered the proposal, his gaze flicking between Darcy and the carriage. Wickham's eyes narrowed slightly, studying him, searching for any sign of hesitation. "You are a curious fellow, Darcy. But I have no interest in your carriage. Very well, but I cannot have your men running off to alert anyone." He flicked a glance at one of the workmen, who lifted his axe with a not-so-subtle threat.

"My carriage and my men will stay where they are."

Wickham frowned, tapping his fingers against his leg as if weighing his options. Finally, he nodded to one of his men. "Fetch the workhorse. Best huntsman in Derbyshire, eh Darcy? You ought to have no trouble backing this one."

The workman disappeared into the trees for a moment, returning with a raw-boned, heavy-built nag, its coat slick with rain. Wickham's smirk grew as the horse was led up to Darcy, clearly expecting him to baulk at the sight of the lumbering, unsaddled beast.

Darcy met Wickham's gaze with an unflinching stare, refusing to be needled. He straightened his shoulders, grasped the horse's lead and a hunk of its coarse mane, and swung aboard with a practised ease that belied the pain searing through his skull. He dared not look back at the carriage where Elizabeth remained hidden, the curtains drawn.

He could only hope that his driver and valet understood and were ready to defend their future mistress if it came to that. Steeling himself, Darcy tightened his grip on the horse's mane and prepared to follow Wickham.

Wickham watched him with a mixture of amusement and curiosity, clearly expecting some sign of weakness. But Darcy kept his expression impassive, his grip on the reins steady despite the pounding in his head. The rain continued to fall, soaking through his clothing, but he ignored it.

With a final glance at the blocked road and the workmen who stood guard over the carriage, Darcy urged the horse forward. The animal moved reluctantly, its hooves slipping in the mud, but Darcy pressed on, his jaw set with grim determination. He had no intention of letting Wickham win. Not this time.

Chapter Thirty-Six

Elizabeth crouched low in the dim confines of the carriage, her breath shallow as she strained to catch every word of the conversation outside. Her heart pounded with fear as she heard Darcy volunteering himself to go with Wickham. The impulse to fling open the door and protest surged through her, but before she could act, her father's firm hand gripped her wrist.

"Elizabeth," he whispered urgently, his voice barely audible over the rain pattering against the carriage roof. "Darcy knows what he is doing. He is trying to protect you. Do not waste his efforts."

Tears of frustration pricked at her eyes, but she nodded, swallowing the protest that threatened to escape her lips. She watched helplessly as Darcy rode off with Wickham, her heart clenching with terror for him. The carriage remained still, both of them holding their breaths and praying on the loyalty and nerve of Darcy's men, knowing the workmen were standing guard nearby.

Through a narrow slit in the curtains and the small window just beneath the driver's seat, Elizabeth could catch occasional glimpses of Giles, Darcy's valet, and the coachman. They sat with an air of casual indifference as though nothing was amiss, but Elizabeth noticed the subtle shift in the coachman's posture. Her breath hitched when she caught the glint of a pistol lying by his side, clearly visible to the workmen. It was a silent but unmistakable warning: Stay away from the gentleman's carriage.

At first, the workmen kept their distance, but as time passed, their respect gave way to insolence. One of them began heckling the coachman and the valet. Elizabeth strained her ears to catch the crude words of the workmen as they grew bolder.

"Oi, what do you reckon a fancy gent like him keeps in that strongbox, eh?" one of the workmen speculated. "Bet it's full of gold, jewels... mayhap even some fancy trinkets from London, eh?"

The second workman chuckled. "Aye, and more than just a few coins, I'd wager. Rich buggars like him always carry more than they need. Probably enough in there to set us both up for life."

"Think they'd notice if we took a peek, eh? Wouldn't take much. Just a quick look inside. Maybe a few coins for our trouble."

The second workman laughed again, his voice dripping with contempt. "You think these soft-handed gents could stop us? Look at 'em. They wouldn't stand a chance if we decided to help ourselves. 'Sides, what's the worst they could do? Wave a handkerchief at us?"

The coachman's voice cut through the workmen's laughter, steady and low. "I'd think carefully before you try anything, lads. There's more than a handkerchief waiting for you if you do."

The first workman scoffed, though there was an edge of uncertainty in his voice. "What's that supposed to mean, eh? You threatening us now?"

The coachman shifted slightly in his seat, the movement drawing Elizabeth's eye back to the glint of the pistol. "I am only advising you," the coachman replied calmly, "some things are not worth the risk. A few coins will do you little good if you are not around to spend them."

There was a brief silence as if the workmen were weighing the threat, their earlier bravado faltering. But the second workman was not ready to give up so easily.

"Big talk for a man sitting up there on a box," he jeered, though his voice lacked the confidence it had before. "But I reckon you're all bluff. Gents like you don't know how to handle real trouble."

"Last warning," the coachman said, his voice colder now, more dangerous. "Keep to yourselves, lads. You'll find nothing here worth losing your lives over."

The workmen laughed, but there was a hint of unease in their voices now. They did not take the warning seriously, but neither did they approach.

Mr Bennet leaned closer to Elizabeth, his voice a mere breath in her ear. "Elizabeth, shift beside me. Quietly, now."

Puzzled, Elizabeth obeyed, moving as stealthily as she could manage. Her heart raced with the fear that any movement might betray their presence. As she shifted, the carriage rocked ever so slightly, but just then, one of the horses stamped its foot and sneezed, providing the perfect cover for her movement.

Once she was beside him, her father reached down and lifted the seat she had just vacated. Elizabeth's eyes widened as she saw the brace of loaded pistols hidden there beside Darcy's strongbox. Her father took one in each hand, his expression grim and determined.

"Keep watch through the curtain," he whispered. "Let me know if the workman on your side of the coach approaches."

Elizabeth nodded, her throat tight. She could feel every second dragging on as she kept her eyes fixed on the workmen, her heart galloping wildly. They were standing too close to the carriage now, their earlier bravado returning as they exchanged glances with each other, growing more insolent with each passing minute.

The coachman broke the silence at last, his voice steady but laced with an edge of impatience. "Much obliged if you'd begin chopping that tree, lads. Your master gave you orders, did he not?"

The workmen scoffed. "And where do you think you're going, then?" one of them sneered, taking a step closer to the carriage. "We're not lifting a finger till we're paid. And we don't get paid 'til Mr Wickham's satisfied."

Elizabeth's grip on the curtain tightened, her breath catching in her throat as the men edged closer. The second workman jeered, waving his axe in the air with a mocking grin. "Why don't you get down here and show us how it's done, eh? Get those pretty hands of yours dirty for once."

Inside the carriage, Mr Bennet's movements were slow and deliberate as he raised one of the pistols, his expression grim. Through the slit in the curtain behind her, Elizabeth caught a glimpse of the coachman's hands tightening around his own pistol, his body tensed and ready. The workmen's patience was wearing thin, and their taunts grew more aggressive as they hovered near the carriage, their greed and frustration clearly getting the better of them.

"How long does it take to dispatch one weakling dandy, eh?" one of the workmen spat. "It's been an hour already. You'd think they'd be done by now."

Dispatch? Exactly what did Wickham want with Darcy? Elizabeth's pulse quickened, her mind racing with the possible outcomes. The situation had become a stalemate, and it couldn't last much longer. Something had to give.

Then, the sound of hooves clattering on the wet road reached her ears, growing louder with each passing second. Someone was coming.

Her father tensed beside her, his grip tightening on the pistol as they both peered out through the window. The rider came into view, and Elizabeth's father hissed in dismay when he recognised him.

"Sir Anthony Mortimer."

Darcy barely managed to find his feet as he slid off the rough-hewn workhorse when they reached Netherfield. The dizziness still swirled through his head like a thick fog and the middle fingers of his right hand twitched involuntarily, but he clenched his fist, determined not to show any further weakness. Wickham dismounted with ease, his smirk firmly in place as he motioned for Darcy to follow him inside.

As they stepped into the study, Darcy's patience was wearing thin, and his nerves frayed to the point of breaking. Wickham's untroubled demeanour only deepened Darcy's frustration, adding fuel to the simmering anger within him. Wickham closed the door behind them, then turned, a calculating look in his eyes as he regarded Darcy's taut posture.

Darcy wasted no time. "Enough of this. I have had more than I can bear of your games, Wickham. State your intentions, and let me be on my way."

Wickham smirked, clearly enjoying the power he held in the moment. "It's not that simple, Darcy. You know that." He moved to the fireplace, casually leaning against the mantel as if they were discussing the weather. "I need your support for this vote, and I am willing to do whatever it takes to secure it."

Darcy's eyes narrowed. "And what exactly do you think you have that could force my hand? We both know what I overheard."

Wickham's gaze sharpened, his smirk widening. "I'm not the only one with secrets, and you're not as inscrutable as you like to think. I've seen the way you've been hiding your little... ailment. The spasms you thought no one noticed, the way your right side betrays you when you're under strain. And the headaches—oh yes, you're not as good at hiding them as you believe."

Darcy's expression hardened, though inwardly, he felt a cold chill. Wickham had been watching him more closely than he had realised.

"I'll not waste any more time, Wickham. I want to know exactly what it is you intend. Bring out Bingley and speak your piece, and then I will be on my way. Unless you do not have him at all. You do not, do you? Else, I would have been greeted by him sitting here, bloodied and trussed up like a Christmas ham."

Wickham leaned against the mantelpiece, inspecting his fingernails with mock disinterest. "Whether or not I have him is irrelevant. What matters, Darcy, is that now, I have you. And I know you're not feeling quite yourself these days."

Wickham pushed away from the mantel, circling Darcy slowly, like a predator stalking its prey. "What is it, Darcy? Sick in the liver? No, it cannot be that. You were always a temperate fellow. It cannot be consumption, for you never coughed a day in your life. Falling sickness? That can be a blasted nuisance."

Darcy remained stone-faced, refusing to give Wickham the satisfaction of a reaction. But Wickham's grin widened, his eyes glinting. "Oh, no, it's something terminal, is it not? You're dying. What a pity."

The air between them grew heavy as Darcy kept his features schooled, but the brief flicker in his eyes betrayed him. Wickham's expression shifted into a knowing sneer. "I see I have guessed correctly."

Wickham studied him, his smile fading into something more serious. "Let me make this simple for you. You will rescind your objections to Sir Anthony and use your influence to ensure his election. In return, I will see to it that your loved ones are left unharmed once you're... gone."

He... he would *dare* hint at that? It was a clear threat to Georgiana, and probably even Richard, if Wickham could get to him. Darcy's jaw clenched, but he remained silent.

"What, nothing to say to that? Oh, I know you like to take your time. Think things over, seek advice from someone you trust. And who could be more valuable than Fitzwilliam? It must be difficult, knowing your cousin was reassigned to Chatham just when you needed him most. Bloody shame, that."

A cold prickle ran along Darcy's spine as the pieces began to fall into place. Somehow, this had all been orchestrated for months—since long before Darcy came to Netherfield. Wickham had taken steps to separate Darcy from the one other person who would see through his lies. But obviously Wickham had connections—powerful enough ones to pull strings at Whitehall—so why would the man now be saying he needed Darcy's help?

Perhaps Wickham had only been hedging his bets in case the one man most likely to expose his little sham should happen to discover him. Darcy clenched his fists, his temples throbbing with each passing second, Wickham's eyes boring into him, probing for any hint of hesitation.

"Why?" Darcy finally asked.

Wickham raised a brow. "Why what, Darcy?"

"Why did you invite me here to try to work upon me? Why involve me further? I haven't half the political power that you have somehow tapped into."

"Oh!" Wickham laughed. "As to that, why, I should say it was a bit of luck, finding out that Bingley was the man who tried to lease the estate first. He may not have remembered me from school, but I certainly knew who *he* was, and a more useful chap for my purposes was never born. Why, anyone I could not charm, he could, and I had all the benefit of the connection. As to *your* invitation..."

Wickham paused, pacing behind a side table to pour himself a glass of something, but he never offered Darcy one. "Well, perhaps that was my one mistake. But I could not resist, you know—the chance for you to see your old friend doing well for himself. I like to think George Darcy was smiling down at my good fortune."

"You are a fraud!" Darcy spat. "A bought man, spending another man's fortune to buy votes! You think my father would have been proud of that?"

Wickham's fingers tightened on his glass. "He wanted a gentleman's life for me. He treated me like a son, like I was his own... in every respect but one. And now I have the one thing that was denied me by birth."

Darcy flung a hand towards the outer hall. "And that is why the first thing you did was have a painting commissioned? To try to legitimize yourself?"

Wickham smiled faintly. "A masterpiece, is it not?"

"What are you trying to prove? What do you think it changes? Georgiana told me," Darcy growled. "She told me everything."

Wickham resumed pacing, clicking his tongue. "I imagine she *thinks* she told you everything, but the one who really learned everything was I. Fascinating girl, Darcy, truly. If she did not think of me like a brother, I think I should have pursued her."

"She thinks of you as a cheat and a liar," Darcy hissed. "And if you go within a mile of her—"

"But that is not for you to say, is it, Darcy?" Wickham rounded to face him once more, wearing a mock frown of concern. "You cannot imagine my shock the first day you turned up on Netherfield's doorstep—pale, shaking, and a full stone underweight. You looked like you had a foot in the grave already, but I will confess, you do mask it decently well—provided your audience is as self-absorbed and unobservant as most people are." Wickham paced closer. "But what will you do when time runs out, Darcy? When the secret can no longer be kept, and pretty Miss Georgie is all alone? Grieving her lost brother?" He smiled and shook his head. "You would not deny her the comfort of a childhood friend, would you?"

Darcy's pulse was drumming in this throat so tightly, he felt he might choke. He wanted to choke anyway, listen to this snake. But letting Wickham gloat was purchasing time—the time needed for Bingley to reach London, for Elizabeth and Mr Bennet to be found by a friendly face.

He took a deliberate breath, steadying himself. "Leave Georgiana out of this. If influence—respect of your peers and my name behind you—is what you seek, I will write to Matlock on your behalf," he said, his tone cool and precise.

"And say what? This is no mere game of popularity, Darcy. I am accountable for a vast deal of money, and I must see it bear fruit. You will have to offer something substantial."

Darcy clenched his teeth. "I will vouch for Sir Anthony's character and his political views. That should suffice for your purposes." He let his words hang, knowing Wickham wouldn't find them enough. It was a starting point, a calculated move.

As he anticipated, Wickham snorted. "A letter? That's all you offer, Darcy? Don't insult me. I need more than words on paper."

Darcy's gaze remained steady, hiding his satisfaction at Wickham's predictability. He needed to press Wickham further, making the next concession seem like a reluctant step. "What more, then? My name, spoken publicly in endorsement? A grand display of support?"

Wickham's eyes gleamed as he sensed a victory. "Exactly. Your presence, your words. You will stand beside Sir Anthony and myself, convincing your acquaintances—especially that meddlesome Bennet—that Sir Anthony is the right choice. Your voice must be heard, Darcy, your influence seen and felt."

Darcy's gut tightened, but his face remained stoic. "Very well," he replied, allowing a trace of fatigue to colour his words, as if conceding reluctantly. "I will use my connections with Matlock and speak to Mr Bennet, Sir William, and whatever other gentlemen you deem necessary. I will arrange the meetings and make the necessary introductions in London, as well."

He paused, his eyes locking with Wickham's, and added with a firm edge, "But you must bring them here to Netherfield yourself to secure their initial support. Immediately."

Wickham laughed. "Darcy, I think you forgot! You are in no position to make demands."

Darcy allowed a faint smile to crack his features. "And as you so astutely pointed out, I am also in no condition to gallivant about the countryside. Time is, as you have guessed, of the essence. If you want my help, go to Longbourn in person and ask for Mr Bennet. Then bring Sir William and Mr Philips and Mr Purvis and Mr Long and whomever else you like to join us here."

Wickham studied Darcy's face, his expression sceptical. "Why not just send a servant?"

"Because you do not understand an academic cynic like Bennet. I do. If you want the man's support, you will not get it without showing up in person," Darcy shot back, his voice edged with irritation.

Wickham hesitated, clearly weighing his options. "No," he decided after a few seconds. "You shall come with me. What better way for you to prove your sincerity?"

That... that was not possible. Mr Bennet would not even *be* at Longbourn, but if Wickham had gone there on an unsuccessful attempt to invite the gentleman to Netherfield, the delay might have been enough for Darcy's needs. But why would he expect Wickham to just conveniently agree to his plan? He needed some other impetus, some means of forcing Wickham's hand...

Darcy blinked hard, trying to clear his vision as a familiar wave of dizziness swept over him. The telltale signs were there—the increasing tremor in his right hand, the sudden pounding in his skull. Another episode was imminent; he could feel it creeping up on him, threatening to rob him of control.

Panic clawed at the edges of his thoughts, but with it came a sliver of inspiration. He could feel the weakness overtaking him, but he was not yet helpless—he could use this. Wickham thrived on exploiting vulnerabilities, but perhaps, just this once, Darcy could turn his own frailty to his advantage.

He let himself sway slightly, his hand rising to his forehead as if succumbing to the pain. His vision blurred, the room spinning ever so slightly, but he steadied himself just enough to make it look intentional. If he could make Wickham believe he was losing control, perhaps he could prompt a decision before his body truly gave out.

Darcy groaned softly, letting his knees buckle a fraction, his hand gripping the edge of the mantel for support. The movement was small but deliberate, a calculated performance that played on Wickham's curiosity. If he could keep Wickham focused on him, on his supposed decline, he might still have a chance to influence the outcome.

"Darcy?" Wickham's voice hinted only at mild interest. "What, er... what say you?"

Darcy looked up, his face pale, his breath ragged. "I do not have time for this, Wickham," he rasped. "If you want my support... you need to act quickly. My condition... I cannot waste what little strength I have left."

Wickham's gaze flickered with calculation. "So, you are closer to the grave than I thought," he muttered under his breath, half to himself.

Darcy seized the moment, letting himself sink further down, making his body appear weaker, more vulnerable. "Make your decision," he urged, his voice strained. "Go to Longbourn and Lucas Lodge and the other principal houses in the area; bring the gentlemen here. I will do as you ask... but only if you act now."

The urgency in his tone, combined with his feigned collapse, seemed to sway Wickham. He nodded slowly, his eyes never leaving Darcy's face. "Very well," he said, finally relenting. "I'll go myself. But know this, Darcy—if you're playing me, you'll regret it. I promise you that."

Darcy managed a weak nod before he collapsed utterly. His ploy had worked. He had bought himself a little more time, and with any luck, it would be enough.

Chapter Thirty-Seven

Elizabeth held her breath as she watched the scene unfold from her vantage point in the carriage. Sir Anthony Mortimer rode past the window, his horse's hooves splashing mud as he halted abruptly before Darcy's carriage. Through the narrow slit in the curtain, she could see him turning his mount to square off with the driver, his expression twisted with impatience.

"Turn this carriage back to Netherfield," Sir Anthony barked, his voice carrying over the rain-soaked landscape. His command was sharp, almost desperate, as though he had little time and even less patience.

Darcy's coachman, who looked to Elizabeth like a seasoned man who had seen his share of rough dealings, kept his seat atop the carriage, his back straight, his expression unyielding. "I am sorry, sir," he replied evenly, his voice steady despite the tension simmering in the air. "But I take my orders from Mr Darcy. He instructed me to remain here and ensure the road is cleared."

Sir Anthony's face darkened at the refusal, his lips curling into a sneer. "Darcy be damned," he snapped. "I have authority here, and I say you will turn this carriage around, or I'll—"

"With all due respect, sir," the coachman interrupted, a boldness in his tone that surprised even Elizabeth. "If you've authority, then perhaps you might order these workmen to get on with clearing the tree. That's what needs doing."

Elizabeth's breath hitched. She could barely make out her father's form beside her, his hand still firm on the pistol under the seat, ready to act if necessary. She glanced back at the scene outside, her pulse racing. For a moment, she dared to hope that Sir Anthony would be reasonable, that he would see the sense in the coachman's words. But that hope shattered in an instant.

Sir Anthony's hand moved swiftly to his coat, and in a flash, he pulled out a pistol, levelling it directly at the coachman. "I will not be defied," he hissed, his eyes wild with a mix of frustration and fury. The pistol glinted in the weak light, its barrel unwavering as he aimed it squarely at the coachman's chest.

Elizabeth stifled a gasp, her hand flying to her mouth to keep silent. Her father was scarcely managing better. His thumbs drew back the hammers on the flintlocks, but the muzzles dipped and wavered.

The coachman held Sir Anthony's furious gaze, his hands still raised in a calm display of surrender. The rain continued to drum against the carriage roof, adding a dull, rhythmic beat to the tension that thickened the air. Elizabeth could hardly breathe, her eyes darting between the men outside, her heart thrumming with fear and uncertainty.

Giles, Darcy's valet, took a tentative step forward, his voice as measured as his movements. "Sir Anthony, surely there is a more civil way to resolve this," he reasoned, his tone even, attempting to appeal to the gentleman's sense of decorum. "We are only following Mr Darcy's instructions. If you would permit us to clear the tree—"

"I said I will not be spoken to by servants!" Sir Anthony snapped, his pistol still trained unwaveringly on the coachman. "Turn this carriage about, or I'll shoot that wheel horse right here!"

The coachman glanced down at the horses, the rain dripping from the brim of his hat. He looked back up at Sir Anthony, a flicker of defiance in his eyes. "A fine beast, that one," he said, his voice steady despite the danger. "Cost Mr Darcy eighty guineas, he did. Shall I tell him where to send the bill?"

Sir Anthony's face twisted in fury, the pistol in his hand shaking with the force of his anger. "Darcy will not be billing anyone for anything unless he cooperates," he thundered, his voice carrying over the steady rain. "And I have no intention of letting his servants run off to parts unknown until the man himself has agreed to my terms!"

Elizabeth could feel her father's steadying hand on her arm, holding her back as she fought the urge to throw open the door and confront Sir Anthony Mortimer herself. But they had agreed to remain hidden, to wait for a moment when escape seemed possible. Now, though, that moment seemed to be slipping further away with every breath she took.

"I beg your pardon, sir, but how shall we 'run off to parts unknown' when the way is blocked?" the coachman replied.

Through the narrow crack in the curtains, Elizabeth watched as Sir Anthony's face grew redder, his patience clearly wearing thin. "I have had enough of your insolence!"

he barked, snapping the muzzle of his pistol back toward the driver. "Turn this carriage around, now, or I will have your head for insubordination!"

The coachman, to his credit, held his ground, though Elizabeth could see the tension in his rigid back, the tightness in his grip on the reins. "I am afraid I cannot do that, sir," he replied calmly. "Mr Darcy ordered me to remain here."

Sir Anthony's eyes narrowed dangerously. "Are all Darcy's servants so obstinate? No, no, man, you must be hiding something for him."

"I assume you sir, there is nothing!"

"Then you will not object to me seeing for myself, will you?" Sir Anthony swung down from his horse, tossing the rein to one of the workmen standing by.

"Sir, I must protest! You would not dare meddle with the gentleman's property!" The coachman had the pistol in his hand now, and Elizabeth shook her head, praying silently that he would not attempt to use it. Sir Anthony would surely fire first if the coachman made any effort to aim.

"I would not touch that flintlock if I were you," Sir Anthony warned as he stepped closer to the carriage. "If you do not wish to cooperate, perhaps I should see what is so valuable inside this carriage that you are willing to risk your lives to protect it."

Elizabeth's heart shuddered to a stop. She exchanged a quick, alarmed glance with her father. Mr Bennet gave her a slight nod, his expression dark.

The coachman, realising the situation was about to spiral out of control, made a last-ditch effort to divert Sir Anthony's attention. "Sir, there's nothing in there but some sensitive correspondence and Mr Darcy's personal effects. If you could just—"

But Sir Anthony wasn't listening. He was already at the carriage door, his hand reaching for the latch. The door swung open with a creak, and Sir Anthony's expression shifted from annoyance to surprise—and then to satisfaction—as his eyes fell on Elizabeth and Mr Bennet inside.

Sir Anthony leaned closer, his eyes narrowing as he took in the unexpected sight. "Well, now," he said slowly, a sly grin forming on his lips. "Mr Bennet, isn't it? Hiding in Mr Darcy's carriage, no less. I wonder what business you have here. Were you planning to rally support from elsewhere before the election, perhaps? And who is this...?" His gaze shifted to Elizabeth, then quickly back to her father—no doubt tracing a resemblance. "Ah, the daughter, of course. Elizabeth Bennet." His smile widened, realisation dawning. "So, Wickham was right. It seems there is more between Darcy and your family than I was led to believe. This does complicate things."

Elizabeth met his gaze with a defiant glare, her pulse quickening. "Sir Anthony, there is no need for this hostility. We are simply trying to make our way safely—"

"Save your breath, Miss Bennet," Sir Anthony cut her off sharply. "Appearances speak for themselves. And it seems to me you're in a rather compromising position, travelling in Mr Darcy's carriage, are you not?"

Elizabeth bristled at his insinuation, but before she could respond, her father spoke up, his voice steady but firm. "Sir Anthony, if it is leverage you seek, using my daughter in this infamous manner will gain you nothing but my deepest contempt. Release us at once, and we can discuss matters like rational men."

Sir Anthony chuckled darkly. "Oh, Mr Bennet, you misunderstand. I have no intention of letting you go just yet. In fact, I think it is high time we return to Netherfield and have a proper discussion—with Mr Darcy present, of course. I am sure he will be delighted to see his guests returned safely."

He stepped back and gestured to the coachman with his pistol. "Turn the carriage around. We are going back to Netherfield."

The coachman hesitated, but a sharp look from Sir Anthony—and the threat of the pistol still aimed squarely at his chest—left him with no choice. Slowly, he began to turn the carriage, the wheels creaking against the muddy road.

As the carriage halted before Netherfield's entrance, Elizabeth's eyes darted to the grand doors, searching for any sign of movement. Sir Anthony's smirk widened, his eyes glinting with satisfaction as he gestured for her and Mr Bennet to disembark. A shiver ran through her, partly from the damp chill of the morning air, but mostly from the cold dread settling in her stomach.

There was no sign of Darcy. Where was he? What had they done to him?

"Come along," Sir Anthony urged, his tone unnervingly light. "I believe Mr Wickham will be quite pleased to see what we've brought him."

Elizabeth glanced at her father. He gave her a brief nod, but his face was now greyer than she had ever seen. They had no choice but to follow, at least for now. Her mind spun, scrambling for any plan that could get them out of this situation. But each thought led back to the same question: Where was Darcy?

As they entered the foyer, Mrs Nicholls emerged from a side door, her expression carefully neutral. She looked at Elizabeth and Mr Bennet, her gaze sharp, almost calculating. Elizabeth felt a flicker of hope. The housekeeper had shown herself to be a decent woman before. Could she be an ally now?

"Ah, you are the housekeeper," Sir Anthony said brusquely, hardly sparing her a glance. "Tell your master I am returned."

Mrs Nicholls hesitated. "The master called for his carriage an hour ago, sir. I do not know how long he intends to stay away."

Sir Anthony scarcely troubled himself to conceal his impatience. "Very well. We shall await him in the drawing room. Let Mr Wickham know as soon as he returns that I have brought him a rather... valuable surprise."

Mrs Nicholls inclined her head, her eyes darting quickly to Elizabeth. There was a fleeting look of understanding there. "Of course, sir," she replied smoothly.

Elizabeth felt a faint stir of relief. Did Mrs Nicholls grasp the seriousness of the situation? The housekeeper discreetly gestured to a younger maid, a girl who moved with quick, practised steps. The maid's eyes flicked from Elizabeth to Mrs Nicholls, and without a word, she slipped away into the shadows of the hall.

Sir Anthony did not appear to notice. He continued to usher Elizabeth and her father into the drawing room, rambling about Wickham's plans and the need for their "cooperation."

Elizabeth scanned the room as they entered. It was empty. No sign of Darcy. A wave of panic rose in her. Where could he be? She needed to find him, to see for herself that he was unharmed.

Her father squeezed her arm gently, his touch steadying. "Stay calm, Lizzy," he murmured, his eyes locked on Sir Anthony.

But calm was the last thing she felt. She cast another glance at Mrs Nicholls, who seemed to be moving more slowly now, perhaps trying to distract Sir Anthony. Was she stalling for time? Was this a signal that help was coming?

Moments passed, each one dragging like an eternity. Then, she caught sight of the younger maid returning, her movements even more urgent, though still quiet and deliberate. She whispered something into Mrs Nicholls's ear. The housekeeper's face remained composed, but Elizabeth could sense a shift.

Mrs Nicholls turned back to Sir Anthony with a professional smile. "Sir, may I suggest that we have tea brought in while we await Mr Wickham?"

Elizabeth's frustration swelled as she was ushered into the drawing room, her eyes darting frantically about for any sign of Darcy. Sir Anthony's face was a mask of irritation, clearly displeased that Wickham had left without warning. Elizabeth tried to focus, to think clearly, but her mind kept circling back to Darcy. She couldn't bear the thought of him suffering alone, potentially at Wickham's mercy.

Mrs Nicholls appeared some minutes later with a silver tea tray, her face carefully composed. She poured the tea with a practised hand, but Elizabeth saw the fleeting look she cast in her direction—a glance that held far more than mere concern.

"Miss Bennet," Mrs Nicholls said softly as she offered her a cup, "perhaps a bit of tea will settle your nerves."

Elizabeth shook her head, her voice coming out in a harsh whisper. "I do not need tea, Mrs Nicholls. I need to know where Mr Darcy is."

Mrs Nicholls poured the tea with a steady hand, but Elizabeth could see the worry etched in the lines around her eyes. As she placed the cup in Elizabeth's trembling fingers, she leaned in just enough to whisper, "Miss Bennet, Mr Darcy is unwell. He is in Mr Wickham's study. We have summoned Mr Jones, and he is with him now."

Elizabeth's heart leapt into her throat. "I must see him," she whispered back urgently, her fingers gripping the teacup so tightly she feared it might shatter.

Mrs Nicholls shook her head, a faint, almost imperceptible movement. "No, miss," she whispered softly, casting a cautious glance towards Sir Anthony. "It would be too great a risk. Mr Jones is doing all that can be done."

Frustration coursed through Elizabeth. Every instinct screamed at her to run to Darcy, to be at his side. But Mrs Nicholls' warning stilled her. She glanced at Sir Anthony, who was pacing by the window, muttering under his breath. He had not yet figured out the exact nature of her connection to Darcy yet, but she could see the calculating look in his eyes as he glanced her way, as if piecing together a puzzle.

Finally, Sir Anthony turned his gaze fully on Mrs Nicholls. "You, there... housekeeper, whatever your name is," he barked, his tone sharp and commanding. "Where is Mr Darcy? If he is still somewhere in this house, I demand to speak with him."

Mrs Nicholls gave a small curtsey, her face composed, betraying nothing. "I regret, sir, that Mr Darcy is not well enough for visitors," she said calmly, but Elizabeth could see the subtle shift in her stance, a protective determination beneath her servant's demeanour.

Sir Anthony's eyes narrowed, flicking between Mrs Nicholls and Elizabeth. Elizabeth's pulse quickened, her mind racing. She needed to find a way to reach Darcy, but she couldn't act rashly—not yet. She took a deep breath, her gaze locking onto Mrs Nicholls, silently pleading for a chance to slip away.

Mrs Nicholls straightened, her eyes darting toward the hallway where more commotion could be heard. "If you'll excuse me, sir," she said with another curtsey, "there appears to be a disturbance in the scullery. I must attend to it."

Elizabeth's eyes followed Mrs Nicholls as she moved toward the door, her mind whirring. The housekeeper was up to something—she had to be. And if Elizabeth had any hope of reaching Darcy, she needed to seize the opportunity.

As Mrs Nicholls slipped out of the room, Sir Anthony's gaze sharpened, fixing on Elizabeth with a cold, calculating stare. He took a step closer, his lips curling into a thin smile. "Miss Bennet," he began, his tone deceptively smooth, "it strikes me as rather curious to find you and your father in Mr Darcy's carriage. And at such an inconvenient time. What exactly is your connection to Mr Darcy?"

Elizabeth straightened, trying to maintain her composure under his scrutinizing gaze. "Mr Darcy is a friend of the family, sir," she replied evenly, willing herself to stay calm. "We were merely returning from a... visit."

"A visit?" Sir Anthony's eyes narrowed, his scepticism clear. "And does this visit have anything to do with your father's recent interest in the election? Or perhaps you have been led to believe Mr Darcy has intentions toward you?"

Mr Bennet, who had been quietly observing the exchange, interjected with a dry laugh. "Ah, Sir Anthony, always quick to the point, I see. As for my interest in the election, it is no secret I am fond of a bit of political theatre. Though I must confess, your particular act has grown a touch stale."

Sir Anthony's expression darkened, but he turned his attention back to Elizabeth. "And what of Mr Darcy's intentions? I would think a gentleman of his standing would have better things to do than meddle in local politics unless there is something—or someone—keeping him here."

Elizabeth bristled at the insinuation, but before she could speak, her father cut in again, his tone laced with sarcasm. "Ah, intentions! A word that can mean so much or so little, depending on the context. I would wager Mr Darcy's intentions are far nobler than yours, Sir Anthony. But then, that would not be saying much, would it?"

A flash of anger crossed Sir Anthony's face, and he stepped closer to Mr Bennet. "You mock me, sir, but you forget your position. I could easily have you arrested for trespassing—or worse. It is not your place to question my motives."

Mr Bennet met his glare with a wry smile, unperturbed. "And yet, here I am, doing just that. You see, Sir Anthony, I have a remarkable talent for not knowing my place."

Sir Anthony's patience was wearing thin, and he turned his focus back to Elizabeth, his eyes narrowing. "Miss Bennet, you will tell me what I want to know. What is the matter with Darcy? Why is he so determined to meddle in matters that do not concern him?"

Elizabeth felt her pulse quicken, but she kept her expression steady. "I am afraid I cannot answer that, sir. Mr Darcy's actions are his own."

Sir Anthony's face twisted with irritation. "Very well," he snapped. "If you will not speak, perhaps your father will reconsider his position. It would be in your best interest to ensure that Mr Darcy withdraws his objections to Sir Anthony's candidacy. I can be quite persuasive when I need to be."

Mr Bennet's eyes flashed with defiance, but he merely smiled. "Persuasive? Is that what they are calling it these days? I always thought it was called something else. Perhaps you should save your breath, Sir Anthony. I doubt Mr Darcy is inclined to take advice from someone like you."

Sir Anthony's eyes blazed with fury, but before he could respond, a loud shout echoed from down the hall, followed by the acrid smell of smoke. Servants began rushing past the open door, their voices raised in alarm. Sir Anthony cursed under his breath, his attention momentarily diverted.

Elizabeth's heart quickened. This was her chance. She turned to her father, giving his hand a quick, urgent squeeze. They had to move, and they had to move now.

Chapter Thirty-Eight

Darcy lay slumped in a chair in Wickham's study, his breathing ragged, his vision hazy from the pain coursing through his skull. Every noise, every movement, sent a sharp throb to his temple, but so far, he had been able to force himself to remain aware, Mr Jones' narcotic concoctions notwithstanding. He had to stay alert, to listen. Wickham would return any moment, and he needed to be ready.

Mr Jones, the apothecary, hovered nearby, his brows furrowed with concern as he poured a small amount of laudanum into a glass. "You should have summoned me weeks ago, Mr Darcy," he said, his tone reproachful. "This condition of yours—whatever it may be—has clearly progressed. You cannot afford to ignore it any longer."

Darcy clenched his jaw, his eyes narrowing. "I am aware of my condition, Mr Jones. More than you could possibly imagine. But I need to remain alert, not drugged. I will not be carted off to Cambridge like some helpless invalid who cannot hold his head up."

The apothecary sighed, placing the glass on the table beside him. "Then, at least allow me to advise you on how to make the journey safely. You must rest, keep yourself calm. And you need to keep well-nourished. The stress—"

"—is unavoidable," Darcy interrupted, his voice sharp. "And if I am to remain alert, then there will be no rest, Mr Jones. Understand this: If I am not fit to handle myself, then I will not be making that journey at all."

Mr Jones opened his mouth to argue, but before he could speak, the distant commotion in the hallway grew louder, followed by the pungent smell of smoke seeping into the room. Darcy's head whipped toward the door, his pulse quickening despite himself. "What in the devil is going on out there?" he muttered.

Mr Jones crossed to the window, peering out cautiously before glancing back at Darcy. "There seems to be some sort of fire somewhere, sir. And the servants... they're running back from the well with buckets, trying to put it out."

“Go into the hall and see what else you can find out,” Darcy ordered, struggling to push himself upright. “But do not let them see your face. If Wickham knows you were here...”

The apothecary nodded, moving quickly to the door. He opened it just enough to peer out, his body blocking Darcy from view. The noise outside grew louder—the shouts, the sound of hurried footsteps—and Mr Jones turned back to Darcy, his expression tense.

“It seems there is quite a commotion. Mr Wickham has just arrived, and he does not look pleased. There is smoke everywhere, and it is causing a great deal of chaos.”

Darcy’s heart sank. This was the worst possible timing. He glanced at the open door, then back at Mr Jones. “You need to leave. Now. And make sure no one sees you.”

“But Mr Darcy—”

“Go, Jones,” Darcy snapped, his voice low but firm. “Do not let Wickham see you. Get out of here while you still can.”

The apothecary hesitated for a moment, then nodded, slipping quietly out of the room and closing the door softly behind him. Darcy listened to the faint sound of his footsteps receding down the hallway, then turned his attention back to the noise outside.

The commotion outside reached his ears first—voices raised, the hurried steps of servants, and then the unmistakable burn of smoke in his eyes. Darcy’s grip on the armrest tightened as he heard the distinct click of footsteps approaching. Wickham’s footsteps. Darcy’s stomach twisted. The door swung open, and there he stood, wet from the rain, his expression dark and furious. Wickham’s eyes darted around the room, then fixed on Darcy, a sneer forming on his lips.

“Darcy,” Wickham said, his voice steady but edged with irritation as he stepped into the room. “Did you really think sending me to Longbourn would keep me away for long? You underestimate me, as always. I know every trick you would try to pull—by now, I would have thought you’d learn that.”

Darcy forced himself to sit straighter, every muscle protesting. He had no intention of letting Wickham see his weakness. “Obviously, you did not know as much as you thought you did,” he replied, his voice steadier than he felt. “But it kept you away long enough, did it not?”

“Long enough for what, Darcy? You are still here and in worse shape than before, if that sickly sweat on your brow is any indication. What did you hope to gain?”

Darcy swallowed, trying to force his vision back to singularity, but there was nothing he could do about the tremor in his hand. “Little enough, I suppose.”

"Where is Bennet?" Wickham stalked closer, towering over Darcy's chair. "You know—you must know. Where have you sent him, Darcy? Off on some errand to undermine me with the neighbourhood?"

Darcy's breathing eased a little. So, Wickham still did not know that Mr Bennet and Elizabeth had been in his carriage. They remained safe. "How should I know? I scarcely know the man, and I am certainly not his keeper."

Wickham's sneer deepened, but before he could respond, a servant rushed in behind him. "Mr Wickham, there's a fire in the scullery! We're trying to contain it, but the kitchens are almost entirely blocked!"

"A fire?" Wickham's eyes flashed with irritation, then suspicion. "Who started it?"

The servant looked uneasy. "I—I don't know, sir. It was an accident..."

Wickham dismissed the servant with a curt wave. "See that it is handled," he snapped before turning back to Darcy. "I suppose you had something to do with this as well?"

Darcy managed a faint smile despite the pounding in his head. "I have been here the entire time, Wickham, incapacitated as you see. I hardly think I could orchestrate a fire from this chair."

Wickham opened his mouth to retort, but before he could speak, another figure appeared in the doorway—Sir Anthony Mortimer. Darcy's heart sank further.

"Well, well, Darcy," Sir Anthony drawled, his tone dripping with false civility. "You've been quite the busy man. It seems we've found some unexpected guests of yours."

Darcy's breath hitched. *Guests?* His mind raced. They could not mean—

His stomach lurched as the door swung open wider, revealing Elizabeth and Mr Bennet standing just outside the threshold. Elizabeth's face was taut with worry, her eyes darting between him and Wickham. Mr Bennet, on the other hand, wore a bemused expression as though he found the whole situation mildly entertaining. Darcy's heart sank. How had they been discovered? They should have been well on their way to safety by now.

Wickham's eyes widened with surprise, the confident mask slipping for just a moment before he regained his composure. "Well, well," he said slowly, his tone sharpening as he assessed the situation. "What have we here?"

"They were hiding in Darcy's carriage," Mortimer replied. Darcy's hair stood on the back of his neck at the way Mortimer's eyes were raking down Elizabeth's body. "Surprised you did not find them yourself, Wickham. And the lady here thought to make for the window when the servants reported smoke. I only just caught her as she was climbing out."

Wickham's gaze snapped back to Darcy, then he rubbed his jaw and began to pace round the Bennets. "Darcy," he murmured, "I confess myself humbled. You yet have the capacity for surprise. So, Miss Bennet and her esteemed father, hiding in Darcy's carriage like thieves in the night. I must admit, this is quite the unexpected reunion."

He forced his expression to remain neutral, though his insides were churning. "Wickham," Darcy said, his voice steady but edged with warning, "leave them out of this. They have nothing to do with our dispute."

Wickham's eyes narrowed, the wheels visibly turning in his mind. "Nothing to do with it? I find that hard to believe, Darcy. Why else would they be here, hidden away in your carriage? Unless..." He turned a calculating gaze toward Mr Bennet. "Unless there's more to this than meets the eye."

"It appears Mr Bennet might have publicly changed his allegiance, don't you think, Wickham?" Sir Anthony asked. "And as for Mr Darcy, well, perhaps Miss Bennet is even more... persuasive than you thought."

Elizabeth's face flushed, but she held her ground, her chin lifting defiantly. "You know nothing of the circumstances," she said, her voice calm but firm.

Wickham's gaze flicked to Elizabeth, then back to Darcy, his mouth curling into a smile that did not reach his eyes. "Oh, I think I know enough," he drawled. "You fell for Darcy—heaven only knows why, for I thought you utterly despised the man. Unless you are fonder of coin than I had given you credit for— and your father did whatever you wished him to do."

Mr Bennet's lips quirked into a small, ironic smile. "I assure you, Mr Wickham, I am no one's pawn. Not Darcy's, nor my daughter's, nor yours. And I came here of my own accord—more for the entertainment, I dare say, than any political machination."

Wickham's eyes darkened, clearly irritated by Mr Bennet's flippant tone. "You think this is a game, old man?" he hissed. "I assure you, the stakes are far higher than you imagine."

Darcy tried to stay upright, his vision blurring as he swayed to his feet. The pain in his head had worsened, a relentless pounding that made every sound sharper, every movement more jarring. He could barely focus, but he had to. He had to protect Elizabeth and Mr Bennet.

Wickham clearly noticed the way Darcy swayed, his steps uncertain. "You do not look well, Darcy," he said casually. "You ought to be resting. I am more than capable of seeing to the lady's comforts."

Darcy watched Wickham's gaze flick to Elizabeth, and a cold dread settled in his stomach. Wickham's expression softened, his lips curving into a smile that might have seemed polite to anyone who did not know him better. He stepped closer to Elizabeth, extending his hand as though to offer her assistance.

"Miss Bennet, forgive my earlier brusqueness. I only wish to ensure your safety, you understand."

Darcy's pulse quickened. He could see the calculated look in Wickham's eyes, the way he was positioning himself. Elizabeth hesitated, glancing at Darcy for reassurance. Darcy wanted to shout at her to keep her distance, but his voice caught in his throat, a wave of dizziness nearly toppling him over.

Wickham's hand moved suddenly, gripping Elizabeth's arm and twisting it behind her back. Her gasp of pain cut through Darcy like a knife. He lurched forward instinctively, but his legs buckled beneath him. Wickham's smile remained in place, his tone still deceptively smooth. "You see, Darcy, it is quite simple. You do as I say, and no one gets hurt."

"Leave her out of this, Wickham!" Darcy growled, his voice hoarse with desperation.

But Wickham ignored him, pushing Elizabeth ahead of him. "Oh, I think not," he said, his tone mockingly light. "You see, you and I are going to have a little chat, and she's going to make sure you stay... cooperative."

Darcy's vision swam, and he fought to stay conscious. He could feel himself slipping, his legs weakening. He looked at Mr Bennet, who was already moving to support him, his expression grim. A male servant rushed forward to help, and together, they kept Darcy on his feet as Wickham forced Elizabeth toward the door.

"Bring him," Wickham ordered over his shoulder. "I want to keep an eye on all of you."

The room was filling with smoke, the air thick and choking. Darcy could barely breathe, his chest tight with panic and pain. He could see the fear in Elizabeth's eyes, even as she tried to remain calm, tried to stay strong. Her courage only fueled his determination. He would not let Wickham win.

As they stumbled toward the door, the servants began to act, moving subtly, quietly, trying to create as much chaos as possible without drawing Wickham's attention. Darcy could see Mrs Nicholls in the corner of his eye, directing the maids and footmen bringing in buckets of water, but... none of them were going towards the scullery, where the fire was supposed to be. She was up to something, he knew it, but what?

The shouts outside grew louder, frantic voices merging with the crackle of fire and the sharp, acrid smell of smoke that now filled the air. The commotion was intensifying, with servants rushing past the door, their faces smeared with soot, carrying buckets of water, their footsteps pounding against the wooden floors in hurried, erratic rhythms. Darcy could feel the heat building from the growing fire, a suffocating warmth that pressed against his skin and made it hard to breathe.

Wickham's composure began to crack. He barked orders at the two workmen who had accompanied him, his voice rising above the din, but there was a tremor of uncertainty beneath his authoritative tone. The chaos was taking its toll on him, eroding the veneer of control he so desperately clung to.

Darcy could feel his own strength waning, the dizziness creeping up on him, threatening to pull him under. His chest tightened, and his breaths came in shallow gasps. But the sight of Elizabeth, her arm wrenched behind her back in Wickham's grip, stirred a fury and desperation that cut through his haze. He could not let Wickham take her. He had to act, and quickly.

Darcy looked at Mr Bennet and the servant who stood beside him. "Help me," he whispered, his voice barely audible over the noise, his eyes fixed on Elizabeth. "We need... a chance."

Mr Bennet nodded, his usually indifferent demeanour is now steely with determination. Darcy saw a flicker of resolve in his eyes—this was not the time for his usual sarcasm or indolence. He understood the gravity of the moment and what was at stake. Mr Bennet shifted slightly, his body moving closer to the door, adopting a position that was deceptively casual yet poised to spring into action.

Darcy drew in a shaky breath, every muscle in his body tensing. His head swam, the pain throbbing in time with his heartbeat, but he forced himself to focus. This might be their only chance. He had to create a distraction.

Just as Wickham reached the doorway, yanking Elizabeth with him, Darcy let himself collapse forward in a controlled fall that scattered bodies ahead of him. Mr Bennet and the footman both stumbled as Darcy's weight collided with the backs of their legs, their bodies crashing into the doorframe with a heavy thud.

"What the—" Wickham spun around, momentarily losing his grip on Elizabeth as he tried to make sense of the sudden chaos.

That brief lapse in concentration was all Darcy needed. With a surge of adrenaline, he hurled himself forward, colliding with Wickham, his shoulder slamming into Wickham's chest with enough force to knock him back against the wall. Elizabeth twisted free, wrenching her arm out of Wickham's loosened grip, and Mr Bennet lunged forward, pulling her behind him. The servant rushed to Darcy's side, steadying him as he swayed, the room spinning around him.

Wickham recovered quickly, his face a mask of rage. "You think you can make a fool of me, Darcy?" he shouted, his voice rising above the noise. "What do you think you stand to win? You are dying!"

Darcy's vision blurred, black spots dancing at the edges, but he planted his feet firmly, refusing to yield. "This is not about winning, Wickham," he rasped, each word a struggle against the pain that threatened to overwhelm him. "It is about getting out of here alive."

The smoke was thicker now, stinging his eyes and filling his lungs with every breath. Servants were dashing past, coughing and shouting, trying to keep the fire from spreading further. Wickham's eyes darted around the smoke-filled hallway, his advantage slipping away with every passing second. "Very well," he muttered, his voice strained, his composure cracking. "We are leaving. But Miss Bennet comes with me."

Wickham lunged for Elizabeth again, but this time, Mr Bennet and the servant were ready. They stepped into his path, forming a wall between him and his quarry. Yet, Elizabeth was not content to merely stand by. Her eyes flashed with defiance as she stepped closer to Wickham, her chin tilted upwards, a sharp rebuke poised on her lips.

"Really, Mr Wickham," Elizabeth drawled, her tone dripping with sarcasm that cut through the chaos like a blade, "is this your grand plan to prove your manhood? Bullying women and elderly men? How bold you are. Truly, the very model of a gentleman."

Wickham's face flushed with anger, his smug expression slipping as her words hit their mark. "You know nothing of what is at stake here, Miss Bennet," he snapped, though his voice wavered ever so slightly.

Elizabeth arched a brow, her eyes narrowing with contempt. "Oh, I know plenty," she retorted, a sharp edge to her voice. "I know you are nothing more than a bought man with a tremendous sense of your own inferiority, trying desperately to play the part of a gentleman. But do go on, Mr Wickham, show us how a true coward carries himself in a crisis."

Wickham's eyes narrowed further, fury sparking in his gaze as he glared at her. "I would watch my tongue if I were you, Miss Bennet," he hissed.

Elizabeth's lips curled into a mocking smile. "Oh, believe me, I would rather watch yours. It does such amusing contortions when you lie. I daresay it is your best skill."

Her words stung, and Wickham's eyes narrowed, a flash of anger crossing his features. He moved again to grab her, but Mr Bennet thrust his arm out, his voice hard with resolve. "Back away, Wickham. You have no business here, and even less with my daughter."

Darcy, struggling to stay upright, forced himself into Wickham's line of sight, his presence a steadying anchor amidst the chaos. "You will not touch my future bride," he rasped, every word a strain. "She stays where she is."

Wickham paused, frustration clear in his expression. He was losing control, the fire's heat now almost unbearable, the smoke choking. His gaze flicked from Darcy to Elizabeth, calculating. She met his stare with unwavering defiance, her posture rigid, her hands clenched into fists at her sides as if ready to strike.

"You think you can command me, Darcy?" Wickham snarled, his bravado slipping. "You, who cannot even stand without shaking?"

Darcy did not respond, but Elizabeth's voice rose again, sharp and mocking. "At least Mr Darcy stands for something, Mr Wickham. Unlike some who slink about in the shadows, preying on the vulnerable."

Wickham's face twisted with rage, but Elizabeth did not waver, her gaze steady and unflinching. The fire's roar was getting louder, the heat oppressive, but she would not be cowed by him.

"Enough of this," Wickham finally barked, his composure slipping as the situation grew more dire. "You will all come with me, or we will see how long your defiance lasts in this inferno."

Elizabeth took a step back, moving closer to Darcy and her father. "We will take our chances here," she said calmly, a final note of defiance in her tone. "At least here, we are not at the mercy of a coward."

Wickham hesitated, his face a mask of fury and indecision. The flames crackled louder, and he could see his advantage slipping away with every moment. For a moment, he seemed about to strike, but then he stepped back, his gaze still locked on Elizabeth.

And then, without another word, he turned and stormed out, leaving them alone in the smoke-filled room.

Darcy could feel the tremor in his own legs, the unsteady wobble that threatened to betray him at any moment. He could not keep this up much longer—his body was nearing its limit, and the fire was spreading too quickly. But he kept his gaze locked on Wickham's retreating back, refusing to show any sign of weakness until the blackguard had gone.

Elizabeth rushed to Darcy's side, her face pale, and eyes wide with concern. "Fitzwilliam!" she cried, her hands moving to steady him, "We need to get you out of here."

Darcy nodded weakly, struggling to stay focused. The heat was becoming unbearable, and the smoke was choking him. "The back door," he murmured, barely able to get the words out. "We need to get to the back door."

Mr Bennet nodded, quickly taking charge. "This way," he urged, moving toward the nearest hallway. "We can make it if we hurry. Keep low and stay close to the walls."

Elizabeth hooked an arm under Darcy's shoulder, helping to support him as they began to move. The servant stayed close behind, ready to catch Darcy if he faltered. The smoke was thick and acrid, stinging their eyes and filling their lungs, but they pressed on, driven by the need to escape.

The group moved through the darkened corridors, the heat intensifying with every step. Flames were visible now, licking at the edges of the wooden beams and creeping along the walls. The crackling of burning wood was a constant, ominous presence, a reminder that time was running out. Darcy's breath was coming in ragged gasps, his strength fading rapidly. He stumbled, his vision swimming, but Elizabeth held him firm, her grip strong and unwavering.

"Almost there," she urged, her voice steady despite the fear she could feel gnawing at her insides. She could see the faint outline of the back door ahead, a small sliver of hope in the midst of the chaos.

As they neared the exit, a sudden burst of flames erupted from a doorway to their left, the heat scorching their skin. Elizabeth shielded Darcy as best she could, her own fear forgot in her determination to protect him. The servant pushed forward, kicking the door open with a forceful shove, revealing the cool night air beyond.

"Go!" Mr Bennet shouted, ushering them through the doorway. "Get him out of here!"

Elizabeth didn't hesitate. She half-dragged, half-carried Darcy through the door, feeling the cool rush of air on her face as they stumbled into the night. The servant followed close behind, slamming the door shut to slow the spread of the fire.

They were outside, but the danger was far from over. Darcy sagged against Elizabeth, his body trembling with the effort it had taken just to get this far. His head was pounding, each beat of his heart sending a fresh wave of pain through his skull. But they were out. They were safe.

"Fitzwilliam," Elizabeth murmured, her voice thick with emotion, "stay with me. Just a little longer. We need to get you away from here."

Darcy nodded, though he was barely conscious. He could feel the darkness closing in, his body finally giving way to the exhaustion that had been clawing at him for so long. But he forced himself to stay awake, to stay alert. He could not leave Elizabeth now. Not after everything.

"We... we need to move," he whispered, his voice barely a breath. "Cannot... stay here."

Mr Bennet joined them, his expression grim but determined. "He's right. Wickham and Mortimer are surely waiting for us to emerge somewhere. There's a path around the side of the house that leads to the stables. Perhaps his carriage is still there to get us further away, and in the chaos of a house fire, I doubt Wickham will be able to spare his energies for us."

Elizabeth nodded. "Then let us go," she said, tightening her grip on Darcy's arm. "Come, my love. Stay with me."

He managed a lopsided grin—at least, it felt like it was probably lopsided because the right side of his mouth did not respond as he would have liked. "As you wish, Mrs Darcy."

Chapter Thirty-Nine

The carriage rattled over the uneven road as Elizabeth tried to wedge her shoulder up under Darcy's to steady him. Her mind was still reeling from the chaos at Netherfield, the thick smoke, the shouts of the servants, and the heat of the fire. But above all, it was the sight of Darcy—his face half-paralyzed, his movements sluggish—that tore at her heart. His hand trembled slightly in hers, and his eyes had grown unfocused.

She watched him with mounting terror. Was it already too late for this doctor in Cambridge to help him? Would he even survive the journey? Certainly, stress and fatigue worsened his symptoms, but how much worse could they get before he collapsed irrevocably?

The carriage lurched to a sudden halt, nearly throwing Darcy, and Elizabeth with him, forward. She glanced out the window and saw a familiar sight—Sir William Lucas's carriage barreling toward them, the horses frothing at the mouth from exertion.

Her father was turning in the rear-facing seat to peer out of the window. "Stay calm, Lizzy," he murmured, his voice low. "We must not appear panicked."

Sir William's carriage drew up alongside theirs, and he leaned out the window, waving frantically to catch their attention. "Mr Darcy!" he called, his voice tinged with alarm. "Do you need assistance? What is happening at Netherfield? I saw the smoke and came as quickly as I could!"

His gaze darted anxiously toward the rising smoke in the distance, then back to the figure slumped in the opposite carriage. It took a moment for reality to sink in—Darcy was there, but he was not alone, nor was he in any position to speak.

Elizabeth tensed, her eyes fixed on Darcy. His lips moved, but no sound came out, and the right side of his face twitched uncontrollably. Her heart twisted painfully at the sight. He was struggling, desperately trying to form words, but the seizure or whatever was gripping him made it impossible.

Sir William's eyes widened further as he took in the scene, shock spreading across his features. "Mr Bennet?" he stammered, finally noticing the older man seated beside Elizabeth. "What on earth—?"

Mr Bennet cut him off with a brisk wave of his hand. "There is no time for explanations, Sir William. Darcy is unwell, and we have been caught in a rather nasty business with Wickham and Sir Anthony. I suggest you turn back at once and raise the alarm. Get the whole of Meryton involved if you must."

Sir William blinked, struggling to comprehend the gravity of what he was hearing. "Wickham, you say? And Sir Anthony? But... the fire—"

Elizabeth glanced up from Darcy, her eyes sharp with urgency. "I assure you, Sir William, the housekeeper has her people well managed. Everyone is quite safe, but they could use help putting out the flames."

"I should say so! Look, let me call for others. I shall drive out to Purvis, and might you—"

"Not now, Sir William," Mr Bennet cut him off. "We need to reach Cambridge as quickly as possible. Please, go back and warn the neighbourhood. Wickham and Sir Anthony are not to be trusted by any measure, and by no means should any responsible man give them his vote."

"But, sir! You speak vague accusations against a good and generous man, who—"

"A corrupt man who has been paid to engineer this entire by-election to place another corrupt man in the House!" Mr Bennet retorted. "I can offer you proofs if you like, but just now, we have a more pressing crisis at hand."

Sir William's gaze flickered back to Darcy, who seemed barely able to hold himself upright. "Yes, it appears so. Mr Darcy, sir, are you... are you quite all right?" he asked, his tone softening with genuine concern. "Do you need anything?"

Mr Bennet leaned forward again, his voice commanding. "Sir William, I assure you, Darcy is in no state to converse. He needs medical attention. Go back to Meryton and do as I have asked. Now."

Sir William hesitated, clearly torn between the instinct to help and the urgency in Mr Bennet's voice. Finally, he nodded. "Very well, Bennet. I shall see to it at once." His eyes flicked briefly back to Elizabeth, noticing the way she clung to Darcy, and he added, almost as an afterthought, "And... congratulations, I suppose, on your daughter's future engagement."

Elizabeth flushed, glancing quickly at her father, who merely raised an eyebrow. The coachman, sensing the exchange had gone on long enough, cracked the reins, and their carriage jolted forward, leaving Sir William staring after them.

As their carriage jolted back into motion, Elizabeth shifted her weight to support Darcy better, but he was too heavy and too limp for her efforts to have much effect. His head lolled to one side, resting awkwardly against her shoulder, and she could feel the uneven rise and fall of his chest, his breath laboured and shallow. Her stomach knotted with every bump and sway of the carriage, each jolt sending a new wave of worry through her. She wanted to do something—anything—to ease his suffering, but she felt utterly helpless.

Her father, noticing her struggle, said nothing at first. He simply unfastened his great-coat, balled it up, and leaned across the carriage to gently place it under Darcy's head. The improvised pillow provided some measure of comfort, and she saw Darcy's tense features relax slightly as his head settled more comfortably.

Elizabeth offered her father a grateful smile, whispering, "Thank you." Mr Bennet nodded curtly, his expression softening just a little in response. He watched Darcy for a moment, his brows furrowed in thought.

"Papa," Elizabeth began quietly, her voice barely audible over the rumble of the carriage wheels, "do you truly think we can make it to Cambridge before nightfall?"

Her father's gaze shifted from Darcy to the road outside, calculating the distance in his mind. "We have little choice," he replied, his tone pragmatic. "We had a late start, and we have already been delayed some two hours from that point. On good roads, it might take eight hours to reach Cambridge, including a stop to change horses. That is a long day of travel even if we had started out at a decent time. But still, I would rather press on if the driver is confident in navigating after dark. Those are well-traveled roads, and there seems a better chance of getting help for Mr Darcy there than taking whatever lodgings we might find along the way and delaying our arrival further."

Elizabeth nodded, though her heart remained heavy with doubt. She glanced back at Darcy, his face pale and drawn, and she squeezed the large, powerful hand that lay nestled in hers.

He tried to smile back at her, but only half his face complied.

DARCY WOKE WITH A start, the dim light filtering through the curtains, unfamiliar and disorienting. His body felt heavy, his limbs sluggish, as if he were submerged in water. The room around him swam in a haze, and a dull ache throbbed behind his eyes. He blinked, trying to clear his vision, but the fog in his mind only seemed to thicken. Where was he? Panic gripped him as the thought struck: *Elizabeth!*

He sat up abruptly, too quickly. A sharp pain shot through his head, and the room tilted violently. He gasped, pressing a hand to his temple to steady himself. The last thing he remembered was being at Netherfield, Wickham's sneering face, the smoke... "Elizabeth!" Where was she? He needed to find her.

"Sir, please—lie back," a familiar voice urged gently, and Darcy turned his head to see Giles standing by the bedside, his expression one of calm concern. "You are safe, sir, and so is Miss Elizabeth. She is just down the hall, on the same floor."

Darcy blinked, trying to process the words, but his mind felt sluggish, as though it were moving through treacle. "Elizabeth... down the hall?" he repeated, his voice rough and hoarse. His heart still pounded, the fear for her safety lingering. "Is she... is she safe?"

"Yes, sir, she is quite safe," Giles reassured him, stepping closer. "She was here not ten minutes ago, asking after you."

The tension in Darcy's chest loosened slightly at Giles's words, a faint sense of relief creeping in. If Elizabeth was well enough to visit, then she must be secure... safe. He took a shaky breath, his body beginning to relax, the pain in his head easing just a little. "Where... where am I?" he managed, his voice still thick with confusion.

"You are in Cambridge, sir, at an inn," Giles explained. "Doctor Pembroke has been sent for and is expected to arrive sometime this morning."

"Pembroke?" Darcy muttered, rubbing a hand over his face. His mind was still clouded, his thoughts slow to form. "How... how did we get here?"

"Mr Bennet helped, sir," Giles replied. "He was instrumental in ensuring we made it to Cambridge."

Darcy frowned, trying to recall the events of the previous day, but his memory was a blur. "Bennet?" he repeated, incredulous. The image of Mr Bennet he remembered was that of a reclusive cynic, a man more inclined to mock than assist. "Bennet helped?"

"Yes, sir," Giles confirmed with a small nod. "He was quite determined to get you to Cambridge, even insisted that we continue through the night rather than stopping."

Darcy blinked again, the fog in his mind slowly beginning to lift. The pieces of the previous day's chaos started to come together, though they still felt distant, as if seen through a thick mist. He struggled to connect his thoughts; his mind was still sluggish from whatever substance had been given to him. "Laudanum?" he guessed, his voice a little clearer now.

Giles nodded again. "A small dose, sir, to help you rest during the journey. You were in considerable pain."

Darcy's hand tightened into a fist against the sheets, frustration simmering beneath the surface. He hated feeling so disconnected from his own body, his own thoughts. "And Elizabeth," he asked again, more insistent this time. "You are sure she is just down the hall?"

"Quite sure, sir," Giles reassured him, his tone steady. "She is eager to see you once you are up and dressed."

Darcy closed his eyes for a moment, willing the remnants of the laudanum to dissipate. He needed to clear his head, to think straight. But more than that, he needed to see Elizabeth. The thought of her waiting for him stirred a sense of urgency, a need to be near her, to reassure himself that she was truly safe.

"Help me up," he said, his voice firm despite the lingering grogginess. "Dress me quickly, Giles. I want to see her."

Giles moved swiftly, his hands deft as he helped Darcy to his feet. The room swayed slightly, but Darcy gritted his teeth, pushing through the dizziness. He could not afford to be weak now—not when Elizabeth needed him. And perhaps, he thought with a faint, determined smile, he needed her even more.

ELIZABETH PACED THE LENGTH of her small room, her footsteps echoing softly against the floorboards. She could not still the anxious tremble in her limbs nor quiet the frantic beating of her heart. She yearned to go to him, to rush down the hall to his side, but she had no right to do so. Not yet. Not as if she were already his wife.

How much easier it would have been if she were! If only she could hold him, comfort him, reassure herself that he was still breathing, still fighting. But they would have to wait a few weeks for that... a few weeks that Darcy might not have, if his condition on the road were any indication. Her legs felt watery at the very thought, and she gripped the back of a chair to steady herself.

She cared nothing for his wealth, his estate, or his connections. None of it mattered if he was destined to die. If there was truly nothing that Doctor Pembroke could do to save him, then she wanted—no, she *needed*—the right to call him her husband before she lost him. Her chest tightened with the weight of her fear, and she cupped a hand over her mouth, realising with a start that she was weeping uncontrollably. She wiped her cheeks hastily, taking a deep breath to steady herself. She could not afford to lose control now, not when the doctor might arrive at any moment to either confirm their fears or give miraculous hope.

Desperate for something—anything—she could control, Elizabeth moved to the small writing desk near the window and sat down. She would write a letter to Charlotte. Jane would have already spoken with her, surely, advising her about Mr Wickham and Sir Anthony, as well as their engagements with Mr Bingley and Mr Darcy. But Elizabeth wanted to tell Charlotte the whole story herself, to provide her own account of everything that had transpired. She also wanted to comfort her friend, knowing how close Charlotte had come to losing her heart to Wickham. Elizabeth feared that Charlotte would be devastated all over again, that she would lapse back into her dark self-pity and the belief that no one truly valued her.

She picked up her pen, her hand trembling slightly, and began to write. She poured her heart onto the page, her words flowing in a torrent of emotion. She wrote of Darcy's bravery, his strength in the face of adversity, and the desperate hope that still flickered in her heart. She prayed that when this nightmare with Mr Darcy's strange condition was resolved—one way or another—she would do whatever she could to see Charlotte happy, to ensure that her friend found the love and respect she so richly deserved.

A sudden knock on the door interrupted her thoughts, and she nearly dropped her pen in surprise. She heard Darcy's voice outside, low and familiar, and her heart soared in her chest. She pushed back from the desk, her chair scraping against the floor, and ran to open the door. She flung it wide, her eyes searching for him, her breath catching in her throat at the sight of his tall, familiar figure standing there.

DARCY HAD BARELY KNOCKED before the door swung open, revealing Elizabeth on the other side, her eyes wide with a mixture of relief and something more intense. She paused for only a fraction of a second before sweeping into his arms, pulling him close with a force that made him forget everything except the warmth of her body pressed against his. He knew very well that he ought not to enter her private room, that propriety dictated he kept his distance, but as she drew him inside, his resolve melted away. The door closed behind them with a quiet click, sealing them in a world of their own making.

Elizabeth's hands were on his face, her fingers tracing the lines of his jaw, the contours of his cheeks, as if checking to see if he was really there, if he was truly well. Her lips found his with an urgency that matched his own, and he kissed her eagerly, his hands moving to her waist, pulling her even closer. She tasted of salt and sweetness, her breath mingling with his in a way that made his heart pound with something other than the exertion of the illness that plagued him.

"How are you feeling today?" she asked between kisses, her voice a soft murmur against his lips.

He pulled back just enough to meet her gaze. "Honestly, I feel dreadful," he said with a wry smile, "but I thought I might spare you the details and instead make a poor attempt at charming you with my wit. It seems the tables have turned, Miss Bennet. It was not long ago that every time we met, you were the one flustered and out of sorts."

She laughed, a bright sound that made his chest ache with affection. "Oh, do not be so sure of yourself, Mr Darcy. My ankle is still black and blue from the other day, and it is terribly tender. I daresay it is ready to revolt at any moment, given a proper excuse."

He chuckled softly, his fingers brushing a stray curl from her face. "Then I shall simply have to carry you everywhere from now on, to prevent any further mishaps."

Elizabeth's eyes sparkled with a playful glint as she wrapped her arms around his neck. "I think I could grow accustomed to that. You are far more reliable than my father's miserable horse, at any rate."

"You trust me that much, do you?"

Elizabeth pulled back just enough to cup his chin in her hand and gaze into his eyes. "Trust? I trust you to the moon and beyond. You are the one person I would believe when all the rest of the world whispered the same lie—I would trust you with my life."

He kissed her again, more slowly this time, savouring the feel of her lips against his. "I have already done that, Elizabeth," he whispered, his voice low and earnest, the words a promise and a plea all at once. "With the full measure of all that I am, I am a lost man without you."

She responded with a soft sigh, her fingers threading through his hair, and for a moment, there was nothing in the world but the two of them, their bodies pressed close, their breaths mingling as one. But then, a quiet knock at the door shattered the stillness, and they broke apart, both of them breathing hard, their hearts racing.

"Mr Darcy," came Giles's voice from the other side, his tone carefully neutral. "Doctor Pembroke has arrived and is ready to examine you."

Darcy closed his eyes briefly, a flicker of frustration crossing his face before he looked back at Elizabeth. She smiled softly, her hand brushing against his cheek. "Go," she whispered, her voice gentle but firm. "Let him help you."

He nodded, pressing a final kiss to her forehead before stepping back. "I will return as soon as I can," he promised, his eyes lingering on hers. "And then we shall speak of many things, Elizabeth. Many things."

With that, he turned and opened the door, his heart heavy with the weight of what was to come but lightened by the feel of her touch still lingering on his skin.

Chapter Forty

Darcy steadied himself against the doorframe as he left Elizabeth's room, his heart still thudding from the fervent embrace they had shared. He could scarcely believe that in the span of only a few days, his entire world had tilted on its axis. The thought of Elizabeth, her lips on his, the warmth of her touch—it brought a rush of strength he had not felt in weeks. But as he stepped into the hall, he came face to face with Mr Bennet.

Mr Bennet arched a brow, taking in Darcy's dishevelled appearance, a faint hint of amusement in his eyes. "Up and about are we, Mr Darcy?" His tone was dry, but there was a note of genuine concern beneath the surface.

Darcy hesitated under the weight of the man's scrutiny. He considered offering some excuse, but what point was there? They both knew what he had been doing, and he could not bring himself to regret it. "Yes, Mr Bennet," he said, inclining his head. "I—" He stopped, feeling a surge of dizziness. "I understand Doctor Pembroke is awaiting me in my room."

"Ah. Then I shall not keep you, sir. My very best wishes for a promising outcome."

Darcy dipped his head and began to walk on, but then paused. "Mr Bennet? I wonder if you might... sit in on the examination? My memory, you see, has been unreliable. Elizabeth will want a full accounting, and I fear I might... not remember everything."

Mr Bennet's eyes softened, and he gave a slight nod. "Of course, Mr Darcy. I am not much for medical jargon, but I dare say I can manage a faithful recounting. Lead the way."

Darcy felt a swell of gratitude. Despite his cynicism and sharp tongue, Mr Bennet had shown himself to be yet another soul in whom he could trust. Together, they entered the room, where Doctor Pembroke was already waiting.

"Mr Darcy," Pembroke greeted him, rising from his chair with a measured nod.

"I am." Darcy inclined his head politely, then gestured to Mr Bennet and Giles, who had walked in behind them. "This is Mr Bennet, my future father-in-law, and Giles, my valet. I desire for them both to sit in on the examination."

"Of course, sir." Pembroke dipped a slight bow to Mr Bennet. "And may I offer my felicitations on the happy event? I hope I will be able to provide you with a promising report, sir."

"So do I. I trust you have been apprised of my condition?"

Pembroke's eyes still flicked between the two men, his expression thoughtful. "I have reviewed the notes and correspondence from your previous physicians. I confess, I have some concerns. I hope to restore you to the lady waiting for you, Mr Darcy, but we must be candid about your situation."

Darcy nodded, his throat tightening as he took a seat. He braced himself for the examination, knowing this might be the moment that sealed his fate. Doctor Pembroke began by asking a series of pointed questions, his tone clinical yet compassionate. "Have your headaches been consistent, or do they come in waves? Is there any recent trauma you can recall that might have precipitated these episodes?"

Darcy rubbed his temple, feeling the familiar throbbing beneath his fingers. "The headaches have been persistent," he said slowly, choosing his words carefully. "Sometimes they dull to a manageable level, but they often return with a vengeance. As for trauma... there was a fall, some months back, from a young horse. I did not think much of it at the time."

Pembroke's brow furrowed. "A fall, you say? And you struck your head?"

Darcy nodded. "Yes, though I did not lose consciousness. At least... not immediately. And the headaches did not commence for some while after that, so I did not believe there was a connection."

The doctor hummed thoughtfully, jotting notes in his ledger. "And the seizures—how frequent have they been?"

"More frequent of late," Darcy admitted, his voice tightening. "They come without warning, and... leave me disoriented."

Pembroke moved closer, peering into Darcy's eyes, checking his pupils for any signs of irregularity. "Any changes in your vision? Blurring, double vision?"

Darcy hesitated. "There have been moments. Flickers at the edge of my sight. And sometimes, I see spots of light."

Pembroke's face remained impassive, but his eyes sharpened with a new intensity. "Mr Darcy," he said carefully, "from what you describe, there is a possibility—indeed, a strong one—that you are suffering from a subdural haematoma rather than a tumour."

Darcy's breath caught. "A... a what?"

"A blood clot, Mr Darcy. Inside the skull and within the outer layer of the brain. A rather serious one, I fear. Given your symptoms and the history of trauma, it is likely that the blood has been accumulating slowly, causing increasing pressure on your brain. This could account for the headaches, the seizures, and the fluctuations in your condition."

Darcy's brow furrowed as he considered the doctor's words. "Why do you suspect a subdural hematoma rather than a tumour?" he asked, his voice steady, though an undercurrent of anxiety rippled through him. "The other physicians I consulted were quite certain it was a tumour."

Doctor Pembroke regarded him carefully, weighing his words before he spoke. "Your symptoms, Mr Darcy, provide crucial clues. A brain tumour typically presents with a gradual onset of symptoms, worsening over months or even years. The symptoms you describe—your persistent headaches, occasional vision disturbances, and seizures—are indeed common with a tumour, but there are inconsistencies. A tumour would likely cause progressive, consistent neurological deficits. You would be experiencing a steady decline rather than the fluctuating nature of your episodes."

He paused, then continued, his tone more measured. "Moreover, you mentioned experiencing a head injury some months ago, which the other doctors may not have fully considered. A subdural hematoma can develop slowly following trauma, particularly if the bleeding is gradual. This would explain the waxing and waning of your symptoms. The moments of clarity interspersed with sudden seizures and worsening headaches—these are more indicative of a clot than a tumour. The acute episodes, the confusion that comes and goes... they point to pressure building intermittently rather than a constant, growing mass."

Darcy nodded slowly, absorbing this new perspective. "So, you believe my condition could be due to a clot pressing on my brain?"

Pembroke inclined his head. "Precisely. And if that is the case, there is a chance—however slim—that we could alleviate your suffering through surgery. The procedure would relieve the pressure and potentially offer you some relief. It is not without risks, as I have said, but if it is indeed a clot, the surgery might offer you more hope than if we were dealing with a tumour."

Darcy's heart pounded. "What manner of surgery?"

Pembroke drew in a deep breath. "Trepanation. It is an ancient practice, but we have perfected it somewhat in recent years. We would bore a small hole into your skull to relieve the pressure. However, Mr Darcy, I must caution you: you may well have waited too long. The procedure itself is dangerous—there is a significant risk that you could die on the table."

"And if we do nothing?"

Pembroke cleared his throat. "Sir, with the increasing severity of your symptoms, I should say your time is... rather limited at best."

Mr Bennet shifted beside him, his face a mask of concern. Darcy glanced at him, then back at Pembroke, his resolve firm. "I will take that risk, Doctor. I would rather die trying to live than linger in this... half-state, in which I will die, anyway. Let us proceed."

Pembroke nodded, his expression grave. "Very well. We shall prepare at once. I will have you taken to my surgery."

Darcy closed his eyes briefly. The decision was made, and there was yet hope—hope for a life, a future that had all but been snatched from him, and the prospect of a new tomorrow with the woman he loved. For Elizabeth... yes, it was worth the chance. Worth risking the terror of perishing this very hour rather than lingering into a slowly sinking abyss with her helplessly looking on.

When he opened his eyes, he found Mr Bennet staring at him, his gaze steady. "Tell Elizabeth... tell her I am doing this for us."

Mr Bennet nodded, his hand resting on Darcy's shoulder. "I will, lad. She will understand."

Darcy managed a faint smile, a flicker of hope lighting his weary eyes. "I pray that she does."

Elizabeth paced the length of her small room in the inn, her hands twisting the fabric of her gown, her mind consumed with dread. Each step was a torture, each tick of the clock on the mantel a cruel reminder of the time passing. She could not bear to sit, not when the vision of Darcy lying on a surgeon's table played endlessly in her mind. The thought of him never waking, of his eyes never opening again to meet hers, sent a fresh wave of terror through her. She had known fear before, but nothing like this.

He had come to her just before leaving for the surgery, his face pale but determined. He had taken her hands, brought them to his lips, and kissed her with a tenderness that left her breathless. It could be the last time, she realised, as a cold shiver ran down her spine. The last time she would ever feel his touch, hear his voice, see the soft light in his eyes when he looked at her. Her breath hitched, and she sank to her knees beside the bed, her hands clasped tightly in prayer.

"Please," she whispered, her voice breaking. "Please, God, do not take him from me. Not now. Not when we have only just begun." Tears streamed down her face, and she pressed her forehead to the mattress, her body trembling with silent sobs. All the other troubles—the flooding in Meryton, Wickham's threats, Sir Anthony's schemes, Charlotte's despair, and even the irritation of Mr Collins looming as a future brother-in-law—all of them seemed so small, so insignificant, compared to the thought of losing Darcy.

The hours dragged on with excruciating slowness. She tried to distract herself, picking up her embroidery only to put it down moments later, her hands too shaky to hold the needle steady. She poured herself a cup of tea, but the mere thought of swallowing made her stomach twist. Pacing had become her only solace, her only way to keep from descending into utter panic.

A knock sounded at the door, and she flew to it, her heart pounding. She flung it open to find her father standing there, looking worn and weary. She searched his face desperately, trying to read any sign of what news he had brought. "Papa?" she whispered, her voice barely more than a breath. "Is he...?"

Mr Bennet stepped inside, his face lined with exhaustion, his hat in his hand. He moved slowly, his fingers working the buttons of his greatcoat, which he tossed onto the bed before sinking heavily into a chair. "Elizabeth," he began, his voice thick with fatigue. "Sit down, my dear."

She couldn't stand the suspense. "No, tell me!" she cried, her hands wringing together. "Tell me the worst, even if I cannot bear it."

He looked up at her, his eyes softening. "He is still alive," he said quietly.

Elizabeth's knees buckled with relief, and she collapsed into the chair opposite him, her hands flying to her mouth to stifle a sob. "Oh, thank God," she breathed, her chest heaving as she tried to steady her racing heart. "But... but how is he? What did the doctor say?"

Mr Bennet rubbed his temples, looking as though he had aged a decade in the last few hours. "It was a most horrifying procedure," he admitted, his voice low. "I was permitted to witness from the back of the room, though I would not wish such a sight on my worst enemy. The surgeon, Pembroke, was thorough and meticulous. He knew what he was about. He believes he found the clot and relieved the pressure on Darcy's brain."

Elizabeth's heart ached at the thought of Darcy enduring such an ordeal. "And now?" she pressed. "Is he in pain? Can he be moved? What is his condition?"

Mr Bennet sighed, his eyes meeting hers with a grim expression. "Darcy is in a great deal of pain, yes. They have given him laudanum to ease it, but the bleeding was severe, and he is weak. Pembroke says he must remain at the surgery for several days, perhaps a week, before he can be moved anywhere safely. They have to be certain there are no further complications, no new bleeding or infection. It is a delicate recovery, and any false move could prove fatal."

Elizabeth felt a fresh wave of anxiety wash over her. "But he will recover? Truly recover?"

Her father hesitated, then nodded slowly. "Pembroke believes he has a chance. A good chance. But he must rest, and we must be vigilant. It will take time, and there are no guarantees. But for now, he is alive, and that is more than I dared to hope for this morning."

Tears welled in Elizabeth's eyes, and she covered her face with her hands, overwhelmed with relief. "Thank you, Papa," she whispered. "Thank you for staying with him."

Mr Bennet reached across the space between them, taking her hand in his. "Before they began the procedure," he said softly, "Darcy asked me to write to his cousin, a colonel stationed in Chatham. He wanted to make certain that his affairs were in order, particularly where you and his sister were concerned, just in case..."

Elizabeth's breath caught at the thought of Darcy preparing for his own death, and she squeezed her father's hand tightly. "Will you write to him?"

Mr Bennet nodded. "I will. But let us hope that by the time the letter arrives, it is unnecessary."

She moved to embrace him, wrapping her arms around his shoulders, feeling the solid comfort of his presence. He kissed her cheek, his expression softening. "Heaven has smiled on you, my dear," he murmured. "It gave you a good man and, perhaps, a way to keep him a little while longer."

Elizabeth clung to his words, her heart filling with a fragile hope. Anything could still happen—that much was true. But for now, Darcy was alive. And that was enough.

DARCY DRIFTED IN AND out of a fog, his mind tangling with the sensation of pain that pulsed through his head in waves. Awareness came slowly, inching into his consciousness like a creeping dawn. He blinked, his vision blurry and unfocused, the dim light of the room doing little to ease the pounding in his skull. His throat felt raw and dry, each breath scraping painfully through his lungs. As the haze began to clear, he saw a figure seated nearby, a familiar form hunched over a book.

"Mr Bennet?" His voice was a rasp, barely more than a whisper. The effort of speaking sent another sharp pang through his temples, and he winced, his hand instinctively moving to his head.

Mr Bennet barely looked up from his book, his expression as placid as ever. "Ah, you are awake, Mr Darcy. Took you long enough," he remarked dryly, though his tone held a note of relief.

"How..." He swallowed against the scratchiness of his throat. "How long?"

"Three days, unless you count the deluded episodes when you opened your eyes, staring about the room but did not speak. I daresay your poor valet is worn to a skeleton keeping watch over you, so I volunteered to take my turn."

"El..." He swallowed again. "Elizabeth?"

"Yes, yes, Lizzy is well and impatiently waiting to speak with you as soon as you are up and about." With that, he calmly closed his book, stood, and made his way to the door. "I shall fetch Pembroke," he added, not bothering to wait for a response before exiting the room.

Darcy let his head fall back against the pillow, his eyes fluttering closed as he tried to manage the pain. It was worse than ever, a relentless throbbing that seemed to echo with every beat of his heart. Yet, as he focused on the sensations running through his body, he noticed something else—the tingling in his arm and hand, the cursed twitching of his face, had vanished. A small victory, he thought, his mind struggling to stay focused amidst the pain.

A few minutes later, the door opened, and Darcy opened his eyes to see Doctor Pembroke entering the room, Mr Bennet just behind him. Pembroke approached the bedside, his gaze assessing as he took in Darcy's condition. "Awake at last, I see," he said with a nod. "How do you feel, Mr Darcy?"

Darcy's lips twisted into a wry smile. "Like I have been trampled by a carriage," he muttered, his voice hoarse. "What... did you do?"

Pembroke pulled up a chair and sat down, his expression serious. "Well, I daresay you may not recall half of what we said when last you were alert. We performed a trepanation, a procedure to relieve the pressure on your brain caused by a blood clot. It was a delicate operation, but I believe we were successful in removing the clot and reducing the pressure."

Darcy absorbed the information slowly, his thoughts sluggish. "And... my recovery?" he asked, his words slurring slightly. "When... can I leave? When can I stand, walk... get into a carriage?"

Pembroke chuckled softly. "You must be patient, Mr Darcy. I know full well you have ample motive to recover quickly, but your body needs time to heal. The banns have not even been read yet, have they?"

Darcy looked questioningly at Mr Bennet, who stood by the window with a smug grin. "Actually, they have," Mr Bennet said with a hint of satisfaction. "I wrote to Mr Harrison in Meryton to notify him of the engagement. The banns for both you and Elizabeth, and for Jane and Mr Bingley, were published for the first time last Sunday."

Darcy felt a foolish grin spread across his face as he relaxed back on the pillow, calculating in his head. Two more Sundays and Elizabeth would be his. He propped himself up again, his determination flaring. "I have to be recovered by then," he insisted, his voice firmer.

Pembroke smiled, a knowing twinkle in his eye. “I think you will be on your feet by then, though perhaps a bit weak. And I would advise you to consider a wig.”

Darcy winced, his hand hesitantly touching the left side of his head. Ah, yes, he remembered that now—Giles had shaved down a considerable thatch of hair before Doctor Pembroke began the surgery. His stomach churned at the thought of touching the wound, but he decided it was a scar he would wear proudly. He had fought for his life and won.

Pembroke nodded approvingly. “I will send in a maid with some broth to strengthen you. Meanwhile, a rather anxious and somewhat belligerent visitor arrived just moments ago, nearly banging down the door in his urgency to see you. Are you well enough for a visitor?”

Darcy raised an eyebrow. “Who is it?”

“I daresay a familiar face. He would not heed *my* reassurances, so perhaps he will appreciate yours.” Pembroke moved to the door, opened it slightly, and exchanged a few words with someone outside. A moment later, the door swung open fully, and Colonel Richard Fitzwilliam strode into the room, his face a mix of concern and relief.

“Darcy!” Richard exclaimed, his voice filled with emotion. “You look like death warmed over, but it is blasted good to see you alive.”

Darcy managed a weak chuckle, overjoyed to see his cousin. “Richard,” he greeted warmly. “It is good to see you, too.” He turned to Mr Bennet, who had closed his book and risen from his seat. “May I introduce Mr Bennet, my future father-in-law?”

Mr Bennet gave a polite bow to Richard, who returned it with a respectful nod. “Ah, so you are Mr Bennet. Jolly glad you wrote to me.”

“As am I, Colonel. And now, I believe someone else will be anxious for word of our Mr Darcy’s recovery.” Mr Bennet excused himself with a brief nod, leaving the room quietly.

As the door closed behind him, Richard took the chair beside Darcy’s bed, his gaze moving from Darcy to the door and back again. “Your, eh… future father-in-law, I understand? Anything you want to tell me, Darcy?”

Darcy grinned despite the pain. “There is a great deal you should hear, and I will tell you all in due time. But I will not speak of Elizabeth. The lady will speak for herself.”

Richard laughed, a warm, genuine sound that filled the room. “That is the best commendation you could give her,” he said, his eyes gleaming with amusement. “I am eager to meet her.”

Darcy’s smile softened. “I am proud that she found me worthy.”

Richard nodded, then leaned forward, his expression turning serious. "But meanwhile, if you are not in too much pain, I would very much like to speak of what happened with Wickham."

Darcy's brow furrowed, his memory still foggy. "I might not recall all the details correctly," he admitted.

Richard waved a hand dismissively. "Mr Bennet's letter did most of that, but have you heard? Wickham is in gaol."

Darcy's eyes widened in surprise, and Richard continued, "Furthermore, 'Sir Anthony' was really a steward for Lord Wexfield up until about a year ago when he suddenly began living the life of a gentleman. I understand he properly goes by the name of Henry Billings, and he is also in gaol."

Darcy managed a faint nod. "Georgiana will be interested to hear that."

"Eh? What's this about Georgie?"

Darcy closed his eyes in an approximation of a head shake. "It can wait. What else? I do not suppose you have spoken with your father?"

"Not in person, no, but the moment I got Mr Bennet's letter, I sent off an express to him about everything Bennet said. I've no doubt that he will make sure Lord Wexfield is now under investigation for fraud in the House of Lords. He has wanted proof for a long while, and now he ought to have it."

Darcy let his head fall back against the pillow, a deep sigh of relief escaping him. "That is all good news. Not because I sought revenge on Wickham but because I am glad to know that the people of Meryton are safe. Now, all I care about is recovering in time to marry Elizabeth."

Richard grinned. "I think that is a worthy goal, cousin. And with your stubbornness, I have no doubt you will achieve it."

Chapter Forty-One

A fortnight had passed, and the carriage wheels creaked softly as they rolled over the frozen Hertfordshire roads, the gentle sway almost lulling Darcy back to sleep. He sat back against the padded seat, a walking stick resting against his knee, his fingers drumming lightly on the handle. The return journey to Hertfordshire had been cold but uneventful, and for that, he was grateful. He was still weak, his body recovering slowly, but he was upright, his faculties clear, and his mind keen once more. The familiar countryside stretched out before him, and he felt a sense of calm settle over him.

Elizabeth sat beside him, her hand twined over his arm and her body keeping him warm. He had struggled almost constantly with feeling chilled during his recovery, but fortunately, the remedy for that particular ailment was a pleasant one. She glanced up at him every so often, her eyes filled with concern and something more tender, more personal.

Darcy met her gaze with a soft smile, feeling a new kind of warmth spread through his chest that had little to do with the winter sun streaming through the carriage window. Opposite them, Mr Bennet sat with Richard, both men engaged in a low conversation that Darcy only half-heard. His focus was entirely on the woman beside him—her touch, her nearness.

As they approached Longbourn, Darcy felt a flicker of anxiety in his chest. He had not set foot in the house since his engagement to Elizabeth, and though he knew the Bennet family had welcomed him with open arms, he could not shake the feeling of stepping into the unknown. Particularly where the mother and younger sisters were concerned.

The carriage drew up to the house, and Darcy's hand tightened on his walking stick as he prepared to disembark. His equilibrium had suffered somewhat since the surgery, but the nausea and unsteadiness were receding a little more each day. Still, he used that walking stick wherever he went, for he had discovered a rather curious benefit to carrying it—with it in his right hand and Elizabeth holding his left elbow, it created a natural barrier to overly convivial and familiar greetings... a thing he would probably always abhor.

Inside, the drawing room was warm and bright, a fire crackling in the hearth. Bingley was already there, waiting eagerly, his face breaking into a broad smile as they entered. "Darcy!" he exclaimed, hurrying forward. "You are looking well! Or, at least, better than I feared."

Darcy chuckled softly, leaning on his stick for support. "I am on the mend, Bingley. Slowly but surely." He exchanged a tender look with Elizabeth, who squeezed his arm gently before stepping away to join her sisters.

Mrs Bennet must have been hovering in the entryway, and she approached now with a look of barely contained excitement. Her greeting, however, was tempered with uncharacteristic restraint. Her voice, usually as sharp and lively as a sparrow's, was unusually gentle. "Mr Darcy," she said, her words deliberate and measured, "how very good it is to see you looking so well. We were all so worried—well, of course, I was worried sick! My poor nerves, you know. But you did not die, after all—Lady Lucas said she was sure you would. I shall be sure to tell her that you are here now, still as wealthy and handsome as ever and looking better than we could have hoped!"

Darcy inclined his head politely. She was still very much as she had always been, but perhaps a muted version of her usual self. Elizabeth or Mr Bennet must have written to impress upon her the importance of maintaining calm for the sake of his recovering head. Across the room, Elizabeth stood near the window, her face bright with relief, and the sight of her eased the lingering tension in his chest.

Lydia and Kitty, however, could hardly contain their excitement at the sight of Colonel Fitzwilliam in his red uniform. Lydia whispered loudly to Kitty, "Look at him! So handsome in his regimentals! I did not know Mr Darcy's cousin was an officer. I should love to hear about his battles and the scarlet-coated soldiers!"

Kitty nodded eagerly, her eyes wide with fascination. "Do you think he might tell us some stories?"

Mr Bennet, observing the scene with his usual air of detached amusement, cleared his throat. "Girls," he said in a tone that allowed no argument, "we are all pleased to have such distinguished guests, and surely you will get to know them soon enough. However. as of this moment, you are not to be considered 'out.' You are not permitted to be in company as if you were."

A chorus of protests erupted from the younger girls. Lydia's face twisted in dismay. "But Papa! That is most unfair! I am nearly sixteen, and Kitty is a year older! Why should we be sent away like children?"

Kitty pouted, her lip trembling with frustration. "Yes, Papa, why should we be banished upstairs when there is such company?"

"Oh, Mr Bennet, must you be so harsh?" his wife pleaded. "The girls are simply delighted by the presence of their future brothers-in-law… not to mention that of a fine, brave officer. Surely, there can be no harm in their hearing a tale or two of gallantry."

Mr Bennet's expression remained unchanged. "I am afraid, Mrs Bennet, that your indulgence has made them forget their manners. As they are not yet 'out,' they have no business being in the company of gentlemen."

Lydia stamped her foot, her frustration boiling over. "But Papa—"

"No," Mr Bennet said more sharply. "Upstairs with you, now. I have had a long journey with far too many people touching me as it is. No offence, Colonel."

Richard chuckled as he drew near the fireplace to warm his hands. "None taken."

Bennet grunted in satisfaction and rounded once more on his daughters. "My head is aching sufficiently to make me consider turning back to Cambridge to ask the good Doctor Pembroke to examine me next. I will not have my nerves further tried today." His tone softened slightly. "But if you are very good, perhaps you might come down later to say farewell to Colonel Fitzwilliam before he leaves."

Lydia and Kitty exchanged disappointed glances but apparently decided it was futile to argue further. With exaggerated sighs and huffs, they turned and made their way out, skirts swishing in indignation.

Mrs Bennet huffed, "Well, I never! Keeping them upstairs as if they were still in pinafores!"

Mr Bennet ignored her muttering and glanced at Darcy, who offered a slight nod of gratitude. The girls' chatter had been the last thing he needed. The imminent arrival of Mr Collins, expected to return soon for his wedding to Mary, loomed over him like a dark cloud and, worse still, hearing Lady Catherine's inevitable reaction. If Collins had spoken of Darcy's engagement to Elizabeth—and he most certainly would have—the news would not sit well with his aunt.

Darcy had no intention of being swayed by her opinions, but the prospect of dealing with her disapproval while he was still yet… tender… was not a pleasant one. But no matter. Having Elizabeth for his own, with a full life to look forward to, was worth whatever inconveniences that might arise along the way. Even meddlesome in-laws.

Tea was served, and Darcy gratefully took a seat on the sofa beside Elizabeth. It really was the simple joys he cherished now. His hands no longer trembled, and his appetite, which had been poor for so long, seemed to have returned in full. The food tasted richer, every bite bursting with flavours that seemed more vivid than ever before. The colours around him felt more vibrant, each hue sharper and more defined, as if the world had been brought into sharper focus.

As his gaze settled on Elizabeth, he was struck anew by her beauty—details he had once been too clouded to fully appreciate now appeared with startling clarity. The fine, auburn streaks in her dark hair caught the light, adding a warm, subtle glow that framed her face. Her skin, touched with the faintest scattering of freckles across her nose, gave her a youthful charm that contrasted with the knowing look in her eyes. And there, beside her mouth, was a small crease—a line that deepened whenever she smiled, a sign of laughter that had come easily to her. It was a detail he had somehow missed before, a mark of the joy and spirit that lived within her, and he found himself utterly captivated. She was even more beautiful than he had realised, a beauty not just of form but of life, resilience, and grace.

Beside him, Bingley was rambling on about something, but Darcy could not focus on his words. He was gesturing toward Darcy, Richard was engaged, and even Mr Bennet was nodding in the periphery of Darcy's vision. But his gaze kept drifting back to Elizabeth, his heart full.

"I say, Darcy, what do you think? A capital plan, I believe, but I should like your opinion. "

Darcy blinked and wrenched his gaze back to Bingley. "I am sorry, Bingley; what did you say?"

Bingley looked concerned. "Are you quite well, Darcy? You seem... distracted."

Darcy smiled and nodded. "Yes, I am. Forgive me, please continue."

Bingley hesitated, then went on. "I have been writing to Mr Northam. You recall—the owner of Netherfield Park. He is seeking damages from Mr Wickham for the destruction caused to his property."

Darcy shook his head. "That does not seem likely to succeed. Wickham is not known for paying his debts, and in this case, the money used to lease the property was probably transferred illicitly, with no proof of who truly backed him."

Richard, who had been quietly sipping his tea, looked up. "Not so, Darcy. I have been corresponding with my father about that," he said. "Lord Wexfield's estate and accounts have been seized. I have put in a word with my father regarding the damages to Netherfield."

Darcy nodded thoughtfully. "Interesting. Well, then, perhaps there is some hope of a remedy there. How bad is the damage?"

Bingley leaned forward, his expression serious. "The western wing of the house is destroyed, but the rest is salvageable. It will take considerable time and money to repair, but efforts have been made to protect the damaged portions from winter weather."

"And the servants?"

Bingley's face brightened. "Ah, I had not finished. I am already in negotiations to lease the house as it is from its current owner. Any arrangements for damages or repairs will be adjusted in the contract through Mr Philips as things develop. I intend to keep all the servants employed, paying their wages even before I move in."

Darcy smiled approvingly. "That will certainly endear you to the household."

Bingley waved a hand dismissively. "I am not seeking praise. I only want to do what is right and restore the house to its former glory. And, once it is habitable, I intend to give it a proper mistress." He glanced shyly at Jane, who blushed and smiled back.

As Darcy took a sip of his tea, his gaze was drawn to Mr Bennet, who had been watching the room with his usual air of detached amusement. Suddenly, Mr Bennet's expression shifted slightly, his eyes narrowing as he caught sight of Mr Hill, the butler, standing discreetly at the doorway, beckoning him over. With a sigh, Mr Bennet set down his cup and muttered, loud enough for Darcy to hear, "Well, it seems everyone is crawling out of the woodwork today to see our poor Mr Darcy's miraculous recovery—and to no doubt share every tedious detail of the election results."

Darcy felt a slight smile tug at his lips, though the mention of the election sent a brief ripple of unease through him. He watched as Mr Bennet made his way to the door, engaging in a brief, whispered exchange with Mr Hill. A moment later, Mr Bennet turned back to the room, clearing his throat to gain everyone's attention. "It seems we have more visitors. Sir William, Lady Lucas, and their daughter, Miss Charlotte Lucas, have come to call."

Darcy's muscles tensed involuntarily; his first thought had been Mr Collins. But as Mr Bennet ushered the Lucases into the drawing room, he relaxed, feeling Elizabeth's hand linger in his own for just a moment longer before she stood to greet her friend.

"Charlotte!" Elizabeth exclaimed, her voice bright with surprise and genuine delight. She moved quickly to embrace Charlotte, her face lighting up with joy. "I did not expect to see you here today. It is so wonderful to see you."

Charlotte returned the embrace warmly, her face brighter and more at ease than Darcy had ever seen. "I had to come," she replied. "We have all been so concerned, with everything that has been happening."

As the ladies exchanged greetings, Darcy's attention shifted to Richard, who had set down his cup with unusual precision, his gaze fixed on Charlotte. His cousin, who had always been so vocal about his practical views on marriage—particularly the need for a substantial dowry—was staring at Charlotte Lucas with an intensity that Darcy found... intriguing.

As Sir William entered the drawing room, his face lit up with the eager expression of a man bursting with news. He bowed briefly to Darcy and then addressed him with a flourish. "Mr Darcy! I trust you have been recovering well, but I wonder, have you heard all the news about the election? Quite an extraordinary outcome, I must say."

Darcy, still easing back into his seat with the support of his cane, gave a polite nod. "I have heard bits and pieces, Sir William, but I would welcome a more detailed account. Please, do enlighten me."

Sir William beamed, clearly pleased to be the bearer of information. "Well, as you know, the election proceeded right after your, ah, unfortunate incident. With Sir Anthony Mortimer withdrawing his candidacy in disgrace, it created quite a stir among the voters. Many believed it would be a simple matter of the next most popular gentleman stepping in, but Mr Robinson—one of our less outspoken candidates—seized the opportunity. I believe rather that his modesty was what secured him the vote—everyone had enough of smooth talk, do you see."

Darcy listened attentively, though he already knew most of this from the letters he had received during his convalescence. But letting Sir William have the pleasure of speaking was temporarily shifting the focus of the room to him rather than his more withdrawn daughter... and permitting Richard a chance to overhear every unguarded and whimsical word out of the lady's mouth.

Sir William turned to Mr Bennet with a pleased look. "Mr Bennet, you must have been informed by now—Mr Robinson won by a narrow margin! And he has already made his announcements as our new Member of Parliament. Quite the upstanding gentleman, by all accounts. He has spoken fervently about integrity and transparency—rather a sharp contrast to his predecessor, if you catch my meaning."

Mr Bennet, who had been leaning back in his chair with a knowing smile, responded with a dry chuckle. "Ah, yes, Mr Robinson. I believe he is keen to make his mark. Though I suspect we shall see just how long these lofty ideals endure once he is properly seated in Westminster."

Lady Lucas, standing beside her husband, nodded in agreement. "Indeed, the whole affair was quite the spectacle. But it is a relief to know that the matter has been settled without further scandal."

Darcy felt a weight lifting from his shoulders at the news, even if he had already known the result. Seeing the genuine relief on the faces around him—the knowledge that Meryton had weathered the storm and emerged relatively unscathed—was more comforting than he had expected. He caught Elizabeth's eye as she watched the conversation unfold, her lips curving in a quiet smile. A sense of contentment, more grounded than any peace, welled up in him—along with a certain eagerness to focus his thoughts on the more immediate delights of impending matrimony.

The room fell into a comfortable buzz of conversation—largely without Darcy's input. His gaze shifted occasionally from the woman who consumed his being to Richard, whose attention had not wavered from Charlotte Lucas. There was something different in his cousin's demeanour, something Darcy had not seen before. Could it be... interest?

Surely not. Miss Lucas had been dealt a terrible injustice in being deemed "plain," for she was no such thing. She only wanted good conversation, which Elizabeth was generously supplying, to make her eyes dance like a candelabra, and her cheeks flush like a dew-kissed rose. And there was nothing wrong with her features or her manner. Why did no one notice this lady? Perhaps the very fact of being overlooked for so many years had been enough to smother her charms and colour his first impression of her... but that impression, clearly, had been mistaken.

But still... *Richard?* A man who had turned down every eligible lady his mother had suggested due to her small fortune? Perhaps there was nothing more than intrigue there, but Darcy doubted it very much.

As he pondered his cousin's newfound fascination, the door to the drawing room opened again, and without even waiting for Mr Hill to introduce him, Mr Collins made his anticipated entrance, his gait as self-important as ever. He glanced around the room, his expression a mix of bewilderment at the large party gathered and smug satisfaction that conversation ceased when he entered... until his eyes landed on Darcy. At that moment, he visibly shuddered, his face contorting into an awkward grimace.

"Mr Bennet," Collins began, his voice hushed but loud enough to be heard by all, "how can you possibly countenance your daughter marrying such a man?"

Darcy, taken aback by the sheer nerve of the man, straightened in his chair. He was prepared to defend himself against whatever absurdities Mr Collins might spout—no doubt a result of Lady Catherine's influence. He opened his mouth to speak, but Collins, with all the grace of a bumbling goose, hurried on.

"My esteemed patroness, Lady Catherine de Bourgh, has expressed her utmost disappointment," Collins declared, his chest puffed up like a pigeon. "She feels that Mr Darcy has let down his family legacy most grievously. Indeed, she has found a more suitable suitor for her daughter, thus sparing Miss de Bourgh the fate of being shackled to a dying man."

Darcy's lips curled into a wry smile. "Then I congratulate Lady Catherine on her discretion. Clearly, she knows what is best for her family."

Mr Bennet, standing beside him, chortled quietly, his shoulders shaking with restrained amusement. "Alas," he confessed, "it does seem that I am in the great lady's debt. I shall take her advice under the most serious consideration."

Elizabeth, across the room, covered her mouth with her hand, her eyes sparkling with barely contained laughter.

Collins, oblivious to the mockery, continued with an air of self-importance. "Lady Catherine, ever so concerned about her family's reputation, remarked upon Mr Darcy's apparent frailty and... lingering sickness. She doubts very much that he shall be able to perform his duties, particularly the matter of producing an heir."

At this, Darcy couldn't help but laugh softly. "I suppose, then, that Lady Catherine has nothing more to fear from me."

Collins blinked, clearly taken aback by Darcy's calm demeanour. He seemed at a loss, looking between Mr Bennet and Darcy, searching for some support.

Mr Bennet, still amused, took pity on the man. "Well, Mr Collins, it seems you and Lady Catherine are both quite mistaken. But I thank you for your concern about my daughter's future. I assure you, we are all quite content with her choice."

Collins, flustered and defeated, stammered a quick greeting to his betrothed, who was still seated beside the fire, and hastily retreated from the room, his self-importance crumbling with every step.

As the door closed behind him, Darcy relaxed back into his chair, a grin tugging at his lips. As a faint twinge of pain pulsed through his head, Darcy instinctively turned his gaze to Elizabeth. The discomfort eased almost immediately, replaced by a sense of calm as he watched her, her cheeks flushing a soft pink each time their eyes met. In her look, all the world made sense.

Epilogue

THE LATE SUMMER SUN cast a warm, golden glow over Pemberley's gardens, where a small clutch of friends and family had gathered to revel in the last of the warm rays for the season. Elizabeth, seated on a blanket spread beneath the shade of a broad oak tree, watched with amusement as Georgiana Darcy tried—and failed—to conceal her nervous excitement about her upcoming journey to London for her come-out ceremony.

"I cannot imagine what all the fuss is about," Elizabeth teased lightly, her smile broadening as Georgiana glanced over with a look of mild horror. "Surely you do not mean to tell me you are nervous, Georgiana? You, who have faced far worse challenges, such as... learning to dance with Richard?"

Richard Fitzwilliam, who was lounging nearby with his wife, Charlotte, chuckled. "Learning to dance with me was indeed a trial," he quipped, taking a sip of his lemonade. "But I dare say she came through it splendidly. And I would wager she will do the same at her come out."

Georgiana blushed, casting a shy smile in her brother's direction. Darcy, who was seated beside Elizabeth, gave his sister an encouraging nod. "You have nothing to fear, Georgiana. You will be the toast of the season, I am certain of it."

Bingley, sitting across from them with Jane, grinned. "Quite right. And you will have all of us there to cheer you on."

"Oh, that is very easy for you to say, Mr Bingley," Georgiana retorted. "You are always easy in company, but I..."

Elizabeth rubbed a hand absently over her stomach and cast a wry grin at the man beside her. "A family characteristic, my dear. But, as you can see, your brother has overcome at least most of his reticence in company. Surely you will do likewise."

"I was not reticent," Darcy quipped. "I was suffering from hideous megrims throughout the entirety of our early acquaintance, yet the woman insists on painting me as retiring and unapproachable in company."

"You still are, my love," she soothed, lacing her hand through his. "But I rather like it when you make that forbidding face, especially when I am standing beside you. It spares me the trouble of speaking with ever so many dull people."

Bingley laughed outright. "You ought to have seen him at school, Mrs Darcy. I daresay, any friends he had were because they were friends of mine first."

"And you were entirely *too* sociable," Darcy muttered, but not without an amused quirk of his brow toward Bingley.

"Ah, yes. And too easily led… I know well my faults, Darcy, and I have repented of them. It is a mercy I have always had you to pull me back to some semblance of rationality when I have quite lost my head."

"That is not entirely true." Darcy sipped his own lemonade. "I cautioned you when the repair estimates for Netherfield came in that you would end up footing half of it, but you plunged ahead anyway."

"Well, it is only because Northam agreed to sell me the property at a tremendous loss to himself. He only wanted to have done with the thing, poor chap. By the by, did I tell you that Mr Bennet has agreed to sell me the farms that Wickham had suggested purchasing?"

Elizabeth straightened. "He did? When was this?'

"Last month, Lizzy," Jane replied. "Just after Mr Collins and Mary announced they would be adding a little 'olive branch' to the family. Papa said, and I quote, 'Let us not burden the poor chap with more than he can manage, eh? And I hope he sires twelve daughters for his trouble.'"

Elizabeth laughed. "That sounds like Papa. Well, Mr Bingley, I am quite certain that you will manage those farms far better than Mr Collins would when he comes into his inheritance."

"*If*, you mean," Jane sighed. "Papa says he means to outlive all of us."

"He just might," Bingley added, rising from the blanket to bring Jane another tarte and refill his lemonade. "With all the work of these last months, I feel like I have aged ten years, but Bennet relaxes in his book room and I think his age regresses every time I meet him."

Richard, catching the tail end of their conversation, turned with a grin. "Speaking of work, Bingley, I hear you are nearly done with the restoration. It seems you have worked a small miracle."

Bingley chuckled, a hint of bashfulness in his expression. "Oh, I would not go so far as to say that. But it is coming along. I am just grateful to see the house standing again. It really is the ideal situation. Just the place I want to raise a family." He followed this with a warm smile at Jane as he reclaimed the seat beside her.

Jane Bingley stiffened. "Charles!" she whispered harshly. "It is too soon!"

"Not a bit of it," Elizabeth insisted. "We all knew the moment you stepped out of the carriage, Jane. And how charming that the cousins will be close in age!"

Jane Bingley bit her lip and slid a cheeky look to her husband. "Indeed, Lizzy. It is only a pity that Derbyshire is not a terribly easy distance from Hertfordshire."

"Nonsense. You forget, we will be wintering in London for Georgiana's Season. My goodness, I hope Lady Matlock is right about that modiste."

"Hmm?" Jane looked puzzled.

"Oh! She swears that a talented modiste will hide..." she swept a hand over her growing middle... "*this*. But do you know, I think perhaps I do not wish to conceal anything. I am rather proud of the fact that I can port around all this ponderous weight, and I have yet to injure my ankle again in the process."

Richard roared in laughter. "Fear not, Mrs Darcy. I am certain you will find some opportunity or other to discomfit yourself, should the need arise."

"Is that an insult, Colonel Fitzwilliam?" she shot back.

"No, the highest esteem, I assure you, Mrs Darcy. One never knows when a little 'mishap' may prove to be a convenient excuse, particularly during one of my mother's soirees." At the sound of Darcy's snort, Richard turned his gaze to his cousin. "And what of you, cousin? Are you prepared for the whirlwind that is to come? I suspect Georgiana's debut will be quite the affair."

Darcy glanced at Georgiana, who was seated nearby with Elizabeth. "I am certain she will do wonderfully," he replied, his tone soft with brotherly affection. "She is ready, even if I am not."

Elizabeth turned to him with a teasing smile. "I daresay it is you who are most anxious about the event, Mr Darcy. Poor Georgiana has been much more rational about the matter than you have."

Darcy chuckled, unable to deny it. "Perhaps you are right, Mrs Darcy. I suppose I still find it difficult to see my little sister grown and ready for society. But enough of such talk, for I see my poor sister is turning a rather pretty shade of pink again at all this attention."

Elizabeth leaned a little closer to Darcy, her arm brushing his ever so slightly. She could feel the warmth of his presence, his steady calm in contrast to the lively chatter around them. With a soft smile, she tilted her head toward him and whispered, "Shall we take a turn about the gardens then, Fitzwilliam? I find I could use a bit of air."

Darcy's eyes met hers, and she saw a playful glimmer in his expression, a contrast to his usual composed demeanour. He nodded, rising from his seat. "A fine idea," he said quietly, offering her his arm. "Cheerio, everyone."

She took it gratefully, feeling the familiar comfort of his strength as they made their way out of the drawing room. As they walked, the sounds of laughter and conversation from their friends faded, replaced by the rustle of leaves and the gentle murmur of the brook nearby. Elizabeth breathed in the fresh air, savouring the tranquillity of the gardens.

They walked in a comfortable silence for a few moments, enjoying the peacefulness that the outdoors always seemed to bring. Elizabeth's heart swelled with affection for the man beside her. It was moments like these—simple, quiet, shared—that she cherished most.

Breaking the silence, she chuckled softly, turning her gaze up to his. "Do you think you shall ever get used to such gatherings, Fitzwilliam? With Georgiana's debut approaching, I fear your patience shall be tested to its limits."

He smiled, a warm and genuine expression that softened his features. "If I am to survive it, I shall need your support, Mrs Darcy."

"You have it, always. Though I must say, I think you could simply feign a headache. You have ample experience in knowing how it is done."

"Feign! Madam, you wound me. Do you not know that deceit of any nature is my particular abhorrence?"

She tilted her head with a teasing grin. "Deceit... and crowds."

"Now, I must protest. When have I ever—"

As they rounded a bend near the stream, she was just distracted enough by provoking her husband that she did not notice the root hidden beneath the grass. Her foot caught on it, and she stumbled forward, a sharp intake of breath escaping her lips as pain shot through her ankle.

"Elizabeth!" Darcy's voice was filled with concern as he quickly caught her up in his arms, though not swiftly enough to prevent her fall.

Elizabeth hobbled a little, tangling her arms about his neck for support and leaning back against his chest as she hissed in pain. There was a fresh rip in her gown, just over the knee, and grass stains on her stockings. But the worst was that blasted ankle... always the same one! A few indelicate words slipped by her defences as she winced against the sharp agony.

Darcy slipped his other arm around her, angling to catch her weight better. "Are you hurt?"

She winced, trying to muster a smile despite the pain. "I am afraid I have been rather clumsy, Fitzwilliam. It seems my ankle has betrayed me once more."

Darcy chuckled softly, though she could see the worry in his eyes. "Perhaps I should carry you back, as I threatened to do before."

A laugh bubbled up from her chest, temporarily overriding the throbbing in her ankle. "If you must. It appears I cannot trust my feet any longer."

Without hesitation, he bent down and scooped her up, cradling her close to his chest. She wrapped her arms around his neck, feeling the steady beat of his heart beneath her cheek. "It seems I am destined to be your rescuer, my dear," he said with a soft smile, "not that I mind in the slightest."

Her fingers lightly traced the line of his collar, and she looked up at him with a playful glint in her eyes. "And I am most grateful for it, Mr Darcy. Always."

KEEP READING FOR A preview of ***The Measure of Honor***. Find out how Darcy overcomes the unthinkable to discover the healing powers of love.

From Alix

THANK YOU FOR INDULGING with me and spending a little time with Darcy and Elizabeth.

I hope you've had a delightful escape to Pemberley. I'd love it if you would share this family with your friends so they can experience a love to last for the ages. As with all my books, I have enabled lending to make it easier to share. If you leave a review for *The Measure of Trust* on Amazon, Goodreads, Book Bub or your own blog, I would love to read it! Email me the link at **Author@AlixJames.com.**

Would you like to read more of Darcy and Elizabeth's romance? I have an angsty Darcy and Elizabeth Forced Marriage romance for you to try next! Dive into ***The Measure of Honor***and swoon and sigh with our favorite couple as they find the love they were destined for!

And if you're hungry for more, including a free ebook of satisfying short tales, stay up to date on upcoming releases and sales by joining my newsletter: https://dashboard.mailerlite.com/forms/249660/73866370936211000/share

ALIX JAMES
MR. DARCY'S
FAIR TRADE
A SWEET PRIDE AND PREJUDICE NOVELLA

About Alix James

Short and satisfying romance for busy readers.

Alix James is an alternate pen name for best-selling Regency author Nicole Clarkston.

Always on the go as a wife, mom, and small business owner, she rarely has time to read a whole novel. She loves coffee with the sunrise and being outdoors. When she does get free time, she likes to read, camp, dream up romantic adventures, and tries to avoid housework.

Each Alix James story is a clean Regency Variation of Darcy and Elizabeth's romance.

Visit her website and sign up for her newsletter at AlixJames.com

Also By Alix James

Unintended

Spirited Away

Indisposed

Love and Other Machines

Elizabeth Bennet: Short and Sassy Compilation

The Mr. Darcy Series:

Mr. Darcy Steals a Kiss

Mr. Darcy and the Governess

Mr. Darcy and the Girl Next Door

Mr. Darcy: Swoonworthy Collection

The Measure of a Man Series:

The Measure of Love

The Measure of Trust

The Measure of Honor

Christmas With Darcy and Elizabeth

How to Get Caught Under the Mistletoe: A Lady's Guide

North and South Variations

Nowhere but North

Northern Rain

No Such Thing as Luck

John and Margaret: Coming Home Collection

Anthologies

Rational Creatures

Falling for Mr Thornton

Spanish Translations

Rumores e Imprudencias

Vacaciones en Londres

Nefasto

Un Compromiso Accidental

Reina del Invierno

Una Mente Noble

Cuando el Sol se Duerm

A lo largo del Camino

Reina del Invierno

Una Mente Noble

El señor Darcy se roba un beso

Italian Translations

Una Vacanza a Londra

Preview the Measure of Honor

"HARRY, IS THAT YOU?" Darcy's voice echoed through the great hall of Pemberley, carrying a note of surprised delight. "What the devil are you doing back so soon? I did not expect you for two days yet."

Harrison William Darcy stood in the doorway, a broad grin spreading across his sun-bronzed face. He looked every inch the dashing officer in his scarlet coat, his dark hair tousled by the wind. "The very same," he replied, his voice warm with laughter. "Have you forgotten what your own brother looks like, Fitz?"

Darcy crossed the hall in quick strides, his usual reserve melting into a rare, affectionate smile. "It has been too long, brother," he said, pulling Harry into a tight embrace. For a moment, the weight of Pemberley, his responsibilities, his worries—all of it—fell away.

Harry clapped his brother on the back with a hearty laugh. "It has, indeed! Too long by half! But I am here now, and I intend to make the most of my leave. No army drills, no orders—just a chance to enjoy the comforts of home."

Darcy stepped back, his eyes scanning his younger brother's face. There was a light in Harry's eyes, the same boyish charm that had always been there, but there was something else too—a shadow, a tension that belied his carefree words. "You seem... different, Harry," Darcy observed, a note of concern creeping into his voice. "Is everything well?"

Harry's smile faltered for just a moment, but then it was back, brighter than before. "Well enough, Fitz," he said, squeezing Darcy's shoulder. "But come, let us not dwell on serious matters. I have stories to tell, and I am eager to hear what you have been up to in my absence. Shall we retire to the study? I could use a drink after the journey."

Darcy nodded, his curiosity piqued, and led the way down the corridor to the study. The room was warm and inviting, the scent of leather-bound books and wood smoke filling the air. Darcy poured them each a glass of brandy, handing one to Harry before taking a seat by the fire.

Harry settled into the opposite chair, stretching out his legs with a contented sigh. "Ah, it is good to be home," he said, taking a sip of his drink. "I must say, Fitz, I have missed this—being here, with you, away from all the noise and chaos."

Darcy smiled. "And I have missed having you here, brother. The halls of Pemberley are far too quiet of late. But tell me, what news do you bring from the front? You look to be in one piece, thank Heaven. I confess, some of your letters have left me quite uneasy. Are things really so bad as all that?"

Harry shifted in his chair, a playful glint returning to his eyes as he leaned forward. "I came here to forget war for a time, Fitz. Tell me, how are things at Pemberley? Has Mrs Reynolds prepared any of her famous treacle tarts? I have been dreaming of them ever since I left France. And what of old Wilkins? Is he still puttering about, or has he finally decided to retire and enjoy his twilight years?"

Darcy chuckled, glad to see his brother's spirits lifting, even if only a little. "Mrs Reynolds is as formidable as ever, and yes, she has indeed made your favourite treacle tarts. I shall see to it that she brings some to you directly. As for Wilkins, he is as stubborn as ever. He insists he has no desire to retire and claims that Pemberley would fall apart without him. I fear we shall have to drag him away from his duties when the time comes."

Harry laughed, a genuine, light-hearted sound. "Good old Wilkins. I cannot imagine this place without him grumbling about the new footmen or lecturing the stable boys on proper etiquette. And what of the neighbours? Are the Farnsworths still bickering over that silly boundary dispute? And the Carters—did they ever manage to settle their daughters, or are they still parading them around like show ponies?"

Darcy smiled wryly. "The Farnsworths are indeed still at odds, though I suspect it is more for sport than any real grievance. As for the Carters, their eldest daughter finally married a minor baronet from Derbyshire, but the younger ones remain, as you say, 'on parade.'" He paused, his gaze growing more serious. "And Uncle Matlock and Lady Catherine are both well enough, though you know as well as I that 'well' is a relative term where our dear aunt is concerned."

Harry grinned, his eyes sparkling with amusement. "Ah, Lady Catherine. Always a joy. And Uncle Matlock? Still pressing you about those parliamentary ambitions?"

Darcy nodded. "As persistent as ever, though I have managed to avoid any firm commitments. For now, at least."

Harry's smile remained, but there was a flicker of something else behind his eyes—an unease, a tension that Darcy had seen earlier. He leaned forward, his voice softening.

"But enough of my affairs, Harry. You have been deflecting long enough. What is really troubling you?"

For a moment, Harry's face froze, his smile becoming almost painfully tight. His eyes flickered with a brief flash of something—fear, perhaps, or reluctance—but then, just as quickly, it vanished. He straightened in his chair, his expression brightening as if a new thought had occurred to him. "You always could read me too well, Fitz. You know, there is something," he began, his tone shifting. "Something rather... important."

Darcy waited, watching his brother closely.

Harry's face softened into a genuine smile. "I have met someone, Fitz. Someone quite remarkable."

Darcy arched an eyebrow, surprised by the sudden shift in topic, but intrigued nonetheless. "Ah, and here I was thinking you had some grave matter to share. So, you have found another pretty girl to occupy your thoughts, have you?"

Harry laughed, shaking his head. "This is different, I assure you. Her name is Elizabeth Bennet."

Darcy's eyebrow arched higher. "Elizabeth Bennet? Not a very distinguished name, is it?"

"The name may not be distinguished, but the lady herself certainly is."

Darcy sighed, leaning back in his chair. "And where, pray tell, did you meet this distinguished lady?"

Harry's smile widened. "I have been stationed in London off and on this past year, you know. And while there, I frequently encountered an old school friend—Charles Bingley."

Darcy squinted, searching his memory. "Bingley? Is that not the son of the woollen miller?"

Harry laughed, nodding. "Yes, yes, but he is also a gentleman of quality, Fitz. You must not be so quick to judge. Bingley is a good man, and he has been quite taken with a young lady from Hertfordshire—a Miss Jane Bennet."

Darcy's frown deepened. "And this Miss Bennet... she has a sister, I suppose?"

Harry's grin grew even wider. "Elizabeth Bennet, yes. And before you ask, no, none of this may sound promising to you, but I assure you, she is quite remarkable. In fact, she is the very woman I have asked to marry me."

Darcy nearly choked on his brandy. He straightened in his chair, his eyes wide with disbelief. "You what? Harry, have you lost your senses? How do you mean to live? Does the lady have a sufficient dowry to support you both?"

Harry's expression sobered slightly. "No, she does not have much in the way of a dowry. But I am expecting a promotion soon, and we intend to live modestly. I believe we will be very happy, Fitz. I am certain of it."

Darcy's face remained sceptical, his brow furrowing. "And what makes you so certain of that, Harry? You have always been too quick to fall for a pretty face."

Harry leaned forward, his expression earnest. "Because she is not like the others, Fitz. She is intelligent, strong-willed, with a lively mind and a wit that matches my own. I believe you will like her—once you meet her."

Darcy sighed, setting his glass down on the table. "I suppose I shall have to meet her, then. But do not expect me to approve of this at once. You know our father always wanted better for you."

Harry chuckled, a mischievous gleam in his eyes. "I know, brother. But do promise to be on your best behaviour. But I believe, once you see her for yourself, you will understand."

Darcy rolled his eyes, a reluctant smile tugging at his lips. "Very well, Harry. I shall reserve my judgment until I meet this Elizabeth Bennet. I shall endeavour to be polite."

Harry laughed, raising his glass in a toast. "That is all I ask, Fitz. To Elizabeth Bennet and the hope that my dear brother might see what I see."

Darcy clinked his glass with Harry's, though his smile remained wary. "To Elizabeth Bennet," he echoed, his voice carrying a note of resigned amusement. "And to you, Harry. May you always find happiness—if not sense."

They both laughed, the sound filling the study with warmth. For a moment, it felt as if nothing could mar this happiness, as if the world was as it should be. But Darcy could not shake the unease that settled in his chest, the nagging feeling that something was amiss. Harry was home, but there was a shadow behind his eyes—a shadow Darcy was determined to understand.

Darcy and Harry had planned a leisurely ride through the estate, a chance to enjoy the crisp morning air and the rolling hills of Pemberley, still lush from the summer rains. It had been too long since they had shared such a carefree moment, and Darcy was determined to make the most of his brother's unexpected visit. They stood by the stable, their horses being prepared by the grooms, as the sunlight filtered through the branches of the nearby trees, casting dappled shadows on the ground.

Harry leaned against the stable door, a contented smile on his face. "It feels good to be home, Fitz," he said softly, his eyes scanning the familiar landscape. "There is something about this place… it calms the soul. I had forgot how much I missed it."

Darcy glanced at his brother, noting the lines of strain around his eyes, the way his shoulders seemed to bear an invisible weight. "I am glad you are here," he replied. "You know Pemberley is not the same without you. And if I had known you were coming early, I would have had a better welcome prepared."

Harry chuckled. "I prefer the surprise, honestly. Gives me a chance to see you without your mask of responsibility." He hesitated, his smile faltering for a brief moment. "But there is something I need to ask of you, Fitz."

Darcy frowned, sensing the shift in Harry's demeanour. "What is it?"

Harry took a deep breath, his gaze fixed on the distant hills. "I want you to arrange a meeting with the family's solicitor," he said quietly.

Darcy's eyebrows knitted together in confusion. "The solicitor? For what purpose?"

Harry was silent for a moment, his expression thoughtful. Then, with a small, almost resigned smile, he turned to face Darcy. "I want to draft a settlement to offer Miss Elizabeth Bennet's father," he explained. "I want to ensure that she will be well cared for, should anything happen to me."

Darcy's face darkened with concern. "Why such morbid thoughts, Harry? You are on leave, not marching into battle. And you know how I feel about this impulsive engagement of yours. You have not even introduced me to the lady yet."

Harry shrugged, his smile growing softer, more introspective. "I just want to be prepared, Fitz. Life is unpredictable, and I want to know that Elizabeth will be safe, no matter what."

Darcy sighed, his hand rubbing his chin thoughtfully. "Very well. I will summon the solicitor. But you must promise me that you are not keeping anything from me. What is truly troubling you, Harry?"

Harry hesitated, his gaze dropping to the ground. For a fleeting moment, the mask slipped, and Darcy saw the shadow of something dark, something weighing heavily on his brother's heart. But then, just as quickly, Harry's smile returned, bright and carefree. "Nothing at all, Fitz," he replied with forced cheerfulness. "Come, let us not dwell on sombre thoughts. The day is too fine for that. Shall we ride?"

Darcy watched him for a moment longer, still sensing the unspoken burden his brother carried. But he nodded, deciding to let the matter rest for now. "Yes," he agreed. "Let us ride. I could use some fresh air myself."

They mounted their horses and set off at a gentle trot, the sun warm on their backs and the soft breeze carrying the scent of late summer blooms. For a while, they rode in companionable silence, the sound of hooves crunching on the gravel path the only noise. It was a moment of peace, a rare reprieve from the worries that usually occupied Darcy's mind.

But as they rode towards the stables, Darcy felt a subtle tension in the air—a stillness that felt unnatural. The horses, usually calm and steady, seemed skittish, their ears flicking back and forth as if sensing something was amiss. The tranquil morning was interrupted by the distant sound of barking dogs, followed by a high-pitched whistle. Darcy glanced towards the sound, noticing a group of stable boys struggling to corral a pair of hounds that had somehow got loose.

"Looks like the hunt was more successful than anticipated," Harry remarked with a grin, his voice light. "The old fox is putting up quite the chase."

Darcy smiled, though his eyes remained on the hounds. "Yes, but those boys should know better than to let them run this close to the stables. It's bound to cause trouble." His gaze shifted to the nearby grooms, who were distracted, watching the commotion with growing concern.

As they continued their ride, Darcy's attention was caught by one of the younger stable hands. The boy was attempting to lead a high-spirited stallion across the yard—a new acquisition from the north, a horse Darcy had been meaning to examine more closely. The stallion was fast, but known for its unpredictable nature, a beast with fire in its veins. Darcy frowned. The boy seemed to be struggling with the animal's bridle, his grip unsteady.

"Easy there," Darcy called out, his voice firm but calm, hoping to steady both the horse and the boy. The stallion's ears twitched, and for a moment, it seemed to settle. But then, a sudden snap—like a whip cracking in the air—broke the fragile calm. The sound was sharp and unexpected, shattering the quiet like a gunshot.

It happened in a heartbeat.

The stallion reared up violently, its eyes wide with panic. The young stable boy lost his grip on the reins, and the horse bolted, charging across the stable yard with wild, frenzied eyes. Darcy's heart leapt into his throat. He saw the boy fall back, his face pale with fear, and the horse careening straight toward them.

"Harry! Watch out!" Darcy's shout cut through the crisp morning air, sharp and urgent.

Harry, caught off guard, turned in the saddle, his bright eyes wide with surprise. There was a split second where their gazes met—a fleeting moment where Darcy saw the realisation dawning in his brother's eyes, the flash of fear that was so out of place on Harry's usually confident face. The horse thundered closer, its hooves pounding the earth, throwing up clods of dirt in its wake.

Instinctively, Harry tried to pull his own horse aside, but the movement was too sudden, too sharp. His mount, startled by the chaos and the scent of fear, reared up on its hind legs, unbalanced by Harry's unexpected shift in weight. Darcy's heart pounded in his chest as he watched his brother struggle to regain control.

The ground beneath them seemed to tilt, time slowing to a crawl. Harry's horse, unable to regain its footing, stumbled backwards. Harry fought to stay in the saddle, his hands gripping the reins tightly, but the force of the movement sent him flying. He was thrown from the horse, his body twisting in mid-air. Darcy reached out, as if he could somehow catch his brother, but he was too far away.

Harry hit the ground with a sickening thud, his head striking a large stone hidden beneath the loose gravel. Darcy's breath caught in his throat. For a moment, everything was silent. The world seemed to hold its breath, waiting for something, anything, to break the stillness.

Then, chaos erupted. The stable hands rushed forward, shouting orders and trying to calm the remaining horses, who were now rearing and whinnying in panic. Darcy leapt from his horse, his boots hitting the ground hard as he sprinted towards his brother.

"Harry!" Darcy's voice was raw with fear as he dropped to his knees beside his brother. Harry lay motionless, his face pale, a dark bruise already forming on his temple where his head had struck the stone. Blood trickled from a cut just above his brow, mingling with the dirt. His chest moved shallowly, each breath a laboured effort.

Darcy's mind raced. He should have seen the danger sooner. He should have noticed the skittishness of the horses, the distraction of the grooms, the stallion's unpredictable temperament. He should have called out sooner, done something, anything, to prevent this.

He felt a cold dread settle in his stomach, his hands shaking as he gently cradled Harry's head. "Stay with me, Harry," he murmured, his voice trembling. "We will get you help. Just stay with me."

Harry's eyes fluttered open, unfocused and filled with pain. "Fitz..." he whispered, his voice barely audible. His hand reached out, grasping weakly at Darcy's coat. "Do not..." Something rattled in his throat. "Eliza..."

But even as the words left his lips, his eyes began to lose focus again, his grip loosening. "Harry, no," Darcy choked out, his voice breaking. "Harry, please, stay with me."

But the stillness in Harry's body was unmistakable. A raw, guttural cry tore from Darcy's throat as he clutched his brother tighter, his voice echoing across the courtyard in a desperate wail. It was as if the earth itself shifted beneath him, the solid ground vanishing into an abyss of grief. The dark reality of what had happened hit him with the force of a tidal wave, knocking the breath from his lungs, leaving him gasping. Harry was gone—his bright, vibrant brother—snuffed out in an instant. There was no bringing him back.

The sudden shock of grief crushed him, a relentless, unbearable force that pinned him to the ground. The guilt wrapped around his heart like a vise, squeezing tighter with each passing second. "I should have stopped it—I should have done something!" Darcy's voice broke, his words barely coherent through the sobs that wracked his body. "It is my fault... all my fault..." His hands trembled as he held Harry close, his tears falling freely, unchecked. He should have been quicker, more vigilant, should have noticed the danger before it was too late. He should have saved his brother from this senseless, cruel accident.

But he hadn't, and now... now Harry was gone forever.

P PRE-ORDER

ALIX JAMES
THE MEASURE OF HONOR
THE MEASURE OF A MAN COLLECTION
BOOK THREE
A PRIDE AND PREJUDICE VARIATION

Printed in Dunstable, United Kingdom

70025210R00231